More Than You Think You Know

CYNDI PERKINS

D1411727

Published 2017 by Beating Windward Press LLC

For contact information, please visit:
BeatingWindward.com

First Edition
ISBN: 978-1-940761-31-2

Table of Contents

Dedication

This book is offered with sincere and humble thanks to family and friends, particularly my husband Scott, who back in 1982 bought his 22-year-old wife an electric typewriter and said, "You want to write? Write."

There are tall ships and small ships,
Ships that sail the sea.
But the best ships of all are friendships,
And may they ever be.

—Traditional nautical toast

Chapter 1: The Getaway

My husband Derek stomps away at his usual impatient double pace, shower bag in one hand, down a three-block pier like it's any other morning in which shit, shave and shower will be followed by the concocting of breakfast in the galley. This will be followed by yet another tedious boat project in preparation for our cruise down the "Great Loop" rivers to the Gulf of Mexico. Derek is more predictable than he thinks. On this day of liberation he moves as always, 220 pounds full speed ahead, broad gait, no motion wasted. Tall, formidable, florid-faced, unwavering in the conviction that he is always right, my husband's walk is a warning to everything in his path: yield or be mowed down. Every line of his form conveys decisiveness, from the red hair shot with steely gray curving back from his high forehead into a rigidly bound ponytail to his size 13 feet perennially clad in the yachtsman's preferred footwear: stretched-out, worn-in brown leather Sperry topsiders with no socks. Even the ever-so-slight slab of belly meat he has acquired in recent years protrudes aggressively.

Gathering my ditch bag, I am relieved that the radio calls, shouting and horn blowing required to summon the drawbridge operators is done for me. No more circling, waiting for timed openings as Derek swears under his breath because something does not immediately yield to him.

Magnanimous in public, Derek generally saves the contemptuous jabs, verbal and physical, for private moments. He can be especially cruel during boat projects. *Chinook's* mast and rigging must come down so we can take the 40-foot sailboat under the fixed bridges spanning the Illinois River. Last time we lowered it I took a metal shackle below the eye. My arms were busy holding up the mast. He was in too much of a hurry to wrap the rigging and secure loose lines. I also took a lot of "did you win the fight?" jokes. "You should see the other guy," Derek said.

During a trip around America's Great Loop two years ago, we learned that the Hammond, Indiana marina is a cheap place to drop the mast. The huge, impersonal complex of alphabetically ordered piers houses more than a thousand power yachts, sailboats, sport fishing boats and trawlers of all makes and models. The private craft are dwarfed by the permanently docked cruise ship suffering a shoddy, second life as a tarted-up gaming casino. The casino has literally been constructed around the mother ship, a bas-relief relic of its former self shrouded by parking decks and brick-tower elevators. It floats but goes nowhere.

Derek is out of sight, but in the quiet morning I still hear him tromping down the metal pier. Then the ponderous black wrought iron gate, heavy enough to amputate a limb, clangs behind him.

If I don't run away, one of these days he's going to kill me. Being murdered surely wouldn't be pleasant, but the fear of dying left me as soon as my kids entered their 20s. It was a relief to be past the biggest horrors like crib death, Make-A-Wish terminal illnesses, pedophile kidnappings and that all-time classic, getting squished in the road running to retrieve a ball. Thanks so much Stephen King: I read *Pet Sematary* on the Christmas Eve that Joey turned two.

When Lisa and Joey were little, I ran the ultimate defense against Derek, getting myself and the kids out of the house as much as possible. Hailey Marie Henderson, Brownie Leader, Elementary Bake Sale Contributor, Hockey Mom, Parent Council Representative and all-around activist for the advancement of young minds and bodies. Derek never hit them. I never gave him an opening.

Raising his stentorian voice subdued them in squalling infancy right through to the beginning of defiant adolescence, when they finally got their mad up. Lisa was the first to shout back and withdraw.

When Derek bought *Chinook* and announced he was resurrecting his childhood love of sailing, both kids cleverly proclaimed it wasn't their bag. This left them plenty of time to throw keggers at the house while Derek and I banged the crap out of ourselves, sailing in gale conditions out on the lake. To sail directly toward the wind, to beat, that's what Derek calls it and that's what it feels like because it basically means flogging yards and yards of maniacally whipping ropes, shackles and sail fabric while pitching and rolling. I think sailing fascinated Derek so much because he found something he couldn't always control. It angered him; he finds perverse and righteous delight in his anger. We learned, gradually, to sail, traveling to remote locations where we hadn't a prayer of getting back in time to break up the illicit juvenile activities going on at the house. My red-headed babies played to their hearts' content and I was home in time to clean up the messes before the destructive revelry resumed the following weekend.

These days Lisa and Joey keep their distance from Derek. I'm envious. And I fear the day they might be asked to come and take care of me. I am not sure that they would, given my long list of failures as a mother.

Derek doesn't hit me that often. In fact, you couldn't even really call what he does hitting. It's more a subliminal passive-aggressive punch, rendered in tight places where I am forced to maneuver around or try to get past him. Eclipsing me in any space, with a raised elbow or a hip shot and a foot kick thrown in for good measure, is usually good enough for him. He occasionally yanks my pony tail or braid, but seems to take greater satisfaction in bruising me "inadvertently."

My time window is narrow, but not impossible. Derek never spends more than a half-hour performing his bathhouse ablutions. He'll discover that the marina card key is gone when he tries to get back onto the dock from the bathhouse. The marina allots two keys, his and hers if you will, but he assured the dockhand that we only need one. Why would we require an extra key when I never go anywhere without him?

"It would just be another thing for you to lose," he said.

So ha-ha Derek. He's shut out and will not be able to get through the 10-foot-high gated, spiked fence that keeps interlopers off the docks. Unless he convinces an entering boater to take pity on him. Derek inspires neither hospitality nor pity. A classic know-it-all, he appears to require neither. Last night when I lifted the card out of the pocket of the ripped, paint-stained faded black cargo shorts that he wears every day, I stifled the impulse to throw both the card key and those ugly shorts into the water. No sense in blowing the $50 key deposit. There will be enough traumas.

I'm figuring an additional 20 minutes for him to search for the key and find a way back to the boat. He can't call me because I don't have my own cell phone.

I chose my escape vessel two days ago when we first arrived at this Lake Michigan port. We'd slogged on through frosty weather, a week-long, contentious sail across Lake Superior, through the Mackinac Straits and down the Michigan side of Lake Michigan, anchoring and docking in various harbors along the way. It's possible to day-hop along the sand-dune strewn coast of Michigan, with a pretty port every 25 miles or less, but Derek was in a hurry. We sailed, ate, slept, and then sailed again until we reached the head of the rivers.

Hammond Marina is not one of those lively ports of call where boaters congregate for potluck dinners and Happy Hour cocktails. Or perhaps it is, on summer weekends. It's deserted on late fall weekdays, aside from after-work boaters preparing to stow their vessels for the winter. We've only seen a handful of people near their boats and no boats going out on the lake.

I don't know if *Seawind* is seaworthy, but she doesn't appear to be leaking anywhere and is sporting a well-maintained unoccupied look: recently established spider webs on the rigging and bowsprit, clotted brown gunk-line on her hull, coagulated slime-green algae on bumpers and the tail-ends of lines dangling in the water. It is Tuesday; if *Seawind* goes out at all it is probably on weekends. Her appearance is as innocuous as her trite name. During my scouting walk on the piers I was initially drawn to a 36-foot red-hulled beauty named *Sea Wolf* and had to remind myself that I was not shopping for an attention-getter. *Seawind*, a 28-30 foot plain white boat with ubiquitous blue Sunbrella dodger, Bimini and sail covers will afford a measure of anonymity. But if the engine doesn't fire, I am screwed. Accomplished sailors may be able to sail out of a tight slip without using the engine, but that skill is beyond my abilities.

One duffle is all I'm allowing myself. There's no time to regret what I leave behind, most of it girly-girl wardrobe packed aboard long ago in anticipation of romantic dinners, Tiki Bar gatherings, dancing in the sand and other magazine-layout occasions that never materialized during our years of cruising. I doubt Derek will notice the absence of the flirty peach sundress, white espadrilles, slinky black trousers et al. These symbols of anticipated celebration were long ago shoved under the cubby beneath the V-berth, sealed in a plastic bag so I didn't have to hear him bitch about "my shit" being in the way.

What I wear, what I read, the products and processes that I consider essential to my everyday existence are considered minor, petty, boring. In the grand drama of my husband's life I am habitually overlooked as an extraneous, clumsy and inconvenient appendage. It has been so for 25 years, about the same length of time that I have been begging for sex on a regular basis. Derek doesn't like sex, something he hid very well prior to our wedding. Doesn't want to have it. Doesn't want to talk about it. I think he sees sex as a sign of weakness. He's kind of grossed out, too, because whenever I peek when he's fucking me he's got this slit-eyed, straining-to-finish look like he can't wait to come and get it over with. I don't know whether it's me or just sex in general. It took me so long to realize that our way of life had been established early on and would never change. During the night sweats and sleeplessness of menopause I have had a lot of time to think about this.

The duffel, actually Joey's old hockey bag, weighs a ton by the time I have stuffed it with the bare necessities. It smells like boy; sweaty shoulder pads, wet wool socks and Ivory soap. The stump of a candle with no wick (for polishing skate blades) is stuck in a crevice and falls into the water when I push the canvas inside out to de-crumb it before inserting my most essential life possessions.

There's more than fashion in my stinky oversized satchel. Derek may never know that I raided the backmost corner of the seaberth locker, a hard-to-reach area not often opened except to cram in spare parts or old gear for just-in-case occasions. From the cache I appropriated the old hand-held GPS, spare auto-pilot and outdated binoculars. Since I haven't been inside *Seawind,* I have no idea how she is equipped. I will have to get along with what I find. There's bound to be a Lake Michigan chart at the very least. Some of the $1,572 in my saved waitress tips may eventually have to be spent on maps and guidebooks. But I am an Information Specialist by profession and I have traveled these waters before. As long as the territory remains familiar I can make do.

Chinook is berthed at the end of Dock P. *Seawind* is in the middle of Dock C. There are no dock carts here and the duffel seems heavier by the minute. I've taken 15 minutes to drag it the length of the main pier, going by the clock on the Jumbotron billboard that looms over Interstate 80 at the casino exit. Time. Temperature. Jackpot. Every recent bruise aches. Panting, breaking a sweat, I try not to breathe through my nose. The soap-and-boiling vegetable smell emanating from the nearby Libby's canning factory induces nausea.

I wish the bag had wheels. I pray no one will see me and offer assistance. Boaters are a helpful lot. A going-gray 110-pound woman dragging duffel from pier P to C would definitely provoke a chivalrous call to action. The unwieldy shape of the bag is actually worse than the weight of it. Weight, I can handle. I may look skinny, but years of hoisting food-laden trays and yanking up sails have added muscle in all the appropriate places. My physique is attractive, or so I've been told. I know that I missed the kind of beauty society deems ideal. As a schoolmate's mom told me in junior high, "You would be so pretty if you had eyebrows." Somewhere in my 30s I realized that I'd been beautiful in my own way and missed the opportunity to enjoy it. In my early 40s I learned that life is not a beauty contest. Nearing 50, I'm doing a rapid wardrobe edit that's more about layers and warmth than style. Derek's contempt for "dolling up" aside, Joey and Lisa's castoff hoodies and sweats get more wear than the flirty peach sundress.

Dock C is deserted. *Seawind's* engine key, attached to one of those floating bobbers favored by cautious mariners and boat brokers, dangles from the ignition. There is another key on the ring. I say a prayer as I insert it into the hatch padlock. The hasp yields easily. *Score!* I pull out the wooden hatchboard.

The interior decorating scheme is lighthouse kitsch run amok. Red, blue and yellow lighthouse pillows, lighthouse curtains, a lighthouse throw tossed on the navy blue salon cushions. Standard for a sloop her size, the engine compartment is behind the companionway steps. The Perkins engine looks clean, with no oil drips or water puddles — a promising sign. I climb back up into the cockpit, reinsert the engine key and turn it. She starts like a champ. The gearshift smoothly kicks into reverse and forward. I spend a few minutes throttling up and down, back and forth, driving *Seawind* in her slip. Good to go.

Sweet Jesus, am I really doing this? Don't think, Hailey. Act.

Grunting, I yank the duffel from the dock to cockpit, and then hop back on the dock to untie all but the middle springline from the dock cleats. *Crap*, I almost forgot the shore power cord, still plugged into its stanchion. That would have been a cute trick, taking the dock with me. I yank the cord and toss it on deck, making a mental note to coil and stow ASAP. *Always Say A Prayer.* Already this is becoming more complicated than imagined.

Seawind is sandwiched in a tight channel with a row of super-size luxury trawlers parked behind her. All is lost if I fumble in reverse. The last time I backed out of a parking space I ended up in a jail cell. Of course that was a car and I was drunk. Still, it could happen this time, too. "Crazed Menopausal Wife Steals Sailboat, Destroys Numerous Vessels at Marina — film at 11."

I pull the last dockline into the boat. Hand on the tiller, engine just a hair above idle, I make my move. *Seawind* putzes in the desired direction, gently arcing to port (that's left to you landlubbers). Backing well to the middle of the channel, I click into forward gear and slowly steam toward the lake. Rounding the corner, I glance back down the main marina channel. No Derek in sight, just *Chinook* placidly floating. I blow her a kiss. A group of gangly teens waves from the concrete jetty that shields the marina from Lake Michigan's turbulent waters. I offer a jaunty hand-to-forehead salute in return. In 100 yards I clear the entrance buoys. *Seawind* motors into the crisp blue water. The green stagnance of the yacht basin and the black dread of my marriage are behind me.

We're off and running. Running at 5 miles per hour. I kick the throttle up a notch. Running away at 5.5 miles per hour. There is no turning back.

Chapter 2: Solo Sail

There's barely a breath of wind on Lake Michigan. The forecast calls for calm, clear, warm weather during the next three days, an Indian summer gift at this time of year, when the Great Lakes can turn nasty in a matter of seconds. Favorable weather expands my options.

Yonder, across the lake to the east, lies a myriad of easily accessed Michigan harbors stretching from Petoskey to Grand Rapids where I could find shelter and privacy, or conversely, be in contact with friends who knew me when I was myself. Maybe they care about me still. But I haven't talked to any of them in years. They couldn't accept the cowed and edited version of Hailey that I became with Derek.

What it comes to is this: I don't want anyone to save me but myself. I don't want to owe anybody anything.

I have tried, and am trying again, to picture a new life in Michigan where a better version of me lives free, fulfilled and at peace. But Michigan sucks right now, economically and spiritually, and so do I, as desperate as the homeless vagrants freezing in abandoned Detroit city schools as menacing dog packs roam the streets. To turn back to Michigan would be turning toward the flat-broke police state that is holding my driver's license and awaiting payment on the thousands of dollars in court penalties and the Michigan Treasury's so-called "responsibility fees" for the fender-bender I caused while under the influence of three Miller Lite beers.

Derek laughed in my face when I broached the topic of his help to pay my debt to society. "You're lucky I bothered to bail you out," he said. To avoid higher insurance payments he took my name off the policy. "You don't have a license, anyway," he pointed out.

Michigan in its current crude, cruel incarnation is as dead to me as the Big Three automakers skulking away from shuttered factories and broken blue-collar dreams, all the while feigning concern for alternative energy sources, the gasping ozone layer and global warming.

A honking, irregular V of Canada Geese passes overhead, animated compasses pointed south. "One way or another, I'm going with you," I tell them.

This jump up the shore is a necessary detour. There's nowhere to go from Lake Michigan's southernmost end. No sand softens the industrial structures that manhandle the natural landscape. Factories spew, ominous nuclear domes and cooling ponds loom exotic on the horizon; near shore the water turns a lurid milk-chocolate brown. The low-tide stench of the ocean is perfume compared to the smell.

Out from Hammond shines the brazen gleam of Chicago's skyline, about 15 miles up the coast. There are thousands of boat slips and mooring balls in the rocking, rolling, designated anchorage that is constantly strafed by the wake of passing commercial and pleasure craft.

Out on Lake Michigan sailing solo I talk to myself and the boat. Boats have souls, just like you and me.

"OK, so we'll mosey up to Shytown and suss out the situation, yes?" I ask *Seawind*.

There are docks to be had in Chicago. It's not an option. I can't afford a marina on my $1,572 nest egg. The tip stash has to get me wherever I'm going, even though I don't know where that is yet. Also, any attention is unwanted; I have to stay where I won't attract it.

The decision to pick up a mooring ball — a floating anchor of sorts attached to a long line bolted to the lake bottom — or to drop anchor from the boat itself, an anchor I've yet to examine closely, can wait. Worst-case scenario, I can simply idle all night out on the lake, free floating as Derek and I once did on the Atlantic Ocean off the shore of Sandy Hook. Deep fog had obscured New York Harbor; rather than enter the shipping lanes we drifted outside the danger zone, waiting for the morning light.

As long as I keep an eye out for lake freighters and avoid the shipping lanes, nothing will slam into me here.

I don't want to go where others will predict I'm headed. This idea of Hailey soloing on a sailboat won't be anyone's first guess. Or anyone's guess. Period. Derek will assume I ran home to mama in Toledo. There's a train station next to the marina and cabs run regularly from the casino. Either option would get me to a bus station. Mom will figure, when I don't show up at her place on the Michigan-Ohio border, that I'm staying with a friend. She doesn't know I don't have any.

I've never been considered the sailor in this family. Sailing is Derek's thing. For a decade, I have taken on the roles of deck monkey, cabin girl and galley slave, cranking a winch here, tugging a line there, poised for docking like a birddog quivering at the edge of the marsh, waiting for the command to retrieve her master's kill. Derek is the king of inarticulate instructions. When I don't understand what he wants me to do, he shouts, as if the higher volume will lead to comprehension. My perceived lack of prowess is a running taunt. "Can't you do any better than that?" "Move!" "Hurry up!" "Oh my God you're useless."

A Canadian sailor out of Thunder Bay once told me, "You know more than you think you know, Miss Hailey Marie." Maybe. But I still have a lot to learn and zero confidence in my boating abilities. Putting Ontario Dan's theory to the test scares me spitless; still, I'm nowhere near ready to turn around. I keep repeating, "You know more than you think you know." Surprisingly, it settles me.

When *Seawind* is a couple of miles offshore in reliably deep water, I dig the autopilot out of my escape sack. "Otto" was stowed in working condition when Derek upgraded to a fancier, sturdier model capable of controlling *Chinook's* steering in heavy seas and freeing us from hand-steering during 12-hour or more travel days. The clever gizmo attaches at the base of a sailboat tiller, allowing steerage at the click of a dial or push of a button, keeping the boat on a set course. "Otto" fits *Seawind's* steering stick to a T, and I take this as a lucky sign. After setting the course and watching the boat steer herself for five minutes, I'm confident we're holding a straight deep-water path up the coast. Chicago is about three hours away at current speed. *Seawind* moves smoothly through the 1-2 foot waves. It's time to acquaint myself with *Seawind's* systems, supplies and provisions. Especially provisions; there will be no going ashore in Chicago.

Popping up on deck for a quick scan and back down below, an exercise by necessity repeated in prairie-dog fashion every five minutes, I complete a preliminary inventory showing one dog-eared copy of Skipper Bob's *Cruising Lake Michigan*, Richardson's Lake Michigan charts, a better set of binoculars than mine, working radar, a decent GPS and a looks-new marine radio. I turn the latter on; it's set on Channel 16, the international hailing and distress frequency. The depth sounder and wind indicator gauges also click on with no problems. I will know how deep the water is and how hard the wind is blowing.

A finicky, matchy-matchy homemaker's touch is strongly evident in the immaculate interior. The royal blue-and-white striped miniature lifering affixed to the teak cabin wall in the salon, a combined living-dining-bedroom, cheerily assures that all are "Welcome Aboard!" The woven galley (kitchen) floor mat features a montage of Lake Michigan lighthouses, as do the kitchen towels and potholders. I haven't peeked in the head (bathroom), yet but I can guess what kind of towels are on the rack. There's probably a lighthouse toilet paper holder with matching night light, too.

There isn't a boater alive who doesn't fall prey to cheesy nautical décor of one kind or another; this vessel seems particularly hard hit. The "less is more" theory of design is not known here. The galley cupboards are full of neatly stacked lighthouse motif plates, bowls and mugs as well as stemless clear plastic wine glasses, no-tip tumblers, a half-full bottle of mid-priced Cabernet, a full bottle of Pusser's Rum, eight cans of Campbell's Select Italian Wedding soup, two cans of salmon, three of water-packed tuna, a half-full packet of saltines (most likely gone stale, because that's what happens to dry crackers on a humid boat) and three cans of Chef Boyardee spaghetti and meatballs. I grab one of the going-brown bananas from the copper mesh hanging produce basket, displacing a mini-swarm of fruit flies. I must not ignore the need for sustenance even if I don't feel hungry.

In a hanging locker redolent with the spring-mountain scent of dryer sheets used to combat must and mildew, I find two size-large sets of men's foul-weather gear and oh, blessed be, a set of women's red foulie bib pants. The lady-sized Neoprene overalls are accompanied by a matching offshore-rated waterproof hooded jacket. I've priced out this gear; the jacket alone is about $350. Derek has a top-of-the-line set of foul weather gear. He's never seen fit to upgrade my sweaty rubber fishing bibs, white footless waders with adjustable elastic straps purchased on eBay for $14. On rainy days I wear the rubber pants paired with an orange vinyl Wal-Mart rain jacket. The pants keep my butt dry but suffocate my lower body, giving literal meaning to "sweatpants." The jacket, a type favored by municipal crossing guards, turns sodden after 10 minutes of steady rain, relentless moisture wicking from the sleeves up in anything more severe than a light drizzle.

"When the going gets tough the wimps go down below," Derek said. "Only serious sailors need serious gear. You're not there yet. Probably won't ever be."

Here, now, on Lake Michigan, I have entered the serious realm, if only on borrowed time on a borrowed boat. I will strive to take good care of *Seawind*, leaving her safely in a place where she can be easily found and reunited with her rightful owners. Like the perfect friend with benefits, our fleeting relationship should end on a mutually positive note with no recriminations, all secrets intact and no harm done.

The jacket fits. It's not needed in 70-degree sunny weather, but I shrug it on over my white turtleneck anyway, having a fashion moment, armored in snazzy competency, very America's Cup. "Hey, fake it 'til you make it," I whisper to myself. "You know more than you think you know."

The deck is stable and comforting beneath my bare feet. Moving forward to check out the anchor system, I make a mental note to rig a jackline while the lake is behaving. If the waves kick up and the ride gets bouncy, the flat, strong length of rope firmly affixed on both ends to a permanent object can be used as a handhold to move around the boat decks. In rough seas, sailors clip on to jacklines from their safety harnesses, allowing them to be fished out if they fall overboard. Since no severe weather is predicted in the near future, I will wait to see if there are any safety harnesses aboard.

The anchor is a hefty Delta, the best of its kind and good for holding in any kind of condition from sand bottom to river mud. Securely lashed to the bow, the anchor is attached to about 100 feet of chain wound around a manual windless. The hoisting mechanism is a bonus as I doubt I could pull up the anchor under my own power. There is also a back-up Danforth plow anchor, a claw-like 20-pound hunk of metal that I have absolutely no faith in after numerous draggings using the same type of anchor on *Chinook* in tidal waters down south. As the water rose or fell every 6 to 12 hours, the boat would swing crazily around in the ensuing current, easily dislodging the Danforth and causing us to drift too close to other boats, too close to shore, too close to shallow water, or, on one rainy night in Georgia, right up onto a muddy reed flat.

"Securité! Securité! Securité! Hello All Stations. This is the U.S. Coast Guard ..." The staticky burst of the radio startles me and I realize that I need to pee. The Coasties are merely reporting an overdue vessel that was supposed to arrive in port several hours ago. Listeners are "advised to keep a sharp lookout and report all sightings to the U.S. Coast Guard."

Roger that, as we say in nautical marine radio lingo.

The only boats on my horizon are a collection of sport-fishing go-fast day-trippers, distinguished world 'round by their *bon vivant* bridge decks where the Captain's chair, accessed by a ladder, perches dizzyingly high above the water, *the better to see the fish, my dear.* "Otto" continues to hold *Seawind's* helm with aplomb; an occasional mechanical "rrhn rrrrhn rrrhn" assuring the device is still on, making minute adjustments to keep us on course.

Down in the head (bathroom to you landlubbers) I perch on a commode nicer than *Chinook's*, featuring a one-button flush instead of the callous-producing elbow-stressing primitive pump handle I am used to.

Surprise, surprise, the bathroom scheme is not lighthouses. It's fish. There are also two framed plaques: "If you sprinkle when you tinkle please be neat and wipe the seat," above which reads, "If it didn't come out of your body, don't put it in the toilet."

I do not flush the toilet paper. It goes into a Ziploc bag thoughtfully positioned next to the toilet in a tiny wastebasket featuring a swathe of striped cartoon clownfish circling its circumference.

It occurs to me that I have no idea how full the holding tank is. *Chinook's* 50-gallon waste tank overflowed on one occasion two years ago. Brown sludge, known to cruisers as the "stain of shame," oozed out of the tank valve onto the starboard (right) middle deck. Gross doesn't even begin to cover it. Pump-out facilities are few and far between and on the rivers. When they can find one, boaters pay as much as $45 a pop to get the toilet tank sucked clean.

I could go in a bucket and dump it overboard. A retired South Carolina doctor that Derek and I met in Tampa bragged about his "virgin holding tank." He'd been sailing for years with his boat rigged to bypass the tank, dumping waste directly into the water. Doc, who keeps his surgical skills sharp by operating on dogs in foreign countries when humans aren't available, informed us that urine is sterile. Fecal material is another matter.

You can actually get a ticket with hefty fine for peeing or pooping, aka "dumping," overboard. Laws vary by body of water. For example, on the Atlantic one must venture a few miles offshore before legally emptying sewage. A sailboat's piddly tank is nothing compared to the Big Boys out there. *Chinook* has skirted around huge sludge slicks deposited by freighters and cruise ships. In contrast, Lake Superior waters are a zero discharge zone. That means nothing is allowed to go in the water. No pee, no poop, not even food. And of course, no trash.

I confess to freely violating this rule playing a game I call "What Floats" with anything biodegradable. Banana and potato peels float. Pasta, meat and coffee grounds sink. Crabs love eggshells, which may float for a while but will eventually sink. "What Floats" is especially amusing and instructive on waters with a strong current. I was preparing to take a dip in the Tennessee River on a hot autumn day until I watched the outer leaves of a head of iceberg lettuce whisked downstream and out of sight in a matter of seconds. "Go ahead, Hailey, jump in," Derek taunted. "If I tie a rope to your ankle I might be able to haul your skinny ass back."

When I first decided to quit smoking cigarettes, (a project still underway after a decade of yo-yo success) I stopped throwing butts in the water. Each Smokey Treat is counted as it is deposited in an empty beer can tucked behind the bailing bucket near the back rail. I am down to five Smokey Treats per day now that I have given up beer. There are two $15 cartons of an off-brand Lights Kings in my ditch bag. Thinking about them makes me want one. To counteract the urge I take a few deep yoga breaths.

Center. Ground. Calm. Clarity. I close my eyes and inhale-exhale to the rhythm of Lake Michigan.

A beer would taste so good right now.

When I was thrown in jail in June for operating under the influence, my sister Layla, a renowned psychiatrist who mostly works these days in the upper echelons of public policy, informed me in cold clinical terms that I "need to evaluate my relationship with alcohol."

So alcohol and I are no longer dating. We aren't even speaking. The break-up ensued quietly after the cop drama at the accident scene and later at the jail, when the nastiest cop came back to take private pictures of me.

Downing three or four or five beers after work had become automatic. It was my habit to have one or two at the restaurant, thriftily using my employee discount, and then two or more when I got home. It felt deserved. As a mother, trapped in a marriage that had been a bad idea to begin with, and an Information Specialist at the Keweenaw Peninsula Tourism Bureau by day, AND a waitress by night. Alcohol softened sharp edges, drowned dissatisfaction. In times of great stress or jubilation a shot of Crown Royal or an Absolut and tonic did not seem overly off the rails. I never suffered blackouts or delirium tremens.

During my court-ordered counseling after the accident I gave all the proper responses to the kind, scholarly, comfortingly zaftig lady psychiatrist. Privately, I decided that if I am an alcoholic, I'm a high-functioning one.

I wanted to see how I functioned without a beer crutch. There have been moments of quiet pleasure in my clarity experiment. But the pain of living with Derek became intolerable. Put simply, it was a lot easier to put up with his constant criticism, harsh judgment and selfishness when I had a buzz on.

While first forming an escape strategy, it occurred to me to choose the illicit lover route. You know, running around instead of running away. As I have done before. As a lot of potential runaways do.

My friend Nancy ran away like that, to another man, and then another. She explained her absences to her husband by explaining that she'd taken up kayaking. He caught on because she always came home dry. Tall, lanky, beautiful Nancy wound up with a divorce that segued into another unfulfilling marriage, followed by more cheating and another divorce.

Then there's my friend Lynnae, a 40-something petite blonde princess searching the internet for her Knight in Shining Armor. She was outraged when one of her internet matches expected to have sex with her on the first date. Never mind that they'd already been having virtual nookie online.

My waitress pals Mary and Patti ran away by closeting themselves in celibate solitude. Sex is too important to me to choose that route. I have firmly believed since womanhood that an orgasm per day is medicinal both psychologically and physically. Never interested in sex, Derek in recent years had degenerated from premature ejaculation to erectile dysfunction. When he did get hard, about twice a month, all attention was paid to getting him off during the brief seconds the sacred erection lasted. While not averse to other drugs of all kinds, Derek thinks Viagra is stupid and dangerous, snorting in derision at commercials that warn of priapism. He wouldn't know what to do with an erection that lasted for more than four minutes, let alone four hours. Once I accomplished my bi-monthly duties as semen receptacle and he was snoring I could sometimes get myself off with a few quick twiddles to the clitoris. More often I had to wait until I was alone behind the locked bathroom door. Other than the occasional hand-held or well-aimed high-pressure shower nozzle, I have never used props other than electric toothbrushes. I've actually considered buying a vibrator. I've checked out the models but resisted an actual purchase in the hope that the real thing will someday be reliably accessible. Sex for one without artificial props does the job for now. Feels less lonely and desperate than electric stimulants. Given the proliferation of erectile enhancement drugs on the market these days, I do not think I am off-base in assuming real-life penises are still available. It would be a certified shame if I never had another lover.

There have been four lovers in the last two decades if I don't count Derek, which I don't. The Cynic, the Carpenter, the Chef, and the Contractor. Each served a purpose. Each affirmed that I was worthy of a lover, that I could inspire lust. It embarrasses me now, my compulsion to prove myself attractive through a series of impermanent affairs with a quartet of men with their own serious dysfunctions. In the end, the mini-escapes provided no lasting relief.

But I digress as the boat pilots herself. Reverie is a dangerous condition on a moving ship. Constant correction is required. A lazy sailor, a preoccupied sailor, a bored sailor is a bad sailor.

Our morning and afternoon together has established a measure of trust and comfort. The wind indicator shows a benevolent 10-15 knot west breeze. Such light airs encourage further bonding with my borrowed ship. Deep yoga breaths in and out, lines in hand, I unfurl the headsail at the tip of the boat, which is rigged so it can be controlled from the cockpit. As the fabric unfolds, *Seawind* tilts almost imperceptibly to starboard. I idle down the engine, disconnect the autopilot and let the wind take us. I'm afraid to shut off the engine for fear it won't start again. Motor-sailing is not regarded as "pure." Derek would be shaking his head and huffing in disgust at my tactics, as he has so many times. But I am grinning. *Seawind* is for now my boat and here and now I am proving myself an able captain.

I am sailing alone.

The citified western shore of Lake Michigan is a concrete contrast to the sandy shorelines, forests and artsy northwoods communities on the opposite side of the lake. Chicago makes itself known by sight, sound, smell and vibration long before the harbor proper is in entry range. There are eight harbors in and around Chicago, encompassing more than 20 miles of shoreline. Skipper Bob's guidebook indicates that there are 1,200 transient mooring balls in Monroe Harbor. I'll wait until sunset to attempt to hook a ball and tie up *Seawind* for the night. Phoneless, I will keep an eye out for any harbor patrol boats collecting mooring fees. Perhaps the expense can be avoided if I arrive late and leave early. I am still too wired to feel hunger or fatigue, but I must eat and sleep — and decide what to do next. *Seawind* cannot make it under the Chicago River & Sanitary Shipping Canal bridges with her mast up.

Catching a mooring ball is a tricky business, even with more than one pair of hands aboard. *Chinook's* maiden mooring took place in Fort Myers Beach, Florida, with Derek at the helm and Yours Truly on the bow, frantically brandishing a long aluminum boathook, trying to nab a floating nylon rope pendant tagged by a numbered ball in the close-packed field of bobbing numbered balls all the while avoiding other moored and maneuvering boats.

"Here — get that one, no, THAT one, can't you do anything right, Jesus Christ you're useless ... it's right there ..." Cringing from the barrage of jeers, derisive laughter, criticism and shouted commands from the cockpit with an audience watching from nearby boats and dinghies, I nearly fell overboard before I managed to snag pendant and accompanying ball. Because Derek thinks that rigging lines and bumpers ahead of time is anal retentive and overly fussy, I was forced to stand there stupidly with the pendant hooked, awaiting my next order. "Get a line, get a line on it. Are you stupid? No, not THAT one..." I finally held up a line from the rope box that met his approval. "Now get it around the Sampson Post — fuck, forget it, I'll do it myself."

The public humiliation of the peanut gallery was actually a comfort. He never hits me when other people are watching.

Many women with otherwise kind husbands give up boating because the captain of the ship is verbally abusive, or as my new "husband" Robin will describe it "an out-and-out asshole the minute they push off from the dock." There's a very popular "Don't Shout" t-shirt specifically designed for long-suffering boat wives. Some enlightened couples invest in "marriage savers," electronic headsets that allow them to communicate calmly, quietly and efficiently via walkie talkie from the steering station to the person stationed on the bow. Other brave wives take seamanship courses and become as competent as their husbands. In Canada, many of the lady sailors choose to man the engine while the male aboard handles docklines and hauls anchor. Early on, I tried to tell Derek that his fortissimo vocal performances turn me into a fumbling bumbler but he is unable to control his hot-tempered cursing. I actually counted how many times he said "Fuck" one day. Forty-seven. The barrage is even worse when he's nervous about his approach into a new harbor; I become the object against which he can smash his uncertainty. I cannot count the times I have docked, anchored or moored with tears clouding my vision, nose running, and red face hot with humiliation. Even kindly comments from the peanut gallery, "Good job little lady!" cannot counteract the ache. Holding back tears still hurts but is now second nature. Derek has no patience with histrionics, or any other expressed emotion. My tears cement his conviction that I am manipulative and whiny. He does not melt when I cry; he freezes. Any sign of weakness makes him angry. Almost everything makes him angry.

"Never again," I say out loud, punching the autopilot button twice to make a slight course adjustment. I am smiling. I do know more than I think I know. "Nice job, *Seawind*!" I pet the tiller.

As the sun begins its late afternoon track across the western sky, I round the outer breakwater of Chicago's magnificent harbor and pull in the headsail, rolling it up in preparation for a solo mooring. The only witnesses are two smallish speedboats fishing just off the Chicago lighthouse pier. I hank and uncoil a line on each side of the vessel, plunking the boathook in the middle of the deck atop the bulkhead for easy grabbing from port or starboard. Back in the cockpit, I shift the engine to idle, allowing momentum to propel the boat alongside the big white floating ball I am angling for on the outermost corner of the mooring field. *Seawind* gently coasts alongside it, miraculously (to me) in hooking range. I hurry forward to secure the ball attached to the line, hooking the looped pendant on my first try. Yay! I thread the rope through the giant bolero, cleat the line back on the boat and let out my breath, which I hadn't realized I was holding. I savor this tiny success that feels huge to me. "You know more than you think you know" may well be my new mantra.

Trepidation does not fully abate as I shut off the engine and sit, rocking in the harbor, absorbing the enormity of the day's ventures. I still wait to be discovered, apprehended, jailed again, publicly reviled, and privately scorned. Every element of my escape thus far has gone smoothly. There must be a pill to swallow amid all this jam. My life has been such that I cannot think otherwise.

Chapter 3: The Four Lovers

Every time I let down my guard and let myself exist without fear, without worry, I pay dearly. So I already know that I cannot afford sleep tonight. *Seawind* does what she can to calm me, placidly floating in the impersonal harbor without a care for my destiny.

The temperature drops 20 degrees when the sun goes down. I slide the hatchboard into place to keep the night air out and rummage around in the galley cupboards for a saucepan to heat a can of Italian wedding soup.

Between hot flashes, self-justifications and the need to figure out what's next, you'd think my monkey mind would be satisfied. But my ego's admittedly sick obsession with lusty adoration sinks me into the fleeting pleasures and lingering shame of my four lovers: the Cynic, the Carpenter, the Chef and the Contractor. I can amuse or horrify myself for hours with rewinds and replays of car accidents and carnal couplings.

My lovers comfort me. It's twisted, but I have continued to run away with them in my mind long after our brief encounters.

A quartet of lovers. Not all at once, and not currently. What do you take me for?

Judge harshly if you will. But each affair was spaced out roughly four years apart, each preceded by the supreme flirtation of deep conversation, each proceeded by car repairs and volleys of self-recrimination. There was a long, righteous dry spell before the Cynic in which I even outlawed masturbation just to see if I could go without touching and orgasms. I lasted two months. At any sexually active age, it is important to remember that the clitoris has more nerve endings than the penis. Doctor Oz recommends sex at least once per week to cut heart attacks and strokes by up to 50 percent. I need not apologize for my libido. It's healthy to have sex. If you are not having sex you are shortening your life span. And when I'm not having sex I am very unhappy.

They were all younger than me and I am still trying to figure out what that means.

Lover number one, the Cynic, was homely and shaggy, with leathery, scaly skin and small, rodent-like yellow teeth. His brown hair, brown eyes and muddy complexion didn't matter. In the looks department I'm no prize myself, especially on the cusp of a half-century. Zits and wrinkles are a vexing combination. My periods are gone but I still get the pre-menstrual pimple between my eyebrows each month. Yoga mavens take heed: it looks like I've succeeded in opening my third eye and it isn't pretty.

The Cynic, a humor columnist with an acid tongue and liberal sensibilities, worked for the local newspaper. I worked as an Information Specialist at the tourism bureau office. The first time he came in, I remember thinking that he resembled Alfred Einstein on methamphetamines. His wicked humor seduced me. It didn't hurt that he considered me brilliant, powerful and attractive.

What woman isn't a sucker for such comments as: "You're gorgeous and you don't even know it, which is doubly attractive," or later on, "I know you would probably like it to be smaller, but from a man's perspective your butt is perfect..."?

The Cynic welcomed verbal sparring matches, produced a string of witty comments for every occasion, had a flair for caricatures of various important personages on the political and social scene and an unerring instinct for whatever behavior our too-infrequent encounters called for, from circumspect admiring comments murmured in my ear at a Kiwanis Club awards banquet, to a full-blown feel-up in the car under cover of darkness in a restaurant parking lot.

Sometime after my fleeting affair with the eccentric Cynic tapered off, due to progressively building guilt, impossible scheduling and his idiocy with motor vehicles — I prefer a man who can fix things, or at least not constantly break them — the Cynic came knocking on my hotel room door after a day-long marketing seminar at Marquette University in Milwaukee. I shut myself in the bathroom and stood under the blast of a hot shower as he pounded away at the cheap, purple-painted metal door. All I could think of was how he'd ground the brake pads on my Chevy Cutlass down to nubbins when I'd had the bad judgment to lend him the vehicle while the family and I were off on vacation in the Wisconsin Dells.

In the ethics seminar the next morning he asked me if I had been in. "I saw a light under the door," he said. "I knocked and knocked."

"I went to bed early," I said. "Wow, I must have been out like a light."

We both knew differently. Wincing at the dandruff on the shoulders of his rumpled black Salvation Army sports jacket, the dead-skin flakes crusting at the corners of his bushy unibrow — and those squirrel teeth! — I'd progressed to the "what-did-I-ever-see-in-him" phase.

I last heard through a mutual acquaintance that the Cynic is living in obscurity on a goat farm in a small, affluent Minnesota community, the pet of a rich divorcee. I will always carry fond memories of his long, slim penis, really the only beautiful part of him, and how fulfilling it felt inside of me in those marvelous pre-AIDS awareness days when sexually transmitted diseases were not an acronym but merely an occupational hazard for ghetto hookers, heroin addicts and gay men riding bareback.

In my defense, I only took lovers when I feared my pussy was going to close up like a pierced ear gone too long without an earring in the opening.

Have I mentioned that Doctor Oz, and Doctor Ruth before him, said that sex is good for you at any age? Just look at those miraculous Blue Zones around the world, where the long-lived joyfully engage in sexual intimacy well into their 90s.

The soup is bubbling. Standing in the galley I eat it straight from the saucepan, spooning broth and slurping bead pasta as I progress to Lover Two, the Carpenter.

The Carpenter came along a few years later, when I just couldn't take Derek's rejection and my self-imposed celibacy any longer. By then I'd found a waitressing job to supplement my piddling income and take my mind off my abysmal home life. It was clear that the things Derek most loved about me were my medical insurance and 401K; my barely-above-minimum-wage salary was an easy target for ridicule. And then the tourism bureau was forced to cut back on staff. Seniority ruled, and despite a satisfactory job performance for four years, as the newest hire I was out.

"You're nothing but a second-class clerk who couldn't cut it and has no future because you didn't have the gumption to finish college," he shouted in my face, spittle hitting my cheeks, when I asked for an extra $20 to go to the grocery store. "Just wait and we'll go together. I know what we need; you'll just buy stupid shit."

I was a sad case for quite some time after I lost my day job, dragging around the house in a limp, flowered-flannel nightgown, fighting the impulse (and not always winning) to pop a beer at 10 a.m. while watching *Regis & Kathy Lee* followed by *Oprah*, *Judge Judy* and *The Price is Right*. Thankfully the agoraphobia was short-lived, but for a couple of months even going to the grocery store was painful. My 401k was spent on COBRA health insurance payments; the unemployment checks barely covered the beer and cigarettes I couldn't seem to do without.

The job that got my paddle back into life's mainstream turned out to be waitressing, bartending and cooking at a dive called the Elbow Room Resort. My Knight-in-Shining-Armor-seeking friend, Elise — going through yet another crisis after a string of not-so-charming princes failed to rescue her and carry her off to Sugar Daddy Land — got me in. Elise didn't want to run away, she yearned to be swept away, preferably on a white steed. The chances of this happening at the Elbow Room were about as likely as Donald Trump shaving his head. But delusion, as well as hope, springs eternal.

Fall had turned to winter. Three hundred inches of snow descended on Michigan's Upper Peninsula. "Larry needs servers to get him through snowmobile season," Elise said. She called to let me know I'd been hired sight unseen on her recommendation. "If you want the job." It seemed like divine timing. At the time.

The "resort," a dive by any standard, no matter how many boxes of frozen crab legs were collecting frost in the walk-in freezer, was situated on the main trailhead at a juncture convenient to sledders from Lower Michigan, the eastern Upper Peninsula, Wisconsin and Chicago. The affluent seemed to enjoy slumming with the mostly motley crew of Elbow Room regulars swilling cans of Old Milwaukee. Tips were surprisingly good.

By the time the Carpenter had dazzled me with his wide, white grin with a teasing, "Are you married? Please, tell me you're not married!", I'd recovered a measure of self-respect and spunk and had grown to embrace the Elbow Room, dark vibe and all, as a welcomed respite from my troubled and troublesome family. Derek had just quit smoking cigarettes by taking up pot, a crop of which was flourishing in our attic and stinking up the house. Whenever visitors commented on the smell I blamed it on the skunks in the woods across the street. Then Derek decided to downsize his boat repair and delivery business, claiming that by cutting overhead and letting his four employees go he could actually make more money with less effort. It was all about "less effort" and "getting out there" on the sailboat when summer finally came again.

My son Joey had embarked on his long and impressive string of petty criminal activities and car wrecks. I didn't know where my sweet baby boy had gone. From age 16 to 18, his favorite expression was "Don't worry about it," the most useless and maddening phrase in the world. Of course I worried, all the time. Joey's indifferent academic performance was depressing. He shrugged off D grades, doing only enough work to get by. I'd been raised to follow the rules and respect my elders; a "B" on the grade card did not make my parents happy.

My daughter Lisa, the older by only 18 months, was also tanking in the grades department and resented the self-defined role of "good" child. She launched an aggressive campaign of rebellion involving tattoos, piercings, and an outlandish rainbow of hair colors favored by her group of friends (appropriately known as the Skittles). Lisa had run out of private schools willing to accommodate her in our neck of the woods. She'd been kicked out of public high school after being spotted in a sinister black trench coat in the faculty parking lot, where she was writing down teacher license plate numbers in a small black notebook.

All this mayhem and sacrilege was of course my fault. It is always the mother's fault, or at least women are conditioned to feel that way. Actually, I thought her boxing nun puppet Sister Mary Margaret Tyson was funny.

About that time I first heard the calling to run away. When I clocked out of work at the Elbow, I occasionally gave in to the strong impulse to drive for miles down US-41 along the shores of Lake Superior toward the Mackinac Bridge, a female Chuck Berry with no particular place to go. On one run I made it all the way to the bridge that links Upper and Lower Michigan, some five hours distant from my Upper Peninsula hamlet, before I snapped to and reluctantly turned around. The irrational dreams that dawn sustained could not survive the bright light of morning. Derek called me crazy and he was correct. Neither one of us connected the quick tears and sudden, drenching bouts of sweat, the night rambles and constant depression with that normal phase of a woman's life known as menopause.

The Carpenter was gorgeous in that aw-shucks-ma'am way, with a dimpled smile, abundant, curly, collar-length soft brown hair that reminded me of Jeff, my first high school boyfriend. The Carpenter was buff and he knew it, although he endearingly deflected compliments with long, downcast eyelashes as women cooed over his small waist, wide shoulders, tight buns and perfectly sculpted biceps. His past career in the Coast Guard fed our mutual interest in plying the high seas and possibly each other.

The Carpenter had a gorgeous penis. I wanted it at my constant beck and call.

Twice divorced with young children whom his wife had custody of, he was deeply into his own guilt trip and desire for isolation. He lived in a rented house trailer on a gravel road down by the Snake River. The mementoes of his family life with two elementary-aged children and his ex-wives were stored in cardboard boxes in the cheaply paneled living room that also featured an outdated console TV, a beat-up floral-print sofa and a Lazy Boy recliner that had seen better days.

I was mainly into the kissing. It annoyed me that he needed to talk and talk and talk until he had exhausted every facet of possible conversation before reaching for me, his palpable reluctance followed by hunger. The kissing satiated me on every level. Derek never enjoyed kissing and when he did deign to pucker up, it wasn't at all pleasant-all clumsy tongue and sticky saliva as if he was unwilling to devote more than a few seconds to such an unsanitary and boring activity. The Carpenter's leisurely, varied kisses, nibbling, slow-paced, then faster, shallow, then deeper, rendered me 14-years-old again, when making out was better than going all the way. The Carpenter could touch my elbow or my jawline and make me shudder. When we finally kissed our way around to it, the eyes-wide-open sex was a revelation.

Astride his brawny body on his bachelor bed, I tossed my hair back, gorgeous, invincible, and irresistible. "Let me look at you — you're so beautiful," he would say, his hands clasping my butt, his brown eyes crinkling at the corners as he smiled that perfect smile. Now I think, gawd, what a cliché. "You look so beautiful." What a pile of hooey. Word to the not-so-wise: "You look so beautiful," and derivations thereof, comprise the oldest line in the world. Men throughout time have said this to women when they are trying, as my mother crudely but accurately puts it, "to get into their pants." If a guy says it to you, he's said it to someone — possibly several someones-before, with the same tone of wonderment. Ouch.

To my shame, the Carpenter with the perfect penis became an obsession. I bought underwear, the sexiest I'd ever owned, for him. My midnight drives shifted to afternoon rambles down his country road on my days off, cruising past the rinky-dink trailers looking for his rusted burgundy Nissan pick-up truck. Once I walked in when he wasn't home and left a scented candle and sexy note.

I looked for that truck everywhere. Every time the lounge door swung open at the Elbow Room, I held my breath, waiting for him to walk in. Then I'd hide my infatuation, "Oh, hey, how's it's going" all casual, pretending not to notice him, as if I'd never agonized over what to wear for him at work that night. I'd taken to wearing tighter pants and shorter tops that showed a hint of my belly when I chose to raise my arms and stretch a certain way. The space behind the bar was a stage for my strutting ego drunk on libido. The butterflies whipped around in my gut every time I saw him or even thought I saw him. Ridiculous. Unrealistic. Debasing.

On one gray, snow-blasted afternoon I showed up at the trailer looking for his arms, his kisses, that delectable member. He was curled up inert on the couch, covered by a knitted afghan. I was the last person he expected or wanted to see. We conversed politely, like strangers. He complimented me on my gray-and-tan Sorel boots. Then he showed me a videotape on the console TV about his crossing of the equator and the shellback initiation that newbie coast guard members are forced to endure. We did not touch. Apparently there was a never-before-midnight rule that I had violated. He had said "come over any time," but he didn't mean it and never expected that I would be pushy enough to take him up on it. Pulling out from his driveway in my hockey mom van I got stuck in a snowdrift. The tow truck bill was $50; I was late picking my son up from hockey practice.

The Carpenter visited the bar less often as winter gave way to the muddy, still snowy, viciously deceitful ugliness that typifies schizoid Michigan Upper Peninsula spring. When he did come in he did not linger waiting for me to go off-duty. Brave in public, insensate in private, I lowered myself even further, writing him a five-page letter explaining that I did not want to leave my family but wanted him anytime, anywhere and "can we make arrangements when I leave for my new job in the summer?" How trite and desperate can a woman get?

I had decided to upscale my culinary labors by taking a waitress job at a gourmet restaurant 60 miles away on the Lake Superior waterfront. Actually, Derek had decided that he didn't want me working at "that sleazy bar" and delivered an ultimatum, complete with foot-stomping (his) and hair yanking (mine).

Because of the two-hour commute down a scenic, curving highway I was able to convince Derek that it would be cheaper and safer to stay in employee housing in the Harbor all week, coming home to the sailboat on weekends for trips to new and familiar harbors.

I never found out how the Carpenter reacted to my ludicrous offer to pencil him in on my schedule. Two weeks after I began working in the harbor Joey, then 18, was convicted of criminal sexual misconduct and my focus was cruelly snapped back to the people I should have been thinking about in the first place.

Chapter 4: A Bad Mother

My son is a cop magnet. He was not born that way. He was not raised that way. Joey is at the essential level a good person. That I persist in believing this makes me a cliché, one in the sad community of jailhouse mothers who continue defending their innocent babies no matter what. Unlike Lisa, who pushed the breast away screaming at two months old and skipped the crawling stage so eager was she to walk away from me, Joey cuddled, snuggled, and clung. Mama's Boy? Perhaps we fit the stereotype. He went from breast to cup at 18 months never having had a bottle, retaining his sunny nature and tender heart long past elementary school days.

As I marveled at Lisa's fierceness, her need to lead, her quick, instinctive grasp of survival skills to hit first and cover all signs of weakness, I saw my second child as an equally worthy polar opposite: a negotiator, a placator, a team player. Going along to get along served Joey well until he (doomed to illustrate yet another dubious cliché) "fell in with the wrong crowd" in junior high.

Joey didn't break into the neighbor's house and steal the coin jug on top of their TV. But he followed the boy in who did the actual stealing and held some of the money for him. He didn't take the pilfered car stereo out of a car in the fairgrounds parking lot, but he bought the hot property and installed it in his car. He didn't drive our family van without a license, but he let a friend who only had a learner's permit take the wheel. He didn't drink the beer, but he let an underage friend carry an open can in the car and a six-pack in the trunk. By the time he was 18, Joey had a rap sheet that would rival any inner city gangster starring in the booming rap songs he blasted on his Walkman. "You're white, you know," Lisa would tell him.

All of his misdeeds were petty offenses, but expensive and frightening nonetheless. "Give the kid this, at least he varies his violations," said Derek.

"He'll grow out of it. I did all this stuff when I was a kid. It was just a different time. The cops didn't bust you for every little thing." I wasn't so sure. Like most teens, Joey continued to believe he was smarter than the adults. His stock comment to me as I freaked out over the latest court notice in the mailbox or the latest cop knocking on the front door continued to be, "Don't worry about it."

What a stupid expression.

Derek wasn't any better. "Snap out of it. Shake it off. You're not the one in jail for chrissakes," he told me.

I knew my daughter's passions: cutting-edge music, tattoos, social protest, philosophy, theology, and hockey. Lisa thrived on the provocative, on being unique. Joey possessed the same incomparably fluid athletic grace and stamina. Like his sister he could play nearly any musical instrument by ear.

Their school days were neatly slotted with a full array of wholesome, time-consuming activities designed to create well-rounded, intelligent, responsible adults. By no means rich, Derek and I still managed to cover travel hockey fees, music lessons and specialty summer camp tuitions seemingly out of nowhere. We made do with a 20-year-old couch, an unfinished home addition that remained unpainted and plywood-floored for the same amount of time, cheap used cars, Goodwill clothing and the cheaper cuts of meat. We slept in rest stops when we could not afford hotel rooms. These normal parental sacrifices, we believed, would result in raising happy, healthy children schooled to succeed.

In the summer of his 18th year I begged Joey to tell me his passion. "There must be something," I entreated my now evasive and incredibly handsome son. "What's your passion? What do you want out of life?"

The answer was not what I wanted to hear. Oh, parents, do be careful what you ask for!

"Cars," he said. "My passion is cars, all right?" He proceeded to spend his high school graduation money on a cherry 1982 Camaro, specifically purchased in homage to his birth year.

On the first glorious May day here in the North Country, the kind of day when the tulips finally decide to open and Yoopers lift their faces to the sun to catch the fever of coming summer, the prize Camaro was t-boned pulling out of the Wal-Mart parking lot by a teen-age flibbergibbet yacking on her cell phone. The car was totaled. Had he been in a flimsier vehicle, Joey would have been maimed or dead. The heavy driver's side door was bowed in like it had been struck by a ship's prow. It was his first and last drive in his dream Camaro.

That was not the worst. On a balmy night in late August after attending the county fair where Once Upon a Time his 4-H club birdhouse won a blue ribbon, Joey went out to a keg party in "da bush," as they say up here. His fellow merry-makers included a comely young lass testing her wings after years of home-schooled seclusion. Under the influence of prescribed anti-depressants mixed with unknown quantities of cheap, illegally purchased beer, she chose Joey as the object of her seduction. "I should have just stayed by the bonfire with my chips and dip," he wrote in one of his letters from county jail.

At the court hearing, it came out that she'd already been with one or two other young men before she approached Joey. In the large crowd of drunken teens, no one had compared notes. Every story revealed in the court depositions was different. Jeanine, a plump little hippie throwback who smelled of sandalwood and thrived on high drama, testified that there had been a gang bang.

Naturally this shocking revelation made front-page headlines in the local newspaper, complete with giant head-shot photos of the three "rapists." I quickly grew tired of explaining to family, friends and enemies that the encounters were not "all at once" and how do you describe to anyone, even a close personal friend, that your son didn't technically have intercourse with an underage, over-medicated girl?

Seeking oasis, I couldn't wait to escape to the harbor. It's a zone unto itself, isolated and insulated. The papers come a day late. Brockway Mountain blocks radio, cell phone and internet reception. Television programming comes direct from space to the harbor's town-owned satellite dishes, which do not pull in any local news channels. Most harborites and vacationers do not care what's on TV anyway, once they get the Weather Channel forecast.

I'm not the first woman to use work as an excuse to run away from an unmanageable family. Rising at 9 a.m. each morning I threw on sweatpants and a tee and walked to the corner grocery store for a large coffee and a banana. Then my stroll to the pay phone near the Christmas Shoppe & Soda Fountain for my morning check-in call to Derek. Our conversations were perfunctory, "Hi how was your night, were you busy at the shop, did Joey hear from his lawyer, talk to you tomorrow."

Each weekday at noon I reported for my job: lunch and dinner shifts at the Der Anker Inn, a grand and gracious gourmet restaurant open from the Memorial Day to the second week in October, featuring German cuisine and fresh Lake Superior fish cooked to succulent deliciousness over a hickory-fired grill.

The food and service were exceptional and tips reflected that. The work was hard and sweaty, physically and mentally taxing. Having a nose on the grindstone can blot out all other concerns. I welcomed the labor as a release.

I could not mother my children. They did not want it. Having been physically pushed away from Lisa and Joey, one in jail and one with fists raised against me, I became a mother of sorts to the young people staying in the harbor in the "Village," a motley collection of house trailers more primitive than the Carpenter's abode, where the Der Anker Inn provided lodging for kitchen and front-of-the-house workers.

From my base on the fold-out couch in the faded blue-and-white aluminum-sided circa 1970s "Girls Trailer," I surveyed all the nocturnal comings and goings, played enthusiastic hostess for after-work wine tastings, presided over euchre tournaments at the drop-leaf kitchen table, dispensed acetaminophen to the hung over and advice to the lovelorn. Safely installed as the mother figure in the Girls Trailer, my reputation impeccable and all monitors off, I found and embraced a wild side I hadn't known I had.

The kids teased me about my living room/bedroom. "I don't mind the lack of privacy," I insisted. "I just wish the couch had a better mattress."

"Hailey, you can sleep in my bed anytime," said one of the chefs who had just come in after closing up the kitchen. I rolled my eyes and we all laughed.

It was absurd. He was in his early 30s; at the time I was 44. His bedroom was at the end of the hall, the rules of the Girls Trailer having been relaxed due to a housing shortage.

Men in their 30s are delicious; it's the best time to enjoy them, after the idiocy of their 20s and before the first cementing of their ways in their 40s. Later I would recognize Chef's random comment as the beginning of our insane summer sex fiesta atop the mountain, in the water, down old logging trails and in any available bed with a lock between us and the world.

He was Lover Number Three, if you're keeping track. I glowed, and could see that I glowed to others with a sexual aura that I never learned how to handle. Derek knew but did not know what he knew. Never one to compliment anything I wear, Derek offered up unsolicited comments radiating disapproval and suspicion. "Why are you putting on makeup?" "Are you wearing THAT?" "How long are we going to have to wait for you to get ready?"

Clearly the Chef had awakened a greedy sensuality that showed in my body, my bearing, my posture. My same old clothes fit me more provocatively. I didn't know it showed until numerous friends asked me if I was working out more or had quit smoking or simply glowed from the experience of sailing on the water with Derek. Sexual healing opened my spirit in a way that showed in my face, my ass, my walk, my smile. A lover's touch and lusty sport-fucking transformed me physically. My unawareness was part of my attractiveness. After so many years of living with a spouse who loathed touch, flinched at hugs and repelled kisses, it was beyond imagination to be ravished.

In that restless fall with Joey out on bail awaiting trial, my daughter announced that she had married at city hall a dysfunctional blob of a plumber's son and required a large ceremony and reception at the local Country Club. Derek coped by numbing himself with a variety of illegal substances, a haze of silence and cannabis smoke broken by brusque instructions to Hailey the Deck Monkey as we sailed the uncalm waters of the lake each weekend. My days off were more work than the 10-hour lunch-dinner split shifts.

Chapter 5: Bang Shang A Lang

"Sex matters too much to you," Derek has told me more than once. "You're like some slutty nympho, grow up." The message drummed into my brain, used to denigrate my being and degrade my priorities, was negated in Chef's lusty, leg-spreading, licking ministrations. Apparently there are others like me, who believe sexuality is extremely important, perhaps making it too important, but then again, I am making up for lost time.

During those six weeks with the chef, driving the winding scenic tree tunnel highway up to work in the harbor I sang along with the radio, celebrating constant cravings and sweet dreams made of this on a damn cold night. "I don't know who you are, but I'm with you," I cooed. Drenching my heart in white, Chef swam through my veins like a fish in a sea of blankets. He was the one to tuck me in at night; my body is a wonderland. "You're my favorite person to sleep with this summer," I told him, snuggled tight, and sensuously spooned, Chef wrapped around me in a secure hold that does not strangle. I was not lost in his arms; I was found there.

Things were bad for my son. The headlines continued without mercy, his mug shot emblazoned on the front page even when the article was only an update on one of the other accused rapists.

Derek sedated himself in drugs or distance, sailing us far from shore each weekend in fair or foul weather, mocking me when I shivered or swore at the wind. Lisa joked (not so funny) that she wanted to change her last name and make the out-of-town move permanent.

Only in Chef's embrace or awaiting his nocturnal visits (I believe these are known as "booty calls" these days) could I sleep. On the nights he wasn't in the harbor or later, when he chose other sleeping companions, I resumed my midnight-to-dawn rambles.

I get a mistrustful, interruptive vibe from Derek during our weekend journeys. I am there but not. The minute my brain skips away to a longed-for sensual state, he is in my face with another question. The minute I recline on the cushions splayed out in the blessed sun, he finds a line to adjust, a sail to tweak, a winch to crank that requires me to move. I'm forever changing positions, forever in the way, blocking the necessary tasks. Or he trumps my reverie by disappearing down below, forcing me to rise and stand watch. He also tempts fate on the bowsprit seat, perching on the rough wood plank, laughing maniacally as the waves engulf his feet and spray slams into his face, hanging on the rails unharnessed, dipping down into the troughs and riding the crests like a daredevil on an unlicensed carnival ride. This brave idiocy is one of the reasons that I married the man. But I weary of worry. Despite extreme lack of affection, my fear of losing Derek in the water is huge. Boating surveys show that many women share my paranoia with good reason. If the captain falls overboard, could we rescue him? And if not, could we get the boat safely to shore? And if we could sail the ship ourselves, where would we go?

I honestly do not know if I could drop the sails, engage the engine, mark where Derek went overboard on the GPS, toss the floating life rings and slings, the flashing floating buoy and find him, a tiny speck in the devouring waves. I would rather fall overboard myself.

Derek laughs at my fear, nasty and derisive, berating my whimpering until he becomes angry with it, as if castigation will impart courage. When I tremble as he stumbles forward in rough seas, it is too disgusting to him to handle, and I am brusquely ordered to take my deepest fears below decks where he doesn't have to look at me. This is where Joey gets his "don't worry about it" from. I do worry. Telling me not to worry doesn't help in the least.

I have splashed, kicking frantically, breaststroke determined, out of this cold, affectionless and unapproving sphere into a third affair. Third is not the charm. Again it costs me in vehicle damage. It's becoming a trend; $165 this time for ripping the muffler system loose while navigating a muddy logging road on a midnight tryst away from the whispers, the harbor rumors that I am unbelievably at the center of.

"I'm old," I grouse to Chef. "Don't they have anything better to talk about than a 44-year-old woman's comings and goings?" My indignant righteousness feels false, shrill, even to me. Chef tells me nobody cares.

We use condoms, but I truly feel dirty, debased. I begin to wonder if God is punishing me.

In the fourth week, my good, pure friend Mariel pulls me aside after work into her cabin for a heart-to-heart. When she asks me what's going on, I tell her I am trying to help Chef with his drinking problem, keep him away from bad influences, and that I can't sleep anyway because I am so wound up over my son's arrest and my daughter's impending wedding reception with the vegetable. She pretends to accept my explanation that Chef and I are just two buddy-buddy comrades weathering storms in our currently tumultuous lives, but doesn't really buy it. "You know when you're not up here he's messing around with Sheila and still with Missy," she gently tells me. I can't stand how deeply she looks into my eyes. I snort derisively, as if all that sex stuff is beneath my dignity.

Mortified by unwanted attention, I manage to stay away from Chef for a week. No sleep. No appetite.

In the sixth week, the hunter quarries his prey. I cannot resist a few more forays with Chef, nights and early mornings of mutual oral worship, explicit language and flirtations with anal sex, which both titillates and terrifies me. I decide that talking about it with finger stimulation is enough experimentation for me, particularly given my partner's nebulous sexual history. Gossip Central has by this time shifted focus to the infidelity and subsequent break-up involving a long-established harbor couple, Jocelyn and Randy. Jocelyn, ever the blonde drama queen of whipping pony tail and breasts quivering with indignation, demands all the attention. I am profoundly grateful to relinquish an unwelcome spotlight.

After the last lunch shift of the season, I load the van with clothes, blankets, coffeemaker, sundry pots and pans and books I never read because I was so busy being a dirty, dirty girl. Derek wants to ship out as soon as I get to the boat, so I'm missing the closing night party. Everyone scheduled to work that night is already on duty and the village is quiet, except for Isis, who's alternately barking and growling to let me know he's keeping an eye on me from behind the screen door of Mariel's cabin.

"Bye Village," I wave at no one as I back out. At the main street corner I see Chef. It's poetically apt, moviesque, one of those happenstances that you couldn't make up or orchestrate. He motions me to stop, leans in the window for a lingering kiss with tongue. "Goodbye," I say, aiming for a devil-may-care laissez-faire disconnection that will salvage my pride. He looks deep into my eyes, regards my expression. "Oh, I'm sure we'll be seeing each other around," he says. Wink. Wink.

"No, we won't," I say. "We move in different circles."

The next time I see Chef three years have gone by and he has a sexy 30-ish Bosnian fiancé. They spend winters in her homeland and summers running the Lodge kitchen out at Isle Royale National Park. I am over my fourth lover, The

Most Dangerous of All, and am embarking on my second year-long cruise on the boat with Derek. True to my previous promiscuous pattern, I've spent an inordinate amount of time looking for my fourth lover's vehicle, a blue compact with license plate number ending URL, which at the time symbolized "You Are Love" to me. I writhe at the sophomoric sappiness of it even now. Chalk it up to the G-string bravado of early menopause.

But would it have been better to have not felt, to have packed up and put away my sexuality, my need to be loved, after I turned 40? Derek has been waiting for me to finally see how silly, awkward, messy and unnecessary sex is, a conclusion he arrived at when he turned 40 nine years before me. He would have been better off begging off and buying me a vibrator. It was Chef who confirmed for me, as he gently traced a clockwise circle on my bare tummy, both of us tumbled on his soft single bed, "Life doesn't really exist without sex. That's basic. Nature, sex and music are my religion."

I never really did belong with Derek, I belonged to him. Safely tucked away in the cold and barren North Country that I am not from and was never meant to be, I settled for this life with this family, going with the flow of what circumstances chose for me. I came to Derek as a physically abused 19-year-old swapping a fiancé who beat me with his fists for a husband who smacks me down with deprecatory words and enforced isolation. After so many years being forced to hide my own thoughts, I scarcely know how to operate independently. And with all the hair yanking it's a wonder I have any left on my head.

Seawind is guiding me as much as I'm piloting her. I know what I am running from but haven't the foggiest where I'm going geographically or emotionally. My stomach growls and I realize I'm starving again despite the soup.

The sailboat bobs in the ever-present wash and echo of ships gone by. I don't believe this water ever settles down, but my surroundings are otherwise placid. No patrol boats, harbor cops or other nosy inquiries in person or by radio. I decide it's OK to let my guard down just a bit. In the galley I open another can of Italian wedding soup, light one of the three burners on the propane stove and spoon dinner direct from the saucepan, washed down with tap water from the "Raspberry Island" plastic tumbler in the series of Michigan lighthouses. There's a filter system beneath the tiny stainless sink (Hey Culligan Man!) and the water has no flavor. Bland's fine, as long as the filter keeps intestinal eructations away. After brief internal debate I switch on the mast light. It isn't always required in designated mooring fields but as a general rule it's best to ensure a vessel is visible to any traffic navigating in the dead of night.

Mañana, tomorrow, the island sailor's favorite expression for putting off what can be done today. Mañana will demand action, vision, decision. My borrowed boat has a cozy V-berth complete with an old patchwork-patterned lighthouse quilt of sublime quality. The downy pillows invite, but the space feels too personal, too intimate for a stranger's slumber. The battery indicator shows plenty of voltage, so I leave the marine radio on, grab the quilt and curl up on the settee cushions in the main salon. Ensconced on the couch, a lighthouse dish towel next to my pillow, I count Heartland Rivers instead of sheep to help me sleep.

"Chicago, Illinois, Mississippi, Missouri, Ohio, Cumberland, Tennessee, Tombigbee, Black Warrior, Alabama, Ten-saw …" by the time I get to Mobile I'm dozing.

Chapter 6: Around Robin

A squawk of unintelligible radio fuzz mercifully rouses me from another jail nightmare. The sun is up. Dust motes dancing in its first rays strike the eastern salon window. Supine, I mop the night-sweats off my forehead and breastbone, coming to consciousness with the admission that today I must figure out where I am going. Instinctively, and rather stupidly, I have continued along the known path of America's Great Circle Loop, where Derek and I were headed before I ran away. He can easily catch up with me if he figures out what I've done.

Does Derek miss me? Is he worried? God, I am so perverse. On this wild escapade designed to put as much distance as possible between us, I feel ambivalent about causing him any pain. I just want him to leave me alone. The love-you-hate-you is probably just another manifestation of menopause. It reminds me of when Richard Nixon died and fond memories arose — "I am not a crook" and all that — or more currently of the deifying of Ronald Reagan who in death achieved the sainthood he never earned as president.

The women generations ahead of me exhibited some pretty bizarre behavior when they were going through "the change" but I am sure this takes the cake. Derek calls it "mental pause" due to my "whore moans." Perhaps he's right and I need my head examined.

I roll off the couch, splash my face with a few pumps of tap water, wiping the sleep crust my mother calls "fish eggs" from the inner corners of my eyes. She's really going to get a kick out of this. She's never liked Derek, proclaiming him "not worth two shits" and she likes me so much that anything I do is AOK with her. Considering the great mother I have, I should have turned out a lot better. Maybe when the menopause is over I can obtain a doctorate, a Cabinet post or earn a Nobel, something to show her that all her aspirations for me were not in vain.

Up to this point, America's Great Loop is one of my more impressive accomplishments.

The Loop encompasses roughly 6,000 miles of Great Lakes, Atlantic Ocean, Gulf of Mexico and sundry notable rivers and canals in eastern North America. The total mileage of the so-called "Loop" depends on where you begin, in my case Lake Superior. From there, Derek and I sailed *Chinook* across Lake Superior from west to east through the Straits of Mackinac that divide Michigan into upper and lower peninsulas. We proceeded south down Lake Michigan's Michigan side around the Indiana bend — the shortest distance across the lake-and along the southeast Illinois border into the rivers that are accessible from the Chicago area. It is 1,300 miles from Chicago to Mobile, Alabama. From there the entire world is accessible, via the Gulf of Mexico. Not a bad destination. The world.

The first of the Heartland Rivers is the Illinois, followed by 218 miles of the Mississippi with its hairpin turns, swirling currents, mud flats and massive commercial barges steaming 'round the bends. A sharp left at the Ohio River junction brings the current strong against upbound boats. Two locks later it's on to the narrow, twisting, ever-green Cumberland River, leading into the locks at Land Between the Lakes, portal to the poetic Tennessee River. The Tennessee merges into the Tennessee-Tombigbee Waterway. Known as the Tenn-Tom, it's a system of natural and man-made water bodies controlled by a dozen locks dropping to sea level at Mobile Bay, land of salt water and tidal influence. From there Loopers hang a left toward Florida, tracing the panhandle and west coast down to the Keys before heading up the Eastern Seaboard and into the Great Lakes.

Derek will definitely resent the interruption in his plans; resent having to look for me. He hates waiting for me for even a second as I hurry along, trying to keep up but forever behind his double-time pace down the aisles. So many places I would have tarried when he rushed along to something he was interested in. But I know better. In Hammond just a few days ago he'd waited outside with a backpack of groceries while I went in the discount liquor outlet to get something non-alcoholic. It was hard to not drink; Derek continued to enjoy cocktail hour every night along with any other boaters we met. I hated to ask him to stop. And for money. But he was almost cheerful.

"Might as well make it worth it. Get some Blue while you're in there." He handed me a $20. Diet tonic water was speedily located. But despite its prodigious stocks the store did not carry his favorite Labatt Blue. I desperately scanned the coolers, unable to decide on an alternative. Budweiser, Corona, El Presidente, Anchor Steam? He doesn't like light beer, says my favorite

Miller Lite tastes like water. Should I choose dark beer, amber bock, wheat ale? Ten minutes passed before I grabbed two 12-packs of Bud and checked out, the line slowed by an array of ghetto-fabulous characters mulling over Lotto numbers. When I emerged Derek had already started back to the boat. I could see him striding angrily, a pissed-off speed walker, two bags of groceries swinging in his hands, backpack loaded with more provisions, two blocks ahead of me. Hampered by tear-blinded eyes and a case of beer I would not be drinking I hustled as fast as I could down the garbage-strewn road paralleling the Libby Foods Factory, past brick walls splashed with obscene graffiti and gang insignia, concrete sidewalks littered with fast-food wrappers, cigarette butts and broken glass, with no hope of catching up.

He turned back once near a refinery yard, shooting a contemptuous disgusted glance in my direction. I am the ball attached to his chain. As I often do in times of stress and sorrow I sang to myself. "I Walk Alone," from Green Day's "Boulevard of Broken Dreams." Suitable for the occasion of the latest humiliation.

"Hey baby, I wanna go where you're going, where's the partay?"

"Maybe she needs some help, do you need some help baby?"

I half-smile and nod stiffly, maintaining firm eye contact with the trash-talking group of black and white dudes hanging out on the next corner. They are likely harmless but my danger antenna is up. The worst thing you can do is appear submissive or scared. "No thanks guys, I got it," I say pleasantly.

"Well, you have a nice day now, OK?" I nod again and keep moving, shoulders, elbows and wrists aching, startled by the only kindness I have known in quite some time. The beer boxes are sweating more than I am. The wet cardboard could give way any time now, spilling aluminum cans into the street. In my haste to catch up with Derek I didn't stop to put them in my backpack.

Derek finally deigns, at great inconvenience to Himself, to stop and wait for me at the railroad tracks across from the marina street entrance. I flush with relief, sweat popping on my forehead, beading between my breasts, wet warmth running down my spine. "I'm sorry," I say to his back. How pathetic, as pathetic as all the apologies needlessly made for years on end. Why am I sorry that I took so long to thoughtfully attempt to choose a beer that he would enjoy?

Scuttling along behind my husband like a proper subservient wife, I receive the first picture of what a life without vitriol and degradation would be. It would look like a weathered wooden shack hanging over a river in a warm place, a rocker tilted on warped floorboards on a rickety but serviceable porch, a flats boat tied to the railing, fishing poles and crab traps neatly stacked by the screen door. I hear the clack of a manual typewriter, smell brackish saltwater tang in the air. There is a woman here who lives alone but is not lonely. The river is the only road to her home. Her backyard is a dense jungle tangle of palmetto, rattling marsh grasses, lovingly nurtured native flowers. A small area has been cleared and fenced in. Melons, tomatoes and sunflowers flourish.

She spends her days writing, reading, thinking, gardening and fishing. Occasional lovers and constant friends come to her by boat.

In somnambulate half-sleep on the couch of a borrowed sailboat I again inhabit my river cabin, a brave pioneer tending her flowers, herbs and vegetables, feisty and fiercely independent as Marjorie Kinnan Rawlings at Cross Creek. It's beautiful. No one yanks me from my reverie. No one is tapping a foot, snorting in annoyance, waiting for me to drop what I am doing and catch up with what's supposedly more important.

Awake but dreaming I am called to the rivers, to a place I think I remember.

Seawind will not be able to enter the Chicago Sanitary Shipping Canal with her mast up. There are numerous bridges, 40 alone within a five-mile section, including a couple of 20-foot fixed bridges that the boat's rigging is too tall to clear. There's a reason that first section of the Illinois River is called "Fifteen Miles of Hell." In addition to the low bridges there are numerous bascule bridges (drawbridges, to you landlubbers) that must be hailed by radio or with blasts on the horn so operators can open or raise them to allow boat traffic through. All the while the tow barges laden with hot blacktop, benzene, scrap metal and smoking wood chips clog the narrow waterway taking precedent over pleasure craft. Said pleasure craft can also be a danger, particularly because of local hooligans who like to toss back a few drinks and mess with the "fancy boats" and unseasoned Loopers who have no business piloting a vessel.

Grabbing the last banana I head up top for a look-see and breakfast. Another boat came in during the night and caught a mooring two balls over. The transom reads *Blackout*, home port New Orleans. The name does not engender confidence, but the boat itself is a different story, radiating the high gloss of both money and care.

Blackout is a fancy steel trawler with elegant swooping lines. She is decked out with all the accoutrements of a long-range cruising vessel: solar panels, wind generator, motorized lift for the Boston Whaler dinghy, a small electric scooter and all the other toys affluent liveaboards require to keep themselves in the style to which they are accustomed. From a distance I cannot tell whether the thin white noodle of a person sitting on the bow in cross-legged meditative pose smoking a cigarette is male or female.

"Helloooo over there — good morning!" the husky, nicotine-sanded voice offers no further clues to gender.

"Good morning," I shout back. "It's a beautiful day!"

"Want coffee?"

Before I can answer, the Whaler drops off its davits into the water, settling neatly into the roll of the constant Chicago Harbor chop. More boats have come out on the water to greet the possibilities of this crisp morning, but I still see no telltale orange Coast Guard dinghies or any other official-looking craft. The skinny person climbs nimbly down to the dinghy, fires up the outboard engine and zips over to *Seawind*.

Such behavior is not uncommon among boaters, a gregarious lot, at times so aggressively friendly that it will send an introvert running for cover. I cannot count how many times I've been subjected to endless male yapping about diesel engines, intake valves, stuffing boxes, seacocks, the merits of inflatable vs. hard dinghies and so on and so on. For as spiteful and impatient as Derek could be with me, he sure liked to gab for hours with anyone who stopped by in quest of solving a boat problem or touting the merits of their boat. Repelling hospitable advances is a definite no-no that will only attract further attention.

Under a blue ball cap intoning the legend "Relax: Cabbage Key," a slightly lunatic elfin face looks up at me, sparkling blue eyes full of fun under sloppy, graying blonde bangs, apple cheeks plumped by an infectious grin, perfect pearly whites. "Permission to come aboard?" It is a husky-voiced she, and she is already halfway up the swim ladder at the stern before I nod.

I can tell right away that this wiry little dynamo doesn't care about fuel pumps, electrical system wiring or holding tank capacity. In her face I see wealth, eccentricity and an ongoing, unstoppable search for happiness. She likes fishing, as evidenced by her Guy Harvey T-shirt hanging loosely over overpriced men's khaki shorts purchased in the apparel department of some West Marine store. Rather than a Hawaiian shirt, she has topped her fashion ensemble with the second alternative in the cliché boater's cruising uniform category, a long-sleeved denim shirt with the name of her boat embroidered on the right hand pocket. The coffee, handed over in an extra-large silver travel mug that also bears the *Blackout* moniker, is very welcome, a shot of normalcy and comfort with an upscale flair. "Thank you so much. I just got up. Haven't gotten around to making coffee yet. I'm Hailey."

"Hi Hailey, I'm Robin."

"So where are you headed? You're a long way from New Orleans."

"Do you mind if I smoke?" She's already pulling a pack of Marlboro Lights out of her denim shirt pocket. "Want one?"

"Sure. Why not, I'm trying to quit but you know how that goes. I'm good for a while, then I'm bad."

"Shit sistah, I'm bad allll the time."

Can't help it, I'm laughing. She's endearingly childlike although she must be close to my age, 40s headed for 50 any year now. Threads of tiny broken capillaries around her nose indicate that she's never turned down a cocktail. It's a lively face that has seen a lot of life, open and assertive.

We puff away companionably. Sometimes a cigarette tastes so good.

"Where are you headed? You don't sound like you're from New Orleans." If I keep asking the questions, maybe I won't have to supply any answers.

"I have no frickin' idea. South, outta this cold. Katrina laid a number on the marina, just completely and totally creamed it. I ran up the rivers ahead of the storm and now that I'm all the way up here I'm ready to go back down to where the butter melts. Lake Michigan is as pretty as I remembered, but I forgot how cold it is up here."

Turns out she's originally from Detroit. She tells me she left her husband, "a real bunghole, to use a nautical phrase," two years prior, just after they'd bought the boat and moved aboard down in the Big Easy. Like Derek and I, they did the Loop. That was enough of the liveaboard life for him. She wanted to keep going.

"I don't need his money and the big-ass house and all the blahdey-blah, La Dee Dah bullcrap that goes with it, so I said screw it. It's the cruising life for me from here on out. He kept the sailboat; I got stuck with the trawler. She's a modified steel work boat. A one-off. No biggie, at heart I'm a stinkpotter not a rag-bagger anyway. What's your deal, why are you single-handing? I am because no one in my family approves of my 'bullheaded and ill-advised meandering' — that's a direct quote from my sister Renee. Nice boat you got here, by the way." She pats the teak cap rail like she's giving a good dog an atta boy.

"Thanks, but it's not mine. I'm sort of watching it for a friend."

"You're from around here. Cool. We can dinghy into town and you can show me the lay of the land."

"No, actually. I'm a Michigander too. From the U.P."

"A Yooper, eh?"

"Sort of. I moved up there to go to school. My husband was — is — a dyed-in-the-wool Yooper, though."

"So where is he?"

"Um…" She's staring at me as I avert my eyes.

"What? Spit it out. Oh my God, is he dead? I'm sorry. I'm so nosy. Renee says I need a mouth monitor."

"No no no, he's not dead."

The cockpit radio speakers crackle. "Securité! Securité! Securité! this is U.S. Coast Guard Chicago, break … Mariners are advised to keep a sharp lookout for a 36-foot sailing vessel *Seawind*, reported missing from its assigned berth at Hammond Marina as of 9/15, 1800 hours Greenwich Mean Time. Mariners are advised to keep a sharp lookout and report all sightings to the U.S. Coast Guard, break …"

"Hole E Shit." Robin laughs, a raspy guffaw. "That's you Miss Priss, isn't it? And you look so innocent!"

"Well, I just borrowed her, honestly. I'm giving her back. I was only trying to get away. I'm such a loser that I only made it this far. I was actually trying to figure out how to get this mast down so I can get down the rivers somewhere where he can't find me. Derek is going to kill me when he finds me. I am so screwed. He'll probably put me away."

The compulsion to blurt out the entire story in its sordid entirety, with rambling sidebars, is strong. As my mother says, I have the tendency to "spill my guts at the drop of a hat." My entire family, with the exception of a tight-lipped father, is so confessional it's a miracle we aren't Catholics.

In my agitation and self-disgust I carelessly toss the cigarette butt overboard.

"Great, add water polluter to my many crimes."

Robin bounces over to my side of the cockpit, lays her long, knotty fingers on my shoulders, and squeezes reflexively. I flinch, reminded of a first-grade teacher who shook me until my bones rattled because my loopy left-handed cursive was too large to contain a full sentence on the prescribed one line.

Robin does not shake me; she is firm, insistent, but gentle. "Get a grip, girlfriend. Time to abandon your stolen vessel, yaarr matey and chop chop!" She climbs down below and zips my duffel.

She can't be serious. She doesn't even know me. The both of us are clearly deranged. Menopause and perhaps something more.

"Robin. No. This is my problem," I insist. "I don't want to drag you into it."

She stares up the companionway shooting me the kind of no-bull look I haven't seen since my mother told me it was fine with her if I left Derek and moved back home.

"Hey, I'm in it, whether you like it or not," she says, climbing back into the cockpit. "No worries. I specialize in strays dogs and lost causes!"

I bid farewell to *Seawind* with a whispered blessing and gratitude as we zoom to *Blackout* at top speed. I have left no trace save for an open chart, a drip-dried saucepan in the drainer, two banana peels and a 6-ply wad of toilet paper. We're doused with spray as the dinghy plows through the medium chop. Seagulls wheel in the cloud-ribboned sky, laughing at my folly.

Robin lifts her face to the promising morning sun, lets out a disco battle cry, "Ooooh ooooh — rivers, here we come!"

Again, I'm being rescued. Along with the relief of having a problem easily and immediately solved for me, there is a sick familiarity to turning over control. If pattern holds true to form, somewhere along the line resentment will set in on both sides of this bizarre equation, the result being dangerous to one or more said parties.

Abuse does not hinder self-awareness, it amplifies. Already I can feel a chronic eagerness to serve kicking in. To be so useful, handy, unobtrusive and pleasant to have around that she will find me indispensable. Already I am wondering — much as I hate to foster my penurious streak — how much money she has and how she earns a living. As one who has never had enough to make it on my own, subsisting from paycheck to paycheck even in the best of times, I hope she will be able to supplement my $1,572. Of course I am not going to mention it. For now. After all, she could easily rob me and dump me off on the side of the river or leave me stranded on a sidewalk in Joliet, Illinois. Will a reward be offered for turning me in to the proper authorities? *Will they swab the peels and toilet paper for DNA?*

Mom would have known better. She's a fan of TV crime procedurals. She'd wipe everything down and take the trash along.

Why do I always imagine the worst? When I try to look forward, it's only ever in anticipation of the next shit that will hit the fan.

"Quit freaking out." Robin has to holler to be heard over the vroom of the outboard engine. She doesn't strike me as the whispering type in any event.

"Sorry."

"I can see it all over your face. And don't apologize. Quit it right now. Jesus, are you ever tightly wound."

"Well, wouldn't you be? I have no idea what I'm doing. We barely know each other."

"Here we are," Robin eases the Whaler up to the stern ladder. "Welcome to your home away from home. Climb up first and open the porch gate. I'll hand up your stuff."

All is aboard in short order. Robin surprises me with her crisp professionalism. And her natural assumption that I'll man the bow. She issues the prepare-to-cast-off order after I gather in the mooring ball pendant. I untie the bowline harness while she fires up the engines, which I later learn are twin Lehman diesels.

Blackout retains a certain dignity and aloof beauty, as if she is above the mud, barnacles, bilge slime and normal grime that inevitably puts its mark on any vessel that's been out cruising for an extended period of time. Her hull is glossy obsidian, her white stay-gripped decks pristine. There's a good explanation for this. The last in a long line of boatyard owners specializing in marine sales & service, Robin ran the detailing end of the family empire. She is an expert on maintaining, restoring, cleaning and polishing woodwork, fiberglass, brass, stainless and virtually every other surface and materials found on boats. She is also a neat freak, which means no nook or cranny on her 44-foot floating home escapes her ministrations. *Blackout* is a pristine custom craft, its solid black, slightly luminescent hard-chined hull embellished with a discreet cranberry cove pin-stripe above and a slightly thicker cranberry boot stripe at the waterline. Her square lines, from the high, rectangular transom (the back end to you landlubbers) to her waist-high bulwarks (the top edge of her sides on either deck) broadcast 'don't mess with me.' Everything is either solid steel or steel-clad. The conventional, four-windowed white pilothouse and its door are steel-plated, as is the lower "doghouse" on the foredeck, the roof, if you will, of the living and navigational quarters. *Blackout's* heavy, blunt, almost militaristic persona is balanced by the sweeping, subtle arch of her pointed bow, emphasized by geometric cranberry-and-white scrollwork. The bikes and dinghies stowed on the flat-top cabin roof also hint at less-than-official business.

Blackout's tastefully spare interior is the antithesis of the stereotypical cruising vessel littered ad nauseum with nautical novelties and bric-a-brac. Nary a dolphin, mermaid, lighthouse, pelican or coconut pirate head in sight. There is no litter of tools or past lives. The only ornamentation works for a living: barometer, clock, compass, burnished brass oil lanterns and a diminutive, shiny red Franklin stove. Solid black, red and white dominate the color scheme. It's simple, sophisticated, warm. Robin directs me to stow my duffle in the V-berth, which currently seems to be doing duty as a combined toolbox and well-organized storage area for cleaning and paper supplies, including a crate of Bounty paper towels, Swiffer Wet Jet refills and several family-size packages of Charmin Extra Strong toilet tissue. There's no time to wonder about sleeping arrangements, although I allow myself a fleeting thought about sexual orientation before heading up top to the pilot house. We have handily cleared the mooring field and are approaching the ship canal entrance.

Despite the incessant traffic and the need to be on alert for close encounters with tugs, tows and other recreational vessels (RVs, as some of the tow pilots call those of our ilk), the journey through Chicago is, as ever, scenic and imposing. The skyline when viewed from the deck of a small boat is otherworldly. Skyscrapers dwarf *Blackout* as we motor through the concrete canyon, wrapped in the din and energy of the Windy City.

We travel in silence, captivated by man-made sounds and scenery, until the canal dumps us into the river proper, the lovely but toxic Illinois. This river is so laden with chemicals that ice will not form on it in winter. Even now a mentholated vaporous mist steams off the water, wisping in the wind as the sun hits the surface. Signs all along the banks warn against touching the water. Even the many herons at the river's edge seem to know better than to wade, perching instead on the tree limbs, rocks and industrial detritus — rotting wooden piers, rusty metal skeletons-that protrude from the shoreline overlooking the cola-colored river. I continually scan the river, the banks. The binoculars are never out of my hands.

Soon the locks begin. In the first 100 miles from Lake Michigan the river drops 140 feet. From Starved Rock Lock to the Mississippi the drop is another 20 feet.

The first lock, the O'Brien, basically serves to keep river water and invasive species including zebra mussels and Asian Carp out of Lake Michigan. In later years, underwater electrical barriers were installed, providing another good reason to keep out of the water.

The green signal light is on, indicating permission to enter the lock chamber. Once we are inside, with just a couple of other smallish boats — neither one *Chinook*, just a ratty-looking 23-foot cabin cruiser and metallic red racing runabout — the gates on either end of the lock close. The drop is slight, maybe a foot, imperceptible to the naked eye but it's a buffer zone. Robin positions the boat as instructed by an attendant, who curtly nods to our "good morning" and silently points to the spot on the smooth concrete wall where he wants us. "Use your words," Robin whispers under her breath as he moves on. "Shhh," I caution, but we're both snickering.

No need for work gloves to handle long lines. A boathook on the walkway railing is enough to hold *Blackout* in place just off the wall. For me this is a familiar duty handled automatically with no need for discussion. It's as if Robin and I have been traveling together for months rather than hours. When the horns sound and the gate opens, Robin lets out another disco whoop, "Oooh oooh." And I join in.

Buh Bye Derek. There's a solid obstacle between you and me. You can get through faster than an invasive Asian Carp. But it will slow you down.

We glide out barely above idle, giving the two smaller craft plenty of leeway to zoom ahead.

"Look at their fishing poles," says Robin.

"They don't actually eat what they catch, do they?" I wonder.

"I wouldn't," she says. "how far did you want to go today? I was thinking Joliet."

"There's a free town dock there in the Veteran's Park," I offer, trying to be of use. "The casino across the river has a sumptuous around-the-world buffet rivaling the Hammond casino. There's also a Wendy's fast-food outlet on the park side of the river and a party store cum gas station within walking distance," I babble. These are all important considerations for your normal Great Loop cruisers, but a boat hijacker on the run should be thinking of something other than shopping and dining. I remind myself that I must lay low, fly under the radar and operate undercover, as my mixed-metaphor flinging family would advise.

"Joliet it is," Robin says with a nod.

Robin doesn't strike me as the incognito type. Even on short acquaintance I don't believe she will turn me in, but she won't be hiding her light under any bushels any time soon, either. It is hard to tell if she knows how to keep quiet about a situation and if she can keep secrets other than her own. Our own secrets seem to be the easiest to keep, even though holding them in does more damage.

"But…"

"What?"

"The last time Derek and I stopped in Joliet for the night there were regular police patrols in the park. A detective even stopped by the boat to see if we needed anything. He came back later with two courtesy blocks of ice, after Derek explained to their mutual great interest how our refrigeration system had shat the bed."

I worry that that detective is still around. I'll definitely need to watch my back and keep an eye out to avoid being recognized.

"Does he beat you?"

"OK, here's the deal. I don't know when, where or even if Derek is looking for me. He won't think I have the guts to get down the rivers on my own and even if I did, why would I? I've got nowhere to go." I can't look at her. It's embarrassing. I follow the foamy line of bow wake breaking the dark, dense, untouchable water. "As far as he's concerned, I'm a helpless dummy. The first place he probably looked was around the boat. Figured I fell off. For all I know he's demanding they drag the harbor bottom in Hammond right now.

"He could be looking for me in Chicago. Or over in Michigan. Or farther downriver. Or not at all. I don't want to get you in trouble. So if you just want to drop me off somewhere it's cool. Thanks for everything — you've already done a lot — but I don't expect you to keep covering my keister or get yourself in a pickle."

"Does he beat you?" Robin narrows her eyes, ready to do battle. How gratifying.

"No, not physically — unless you count this passive-aggressive thing he does with his body, invading all the space. Also pony-tail pulling. He just, I don't know, swallows me up, like there's no room to have a thought or action of my own. He eclipses me. He *Gaslights* me. You know, the old movie where the husband tries to make the wife think she's crazy? Everything that I think is important he thinks is wrong and stupid. Everything has to be his way. Everything I do is ridiculous. He's so impatient with everyone but himself. It's hard to explain — but I just couldn't take it one more day."

"Well, if anybody official or otherwise bugs us at the docks, we'll just keep going," Robin says, extracting a cig from the pack in her shirt pocket. "We aren't going to run into any cops out here. Let's not worry about them right now."

"And," she adds, "crowding you out and pulling your hair *is* physical abuse and mental abuse is real and every bit as damaging. I saw it on *Oprah.*"

She's right — about the police, anyway. You rarely, if ever, see the Coast Guard on the rivers. This is the lexicon of the U.S. Army Corps of Engineers, which is chiefly consumed with the business of dredging, clearing and shoring up the waterway, along with controlling commercial traffic and operating the locks and accompanying dams. If you are sick of seeing cops, and Lord knows I am, the river is a good place to be.

"Heads-up," Robin barks. A double-wide barge of stinking asphalt is hurtling towards us on the right. Behind us, to the left, a single-wide barge of hot-top is preparing to run up our port side. *Blackout* is the meat in a tow-barge sandwich. There is no choice but to continue on our path up the middle. But the motley cabin cruiser that was with us in the locks has stalled. Its engine dead, it's turned sideways to the current with no room to maneuver. The tow wash is pushing it backward, directly into *Blackout's* bow, as its captain tries to engage the engine.

The impact is a solid thunk that can be heard over the AC/DC blaring on the cabin cruiser's stereo and the cursing of its young-dude crew. The hapless mariners scramble to put down their Bacardi bottles and longneck beers to fend off. The much-lighter fiberglass cabin cruiser won't hurt *Blackout's* thick steel hull. Thankfully the tows have passed. But the collision pushes *Blackout* into a parked barge tied at a nearby pier, taking a chunk out of her stern transom paint and bashing in a corner of the rub rail.

I grab a boathook and rush up front, poking at whatever the tip of the hook can reach to shove the errant boat out of our way. "Watch where the hell you're going," I holler at the dudes in their flowered surfer shorts and mirrored sunglasses.

"Take it easy, lady, this happens all the time," a dreadlocked 20-something says, laughing.

"Not to me it doesn't," I scream back, although we are so close that my irate spittle may have hit his liquored-up baby face. Say it don't spray it doesn't apply in these situations. "If you can't control your boat you should stay off the water."

Blessedly the river is still clear of oncoming commercial traffic and we are able to ease back out with no further encounters. The cabin cruiser finally fires up and speeds off ahead of us.

There are those, mostly non-boaters, who think of the Loop as a relaxing ramble down lazy rivers to tropical climates; I wonder what they would make of this dark version of *National Lampoon's Family Vacation*.

"Remind me to never piss you off," says Robin. Grab me a beer, would you please? That deserves a drink."

After her first sip, she comments, "If Derek thinks you can't handle a boat, his head's up his ass."

Chapter 7: It's Noon Somewhere

Robin takes the soundtrack of her life seriously. She asks me to take the wheel while she flicks on the stereo. Sheryl Crow sings about liking a good beer buzz early in the morning.

I like it, too. Or used to, anyway. I wonder how long I'll continue this experiment with total clarity now that court-ordered sanctions are not particularly applicable. My spurned lover, Alcohol, is calling me: "Come back Hailey, all is forgiven."

Robin is an instigator.

"Grab me another cold one. And get one for yourself, if you like beer. 'It's Five O'clock Somewhere.'"

"Yeah, I do. I even have one of those t-shirts with the Benjamin Franklin quote about beer being God's way of showing us that He wants us to be happy. But I got a DUI right before we left on our boat trip. I've been on the wagon ever since."

Robin eyes me with suspicion for the first time. "Well, I'd like another one, if you don't mind."

Blackout's stainless steel galley appliances include an additional built-in refrigerated cooler devoted to beer. There must be five cases of Miller Lite cans in it. Miller Lite is my brand of choice. Just my luck Robin isn't one of those penny-pinching cruisers who drinks whatever swill is on sale. It would be easy to turn down Old Milwaukee, Busch Light, Schlitz or Florida's favorite cheap beer, Natural Ice, aka "Natty Ice."

"Have you noticed how Pabst Blue Ribbon is making a comeback?" I call to Robin. "And whatever happened to regular Coors?"

I bring up to the pilothouse a comfortably familiar can, nestled in a foam koozie advertising a Detroit-area bar. She raises her eyebrows, questioning before she pops the top, "This gonna bother you?"

"No. I may have one later. But I'll wait for right now. I'm trained not to drink underway."

Technically I am still on probation. No alcohol, no drugs not prescribed by a physician, random urine testing by any probation officer, cop or authority figure who feels like springing it on me. The fear of being jailed again is somewhat irrational, but it's unquestionably, regularly there, a deep dread that hammerlocks the muscles at the base of my skull. I wonder if my total identification with Joey's trips to jail was a self-fulfilling prophecy. Perhaps I destined myself to spend at least one night as an inmate in the county pokey.

In my county jail mugshot I am smiling, pleading, placating, as if a big mistake not mine has been made and will be rectified in short order. It's pathetic. Only the tight ligaments cording my neck above my collar bone convey tension. My pupils are dilated after being brought out from a dark cell in the women's section into the harsh, unforgiving lights of the booking area. Escaping tendrils poke willy-nilly from my waitress braids threaded with gray. I am a diminutive, freaked-out Pippi Longstocking, thoroughly cowed by the lying sack of crap small-town cop who decided to make my arrest as unpleasant as possible. There's a county jail website on the internet. The booking photos remain online, organized by date. Derek set my mug as the desktop wallpaper on our home computer. Funny, right?

In my little town up North, any number of police officers that I know on at least a nodding basis could have apprehended me on that fateful night. The luck of the draw served up a bandy-legged mite with myopic eyes behind Coke-bottle glasses, with giant ears and a Napoleon complex to match. "By the Book Ricky," they call him, or "Ricky the Dick." We have a history. He's the same cop who has dogged my son from time to time purely for shits and giggles. A month before Derek and I left on *Chinook* he came nosing for Joey at the house, sniffing at the front door like an overly eager bomb dog. Derek ordered him off the property simply by noting that it is out of his jurisdiction.

By the Book Ricky came back to the cell a couple of hours after my official photo session in the front room. He wanted to take extra pictures with his own camera. He's probably beating off to the images of me cowering and trying to block my face right now or has my mugshot head superimposed atop some hapless big-boobed bimbo on an amateur porn site.

After Ricky's photo session a fresh round of drunks entered the jail. All male. All in various states of escalating emotion. A happy young lad laughed, burped and laughed again as he was booked in just around the corner from my cell. In the drunk tank, alumni from hockey teams and high schools fell on each other like long-lost bosom buddies. I was reminded of how one Saturday night Joey and his then-girlfriend Kirsten ended up spending an evening in mutual incarceration. He was serving a fleeing and eluding sentence. She'd just earned her first DUI after a string of MIPs (Minor In Possession). One in three American kids is arrested by the time they are 23. I was relieved that Joey wasn't keeping me company on that particular Saturday night.

I tell Robin all this with humility, tongue loosened and embarrassment diverted by the active routine of a traveling day on the river. Watching the water and minding the charts instead of each other's faces makes it easier to get the words out. It's as if not knowing each other has cleared the way for intimate revelation.

Robin feels it too. She tells me about the lupus.

I don't know anything about it and since she hates the internet, bad news, research, follow-up visits and second opinions, she doesn't know much more than I do.

"My joints are inflamed. I tire easily. And I'm not supposed to stay out in the sun," she says. "Lupus isn't fatal, but there's no cure for it."

"What do you take for it? If you don't mind me asking." I'm not sure what's what but there are four or five prescription bottles in *Blackout's* medicine cabinet, along with pain patches and a veritable drug-store shelf of over-the-counter pain relievers.

"Let's see ..." she ticks the inventory off on her fingers. "If the Aleve and Motrin don't do the trick I've got prescription NSAIDS, anti-inflammatories, that are stronger. Then there are the anti-malarial pills that upset my stomach so I don't take as many as I'm supposed to. And then we have the immune suppressant, which gives me nausea, diarrhea and sometimes a fever. It's also extremely expensive. There's supposed to be a new brand coming out called Benlysta that they want me to try once it goes through trials.

"And then the steroids, corticosteroids, I guess they're called. Not like body builders take. There are so many long-term side effects that I can't remember them all. The worst are the bruising and the mood swings, although the occasional euphoria rocks. But the weight gain sucks. You just get fat in select areas, like your abdomen and the back of your neck and your face. But the nausea and diarrhea help with that."

"Sounds awful," I say.

"I hate the fucking steroids. My cheeks get fat like a chipmunk's and I turn into a raving bitch. I only take steroids if I feel a flare coming on or if I have to after a flare," she explains, "and I have the pain patches to put on my calves and the arches of my feet so I can last longer walking."

"How often do you have flare-ups?" I ask.

"Not that often, but when they come, oh boy. And I've had seizures a few times. My last flare was last winter. I couldn't walk for five days. The doctors just keep referring me to rheumatologists and neurologists and all they ever do is prescribe drugs I don't want to take that cost a lot of money. And they never tell me what's causing the problem."

Feeling mutually devil-may-care, Robin and I decide to wave at every boat that passes by and every living thing we see ashore. We bark at dogs. We imitate the herons; there are more of them than I have ever seen on any given day anywhere, great gray bearded creatures majestically surveying the water with Zenlike concentration. Road and railway bridges arch over the trail ahead of us. To port and starboard functioning factories spew white, gray or brown smoke. The dead factories sprouting rust, vines curling around the smashed eyes of panoramic windows are beautiful in a stark way, yards littered with skeletal iron, rotted coils of rope thick as a brawny man's arm moldering on abandoned piers awaiting barges that no longer stop at decayed piers. Corrugated outtake pipes gush foamy brown water. Terraced levees cascade man-made waterfalls into the river.

Our second lock of the day, aptly named "Lockport," is a much larger drop, approximately 40 feet. The friendly tenders beckon *Blackout* into the well, handing down two lines, fore and aft. Right before the gates close the motley cabin cruiser and the four Bozos who smashed into us zoom in. Sirens go off as the gates close and I join Robin in the disco whoop.

"No ropes. We'll just float," yells the cabin cruiser skipper, driving too fast up to the head of the lock past *Blackout* and a couple of other large motor yachts and a sailboat that have been waiting on us. The happy-go-lucky cabin cruiser crew runs up the center of the chamber, now grooving to Pearl Jam, inciting a small panic. The middle-aged vigilant crews conscientiously grip their boathooks, gloved hands clutching the lines.

Looking back at the stern from my position up front, I barely have time to register that Robin is nowhere to be seen but has firmly lashed the lockline to a back cleat. As we drop, the ropes must be paid out or the tied line on the cleat will hang the boat up by the ass end as the water recedes beneath it. The lock machinery hums; as the tension on the line increases the boat cleat actually groans.

"Robin? Hey?"

She emerges from inside the boat where she was doing God knows what, maybe using the head. "Grab a knife, you gotta cut that back line," I holler. "Cut it now. Hurry!"

The rope fibers twang like guitar strings as Robin frantically saws through the thick, straining rope. The jerks in the cabin cruiser hee-haw maniacally; this is a far better show than their own.

Breathing deep, I stifle the strong urge to vault back to help her. It is slightly reassuring that she had a knife handy. Despite my distaste for sharp objects, it's essential to have cutting tools available everywhere on a boat. Robin is completely calm. "I'm so sorry, guys, please throw me another line-a line, yeah!" she shouts between cupped hands up to the lip of the lockwall. We've dropped about 20 feet down in the chamber; the tenders on the sidewalk are no longer visible. A grinning face peers down, and in short order a replacement rope drops over the slimy wall. *Blackout's* stern has drifted too far away for Robin to reach it. "Try the boathook," I yell, but *Blackout's* derriere is swinging out into the center of the lock. She clips the middle of the free-floating cabin cruiser with a satisfying "Donk." Two boozy Bozos land in the water. There is applause.

Now that *Blackout* is not going to come crashing down on them, the boats across, behind and in front of us on the walls are more entertained than alarmed, clapping and laughing as the flailing young men paddle about ineffectively.

"Hey, it says no swimming in the locks, can't you read?" catcalls the sailor two boats behind us as the chastened cabin cruiser crew fishes out the soggy dudes.

Robin apologizes to the lock tender again. "I am so sorry. Let me buy you some new line," she shouts up, genuflecting as if speaking to Oz the Great and Terrible.

Again a friendly face appears over the lip of the sidewalk. "It's OK. Ain't the first time this happened. We got more lines. You travel safe now, OK?"

I'm trembling. "What were you doing?"

"Had to pee," she says.

"I am so sick of collisions," I mutter.

"Relax. Happens again, I'll just whiz in the scupper drain."

The bell rings. The gate opens. I shove off the wall. Flip the bow bumper back on deck. Stare straight ahead. Let her disco whoop alone. "What crawled up your butt and died?"

"Nothing. Replaying my fall from grace." I coil the bowline, and peel off my gloves and life jacket.

"So did you wreck the car? Kill somebody?"

"She accused me of trying to kill her. Said I ran into her SUV so hard it knocked her flip-flop off. I bumped the ass-end of her Truckasaurus, which, I might add, was illegally parked. And she was drunk, too."

"Did she get in trouble?" The river is uniformly deep here. No need to mind the markers. And traffic has eased up.

"This runty cop-everybody in town calls him Ricky the Dick-believed her. She's young and pretty. And she called in the accident." Whoever has the smartest phone wins. I'm not allowed to have my own phone. Derek's rule. And at my age I've forgotten how to have histrionics while maintaining a beguiling cuteness.

"He breathalyzed us both. Made us do the ABCs backward. Walk the line. Then he told Drama Queen she had to wait 45 minutes to drive. I got the handcuffs, and a ride to jail."

"I've always wondered what it's like," Robin says, sliding *Blackout* to port to let another asphalt dredge glide by.

"They call the county jail 'no-tell hotel.' It's not as scary as prison." They took my Citizen Ecowatch, diamond studs, vintage rhinestone bracelet and engagement ring. My wedding band could not be tugged off. My white-and-purple mottled knuckles were too swollen. I stopped shivering when they put me in the heated cop cruiser, another black SUV, but was still cold to the core when we got to the jail. Nevertheless I was not allowed to keep the two sweatshirts I had earlier pulled from my boat rucksack in the back of the car as the chill of the night dew bit my bones at the "crime scene."

"Did they take your belt and shoelaces?"

"Yeah. They let me keep my red bra, which I could have handily hung myself with — four years old with quite a bit of give."

But physical suicide is not my scene. On that night I protested nothing, did not cry, complied cheerfully and died inside.

"I used to think I'd made a model prisoner. I love to read. No one would be yelling 'get your nose out of that book!'"

Robin lit another cigarette.

"I didn't think about jail a lot, until Joey started building a rap sheet." Being a Rules Girl, I avoided trouble like the plague. But occasionally, after a prison-themed movie of the week or a magazine article on the subject, I thought about what it would be like to be locked away. There I'd be, stoic, a little heroic even, sinking into important literary works, and dwelling in interior intellect — a world of ideas from which I would dreamily rise from time to time for a daily workout and occasional shower. Sure, I'd miss filet mignon, fresh cantaloupe, and Key West pink shrimp. But I don't get to eat all those things every day anyway, and having eaten them on occasion I would have the memory of how they tasted.

From my son, I learned that jail involves long, boring periods of tedium in which modern-day inmates watch re-runs of *The Simpsons*, *That '70s Show*, and *Family Guy* all afternoon on the communal TV set positioned outside the cells so all the prisoners have a decent view of the screen. When he was in jail I brought in some board games to "donate," seeing as inmates aren't allowed personal possessions or gifts other than socks, undies, t-shirts and in cool weather possibly a sweatshirt depending on the mood of the supervising guards. Anything else brought in must be a general gift to the facility.

"They played Clue and Monopoly for a week or so," I told Robin. "Then the fighting started over whodunit and how many hotels on Boardwalk. The guards took the games away."

Shut in my cell, I immediately understood that it would take quite some time to settle into any sort of personal routine let alone cope with group dynamics. Contentedly reading away a jail sentence was a bunch of idealistic claptrap. In jail, you don't feel like yourself. You feel like nothing. What my mom calls "the black mood" is all-enveloping. The dullness of not feeling trades places with the shifting shapes of self-defeating suicidal thought processes: righteous and impotent anger, the aforementioned self-loathing, numbness approaching catatonia, all states of mind that do not foster peace, forgiveness or anything approaching happiness.

Having been widely seminared in the corporate world, I knew I should be mentally formulating a proactive action plan with strategic goals. If, for example, I truly did have to stay over the weekend, I would ask how one went about purchasing pen and paper. I would stop beating myself up. I would find an aggressive attorney to challenge the blood-alcohol test, the results which at this point were unknown to me. And I would never, ever, never drive drunk again. In fact, I would never drink again.

"My lawyer had a needlepoint pillow in his office embroidered with the cryptic motto: 'Lawyers: Don't drive drunk without one.'"

Robin laughs. "Did he get you out?"

Even if I'd had a cell phone on the night I fell from grace, it would have done me no good.

"No. He's dead. He hung himself from the township water tower six days prior. Joey and I found him."

In my cell I remember wishing that I was truly drunk, blotto, blitzed, smashed, because I could not will away the image of Mark's lolling head, pasty face, livid purple ligature marks visible under the rope around his neck. He was a tall man; his toes brushed the ground, one leather sandal on, one off. He had one hand in the pocket of his plaid preppy shorts, heavy gold wristwatch marking time.

The body looked like a stuffed dummy. Mark was a heavy man and his dead weight did not sway as it hung limply from the long rope dangling from the very top of the water tower down to just inside the right of the aluminum fencing encasing the tower base. From four feet away he still looked fake, a macabre joke fashioned for amusement by the out-of-town crew hired to paint the tower. Joey had gone out earlier to ride his motorcycle; I was on my morning walk when I saw he'd stopped on the trail next to the tower. "Mom?"

"What's this?" I said, coming closer, motioning for Joey to stay back.

"Is it real?"

"Yes, honey. Just stay back now." I could see the dark hair on the arms ruffling in the warm breeze. Birds cawed, chittered and cheeped in the bordering cedar and pine thicket. He didn't smell and he wasn't rigid. His head canted left over the efficiently tied noose that made terrible use of the thick ropes the tower painters had rigged. A tall white plastic industrial bucket was tipped at his feet; a folding chair had collapsed. He had climbed onto the bucket, which had been placed on the chair.

"Looks like he literally kicked the bucket," remarked Joey, his back to the scene, pulling out his cell phone — Derek couldn't stop *him* from having one.

The corpse was wearing sunglasses, a mercy. I don't remember what color his polo shirt was. His hair was black, thick and full, peppered with silvery-gray. His chest did not rise and fall.

I heard car doors slam. "Uh, you might want to not come any closer," I heard Joey tell the arriving onlookers. "There's a dead guy. I already called 911."

Even in such an undignified position, the corpse maintained a certain arrogance: a fine, upstanding man-about-town in his 50s, dressed down for the weekend, perhaps for a round of golf with drinks at the 19th Hole to follow. Mark's car was parked nearby, a new-model Jeep Wagoneer with a kayak-carrier on top. Later I saw a middle-aged woman and a younger woman — his wife and daughter-removing a laptop and some other items from the vehicle. I didn't know them well. I knew him from one brief visit to his office to talk about Joey — on his advice we'd gone with another lawyer who specialized in youthful offenders — and from a score of visits he'd made to the Elbow Room while I was working there. He was disdainful of our liquor selection, but liked to do his drinking out of town, especially after we made a point of stocking Glendfiddich especially for him.

How long had Mark been hanging? Why did he want to die? Why did he choose to die there? Did the long swaying ropes call to him as he drove past the water tower? Was he fatally ill? In deep financial trouble? Was there no other way out?

A pick-up truck with two porky little kids and their chubby parents pulled off the road, joining the other car that had stopped. In a small town, death scenes have a way of gathering steam. As the children toddled forward, one of the boys clutching a red plastic fire truck, I shooed them back. "If you could please stand back, show a little respect, please," I asked the parents, still herding the kids away from the corpse dangling there like a life-size swollen Cabbage Patch doll.

Later, after the cops had taken our names and excused us from the scene, I cursed my Information Specialist instinct for details that could not be purged from my relentlessly fact-gathering brain. Pacing in the living room alone later that afternoon, I nearly jumped out of my skin when a bird hit the window. A particular type of berry on the front-yard bushes makes them crazy in the harvest season. The collisions, two or three a week when the red and orange berries are ripe, are often fatal, although some lie there on the front porch, dazed, slowly coming back like a contender in the ring woozy after a knockout, collecting themselves and flying away. Don't the waxwings and woodpeckers, the chickadees and sparrows know that all is not as it seems?

The resonance of the bang, the puff of feathers glued to the picture window, the wisps of dander oscillating in sunlight motes indicated — before I even looked at the porch floor beneath — that this bird, an already stiffening flicker, would not take wing again. I forced myself to grab the shovel immediately, scooping up the lifeless light corpse, tossing it into the cedar thicket across the street.

"A few hours later, my mom calls from Florida. Dad's lung cancer is now Stage IV. 'We are all terminal,'" she says.

"I didn't realize how much this shit affected me," I tell Robin. "I couldn't cry. I didn't sleep. Food repulsed me. My dead lawyer, the dead bird, my dying father — all of a sudden it'd hit me, I'd shake it off with a happy face for the restaurant shift, then I'd come home and have a few beers — no, a lot of beers. And when the beers quit working, I switched to vodka. And when coming home made me sad, I did my drinking in other places."

I'd stumble onto the boat at the marina at four in the morning or fall onto the couch at home, praying that I could focus on the words in a book and read myself into oblivious slumber. "Of course we all know that the more you tell yourself to go to sleep the more elusive it gets, right?"

"Especially with all this menopause crap on top of it," nods Robin.

"I acted my way through the day, perky, cheerful Hailey, going that extra smile. And I drank, and I drove."

Frantic to celebrate something, anything, I went to the liveliest local bar in town one Friday night for a co-worker's going-away party even though I was exhausted. All the other staff had clocked out and gone ahead of me. I had a late table; the bartender, head chef and I were the only ones left in the place when we finally locked the doors. "I'd already had two beers at the restaurant," I explained to Robin (who has at least four before lunch every day), "and then I had another at the bar."

Of course I felt OK to drive when I left the bar. Of course I was totally delusional.

"Well it doesn't sound to me like you could have been legally drunk," says Robin.

"If I was, I sobered up quick in that cell." Shivering, hollow, I waited for daylight. There were steel bars all around me. Even the dim bulb in the hall had a cage around it. Finally I smelled coffee brewing as thin morning light cued up on the yellow brick towers on the portion of the gothic courthouse next door visible from my thin, slatted window. A tray slid into place on the metal depression built into the cell door. I regarded the paper-towel-wrapped toast, milk carton and fun-size box of Froot Loops with contempt. But I was too cold to ignore the Styrofoam cup of hot coffee.

Wrapped in my ugly jail serape I sipped, face to the courthouse towers watching what I could see of the sunrise. Soon after I gave up the struggle with my bursting bladder and peed for the camera into the metal toilet bowl, sacrificing privacy and personal dignity. The guards watched me urinate. If this was happening in the outside world it would be against the law. In here it is the law.

"I remember thinking that I am nothing. I hated myself. I wished I was dead."

Robin shakes her head. Sips her beer.

Derek bailed me out at 9 a.m. and was already gone by the time the deputy opened the cell door. I walked home. Before a hot shower I stepped on the scale. My weight had plummeted to 95 pounds.

"That's why you registered on the alcohol Richter scale," says Robin. "And that's why I got a top-of-the-line bike with a rack large enough for a 12-pack 15 years ago."

"What really gets me is why I went out that night at all. I have not seen Krystal since. Clearly she wasn't a friend, just a work buddy."

Clearly I was on the prowl for Lover Number Four. He was the most dangerous of all. You just never knew where you'd run into him; there were four or five places he liked to go and I seldom had time to look for him after work and between family obligations.

"Krystal was just a lame excuse to look for nookie from my latest paramour."

"You really enjoy beating yourself up," Robin shakes her head.

Blackout comes alongside the Joliet town dock after dark, Robin slowing to idle, the boat hovering just off the edge of the crumbling facewall to wait for a three-by-three tow barge to thrum by, search beacons sweeping the channel like a gulag escape scene in an old war movie, white backwash boiling behind it. Two other power yachts in the 50-foot range and the same sailboat we saw in the locks lurch into the aggregate pier, bumping as the wake rolls under us, rubber fenders squirting up. The sailboat's metal rigging clangs in protest.

The obnoxious wake rolls everything from the oranges on the countertop to my stomach contents. All items on *Blackout's* deck are securely lashed; we haven't done such a thorough job of stowing items below. Magazines slide off the salon couch. Shoes tumble across the cabin, accompanied by the rattle of saucepans in the drainer and the disturbing clink of bottles and glassware which most boaters are not foolish enough to keep aboard. I make a mental note to put clean socks over any bottles and layer towels between glassware. Prevents breakage and the repetitive clinking that drives me up a wall.

When our nerves and the boat have settled, Robin nudges *Blackout* closer using its bow thrusters, a stabilizing force foreign to most rag-baggers, as sailors are sometimes called. I step from deck to pier taking care with my footing as tiny rocks break loose and plunk into the water in mini-landslides. As I secure bowlines Robin takes up the all-important mid-ship springline and adjusts the stern tie-up. There are a limited amount of cleats and giant metal bollards here and as is so often the case on the rivers, tying up requires some creativity. "Stay there; we're going to loop the lines back onto the boat, OK?" I hiss in a stage whisper to Robin, so as to not disturb the neighbors who are apparently retired for the evening or trying to get back to sleep after the tow wake.

"Hey little lady, how you doin'?" The panhandler is in my face before I realize he's crept up on me. "That sure is a nice boat, how much you pay for somethin' like that?"

The panhandler is cocky, aggressive and standing way too close. I just want to get *Blackout* tied up and duck back below as fast as possible.

"This old thing? It's a 1977. About $200," I say to indicate we don't have any money to spare. Everyone always thinks boaters are loaded. "It leaks so we have to keep bailing it out."

"Huh huh," he laughs uncertainly and stupidly, hands stuffed in a quilted plaid jacket, steam puffing out his nostrils in the cold night. "If you could just spare a couple bucks, my girl left me ..."

"Hey Hailey, I'm shutting down the computer," Robin yells from the pilothouse, ruining my floating-paupers ruse. "Bring the other GPS in from the deck locker."

The panhandler smiles, refraining from rubbing his hands together.

Then his cell phone rings and I smile.

"Nice phone, buddy. Go peddle your bullshit somewhere else, OK? Call whoever pays your cell phone bill for help."

"I didn't come over here to talk to you," he says, straightening his shoulders and puffing up his chubby chest. The words "Uppity White Bitch" are not spoken, but the implication is clear. "I came here to talk to your husband."

If I was a dog, the ruff on my neck would be quivering. I can't afford to make a scene and attract attention. The last thing I need is for a crazy homeless beggar to squawk until the cops come poking around. "My husband doesn't talk to beggars." That came out way snottier than I intended.

"I am not a beggar!" He stepped closer to the rear of the boat, yelling through the back door "Heyyyy — Hello in there, sir?"

Robin thundered out, twiggy but authoritative, scrunching her forehead as if she isn't welcoming the interruption from the engine room or navigation station. Her deep voice and androgynous upper-class fishing attire completely convince the panhandler that he's appealing to the sane male aboard.

I'm worried that if stray dogs and lost causes are her forte, I may be looking at our newest crew member "He just wants money, honey." *Keep a straight face, Hailey.* "I already told him that we don't have any to spare. He said he was broke. And then his cell phone rang."

"Wait a minute," he insists. "She called me a beggar. That is not how you treat people."

"Well, weren't you asking for money?" I've got a hand on a cocked-out hip, body language hostile. "Wouldn't that be begging? So by definition, you would be a beggar."

He ignores me. "Listen here, sir, I have just recently been stranded; my personal property was stolen and when I tried to recover it they put me off the boat. My mama's sick over in Memphis. My girlfriend won't come get me. She's mad. I'm just trying to scrape up the cash for a one-way bus ticket."

His cell phone rings again. "Excuse me ma'am, sir, I got to take this."

Robin laughs as she produces a $20 from the right-hip pocket of her cargo shorts. (Robin won't wear pants without pockets. Later I will find out that she prefers boxers to briefs. Her favorite pair features Snoopy.)

"That was a GOOD story. I'm paying him for that story," she says to me in a no-arguments tone of voice I will come to know well.

The beggar, his back to us a few steps away, mutters in low, urgent tones, talking into the receiver. He looks up in annoyance when she whistles, but revives a civil attitude and a rapid approach when she proffers the cash.

"Here you go sir, good luck to you," she snaps out, making her voice deeper than it usually is.

"Bless you sir, thank you," the beggar nods, shooting me a vindicated smirk. "Do you take this boat all the way to the Gulf of Mexico?"

"Great. He wants to chat," I mutter under my breath.

A statuesque woman steps into the pool of the overhead dock lights. Her 5'10" silhouette is all curves, sturdy power thighs, admirable breasts (which we will later learn are 34Ds thoughtfully augmented by one of the better plastic surgeons serving the Las Vegas modeling, dancing and hooking community).

"I think you got what you came for, Mister, so why don't you make like a tree and leaf?" Her voice is Midwest with a tiny hint of southern twang. The night lights catch-and-glow at the tips of the tendrils escaping from a pony tail. Her eyes catch the ambient light, too, gleaming wide, full of intention and spirit.

It appears Joliet Veterans Park has a blonde Amazon holding the fort.

"Go on now, buh-bye," she shoos the beggar away with gestures that display exceptionally well-groomed hands tipped by a French manicure. I admire her tone of sweet menace. Very disarming. The beggar retreats.

"Thanks," I say, offering a hand, which she can't grip because hers are full. "I'm Hailey and this is Captain Robin."

"Trish," she says and drops the Hello Kitty duffle bag and Louis Vuitton satchel. Behind her we spot a hard blue train case and a big green canvas rucksack. Uh-oh.

"What's up with the luggage?" asks Robin.

"I am leaving the man on that big yacht up yonder," says Trish.

There are two. "Which one?" I ask.

"The big sky-blue yacht with the navy-blue awnings," she clarifies. "I've been traveling with that guy since Vegas, but we just came from Chicago. I haven't even really known him long enough to call it leaving."

"Hailey's running away, too," announces Robin.

Trish smiles at me, but I cringe. Robin can't even keep a secret for 24 hours. To change the subject away from me, I ask, "You're from Las Vegas?"

"Who's from Vegas?" she says, rolling her eyes. "I grew up in Grand Rapids. Michigan."

At this Robin snorts. "No shit. We're from Michigan too!"

The snort is contagious. And as it often does, laughter clears the air. "Come on aboard and have a beer," Robin invites.

"Where do I get on?" It's clear that she hasn't been around boats for very long.

As I step toward the gangway door she follows along on the sidewalk in tottering Five-inch spiked boots. "Take your boots off, sit down on the side of the pier and I'll help you over," I instruct. "Those are definitely not boat shoes. And this wall is super crumbly."

"Hand over your stuff first," says Robin. "It'll get ripped off out here." Trish hands over the garish zippered kitty carry-all, the Samsonite train case, the Louis Vuitton satchel and the green rucksack that weighs at least 40 pounds.

Once the baggage is toted down the side deck and deposited on the back deck, there's very little room to move, so we migrate into the living room, which is what I persist in calling the salon.

"Sit," says Robin, and we do, after I grab a beer for Trish-and one for myself. "So do you need a ride?" Robin asks, taking a swallow of the Lite she's already working on.

"Jesus, Rob!" I say. "Way to cut through the niceties."

Trish looks at me long and hard.

"I did *not* run away. I just went. What's your story?"

"We can call you a cab, or figure out the bus schedules or whatever you'd like to do," I rush to offer options. Anything to get her off my least favorite subject. Me.

Give her this, she can take a hint. "Well where are you two going? I might be headed in the same direction, that being anywhere but here. That Harry is a piece of work. We left Chicago a week ago and have been here ever since. Harry likes the casino across the bridge. He prefers Harrah's to a hard-on. Can't stay with that old codger, but I love the boating part. So what do you say, ladies? I can chip in on gas and groceries."

Robin and I look at each other and shrug. What the hell.

"I guess I should be grateful," she continues. "Until I got him to the blackjack tables all he wanted to do was pop his little blue boner pills and make whoopee. He expected me to do all the work, of course."

But Trish, a recent citizen of Sin City, has had her fill of the gaming life. "I did it all," she tells us, taking a sip of beer and stifling a delicate burp against the back of her hand. Her specialties were hooking and hairdressing. She danced professionally, too, landing in Vegas after traveling the upper Northwest stripping circuit at a variety of gentleman's clubs, which for the most part were not gentile. "In Moose Jaw, Saskatchewan they didn't have a stage; we had to dance on the pool table," she says. "But the clientele was extremely kind and the tips were excellent."

Vegas, however, was another story. "Too much competition, too many roughnecks, too many times I got screwed out of money that was coming to me," she says, shaking her head. "So I auditioned at the Chicken Ranch. At least in the legal places everything is regulated, you get decent pay and regular time off." She sighs. "You can only put up with that lifestyle for so long. It just got sad. And I got tired of hiding it from my family."

"Where are they?" Robin wants to know.

"Grand Rapids. Big-time Bible bangers. I call my mom every Christmas."

"That's more often than I talk to my family," says Robin. "My brothers and sisters disapprove of my boat bum lifestyle. With my mom and dad gone, there's nobody left to stick up for me."

"You get to a certain age and you realize that you have to do what's best for you, not what everybody else thinks is best for you," says Trish.

Am I not the only one who is just starting to figure this out?

Trish and I assumed Robin'd sleep in *Blackout's* master suite, but she set us straight. "I never sleep in that bed. Bad memories. One of you take it — or both. It's big enough. Sorry, the guest berth is covered with tools and boat parts."

The suite has a great bed, a custom square mattress, unusual in shape and size in the boating world, where beds are usually V-shaped or narrow rectangles in the Pullman style. The navy-blue high thread-count sheets and pillowcases are lush and soft. The navy comforter is neither too heavy nor too light, except when I have a hot flash. There isn't a blanket in the world that can stay on me during one of those surges.

Robin and I often meet on the back deck for a smoke — our little Hot Flash Club. Smoking cigarettes reportedly makes menopausal symptoms worse, but it sure doesn't feel that way in the wee hours when your brain won't be quiet and sleep is only a dream.

Chapter 8: Rollin' on the River

The first night out, we docked at the Spring Brook Marina gratis due to Robin's family business connections with the boat brokerage there. Derek and I had never stayed there, so I could relax. But the following evening tie-ups were at the popular municipal docks in Hennepin and Peoria and at Logsdon Tug Service in Beardstown, Illinois. So I laid low until I was sure I didn't know anyone. Of course, I still wasn't safe. How many times have I had someone walk up to me and start chatting and I had no idea who they are but they remember me like it was yesterday? It happens to boaters all the time. We're watchers. With binoculars.

At Beardstown a wide beast of a custom-made sailboat, *Beluga*, docked in front of us. Thanks to the Swedish couple's generous pouring of copious amounts of Beefeater's gin and tonic, I abandoned all worries of being recognized. We were all three sheets to the wind by the time the sun went down. I did not remember the young sporty blonde Swedish couple's name the next morning, only a heated monologue from the captain regarding the vast difference between shrimp and prawns. He took great umbrage with anyone who considered the two the same. "They are an entirely different species."

In the morning, Robin swore extravagantly when she saw the wood ash and half-burned composite chips blown in smudgy drifts all over *Blackout's* decks, coagulating in the drains and scuppers. That's what you get in Beardstown. But there are perks, too, including plenty of ice for the non-electric beer cooler from the machines out back of the office, a blue-collar neighborhood bar a couple of blocks away and a friendly barber just off the quaint red-bricked town square, who gave us a ride to the Wal-Mart on the highway outside of town.

"We used to have a couple of markets right downtown, with a good butcher. Now Wally World is the only place to buy groceries. Drove the mom-and-pop shops out of business," Larry the barber tells us, posting a "back in 20 minutes sign" on his door.

In Grafton, Illinois we obtained overnight dockage on Mel's Riverdock restaurant's floating pier for the price of a meal. The Riverdock is known for beef brisket and baked goods, especially banana cream pie. There are definite advantages to power-boating in these parts; late arrivals often do not find space on the dock. *Blackout* easily passed up the three sailboats we spotted earlier in the day, drifting dreamlike through a raft of white pelicans, joining the snowbirds migrating steadily south. As we motored through the flock it rose as a single entity, wheeling and swooping soundlessly over the water, surface-diving for sustenance stirred by *Blackout's* propellers. Grafton has flooded so many times that in recent years the City Fathers prohibited building along the banks. "I feel like we're in a *National Geographic* magazine," Trish said. She wouldn't believe they were pelicans until we showed her the entry in Robin's bird guide.

"The brown pelicans don't come up this far," I explained. "We're truly south when we start to see them." We are very much in touch with the land side of the world here, as we have been for the majority of our route down the Illinois. The connection will be broken as soon as we pass through the lock after Alton.

Eighty-six miles, four locks and five days from our meeting with Trish in Joliet, we have made it to Alton, gateway to the Mississippi River. Alton is an old town, featuring the characteristic red-bricked architecture of this region where the Mormons first settled, its wide sidewalks perfect for strolling. Alton marina is a strikingly modern contrast, the blue-roofed edifice protected from river surge by a sturdy man-made breakwall that runs its entire length to the highway bridge topped by a superstructure of metal supports that stretch skyward like monolithic spider webs.

After Alton, there won't be any easy stops or impromptu pull-overs on the lower rivers. We'll have to anchor. Trish accepts this matter-of-factly if not cheerfully. Never having boated before her travels on *Blue Angel*, she simply takes anything Robin and I say regarding nautical matters as the gospel truth.

Shoreside amenities are few and far between, especially at this time of year along the Heartland Rivers. Locals are pulling out their boats for the winter and most marinas shut off the water before they close to avoid frozen pipes. The Mississippi in any season does not cater to pleasure boaters. Robin hates anchoring out. "I can't sleep. I'm afraid we're going to drag," she complains. "Or somebody will run into us in the middle of the night."

I like anchoring out. It's like floating on your own island, self-contained. No one can walk up and gawk at you through the windows. *Blackout* has a top-rated anchor on an all-chain rode. Once it's deployed, we aren't dragging anywhere.

"So, how many more locks?" Trish asks. She's become the official recording secretary and log keeper (in a Hello Kitty notebook) for our trip.

"We're only getting started," I tell her. "We've got the Ohio and Kentucky locks. Then 10 more locks on the way to Mobile. And enjoy the bathroom here because they are as nice as it gets. There's nothing even half as plush as this for the rest of the trip. You're gonna need a broom to fend off the spiders and a big spray bottle of disinfectant before you step into most of the showers from here on down."

The Alton Marina's bathrooms are decadent, luxurious compared to what's available on the rest of the rivers. Women have been known to weep with joy and gratitude at the mere sight of the individual floating private suites featuring hardwood floors, vanity sinks with lighted make-up mirrors, sparkling stalls equipped with massaging shower heads and dispensers featuring a better brand of shampoo/conditioner/body wash/lotion and last but not least, a spotless commode. After days of roughing it, these facilities are a blessing for those in need of a root touch-up, facial hair bleaching, eyebrow tweezing or any of the other quirky beauty routines that cannot easily be accomplished in tight, dim quarters at sea, or in our case, on the river.

I've avoided the marina office and store, trying to limit my interaction with anyone who might remember Derek and me, or have been alerted to my runaway, boat-thieving status. But there's nothing that can make me avoid these splendid bathrooms suites.

Hearing that, Trish cloistered the three of us in one of them.

Her tools of the trade: foils, long-toothed pick, brush applicators, combs of various sizes from wide to rattail, are laid out on the white marble vanity top as neatly and deliberately as surgical instruments. Trish pulls on latex gloves with a snap, instructing Robin to "sit still and don't fidget." "You can't be walking around with that shabby gray hair." Trish mixes color with a plastic spoon, squirting dollops of goo from various numbered squeeze-tubes into a small ceramic bowl. "Why do you want to look like a washed-out old lady?"

Robin and I are both hair-dye virgins. Only recently have I noticed silver-white tufts at my hairline just above the ears and sprouting out of my center part. Robin's hair is a uniformly cigarette-ash gray and as she has informed us multiple times she doesn't care.

"I wear a hat all the time anyway," she says. "I don't have the time or desire to primp."

Comedian and commentator Joy Behar once mentioned on ABC TV's *The View* that the ability to color our hair has changed the world for women, skewing the definition of age as previously defined by the stage when we go gray. "Why would you want to look so washed out?" Trish repeats. "Seriously, that bum thought you were a man."

"That's my voice," Robin insists. "My nieces and nephews call me Uncle Robin. All the Miss Clairol in the world is not gonna change that."

Trish the Beautician is in full-out makeover mode. Rob is getting a new look whether she likes it or not.

"Don't try to put mascara on her, she might bite you." Trish laughs but I'm serious.

"No makeup today, or any day. Except on Halloween." Robin hunches over, pulling her voluminous denim shirt close, enveloping her bony knees.

"Settle down Uncle Robin, I'm not going there today so put your feet back on the floor and relax so I don't paint your ears. One step at a time, dear Jesus ..."

Trish meticulously daubs the natural middle part with a foam applicator brush, a nearly perfect straight line up the middle of Robin's scalp where all the gray hairs are standing at attention.

I haven't done anything about my gray hair but I'm intrigued by the possibilities and eager to take my place at the vanity sink when Trish has finished. "We'll have to do her first so she doesn't escape," Trish had decided.

What gets me about gray hair is that it's so springy, hard to tame and impossible to ignore. It's like pubic hair really, crisp, tough and bushy if you let it get out of hand. As Trish explains it, gray hair is really just a bunch of empty hair follicles. "Your follicles are like tubes filled with pigment. As we age we lose the pigment. The color fills the tubes back up."

"Huh. So I've got more empty tubes than I thought," I say, patting my abdomen where there are still tubes but no uterus.

"We could go black, blue, purple or red with your gray tones, Hailey. Black is very Morticia Adams — a bit harsh for anyone over 40. Blue is old-school, aka the classic blue-haired ladies, and the red may turn orangey-brassy. I could use violet tones to enhance the gray," Trish muses, eyes roaming over her ointments, gels and unguents like an oil-color painter preparing a palette for a masterpiece. She finally settled on "blonding the ash for Robin," since her natural color is — or was — ash blonde. Rob's hair, which she impatiently chops at with any type of scissors that come to hand whenever it gets in her eyes or touches her collar, is already so short that there is no way to refine the style. And I secretly worry that Trish spent too much time at the Chicken Ranch and in Vegas, where there is a different standard for what is considered normal hair color. If the color is too showy, it will freak Robin out. Oh wait, she's already freaking out, folded rows of foils bristling off her head. She resembles a wired-up, agitated porcupine.

"Breathe, Rob," I tell her. "The color is on now, so deal with it."

"I need a smoke," she whines.

"Honey, it's gonna look so good," says Trish. "I promise."

"I'm only doing this to shut you two up," snarls Robin, in what is a very unappreciative tone for the salon-quality service we are receiving free of charge. "Now shove over; it's Hailey's turn."

"Hey, watch it," I mutter, as Robin elbows her way out of the hot seat. The suite is nice, but three people are a tight fit and it makes me miss my sister Layla. Whoever thought I'd one day wax nostalgic over the two of us fighting for mirror space getting spruced up for school in our one-bathroom home at the lake? Eventually my dad put in a half-bath where, as he so poetically put it, he could "shit and shave in peace in the morning."

I have already chosen my custom shade, mulling over the color charts Trish produced from her bag, along with the cornucopia of beauty potions, lotions and liquids. She is carrying more product than clothing. "I have my priorities," she says. The Hello Kitty Case houses an actual bonnet hairdryer. Robin finds it amusing, but warns us to never plug it into the boat. "No curling irons, either," she says. "The DC system can't handle it. We'd blow a fuse for sure."

The train case is chock full of make-up, everything Mac, Maybelline, Mary Kay, Rimmel, Sephora, Covergirl and even Avon have to offer in the way of liner, mascara, blush, eye shadow, brow pencils, eyelash curlers and the like, along with an impressive collection of false eyelashes in startling lengths for all occasions. There are numerous vitamin and herbal supplement vials, too, including the captivatingly titled "Female Caps."

"Those are for perimenopause," says Trish. "My mom got menopause early and I think I am, too. A couple of these babies every day keep the hot flashes away."

"Do they really work?" Trish and Robin have seen my rivers of night sweat. I've warned them about the irrational bouts of anger and weepiness. "I'll try just about anything at this point." Maybe there's a pill I can pop that will take me back, happy, to Derek and the kids.

"They work for me and you're welcome to try them," says Trish, "I carry a year's supply; we'll just have to restock somewhere because I can't do without 'em. The last time I let myself run out I was miserable. Felt like my brain was going to whirl right out of my head it was whipping around so hard at night thinking overwhelming thoughts. And I'd cry at the drop of a hat at TV commercials or the sight of a puppy."

"We know the feeling," I say. Robin snorts.

"You try 'em Hailey, I take enough pills as it is," she says.

Trish gently works a wide-toothed detangling comb up from tips to roots on my shower-damp hair as I sit before the mirror trying to ignore the crow's feet and lines around my mouth that show even in the warm, flattering light. "You're definitely going to take a lot longer, Miss Hailey" says Trish, sectioning, painting and humming, gloved hands working deftly. No cut today."

We will wait for the appropriate moon date that favors maximum growth and health. I have always cut my hair before the full moon to encourage growth. She has no objection to the theory although it's the first time she's heard it.

"It's a little cuckoo, but then again, you do have a nice thick head of hair," she says. "And I suppose that if the moon can affect sea tides and how plants grow … come to think of it, in my experience hair does grow faster in the summer."

"How much longer?" asks Robin, holding her cigarettes.

"About 20 minutes and you can rinse it out in the shower," says Trish. "We can fix a plastic cap and your ball cap over it if you want to go out and have a smoke. But I can't guarantee you won't get laughed at."

"I'll wait," she says, huffing dramatically again to emphasize her disgust with the beautification project.

She swigs her beer. Even here, jammed in a marina shower suite, the beer is ever-present. "What is this lupus? Why did I get it? I still don't know and I've supposedly had it for almost nine years."

"What about diet and supplements?" The question is barely out of my mouth before a spray of beer comes out of hers. "Get real. I have to swallow enough crap as it is. I only eat what I like to eat."

Robin's list of acceptable foods includes chicken strips with ranch dressing dip, lobster tails, well-done beef tenderloin, plain-cheese pizza and the aptly named "Heart Attack Dip" a concoction of melted cheese, tortilla chips and pepperoni with yet more cheese on top of it, microwaved until gooey. I have to agree. It's delish. She ostentatiously gags at the sight of anything green on her plate, be it a lettuce leaf or a single sprig of parsley.

"So, Miss Hailey, you gonna tell me about that husband of yours coming after us?" Trish asks. "How dangerous is he? Give it up."

Playing beauty salon in the private bathroom suite is the perfect time to fill Trish in on the vainglorious, snot-nosed eternal kid yelling 'Hey hey, look at ME,' always craving the spotlight, always pointing out my mistakes to make himself look better. How anything that broke on the boat or in the house or the car was my fault. How I was always in the way, my "giant ass" blocking the view.

How he constantly ordered me "don't worry about that," "don't cry," "shut up," "get out," "move." How when I didn't move fast enough I was hit with ropes, shackles, elbows, big feet stomping on whatever part of me was in the way.

"He resents having to wait for anything. He takes traffic jams personally. He says "Fuck" hundreds of times a day. He doesn't believe in clothes dryers, dishwashers, Christmas or birthday presents. He doesn't think that rules apply to him. He thinks he can fish without a license and fudge on his taxes. He says the autopilot handles the boat better than I do and he yells at me if I take it off to steer around a log or a crab pot. When he's at the tiller, we run out of the channel because he has ADD and doesn't pay attention. He spends all his money on fancy toys for himself, like that guitar he barely learned to play and gave up after a year. He doesn't like museums and he won't go to weddings or funerals. And he acts like this completely different nice guy when anyone else is around."

"He sounds like a one-upper and a put-downer," says Trish. "Does he hit you accidentally or on purpose?"

"He pretends he doesn't hit me at all."

"Well," she says, "I can see why you want to get away from him, although you certainly picked a slow, weird way to do it. The question is will he let you go?"

An hour later, Rob and I are rinsed off, blown dry and styled. Miracle of miracles, Robin even let Trish take the curling iron to her pixie-do. We stand in front of the mirror, smiling. The lights catch the coppery sheen of my carefully applied lowlights; loose curls tumble to my shoulders in sensual disarray. I still look like me, only better, more vibrant. "I love it," I tell Trish, turning for a big hug. "Thank you so much!"

"Damn, you know your stuff," Robin admits, gingerly turning her head side to side as if afraid she'll dislodge something, admiring the artfully fluffed shiny blond cap gracing her head, making her neck appear willowy instead of "like a pipe cleaner with a big balloon head on top" (her words, not ours). "Won't last, but while it does, the boys better watch out!"

"Hardy har har. OK you two, get outta here — I gotta do me now," Trish orders, peeling off her clothes and hopping into the shower stall. "Because if you girls think this color is natural, you've got another thing comin'!"

But Robin and I stay put, astonished by the thin blonde line of pubic hair pointing toward her exposed clit.

"This is the Vegas Showgirl Shave, ladies. Bushes and G-strings don't mix," Trish responded, with no embarrassment regarding her rather prominently displayed "love button." "Now shoo. There's nothing sadder than a stylist with bad hair."

Chapter 9: Current Events

"This Mississippi has kicked the pretty outta me," Trish grouses a few days, two locks and 44.4 miles later, shrugging on the same nondescript gray hooded sweatshirt that she's been wearing since we left Alton. She steps onto the rear deck, aka "the back porch," somehow managing to keep her coffee mug level in one hand while balancing toast and a Good Housekeeping magazine in the other. Unlike Robin and me she's consistently sure-footed, moving about with solid coordination and the uncanny ability to remain upright no matter how vigorously *Blackout* rocks and flounders in the wake and wash of passing tows and speeding power yachts, bows high, up on plane.

I'd been led to believe that I was the klutziest boater on Earth. But Derek never met Robin. Like me, she's forever banging into hard surfaces. Our shins, elbows, upper thighs, hipbones and sundry other areas are covered with bruises of varying shades of black, blue, purple and yellow.

"You can blame yours on lupus," I tell her. "What's my excuse?"

Trish squinches her lips into a moue of distaste as she watches the river, where tree trunks and phone poles pinion and batter, herding and plowing smaller branches and other floating detritus into a raft of wired wooden tumbleweeds. Some of the big oaks defy all remora, allowing nothing to cling as they plow along like unmanned native dugouts.

"Creepy," Trish points, as a naked plastic baby doll with one eye drifts by tangled in some plastic fishing line and a macabre noose of yellow braided poly rope. I shiver and sip my coffee from a mug proclaiming the merits of a yacht brokerage in Boca Raton, Florida. From Rob's eclectic collection Trish has chosen a mug from Daffy Doug's Dollar Store in Marathon, Florida.

For three days the river and its banks have eluded us, cloaked invisible in sodden low-hanging gray vapor irrigated by a steadily weeping sky that drizzles between downpours. Having completed the jaunt from Alton to Hoppies Marina with no more discomfort than enduring the burning pig manure stench wafting from the fields, we are now officially sidelined at Hoppies Marina waiting for the fog and rain to clear so we can safely navigate the upcoming 400-mile stretch of river. It's unforgiving. Downright mean. And landings aren't easy to come by. Or anchorages.

You can travel on the river in the fog but you're taking your boat and your life in your hands. Even the tows don't move when it's foggy. Especially when the current is running hard, water brimming with flotsam and jetsam.

Several boats are holed up at Hoppies. We exchange hellos — I nod from a distance and keep my hood up-with the boats closest to us. A 65-foot riverboat named *Slo-poke*, complete with spiral water slide and a potted garden of tomato plants and petunias in full bloom on the top deck. Sixty-five feet might seem extravagant, but *Slo-poke* houses a big family — Mom, Dad, and a stair-stepped progression of five children aged two to 21. Behind us is a 40-foot crimson Nordic Tug named *Newfie Bullet*, owned by gangly Jack, a 70-something silver-haired blue-eyed charmer, and his wife Dee. "I wanted to name the boat *Red Jacket*, but Dee wouldn't let me," he says, chuckling.

"Too obvious," says Dee.

The weather soothes my worries about nightly dock parties and potlucks. We gathered under the covered fueling area/lounge with dishes to pass on the first night we arrived and the dock filled up. It's too cold and wet to socialize outdoors. No indoor space is large enough. A few boaters have invited us for dinner, which Robin and I have been able to avoid. She doesn't like dinner parties. She's afraid she may be offered something gross, like rare meat or broccoli. I'm not getting anywhere near discussions about Loops or anything else that may trigger memories or questions.

Trish is our willing stand-in. But for the most part everyone is focused on their own boats, the weather and being grumpy. So Hoppies Marina is relatively quiet and I can remain anonymous.

Although "marina" is a rather grand term for the three anchored barges that comprise the docks, connected by steel cables strung and fastened to the towering cliff above. The shore, and the nearby town of Kimmswick, Missouri are accessed by a sharply angled metal dock adjusted to the rise and fall of the relentless river. Owners Hoppie, a thin man with the kind and patient eyes of a tolerant hound dog, and his outspoken wife, Fern, provide dock space and dispense fuel as well as wisdom to pleasure boats plying the river. There is no bathhouse. I used the shore bathroom inside the Quonset mechanics building once, but found that peeing next to the rattling train tracks into a bowl with dubious stains that I tried to convince myself were just rust severely inhibited my flow. Just the sight of it would have constipated Robin for a week, so I told her to steer clear. We are all using the head on the boat, which means that sooner rather than later we will need a tank pump-out.

So far I've avoided Fern and Hoppie. It's egotistical to think that they would remember me. Hoppies Marina Service was established by the Hopkins family in 1934. Sure, it's the only fuel stop for the next 400 miles, so Derek and I have stayed here a few times, but so have hundreds of other boaters. Still, I am not taking any chances.

We sent Trish to Fern's River School, where the forthright matriarch provides all the do-and-don't tips for getting us off this river and safely on to the next leg of the downstream journey. Trishie argued that Robin should go, too. "So what if you've already been. Ever heard of a refresher course?"

"I'm bored, but not that damn bored," Robin responded. We all know why I shouldn't go.

Aside from Fern's famous River School, there isn't much to do in Kimmswick. We're all read out. Robin just keeps playing a John Mayer CD over and over while wiping the constant condensation off the windows in the salon, where the little Ben Franklin stove crackles, the only merry element in sight on yet another somber morning.

"We might need to DO something pretty soon, even if it's bad," Robin informs us, shouting from the interior.

"I hear you, Rob," Trish hollers then aside to me, "What I'm hearing is OCD and ADD." She raises her voice again. "What time is breakfast?"

"Ooh ooh ooh. Oooh Oooh Oooh," Robin sings along with Mayer. The soulful emanations (more like "so foul" Trish says) lost their charm two hours ago. Restless from the travel delay, we are all getting up well before dawn, something none of us are accustomed to.

"Rob, find another CD please. Anything."

I can hear her shuffling through the audio cupboard. "Is "A Jimmy Buffett Christmas" OK?"

"God no."

More shuffling. On my boat we used remote control to effortlessly change the music. It strikes me as unreasonable on my part to now appreciate Derek's cleverness with gadgets. He was very adept at fixing anything that broke and hooking up systems that operated at the touch of a button. Why, if he hadn't hit me with words and punched me with his fists, you could almost have considered me spoiled.

Michael Jackson's "Thriller" bangs out of the speakers. Robin has every Jackson CD. Loves the King of Pop. "This is good for Halloween, right?"

"That might be just enough to send me out into this endless wet," Trish pulls the drawstring of her hood tight around her face. She looks like Kenny the faceless kid on *South Park*.

We've played endless rounds of euchre, consumed every last salty or sweet processed food snack on the boat and aimlessly wandered around getting wet on the few streets of the muddy but charming little town.

At the Blue Owl Café, Robin and the waitresses, who are clad in Little House on the Prairie dresses with immaculate white-flounced aprons, have a standing taunt. "Do I have an accent?"

"Yes, you have an accent."

"Naw sugar, y'all have an accent."

This is the highlight of Rob's day. Going out to breakfast, she tells us, has always been her thing. Like an anxious mother stuffing nutrition into an underdeveloped and hyperactive preemie toddler, I am hard-pressed to stop praising her when she eats or to prod her to "take just one more bite," as her well-done hamburger patty or fried chicken strips congeal on the plate. If there is a dog, cat, duck or heron around, she will feed them her food. And she is *so* thin.

There is no need to tempt her tastebuds at the Blue Owl, where amidst the lighted bakery cases heaped oversized apple bomb pies drenched in caramel, berry-erupting muffins bigger than a lumberjack's fist and glossy doughnuts shining with glaze and sprinkles, Robin devours omelets and bacon and fruit crepes with the gusto of the aforementioned lumberjack. The soothing melodies of the live dulcimer band lull us into sitting with yet more steaming mugs of coffee long after our plates have been cleared.

The Owl shuts at 2 p.m. at which time the antiquing mavens south of St. Louis make the rounds of the many gift shops and historical exhibits that compose the town. Candy, candle and soap emporiums issue delectable smells into the narrow streets, fragrant replacements for the blacksmith, hardware, general store and saloons that were here in days of yore.

Trish and I particularly enjoy the wine shop, where regular afternoon tastings render us jolly and full of confidence. Despite our limited funds, we cannot afford to wear out our welcome and so kick in ten bucks each to purchase a recommended cabernet, a local domestic vintage we pronounce delicious. Rob likes wine about as much as she likes me bugging her to eat. She instead prefers to gloat over the cases of "award-winning pilsner" she stows in *Blackout's* engine room, rendering us impervious to the constrictions of the dry counties coming up on our next leg of the rivers.

She'd buy us wine if we asked. "You'll piss me off. If there's something you need get it," she has told us many times, separately and together. She foots the breakfast bill every morning including an outrageous tip; the Blue Owl isn't cheap. Trish and I tactfully declined to go on the second morning, because we cannot afford to eat out every day. "I want you to come with me. Don't you like it?" Yes and yes. So we go, but never take this generosity for granted.

There are none of what Trish calls "real stores" in Kimmswick. No groceries or discount superstores.

We hear Robin clattering around in the galley. "What time do you guys want to go for breakfast?" she calls.

"Just let us know when you're ready," Trish shouts through the door. She looks at me, lowering her voice. "Miss Robin is rearranging the cupboards. Again. Well at least she's not running that darn Roomba. Again."

Robin adores her robot vacuum; we're always tripping over it or being startled as it comes whirring from around the corner or under the couch. "She's scared to use the hand-held for a little while, anyway," I note, and we both snicker, remembering the scene at the dock when Rob emptied the sweeper bag without regard for wind direction, velocity or the classic snotty yachtsman in his admiral's cap applying a tad more varnish to his Bristol brightwork which was promptly besmirched by a clot of carpet fuzz, assorted lint, toast crumbs and three colors of hair strands in varying lengths.

"He was an idiot, anyway," Robin calls out back. "Who varnishes wood in the rain?"

"It's a good thing there was such a heavy fog, he never saw where it came from," Trish reminds her. "And it wasn't raining then; it was only misting a little."

"Whatevs, Home Slice," Rob says, and we laugh again. She has no business trying to speak gangsta and it never fails to crack us up when she tries.

"This reminds me of Joey." Words fascinate my son; we've spent many road trips pointing out to each other misspellings and grammatical errors on roadside billboards and restaurant menus. He has a good ear for modern colloquialisms and is always reminding me that I don't. "I gave him a 'Holla Back!' once," I tell the girls. "He ordered me to not, under any circumstances say that again. Ever."

"I hope I get to have kids someday.," says Trish. "Obviously not gonna happen around here. Not a pretty penis in sight, let alone husband material."

"Not a swanky frank in the neighborhood," I agree. "You can always hit on a lockmaster or one of those burly attendants. I've seen you eyeing the ladders, like you could just climb right on up and get yourself a real man!"

"Yeah, right," she shakes her head to the contrary. "Not my type."

"Well, I'm no advertisement for what a marriage should look like," I tell her, treading lightly. "And honestly, I don't know that you want kids. They're a lot of heartache. And they may grow up to hate you."

Trish sets her mug down on the grill top. "Don't you say that."

"Lisa hates me."

She takes me by the shoulders. "It will get better. She'll come around."

"Thanks, sweetie. But I don't know about that. Now change the subject before I start blubbering."

"OK," she turns to Rob, "We headed to New Orleans?"

Robin shrugs and says, "South."

"Hailey, where are you going?"

"I honestly don't know yet, but where I end up doesn't have to be where you end up. Or where Robin lands. I'm really sorry if you feel we dragged you into this open-ended thing, but we're at loose ends right now and that's the truth," I say.

"Yeah, right, like you dragged me into this. Besides, I am having fun, even though not taking showers every day is an affront to my feminine sensibilities." Pensive, she picks a fleck of lint off the arm of my fleece jacket. "Please tell me we're gonna stick together on this. I cannot imagine bailing before we come to the end of whatever story this is — or the end of Robin's beer, whichever comes first."

I snicker. "Well I'm just in it for the free breakfasts. And to take care of Robin when she derfs. That's the real fun."

Lupus makes for unsteady pegs. Combined with a 9-5 Miller Lite schedule, "derfs," as Robin calls the bruising stumbles and falls, are a weekly if not daily occurrence, complete with bloody lips, black eyes, cracked ribs and peed pants. I'm familiar with all of the above, but not this form of domestic self-abuse.

Trish and I see the elephant in the room. But since we are all on a free-will odyssey, we can't bring ourselves to stage an intervention.

Perhaps we envy Robin her freedom to spout, despite the beer that fuels it, with no artifice and no guilt. Under cover of a Kelly Clarkson freedom anthem (Robin switched it up), Trish says, "I read a couple of magazine articles. Rob's right. Lupus isn't fatal. But alcoholism is."

The fourth day at Kimmswick dawns clear.

The stars are still out when we get up; even Trish, who likes to sleep in, is on deck wrapped in fleece and raring to go, her breath fogging in the chilly air. She mimics smoking a cigarette, shaking her head as I stub my one allowed smoke of the morning out in the butt can. By example I am trying to get Robin to stop tossing hers in the water.

My grubby red turtleneck is rolled up over my chin, sunglasses on, jacket hood up, gloves on. Robin cackled as she watched me layer two pairs of sweatpants over black tights. "You look like the Michelin Man." Rob's still wearing cargo shorts. She gave away all of her pants when she left Michigan, convinced she would never travel anywhere cold again. When it's frosty she stays inside with the heater blasting.

Bundled as I am, I can still move fast enough to catch the lines as Hoppie unties and tosses the ropes. He shoves *Blackout* into the current, which merrily grabs the keel and catapults the 40,000-pound, 44-foot steel craft out into the rushing river as if it were no bigger or heavier than a dime-store rubber ducky.

"And awwwayy we go!" Robin hollers from the helm, like some anorexic Jackie Gleason. "Holy crap, we're going 7 in neutral," she announces. We are gape-mouthed at the sheer force of the water.

Even with powerful dual engines it would be a formidable task to go against the rush of the muddy water, bubbling and swirling like some dark brew at boiling point. The straightaways are tepid going compared to the "turbulent corners" Fern famously warns of in her River School.

"You do not, repeat DO NOT, want to catch a tow on a turbulent corner," she tells her attentive students. "Your boat's gonna dance, believe me, it will."

I know this because despite my current desire to remain persona non grata, Trish has written the quote down and emphasized it with pink highlighter in her Hello Kitty loose-leaf notebook, which she has placed on the navigation table next to the paper charts.

"You're turning into quite the little navigator," Robin praises.

"Watch it, pipsqueak, I've got at least a foot of height and four bra cup sizes on you," Trish says, winking from behind her pixie-framed crystal encrusted reading glasses, one of her recent finds at a Dollar General Store somewhere upriver. She has not entirely abandoned her fashion standards, although the false eyelashes have been relegated to the "Louie Vitton" satchel. With just an artful smudge of shadow and liner-"I have to wear some makeup or my eyes just disappear"-and a dusting of blush, this 40-something could easily pass for 30. Not that anyone's counting.

"Now watch, you guys, we should be able to see the Kakka Lock soon, so keep an eye out," Robin says.

"Coming up on a turbulent corner," announces Trish, as I scan the shoreline with the binos.

"Tow. Coming fast!"

Robin has angled *Blackout* to the inside corner of a tight curve where the water roils with riled-up current, just as the lead tow of a triple-wide barge pokes its iron nose around the blind corner. "Christ, there isn't even time to hail it," she mutters. "Shee-ut." Cig clamped between her front teeth, two hands on the wheel, we ride so close to the metal monster that you could reach out and slap it. "Hang on girls!"

"Fern says to take it on the red line," Trish instructs urgently. "Pass on the inside bend. And don't tell him the river mile, they don't go by that ..."

"He's gonna see us in a minute," Robin says tensely, both hands on the wheel, cigarette still clamped between her teeth. We're cranked over as far as we can be without running up on the bank.

"Come on now, come on, yougottagimmesomeroom," comes the terse radio command from the tow captain. At least he's spotted us.

"Better on the inside bend than outside, at least," I mumble, rushing forward, one hand on the rail, to make sure everything is securely tied down. The tow wash will churn hardest on the outside curve. The wake won't hit us on the inside until the business end of the beast has passed. And if Robin can maintain enough control to cut perpendicular across the wash, we'll ride it out just fine. I look up at the tow's pilot house. A mounted plaque announced the vessel's name: *Tom Jump*. The captain waves. I nod in return, planting my fanny on the anchor box, legs braced.

The prop wash is a foaming mass. Logs shoot out, airborne, from beneath the *Tom Jump*'s stern, as if the barge is chucking missiles at us deliberately. Robin gamely fights for steerage. Evading a fencepost, a section of plastic floating dock and a deflated yellow strip of plastic containment boom, she deftly cuts left, crossing the larger vessel's wake, angling toward the opposite bank.

"There it is!" I point toward the channel leading to Kaskaskia Lock & Dam.

"Christ, what next?" says Robin, stubbing out her cigarette and turning for the entrance.

Chapter 10: Locka Locka Locka

The relief from the uneasy motion of the Mississippi proper is immediate. This 325-mile tributary is a small thing in comparison. The lock wall where the Skipper Bob guidebook and Fern say it's OK to tie up for the night is directly ahead, a concrete and rip-rap T protruding from the dirt-hill shoreline slightly to the right. Boats going through the lock enter to the left.

"Call the Kakka lockmaster," Rob instructs.

"It's Kass-Kass-Key-Ah!" Trish and I correct in unison, high-fiving each other at the inadvertent synchronicity. Robin is verbally challenged. She persists in calling the floating bollards that we lasso in the locks for raising or lowering "ballards" and keeps us howling over various other mispronunciations.

The Kaskaskia Lockmaster doesn't see all that much traffic; clearly pleasure boats seeking a night's sanctuary off the main river is the highlight of his day. As Fern noted, "He's kinda lonesome, so invite him down there." As expected, the courtly gent relays permission to tie up and then comes out of his perch in the control tower to grab our lines. I keep my head down, adjusting bumpers, uncoiling rope, then hang back on the stern and let Trish take the lead. Thankfully I don't recognize him. Might be a new tender.

"Good evening ladies and gentleman. Now, y'all are welcome to get out and stretch your legs here on the lockwall, but you must be back on your vessel before dark."

"Roger that," Trish responds coquettishly. "Care to join us for an adult beverage when you're off work?" He's cute, in a rugged, stocky sort of way, with sandy, short hair and no wedding ring. About the right age for her. Harmless fun, I decide, watching Trishie practice her wiles.

"That's real nice of you, sweetheart, but unfortunately I'll be working all night. Any more pleasure craft pullin' in that you know of?"

"Let's see — there was one boat ahead of us — and I think three more were planning on leaving Hoppies today." Trish attempts to toss her come-hither locks, apparently forgetting that she hasn't shampooed in four days and has covered her greasy scalp with a flowered babushka scarf. The scarf has slipped sideways, giving her an off-kilter, slightly manic silhouette.

There's only room for so many boats at the sparse anchorages and docks in the stretch ahead of us. Trish collected intel by brazen knocking on hulls the night before we left. An insular group of terse, parlez-vousing Quebec-ers had decided to stay another day so they could all travel together.

"Well," the lockmaster smiles. "There should be enough room for everybody. Y'all tell them about stretching their legs and so forth, all right?"

"Okey dokey, will do," says Trish. "Thank you kindly for your hospitality!"

"One more thing, where y'all headed? Need your documentation number or registration."

"Five eight one six nine five," Robin reels off from memory, deliberately lowering her voice an octave from normal

"Thank you, sir." He notes the info on his clipboard. "Destination?"

With Trishie's gamin-blond handiwork hidden, Robin does indeed pass for a man. She does not correct him. Trish and I are doing our best to suppress the giggles.

"Back to New Orleans. Been stuck up north ever since Katrina. Time to get back," she nearly growls. With her denim ball cap brim pulled low, the effect is decidedly if comically masculine, slightly bowed legs protruding from baggy, shin-length khaki cargo shorts, long sleeve denim shirt topped by the ubiquitous Guy Harvey t-shirt.

"Hurricane Katrina, a helluva tragedy. Glad you got your boat out of there in one piece," he says. "You have a good night, now."

"You too," we chorus, chortling like ninnies the minute he's out of earshot.

The 65-foot riverboat *Slo-poke* glides into the river majestically and slides in behind us, followed by a sailboat.

A smaller sailboat, motoring right for us. There weren't any sailboats at Hoppies. I stop breathing. My throat closes. Sweat pops under my arms and on my breast bone. This is not a hot flash. It's terror. *I've been kidding myself about doing the unexpected. Totally predictable. Here he is. Derek knows more about me than I think he does.* But it is a pretty 32-foot sailboat with the cheerful name of *Chip Ahoy*.

I pull in air like an asthmatic hitting her inhaler. A half-hour later the 40-foot Nordic Tug *Newfie Bullet* takes up the last available spot on the wall. gangly Jack says it's nice to see us again and promptly unpacks his accordion.

The rain kept everyone inside their own boats at Hoppies. In clear weather on a calm river, they're all in a more social frame of mind. We spend Happy Hour drinking Robin's beer and eating Dee's snack of Rold Gold pretzel twists dipped in her special horseradish mustard. Everybody polkas to such timeless hits as "Edelweiss" and "Roll Out the Barrel." *Slo-poke's* rackety family steals the spotlight and I relax enough to enjoy a twirl with Trishie around our makeshift dance floor.

The need to remain persona non grata will be easier after one more night on the Mississippi. The bottleneck of the linear path will ease, while not entirely diminishing, as boaters strike out on slightly different routes and varied timetables. There is still only one way to get to the Gulf, but some will choose, or be forced by the inevitable breakdowns of both boats and crews, to stay longer in places that have marinas with repair and storage facilities. I remember the letdown when the pack scattered during my first Loop. There had been safety and comfort in numbers. Derek did not yell or manhandle me as much when there was an audience. And sometimes I could escape for an hour or so, into the laundry room, for a walk with the lady boaters or once even out to girls-only lunch at a Paducah deli. I winced, remembering how I'd had to beg to go. "It will look funny if I don't, Derek. Everyone else is going."

Dark falls. After Jack's swan song, the virtuoso "Polka Symphony" we obey the lockmaster, retiring to our floating homes. Gas-powered generators grumble to life, lamps are lit, curtains closed. The air smells like steak and spaghetti. A *Slo-poke* baby wails briefly. Another night on the river.

"Good night Robin."

"G'night Trishie."

"Nighty Night, Hailey."

"Good night ladies," I trill.

"We're the freakin' Waltons all right," opines Rob before punching her pillow into shape and turning her back to us on the couch.

"Maybe those pills of yours will kick in and I'll be able to snooze tonight," I tell Trish. By now she is used to my post-midnight menopausal ministrations: kicking off the covers, wiping the sweat away with a dish towel that I keep handy under my pillow, rising to prowl around when my mind won't stop running in pointless, worried circles.

"Yeah, and maybe I'll get lucky tomorrow."

"Fat chance," I snicker. "But keep the faith. Maybe you'll get lucky in Kentucky."

Trish is shaking with silent laughter.

"Get it?" I ask. "Lucky in Kentucky!"

A little pig squeak escapes out her nose.

"Did you just snort?"

She laughs harder. It feels good to be free to be silly.

The jail dream wakes me at 3 a.m. Rob is already on the porch, staring out at the night, puffing away.

"Welcome Comrade in Mental Pause," I whisper. "Where can we get some hormones?" I wipe my wet bangs off my forehead. In the chill the steam rolls off my overheated body. "Can you see this?" I ask her.

"It fogs up my friggin' glasses. How long does this shit last?" she asks.

"Years and years, as far as I know. My mom says it builds slow, peaks and then eases off. Nobody talked about it very much back when it started for her, so she just thought she was going nuts. She's a retired paralegal; wore those 80s power suits, high-heeled pumps, the whole nine yards. Her favorite pumps were black suede. She would sweat right through them. Drenched so many blouses she started wearing sweat pads along with those big shoulder pads. Said she felt like a linebacker, but she was tired of dry-cleaning bills and ruining clothes. And my mother-in-law, when she got 'the change'? She went totally out of character. Drinking a bottle of wine instead of a glass, out dancing at the clubs, found herself a Harley-riding boyfriend that we caught her smoking a joint with."

"Pretty wild," Rob swigs from her beer can.

"At least she was a happy kook. Better than my friend Susan. She cried over everything — the Packers coming on the field before the football game, Amber Alerts for lost children, Al Gore's lost election-she was a real mess." God, I miss my Reiki-healing, crystal-rubbing, dolphin-channeling Goddess Shaman friend! Maybe she could send us some hormones, or an herbal potion to chase away the nightmares and stabilize our sweat glands.

"Tomorrow, well, today, Cape Girardeau. Top off the fuel. There's that floating dock."

"Stay there, or Little River Diversion?" That's where Derek and I always anchored.

"We'll see what it's like. I'll give 'em a call later this morning."

"Remember, Trish and I want to kick in on the fuel."

She bristles, offended. "Don't worry about it."

That expression I hate, again. Does no good. I do not require permission to worry.

"I'm gonna try and get some shut-eye. We'll be rollin' on the river in a couple hours," says my captain.

"Damn skippy, Skipper."

***

The ocean doesn't have a patent on wind against current. That's what the river serves up the next morning. It hits us the minute we motor out of Kaskaskia's shelter back onto the Mississippi. Beating into the wind against the flow of the current is a sailor's worst nightmare. In a power yacht, however, we make real progress, keeping a tight focus on turbulent corners, the rafts of junk in the water and the wide tow barge configurations pushing ton after ton of raw goods up and down river. Often the pilots acknowledge us with a barked "meet you on the ones" (to the left) or "take you on the twos" (to the right). Others don't talk; apparently it is beneath their dignity to deign to speak to recreational vessels. Operating on the you-big-we-little theory helps in those situations. We keep our ears out for one of the scariest scenarios, the so-called "bump and run," which in tow lingo means a barge has come loose and is free-floating in the river.

"Huckleberry Finn would have been run over down here," Trish observes, exhaling after another tow encounter. When she read in one of the guidebooks that it takes a quarter-mile for a tow-barge to even begin to slow down let alone stop she gained a new respect for the behemoths of which we are seeing 30 or more a day — and a new fear.

"They don't want to run us over, Trishie. They really don't. Think of the paperwork, the lawsuits, why, it would ruin their whole day!"

"And the mean ones, they're just dickin' with us," Robin adds. "All in a day's work. Breaks the monotony."

"Speaking of which, how 'bout some lunch?" Trish rises from the co-pilot's chair, making for the galley. She's as taken with the luxurious layout as I am and a far better cook. "Let me go see what I can rustle up."

The constant strain of keeping watch is wearing on all of us. I try to be grateful for the distraction from my dire personal situation. I remind myself that I'd much rather have a dozen tow-barges running at us in a super-size game of Chicken than Derek, coming for me, behind or ahead somewhere, waiting to pounce.

I can just hear him: "Police, arrest that woman!"

"Log to port," I snap, as Robin adroitly swerves around another partially submerged obstacle.

"That's got you, sucka," she mumbles, turning neatly back to starboard. "How far to the Cape?"

"Five miles. Want me to try and get the fuel dock?" Robin and Trish have phones. Signal is iffy; neither one cares. But when we have reception it's often the best way to reach marinas and fueling stops. Many are not big on answering radio hails, especially in off-season.

"See how late he's open."

After seven rings, someone picks up.

"They're there until five; we'll make it. But they don't even wanna see us near the dock unless we're taking on more than 100 gallons. The guy was adamant."

"No sweat," says Rob. "What's his price on diesel?"

"Shit, I didn't even ask. Want me to call back?"

"Nah." And she shoots me that look again, the one that says we are not discussing money or lack thereof or chipping in, again. So I let it ride. *Blackout* carries up to 325 gallons of fuel in two 150-gallon saddle tanks and a 25-gallon day tank. One fill-up would completely drain my stockpiled tips.

The crinkle of a plastic bag perks us up like two dogs waiting for Pup-Peronis or Liv-a-Snaps.

"Girls!" Trish climbs up the pilothouse steps triumphant. "Look what I found." She brandishes a family-size bag of Fritos.

"Hurray! I thought we cleaned out all the crunchy snacks. Were you holding out on us?"

"Well, Miss Hailey, these were hiding in the cupboard. Miss Robin here must have shoved them out of sight during her constant rearranging. We now have the perfect accompaniment to today's luncheon special, ta da! Ham and Swiss on rye."

Trish and I devour the thick-layered sandwiches on Blue Owl bread. Rob picks the ham out of hers, concocting what she calls a "ham roll-up," turns up her nose at the lettuce but wolfs down at least half the bag of chips. At least she's taking in calories, something to balance the beer IV. Her ability to function coherently continually amazes me. It's heroic, tragic and bizarre. And since we are not discussing Derek, or money or any other touchy subjects, it follows that we are not going to talk about her nutritional deficits or the next lupus flare-up, whenever it may come.

A series of swooping bends and wide curves precede Cape Girardeau. Commercial traffic increases, along with merging Loopers and Snowbirds sprinting for one of only two possible stops for the night: Little River Diversion Channel or the floating fuel dock, the latter at best a maybe. Two of the yachts from last night are ahead of us. The sailboat *Chip Ahoy* is behind. A new cruiser appears on the scene in a silver pontoon, its cabin rimmed by a gaily-colored awning festooned with strings of chili-pepper lights. A very large, rotund man with a fuzzy aureole of platinum hair pops out of the pilothouse cradling a tiny, fluffy white dog in one arm as he frantically waves with the other. A vinyl banner tied to a side rail advertises the boat name: *Garage Mahal*. As he runs alongside *Blackout* we see that he's hauling a blue metallic ski boat on the hip, tied to the starboard side. "Where did he come from?" Robin wonders. "That's one hell of a dinghy."

"I saw him at Alton," Trish says. "I forget his name, but his dog is named Precious. Isn't she cute? He said she fell off in the Missouri River so he dove off after her and let that raft ground up on the shore. He's videotaping this whole trip for posterity. His wife and kids wouldn't come along with him, so he's gonna make 'em sit and watch every minute of tape when he gets back home to Nebraska."

"And you thought I was weird," Robin says, shaking her head.

"Not as weird as he is," Trish affirms. "He travels without charts. Says he buys the chart for a particular waterway after he's traveled through it, just to have a record of where he's been. Fancies himself a pioneer explorer or something."

We can see the Cape Girardeau town levee, a massive, angled concrete slab designed to hold back the fury of a Mississippi flood. It's decorated with a colorful mural depicting prominent Missourians. I scan in vain for a portrait of hometown boy Rush Limbaugh.

"There's the dock," I point. Trish passes the binos. As soon as I have a fix I can see that staying there overnight isn't an option. Tow traffic keeps the river rocking with constant wave action. The wind is compounding the unrest. Even at a distance I can spot the docks heaving up and down. The motion at this dock is reportedly so violent that it has snapped lines, emptied stomachs and caused boats to flee back out into the river at night because they couldn't take it anymore.

I wave my hand at Rob's lit cigarette. "Put that out before we pull in." From a storage locker I pull out a couple of absorbent fuel pads, which resemble deluxe-size diapers. "Where's your tool of special purpose?"

"OK, wifey, what's a tool of special purpose?"

"It sounds slightly sexual, to me," says Trish, mugging and leering.

"Get your minds out of the gutter! You know, the doo-dad to loosen the fuel cap. I thought I'd pump for us. It's going to be a sporty situation. Between the weather and tow traffic that dock's bouncing like nobody's business."

"Don't need a tool of special whatever. The cap unscrews by hand. Port side. I'm not gonna turn in this current, so we'll have to drag the hose across."

"Roger that." The wind is strong, coming straight at us, blasting my face as I step on deck to ready the lines for tie-up. Trish is on the phone with the fuel dock; we have permission to come on in. The waves have not subsided. Combined with the tow wake it's like riding a bucking bronco in a washing machine.

"It's a treat to beat your feet on the Mississippi mud..." I sing the only part of the song I remember from my childhood, adding my own line "Looking forward to beating it out of here." I have a tendency to sing, hum or whistle when I'm nervous. Derek hates that.

I'm tense. Scared, even. The dock is heaving a full three-to-five feet up before smashing down into the water again. My former role in such situations was to hand over the tool of special purpose and "stay the hell out of the way." Robin's counting on me without doubt as she closes in on the floating dock. An unsmiling attendant, a young, tubby guy in blue coveralls, motions me to toss the lines. I hit the dock on the first try (yes!) and he hauls us in. The nozzle is heavy, handed over with no greeting or intent to invite anyone to disembark from the now violently rocking *Blackout*. Our ship rises up as the dock smacks down into the wave troughs. Then we're down in the water and I'm looking up at the dock. On my knees, I twist off the cap and shove the nozzle into the tank. The pump clicks on the faraway shore. "Tell me when it's full," I rise to a crouch, yelling over to Mr. Friendly. Braced like a firefighter I wrestle the hose into a better position. I'm grinning. Someone — a few people, actually — assumed that I could do what even I wasn't sure I could handle. It feels like a victory. "You know more than you think you know," I whisper to myself.

The sun is sinking as we conclude Robin's $1,200 credit card transaction. Her only comment about the $4 per gallon price was that she wished she'd gotten more fuel at Hoppies.

The second we untie, the current propels us forward at a brisk 12 miles per hour. "I can't slow this train down," Rob hoots, laughing.

"We can't miss the opening," I warn. "Keep a sharp eye to starboard, to the right, Trishie. The marker isn't always there. The entrance could be narrow or it could be wide. I've seen both." Created to accommodate overflow, Little River Diversion is always in flux.

"Can you take it for a minute?" Robin asks. I grab the wheel, still scanning the right descending bank. A minute later, a song pours out of the speakers. It takes me a minute-"Lonesome Loser," by the Little River Band. "Very funny, Rob."

"Little River Diversion Band," she says, winking.

"Shit!" We missed it. Robin guns the engines, giving it all we've got to turn back, angled perpendicular to the current, which is running 4-5 miles per hour against us. "Are we moving?" She groans.

"I'm sorry," I say. "I was watching, but the green marker is missing ." I wait for the snide comment, the scalding putdown, the sarcastic critique of my navigation skills or lack thereof.

"Chill out on the Blame Game, lady. I didn't see it either," Robin says. "Me neither," says Trish.

Painfully, slowly, *Blackout* corrects course, inching across the raging current toward the brown ditch.

"One, two, three — five boats, including the wacky pontoon dude. Looks pretty wide though," Trish says, adjusting the binoculars, peering into the canal.

I key up the radio mike. "To the boats in Little River Diversion, to the boats in Little River Diversion, you got any room in there?"

Ten seconds of silence. I'm familiar with the delay syndrome; it's part of the boating experience. Everyone is waiting for somebody else to answer the question. So nobody answers or everybody steps on each other and garbles the radio talk. Finally, *Chip Ahoy* responds. "Yeah, we're stacked up pretty good, but we'll fit you in. Plenty of depth, I got seven feet, but it thins out ahead of me." The sailboat must have passed us when we were fueling.

We thread our way into the notch, working *Blackout* around the yacht whose skipper unthinkingly plopped the anchor smack dab in the middle of the entrance. The sun is down, but the ambient light of the fading day graces us with decent visibility.

Three boats down there's a vacant space where we'll fit, barely. Overhanging tree branches from both sides of the skinny canal scrape the upper deck. Blessing the electric windlass that lowers and raises the anchor automatically, at Robin's signal I hit the button that drops the hook. Holding is good here, in sticky muck composed of we-do-not-want-to-know-what. A thicket of deciduous trees, mostly oak, creeping vines and poplar saplings crowds up to the shoreline. The prescribed 4-to-1 anchoring scope is not possible here — letting out too much chain would allow us to swing up on the bank or into the boats behind or ahead of us — but I put out as much as I can to allow for depth fluctuation if the river rises overnight. Fern is succinct with her instructions regarding this stop: "Get out of here in a hard downpour. You don't want to be in there when the runoff comes from Cape Girardeau." I'm grateful there's no rain in the forecast. Now if it would only warm up. I'm tired of wearing 10 pounds of clothes.

At my thumbs-up, Rob cuts the engine. It's my favorite part of anchoring out, that still moment when the machines stop and the noise of the day, the vibrations that you become so accustomed to that you cease to notice them, stop. The forest rustles, chuckles, hoots, rushes.

"We're 110 miles from Hoppies. Paducah is 90 miles and two locks away," Trish announces as she sits at the map table, scrupulously filling in the log for the day.

An inhuman scream raises our hackles. Trishie's eyes are as wide as an owl's. She blinks. "What on God's green Earth is out there?"

"Who Who Whooo's out there?" Robin laughs.

"Well I hope nothing tries to get on board," Trish frets.

"No worries," I reassure. "Whatever is making that noise is a long way into the woods and more than likely doesn't swim. Sound carries on the water."

I take my turn in the galley, producing Velveeta shells and cheese mixed with cut-up hot dogs. As usual Robin turns up her nose at the accompanying green salad in which I used the last of our tomatoes, but to my gratification eats two helpings of the macaroni casserole.

We turn in early. No jail dreams. And the night sweats are but a mild one-time trickle. Maybe those pills are working. I simply mop my breastbone with the dish towel, turn back on my side and fall back into untroubled slumber.

The Ohio River transit is a 60-mile-long buzz kill. Turning the corner off the Miss and onto the Ohio is like hitting a brick wall. The five-knot current that was sweeping *Blackout* along at 10-12 mph is now a three-knot current against us. Chugging away at 6 mph we begin to wonder how long it will take to get to the first of the two locks. Rob impatiently strays from one side of the bank to the other, looking for the lesser current.

Trish is stir crazy. There isn't anything to see or do. At the Mississippi turn-off, the big docks of Quaker Oats and other commercial operations held her interest briefly, as did the shoreline sighting of Cairo.

"That's Cairo, like Egypt?"

"Actually it's Kay-row," I tell her. "And there's nothing there. A sailing friend that Derek and I traveled with on the last Loop, Todd O. Smith, pulled over here and went ashore. He loved the little towns on the Loop and was traveling solo, so he would just stop whenever he felt like it and go looking for company. He said you could roll a bowling ball down Main Street. Boarded-up storefronts, no life to speak of."

"Thanks for the tutorial, Professor Henderson," intones Robin, "We are grateful to have an Information Specialist aboard, but we got bigger issues here. "Beer."

Bob Marley's "Jammin'" oozes relax mode from the speakers, but Rob's tone is decidedly not mellow.

The patchwork of dry counties along the Heartland river route has caused consternation among many a liquor-loving boater. Happy Hour disciples regard the sundowner as an essential component of the cruising life.

Having been here before, Rob knows that Paducah, Kentucky is the last place to procure spirits, or in her case, cases of beer, before we dock at

Green Turtle Bay in the very dry county in the very dry town of Grand Rivers, Kentucky.

There's no reliable place to anchor or dock in Paducah. The normal procedure is to go straight to Green Turtle and drive back to Paducah in the courtesy van, for which there is always a lengthy waiting list.

I have my own concerns about Green Turtle. I've made friends there. There are people to avoid. Slipping by undetected is not going to be fun or easy. In fact it's highly unlikely.

Trish is at the wheel; Rob's shuffling through CDs again. The Eagles, "Take it Easy."

Uh-oh. Another song clue. I know she's got The Big E in mind.

"Does the Rolling Thunder still exist?" I call back into the salon. "Words come to mind. Metal docks. Nightmare."

"You worry too much," is all she says.

We catch our first break of the day at Lock & Dam 53. When we contact the lockmaster on marine radio Channel 13, he informs us that the water is high enough to pass over the dam itself without locking through. "Just stay inside the buoys and you'll be fine; current's not too strong today," he says.

"Huge time saver," says Robin. "No problem hitting the Big E before dark."

Trish is elated to be "driving the boat." Robin coaches her through the channel as we pass by the old lock and the new "53" under construction that will eventually replace both this lock and the one ahead. The banks are pastoral, green hills rolling down to a yellowed tan shore of muddy sand. A flock of wild turkeys jogs unconcerned along the water's edge. Twenty miles upriver, we spot the Superman water tower heralding the town of Metropolis. Word has it that shallow-draft boats can pull up at a decomposing but still useable public dock here, clamber over the busted timbers to shore and hike to town. Since we don't know if there's beer to be had, and even if there was it would be a two-mile hike to town and back, we motor on by.

The second and final lock on our Ohio transit is a couple of miles ahead. "Cross your fingers, maybe they're letting boats pass over the dam here, too," Robin says.

No such luck.

We don't need to radio the lockmaster. It's obvious we'll have to lock through. There's a veritable fleet of sailboats and power yachts milling around just clear of the entrance. I train the binoculars on each and every one, reading names off transoms, eyeballing the occupants, praying for unfamiliar boats. I look for Derek. Every time I see a sailboat the same size as *Chinook* my gut tightens. When I was a teenager, a blue racer slithered over my bare belly while

I was sunbathing, my blanket the snake's closest path to the marshes of the tiny lake of my grandparent's summer cabin. It's that kind of queasy thrill. Like I just had a close call with something that bites. And the only reason I'm safe is because the viper chose to keep moving.

All this time I've been looking behind me. What if he got ahead while I was watching my back? He could be in another boat. A faster boat. Or he's working with the Coast Guard or Corps of Engineers. *He called the locks. They're waiting.*

Stealing *Seawind* was obvious and idiotic. Three women on a boat screams for attention.

"Crap," says Rob. I key up the mike. "Lock 52, Lock 52, this is pleasure vessel *Blackout*."

We are informed in a businesslike, don't-bother-me-with-stupid questions tone that one downbound tow-barge is currently locking through and will be followed by two more. Then, and only then, will the RVs be welcomed into the chamber for the 12-foot rise.

"Locking up sucks," says Robin.

"Agreed." It's a lot more turbulent than locking down. It requires more effort and energy to keep the boat from banging into the concrete walls as tons of pressurized water floods the chamber. No "ballards" here. Older locks like this one require boaters to use their own lines, which mean one of us — probably me — will have to heave two long ropes up the wall to the attendant, who then loops the lines around fixed cleats before passing them back down. It's an impotent wish but I still bitch to myself because the new, easier lock isn't ready yet.

A 45-foot wooden sailboat with an emerald hull, embellished fore and aft with lavish gold scrolling parts from the waiting pack, beelines toward *Blackout*. There is a figurehead proudly mounted on the bowsprit. As the sailboat pulls closer we are treated to the sight of a well-crafted, topless, buxom, long-haired blonde mermaid. Her blue eyes are crossed.

"Check out that statue. I don't know whether to laugh or barf," says Trish.

"Don't do either," I advise. The carved nameplate on the curvy wineglass stern is embossed with the improbable name *Elohssa Repus*. The ship circles *Blackout*. "Good afternoon, ladies!" leers a long-haired middle-aged Ted Nugent-type dressed in camouflage fatigues, a Detroit Tigers ball cap atop his long curly red-brown hair. His companions, incongruously attired in pale yellow Izod polo shirts and impeccable creased khaki trousers, nod distantly, as if to say "we're not with him and are certainly not hitting on you." The patrician with artfully graying temples is handsome in a slicked-back I-hobnob-with-politicians-and-play-the-stock-market way, an older version of the other man, who is perhaps his son, or maybe a nephew.

"How much longer d'ya think we're gonna be waitin' on this lock? I figure I got time for at least one more," 1980s Camo-Rocker man says, raising his Busch Light beer can in mock salute. The polo pair looks pained.

Trish pantomimes a shrug, holds a hand up to her ear. "If we pretend we can't hear him, maybe he'll go away," she stage whispers. We're both on deck organizing lines and bumpers. It's trickier than it looks to arrange the bumpers so that they don't squirt out or get smashed when the power of the rising water pushes the boat up in the lock and hard against the wall. The worst is placing a bumper in the wrong spot. It just dangles off the side, useless, as you shove against the wall at the pinch point, using every muscle fiber in your arms and shoulders. A bad lock-through with incorrectly placed bumpers will tighten your triceps and ache in your neck for days.

"I've cried in this lock," I tell Trishie. In the dark of night I'd blindly tossed the line one, two, three, four times before it hit the sill of the sidewalk above, where the lights and kind voices beckoned. "*Chinook* was cut off at the knees by the current. We could only make two-three miles an hour once we got on the Ohio. So we had to travel in the dark. Other boaters guided us into the marina docks using their flashlights."

Trish, fresh from Fern's warning to never travel the rivers unless you can see the water ahead and both banks, is shaking her head. "That must have been so scary."

"Derek laughs about it. He likes telling the story." But the things that were said and done wounded me forever.

Robin remains closeted in the pilothouse at the helm. It takes more energy and skill to sit and spin, holding the vessel in stationary position in moving water, than it does to proceed forward underway. And at times like this Rob has little patience for anything, let alone "yay-hoos," as she refers to men of Ted's ilk.

Elohssa Repus edges closer. "Where you stoppin' tonight?" Ted is persistent; the bold, brash approach must have worked for him somewhere along the line. I have finally worked out what the boat name is spelled backward. "Super Asshole. How appropriate," I remark to Trishie, moving my lips as little as possible. She snickers.

"Did you name your boat after yourself?" she hollers.

"Sure did. I call it like it is, pretty lady," he shouts back. "These two fine gentlemen here are thinking about changing her name, though. Ain't that a pity? But I guess it won't go over too well in, where'd you say?" he glances at the clearly uncomfortable skipper and his son or nephew. "Oh yeah, Marco Island."

They just bought the boat and being new to sailing have commissioned this Super Asshole to pilot them down the rivers and across the Florida panhandle to Marco Island, on Florida's West Coast.

"Funny, they seem more like the Kennebunkport type," I say to Trish, who is not at all graciously receiving a thorough once-over from Ted the lech. She throws back her shoulders, fists her hands on her hips and gives him a hard, tight-lipped smile.

"No disrespect, Peaches. I'm just likin' what I see."

"You look any longer and I'm starting the meter," she announces.

He cups his crotch. Licks his lips.

"That's it." Trish heads for the pilot house. "Where's that flare gun?"

The marine radio crackles static, short-circuiting the altercation. Finally the lockmaster announces that the gates are open and we're to file in, in our current order, "at which time I will assign you a spot. Everyone on board is to be wearing a flotation device."

"To the Lock 53 Lockmaster, this is *Misty Blue*, *Misty Blue*, is that port or starboard tie?" asks a worried female voice from one of the yachts well ahead of *Blackout*.

"We have a lot of boats today, ma'am, I will advise you what side to tie up on when you enter the lock. Understood?"

"Roger that," she utters, clearly disappointed by the lack of advance notice as well as being treated like an overly concerned novice.

"I remember her," says Trish. "She was at Hoppies. Made that awesome crab dip. Remember when we had the cruisers' party?"

"I remember Helen," I say. Usually I'm bad with names, but it was written in a terrific book she lent us, *White Oleander*. She didn't ask me any questions at the one potluck the rain-soaked boaters waiting out the fog at Hoppies had managed to pull together. She was focused on how tired she was of living on a boat. "Every time I need something I have to move something else out of the way to get it," she said. "I don't know how people do this for years and years." The promise of winter in Florida wasn't an adequate tradeoff for her grandkids or her house. "I miss them," she said.

"Helen is not going to like tossing a rope 12 feet up to the sidewalk," I say. Undeterred by our obvious lack of interest, Ted circles around one more time shouting "see you on down the road, ladies" and revs forward to cut in line in front of *Chip Ahoy*, *Misty Blue* and *Garage Mahal*.

"I hope they got their catcher's mitts on," says Trish, clicking the buckles on her personal flotation device. *Blackout* is equipped with the newest light model PFDs, more like parachute harnesses than traditional orange life jackets. Each has two breast-level floats on the front that automatically inflate like mini-airbags at the pull of a cord. Trish is particularly taken with her leopard-print model; wants to wear it all the time. Like most long-time boaters, Robin and I are rather blasé about lifejackets, donning them only in rough conditions or as demanded by the Lockmasters, who vary from lax to stringent in enforcing the PFD rule. This Lockmaster apparently takes safety very seriously.

Trish and I are also wearing fingerless sailing gloves, for better grip, less chance of abrasion and because, as she notes, "they look really cool."

Elohssa Repus has already broken one rule, darting ahead of three vessels. "No cuts, Mister," broadcasts a snarling skipper from one of the boats ahead.

This is better than *Peyton Place*.

"Look, he's flipping off that boat," says Trish, eyeing the scene with the binos.

"Oh brother. I hope he's not going to be next to us in the lock." Even Derek would not behave this badly.

As we clear the gates, the lockmaster requests the usual documentation info and directs us to the starboard side, right behind *Elohssa Repus*. I drop the fenders down, three big round orange bumpers holding us off the scummy cement wall. It only takes me two tosses to secure the bowline. "All right! Now let's get the back line," encourages the attendant, nodding to Trish. "Upsy Daisy!" With a huge grunt, she flings the line. It hits the lip of the sidewalk and flops back down. "Crap," Trish mutters.

"You can do it, Trishie, just give it all you got," I cheer her on. The second throw hits the wall, well below the mark. "Shake it off, lady, third time's the charm!"

With a guttural "Heeyah!" Trish lets loose, rope unfurling as it flies upward, landing neatly in the attendant's outstretched hand.

"Good one!" he says.

She's huffing and puffing. "I'm already pooped," she announces, picking up a boathook and preparing to fend off. My boathook in hand, I brace for the sound of the siren that announces the lift's commencement. Robin and I have schooled Trish in the proper disco hoot "Oooh Ooh," shaking our groove things and whipping the loose end of the line around our heads like rodeo cowgirls when the siren goes off. It breaks the tension. We have also worked up a hearty rendition of "Roll Out the Bollards." Sounds better with three-part harmony.

"*Blackout* secure." Rob announces over the radio.

We wait. There's a problem. *Elohssa Repus* is drifting. Ted stands on the bow holding a single rope and arguing with someone up on the lockwall. I strain to hear.

"That's OK, we only need one line!" he's shouting.

The attendant is shaking his head.

"He's not wearing a life jacket," Trish notes.

"Oh for chrissake," growls Robin. Don't mess with her when she's on a beer mission.

"Ladies and gentlemen, I apologize for the delay," the Lockmaster announces on the radio. "We got some knuckleheads here who don't know how to follow the rules."

We wait around another 20 minutes, the exhaust from boat engines hazing in the chamber. Finally, a silver aluminum skiff putts into the concrete canyon, manned by two stern-looking men in navy uniforms. *Fuck.* Head down, I edge closer to the lockwall, wishing for one of Robin's ball caps. I squat down below the gunnel, hidden by the pilothouse. I've got a sight line over the bottom rim of the windows.

One of water cops, or guards, or whatever they are, points authoritatively. At Ted. "Out!"

I start breathing again.

Ted's shift from rebellious to contrite is as immediate as my relief. A puffy orange life jacket is hastily procured, a second line handed up by the younger patrician, who appears to be suffering from extreme social-emotional discomfort. Either that or his puffy orange life vest is choking him. The older patrician remains ensconced in the cockpit in his puffy orange jacket, stiff with outrage.

"I'm sorry. I apologize," Ted is falling over himself to make amends. Regardless, the sailboat is escorted out of the lock, accompanied by whistles, cheers and applause from waiting boats.

"Wow, don't mess with the Lockmaster," says Trish, wide-eyed again. She stands up from what she calls her "pushin' cushion" and resumes the lock-up position.

Still we wait.

"Come on, close the damn gates," Robin mutters darkly. "This is ridiculous."

Ten minutes later the Lockmaster announces "Ladies and gentlemen, we sure do appreciate your patience. The knuckleheads have seen the light."

With downcast faces, two lines and all hands on deck in life jackets, the sailboat resumes its assigned parking space on the wall in front of us.

"What a monumental waste of time," snarls Robin. She barely chimes in on the "oooh ooh" when the siren blows.

There is no way I'll be able to argue her out of the Big E.

Robin has a connection. She calls a dude named "Black Ray." Has his home number. "Met him on the last trip down," is all she will say.

We anchor out just off the channel, not too close to where the jerry-rigged floating metal dock of yore, since demolished by high water, was attached by cables to the river bottom. No telling what lies below, or just beneath the surface at the Big E. The unorthodox metal dock that was erected here for a few years before the river washed it away was cobbled together from a scrap-metal yard. The bits and pieces could have ended up anywhere in the unreadable brown water. It would be easy to hook a giant hunk of rip-rap or re-rod and lose the anchor. The riverbank here rises mountain-like, carved soft-sand cliffs, sparsely vegetated by spindly weeds and the most tenacious species of wildflowers. A rickety, narrow, impossibly canted set of 200 or more steel and aluminum steps in various states of rust, contrived from whatever was handy at the junkyard, hangs on for dear life, which is what anyone foolish enough to use it does, finding anything to grip in the absence of handrails. God only knows how Black Ray got the cases of beer down that death-trap to the water's edge. I didn't have time to do anything but glance over occasionally to make sure the delivery had arrived. It takes us an hour to offload from the top deck the 11-foot Boston Whaler that serves as *Blackout's* dinghy. The electric hoist attached to the crane davit worked like a charm and good thing, because there's no way we could muscle the Whaler off on our own. The Johnson outboard cranks on the first pull. "You drive," Robin says, so I do, without mentioning that I've never been allowed to run *Chinook's* tender on my own. It's dark enough to turn on the red, green and white running lights as we zip the Whaler in to shore at the base of the rickety stairwell. Black Ray and another burly dude load 20 cases of beer into the dink. "Come to Mama," Rob croons. She pays with a rolled wad of bills passed in a handshake as I steady the dink in the rocking wash of yet another passing tow-barge.

It's bumpy, but we're well off the shipping channel and the anchor seems to be holding without being fouled on anything. So we decide we'll stay put for the night. There's a day dock up in Paducah, but it's normally packed with small bass boats and in any event for some reason the town discourages overnight guests on the waterfront.

I am handing the last case up to Trish, who then passes it to Robin for can-by-can stashing in the coolers, when the dim outline of a sailboat draws near. Ted and the polo boys again.

"Well lookee who's here. Hey ladies! Say, gorgeous, are you tired?"

He's talking to me.

"No, not particularly." Even I can hear the prissy tone in my voice.

"Well then you must be in very good shape, because you've been running through my mind all day," Ted says, hee-hawing like the donkey's ass he is.

"Wow, that's quite a line," I respond. "Come to think of it, I am exhausted. Good night, gentlemen."

"Aw, come on, gorgeous, don't be cruel. How's about inviting me over for a drink with you and your hot friend? We could have us a par-tay." He winks. Gross.

Robin steps out of the cabin. "You need any help, Hailey? Is this guy bothering you?"

"Is it OK if we anchor somewhere in around here sir?" I hear him asking Rob as I head into the salon. It's definitely Miller Time. "We went all the way to Paducah but there was no room at the inn, so to speak."

"Go ahead, knock yourself out," she says in her deepest voice, considerably cheered by the replenished barley pop reserves and her manly control of the situation. "Just make sure you're at least four boat lengths away. And set that hook. There'll be hell to pay if you drag down on me. Steel hulls aren't forgiving. Neither am I."

Nobody feels like cooking. We have the last of the Fritos, a half-pack of pepperoni slices and beer for dinner. Trish disapproves. "What's for breakfast tomorrow? Beer, cigarettes and phlegm?"

"Awww, come on, cheer up," Robin grabs her in a headlock and administers a noogie, which is the closest she ever gets to hugging. "We'll clean up our act tomorrow. Promise. I'll even eat something green, how's that?"

"Shush," says Trish, only slightly mollified. "Hand over one of those beers. If you can't beat 'em ..."

Chapter 11: What about John?

John is strumming the notes to John Prine's "Level-Headed Dancer" on the same battered Ibanez acoustic guitar I remember from previous visits to Green Turtle Bay Marina. The corn-whiskey fed, slightly balding Kentucky boy is plying us with Schlitz beer. Trish sings along with him in a strong, pleasing alto, exhorting us to move to the country, eat peaches, blow up our TVs and find Jesus.

I expected to run into John during our stop here; he's managed the boatyard for years and is constantly on and off the docks tending to customers. He's also Commodore of the local yacht club and keeps his sailboat *Wild Hair* at the marina across the peninsula on Kentucky Lake. There was no other choice but to stop here. It's the only option for boats 30 feet or larger. The other marinas are either too small or too shallow.

So as soon as we tied up *Blackout*, I went over to the boatyard offices to say howdy and give him a story about Derek having too much work this year and me doing the loop with some girlfriends. I even ask him to come meet my traveling companions after he clocked out for the day.

It was risky. John and Derek hit it off from the second John saw the guitar on *Chinook*. Derek bought it just before the trip, intending to learn to play. It was another impulse that given his short attention span would probably result in pawning the instrument off in one of the shops along the Intracoastal Waterway. John could play fairly well though. He picked for hours after showing us how to run the boat engine's stuffing box efficiently (it should drip, not stream).

I don't think Derek saved John's number in his cell phone. He wouldn't go to the bother. He instructs me to write contacts down in our address book, which I took with me. But I left our business-card black books on *Chinook*.

John's yard-manager card is in one of them. Derek can find it if he looks. Which is unlikely.

Odds are Derek hasn't called John. But John might down a few more beers and decide it would be fun to call Derek. He's definitely a drink-and-dial guy. I'm sure he has Derek's number from last year's repair invoice or other office records.

Robin is holding up like a hard-core stoic but we can tell she's hurting physically. Her movements are stiff. She's short of breath and shorter tempered. Though I've never seen one, I'm 98.7-percent sure that a full-fledged lupus flare-up is brewing. If Robin's incapacitated where does that leave me?

Yesterday morning while she was pulling on ugly gray tube socks banded at the tops with royal blue stripes I noticed the white adhesive pain patches on the soles of her feet.

The socks are not exactly a fashion statement when paired with deck shoes and cargo shorts. But October mornings in Kentucky are chilly, the dew cloying and heavy. Footies lack sufficient ankle coverage. Besides, Rob is one of the few women I've met in my life who honestly doesn't give a crap how she looks. "As long as I'm warm and clean, that ought to be good enough," she says anytime Trish and I try to "fancy her up."

Her appetite? Zilch. Except for the beer, the omnipresent beer.

"Schitz, happens," she grumbled good-naturedly when I warned her about John's rule: "Anybody who drinks with me drinks my beer."

When he showed up at 5 p.m. she grudgingly accepted a Schlitz, downing it quickly like bad-tasting medicine. She grimaced then burped. John joked with her a little, "See, ain't that better than the crap you drink? Damn, that light beer isn't really beer at all. Might as well drink water."

John has eyes for Trish, and she for him. We couldn't begrudge either one of them their mutual attraction.

"Let it fly," Robin whispered.

"Maybe there's someone around here for you," I tease.

"Getting laid is the last thing on my mind."

All Robin seems to care about lately is the stray black dog, a female Labrador mix that the marina staff informally adopted. The meek little thing had a water dish and food bowl in the front of the accounting and yacht sales office in the boatyard, near the prop garden, where amidst petunias, marigolds and red geraniums rests the chunked, snapped and corroded remnants of engine propellers beaten up by bottom obstacles and floating deadheads.

Robin named the dog KC, as in "KC and the Sunshine Band." Nobody seems to know or care where KC had come from. After a few visits to *Blackout*,

KC figured out we weren't going anywhere fast and we became family. The black dog with short legs, a broad chest with a V of ruffled ebony fur, and long silky ears was more often on the boat than anywhere else.

"Wasn't she the good girl?" Trish asks. KC pants obligingly, placing her head on Rob's lap, plumed tail wagging a mile a minute.

"She's the sunshine, yes she is," Robin croons. KC snuggles in. She is never far from Robin. I wonder if she can sense an impending flare-up the way some dogs can detect cancer.

KC moans low in her throat, a twisty, gargly sigh. We've never heard her bark. She talks, low communicative noises, deep frequencies that rise in her throat up from her belly. She also has a high whine in nearly perfect pitch.

"She's talking to me," Rob says.

"Yep. She's telling you to eat," I say, balancing on her lap a plate of scrambled eggs topped with melted American cheese product. "You need your strength to battle the Laundry Bitches. So hang on to this and dig in!"

About the Laundry Bitches: there are a few at every marina this time of year. Washers and dryers are at a premium during fall migration. Ladies accustomed to doing laundry at home in their own clean, private washers and dryers whenever they please are prone to severe separation anxiety. They aren't used to overflowing hampers or standing in line with a plastic bag full of quarters. Cycle 20 to 50 women who are running out of clean undies and time through a tiny room equipped with two washers and one dryer, and you'll hear a continual stream of gossip, speculation and dirty laundry of another variety being aired.

The Laundry Bitches think they have the system figured out. They're the first to tell you where you are in the line and which washer will be open next. They offer unsolicited advice on the hottest dryer, the longest washing cycle and where you should stow your basket or bag. They smile as they instruct, although they are not particularly friendly. They enjoy directing, questioning and holding forth. But they won't watch your laundry for you. It's your duty to stand and wait and pretend to be interested in their stories.

Woe to the boater who throws a load in the washer or dryer and is not there to immediately empty the machine as soon as it stops. The hapless launderer will face the passive-aggressive ire of the Laundry Bitches, those mavens of the machines full of insincere jocularity and an overbearing fervor for enforcement of the rules.

It's a danger spot for me, even if I just dart in to see if there's a machine open. They love to lovingly bash their better halves, as in, "Al worked in the engine room all day and talked about it all night. Men and their boats!" (simpatico chorus of titters).

"I stole a boat and ditched my rotten husband" might be more of a conversation stopper than starter. Especially if anyone remembers Derek and me.

A few of the women hovering around the "Laundry Mat," look familiar, but maybe it's more the type than specific individuals. They're hyper-focused on cleaning every washable item in their boats: rugs, blankets, bumper covers, pot holders, you name it, it's being laundered with a vengeance. They dissect whoever has just left the room, the people in the boats on their pier, the condition of the clothes they see, the right kind of fabric softener-any idle topic that can keep them occupied while they wait out agitate, spin and fluff cycles.

Yesterday Robin broke the most serious code in the laundry etiquette book: she left a load in the dryer. The strident one I call High Bitch of the Laundry Mat, accosted her when she went to retrieve it.

"I folded your clothes. You were holding up the line," the indignant matron informed her, the shelf of her ample bosom literally quivering with outrage. Then to me, not missing a beat, "You look familiar. Which boat are you on?"

"Thank you so much!" Robin gushed, "I really, really, appreciate it. Hailey, look how nicely she folded everything!" Then to me, as we beat a hasty retreat, "They're rags. She folded my rags in precise thirds."

"The Gladys Kravitz of the Laundry Mat," I say. "I wish you hadn't said my name."

"Shit. Sorry." She brightens. "She was so busy reaming me a new one she probably didn't even hear it."

I don't think either one of us buys that. But the laundry's done, we're leaving soon and I'll just stay away from the High Bitch of the Laundry Mat and her court.

Rob gets a few forkfuls of egg down; KC eats most of it, hand-fed by her adoring mistress.

"Hailey? There's a gangplank down in the engine room. It's pretty easy to assemble. It'll make it easier for her to get on and off."

"Aye aye, Cap. I'll set it up after breakfast. Just remember, somebody could claim her at any second. If you get too attached ..."

Robin's a goner. She's dozing on the couch, KC curled protectively in the curve of her belly, both of them snug under the comforter.

"What a pair," whispers Trish, snapping a phone photo as she comes in from her "power walk around the resort," also known as sneaking off to see John.

"Get a grip," I retort, when she tries to tell me she was toning up and taking in the scenery. "I know you were over in the boatyard flirting with John."

"He has a Kool-Aid smile," Trish has her own dreamy smile going.

"What's that?" I've never heard the expression.

"Oh, something my Aunt Ada used to say, some manner of Florida Cracker colloquialism."

"Whoa — is that a word?" Robin mumbles.

"You've heard of Kool-Aid, sleepyhead." Trish rolls her eyes.

"No, I mean the giant, show-off word," Rob says, more alertly. The sarcasm doesn't warrant a response. Her vocabulary is just as extensive as ours and in a good mood she'd be batting around her own 75-cent words. She's hurting.

"Somebody woke up on the wrong side of the bed," Trish observes gently. "Why don't you go on down and stretch out in the cabin? We'll keep the noise down so you can rest."

Now that we're at the docks with hot showers and other accoutrements available, Trish is in full-lashed, uplifted-boob regalia. Packed into her tightest jeans and a deep-cut form-fitting lilac t-shirt, her glorious curly mane is held back from her face by a jeweled band. She has the glow of a woman pursued by an ardent suitor. For his sake, I hope John has a pretty penis. I have a feeling that we'll soon hear more about that than Robin wants to.

Already the sexual overtones are heightened by my discovery of the Chicken Ranch "Pleasure Menu" and a typewritten copy of the official "House Rules" that I discovered while rooting around — with permission to find a shirt that might fit me — in Trishie's duffle.

"Who's Valentine?" I asked.

"That was my working name," Trish says.

"So you're the one who drew the little hearts all over this and wrote 'It is customary to tip'?"

"Yep, that's me."

"Let me see," says Robin. I plop down next to her on the couch so we can read the Pleasure Menu together:

Appetizers
Massage-Exchange Massage — Breast Massage — Lingerie Show — Bubble Bath — French Oil Massage
A La Carte
Body French — Full French — Around the World French — Hot and Cold French — Devices of Pleasure
Ranch Specialties
VIP Lounge — XXX Movies — Mirror Room — Jacuzzi Party Rooms
Entrees
Straight Lay — Half and Half — Combo Half and Half — 69 Party — Two Girl Show — Two Girl Party — Fantasy Session — Salt & Pepper Party

<u>*Desserts*</u>
Banana French — Frappe French — Flavored Pussy Party — Shower Party
<u>*Entrees To Go*</u>
Out-Dates — Escort Services

"Did you have to do whatever the customer ordered?" I'm not judging, just curious.

Trish tosses her hair. "We were never forced to do anything we didn't want to do. And Lord knows, there were girls there willing to do anything, as long as the price was right."

"Some of this stuff sounds pretty kinky," Robin says.

"Kinky is in the eye of the beholder." Trish laughs, but there's a cynical edge, a hard gleam in her eye. Suddenly I feel extremely grateful that she's here with us, out of that life. "Most men want to talk, then they want a blow job, then they want to talk some more."

"Sounds like marriage," says Robin.

"How long did you work at the Ranch?" I ask.

"Two years. That was enough. I saw the writing on the wall, made good money and got out. The hookers say that five years is the limit. After that your face changes. You're jaded. The clients can see it, anyone can see it. The nastiness doesn't wipe off anymore. Although," she muses, "blow jobs are a great facial exercise. All that sucking defines the cheekbones."

"You quit without any hassles?"

"Hailey, it's a brothel, not a harem. I never saw any woman held there against her will. And the medical and vacation benefits were excellent."

Trishie's phone sounds the five-note tone that signals a text message.

"Who dat?" says Robin.

"It's John." While she's texting him back, Rob and I peruse the Chicken Ranch Rules:

Rule 1: Ladies in Line-up:

a) <u>*NO*</u> *smoking or holding cigarettes behind your backs. (If you happen to burn someone's dress in Line-up, you will pay for it.)*

b) <u>*NO*</u> *chewing gum, eating or holding drinks.*

c) <u>*No*</u> *Laughing in Line-up. (It makes customers feel uncomfortable)*

d) No more than one girl in black per shift.

e) <u>*Do Not*</u> *wear the same clothes everyday!! Use variety.*

f) <u>*Must*</u> *have hands behind your back, holding only your purse.*

Rule 2: You are to take customer by the arm or hand and take them to your hallway. When your party is over take your customer over to the bar or entrance *way and tell them to come back and see you. <u>Always</u> make them feel welcome. The customer is your money!*

    Rule 3: Girls are to go through parlor when booking money or signing out, even though there is a Line-up.

    Rule 4: Nylons are to be worn by all girls unless you have a nice tan. If you have Lumpy Legs, nylons are a <u>must</u> even with a tan.

    Rule 5: Heels are to be worn unless you have <u>2</u> Doctor's Excuses. One from a chiropractor and one from Dr. Nelson. Even then an effort must be made to wear heels on weekends & Holidays.

    Rule 6: <u>No</u> books or games when <u>2</u> or more customers are in-house.

    Rule 7: If you have a customer that wants a 69 party & you are on your period, or a special party that you don't do — don't let that customer walk — tell him you will get another girl for him (Leave Man In Your Room)

    Rule 8: Clean up your own mess in parlor (kitchen at night). Floormaids aren't here to pick up after you. Throw away soda cans. No eating soup & chips in parlor.

    Rule 9: Ask your floormaid if you can go to your room or kitchen.

    Rule 10: Girls are being late for the floor. <u>This Must Stop</u>. Some girls are goofing off too much. <u>This Must Stop</u>.

    Rule 11: Girls out of C&E halls, take customers through B&F hallways, so Floormaids can see you and your customer.

    Rule 12: Vacations are required after 3-4 weeks. You have to leave for 5 days or more days.

    Mr. Conforte wants short timing stopped!! Make sure your customer is happy and walks out of here with a smile on his face and comes back to see you.

"I bet you were one of the goof-offs," Robin guesses.

"Nope. I'm a Rules Girl. I was strictly business."

"So girls," clearly she's weary of the subject, "John wants us to come over to his place for a cook-out."

"I dunno," I say. "Robin needs to rest. I'll stay with her."

"I'm fine," Rob insists. "You two go."

I've been to John's house, when it was John and his ex-wife Laura's. Ivy twines up the walls of the red-brick ranch with attached garage. It's tucked back in a cul-de-sac on a winding country road bordering Kentucky Lake, perched on a forested hillside, the back porch hanging over the water. Furnished in restful beige-and-cream tones. Laura filled it with hardbound books, hand-stitched needlepoint pillows, crocheted throws, silk flower arrangements and Hummel figurines. A vintage Grandfather clock kept time.

Laura is afraid of the water. They never had children, although she wanted them. It isn't surprising to me that they are separated.

They had separate spaces in their house. John's smoking den was a screened-in porch off the garage, chock-full of sailing trophies, yacht club regalia and Tiki Bar slogans: "I don't skinny dip, I chunky dunk," "It's Five O'clock Somewhere," "My Attitude Depends on My Latitude." I wonder if he's moved that stuff into the house.

The garage walls were covered with racing news bulletins, clippings and framed photos of John's past and present boats, *WhodaCap'n*, *Dagnabit* and *Wild Hair*, small, swift craft built for speed with a modicum of comfort for the occasional overnights in the bays of Land Between the Lakes.

"Hailey, meet my wife Laura," John said. "You can learn a lot from her, Laura. This is a lady who ain't afraid to heel."

I laughed, uncomfortable with the surly cant of his voice. "Actually, I don't like it when the boat tips. Derek's the one who really loves sailing," I demurred. "It's his world; I'm just along for the ride."

Laura managed a medical-supply warehouse. She'd just come home from work and was still in her neatly tailored pantsuit and crisp white blouse, her black hair carefully French-braided, a long, glossy plait halfway down her back.

"Welcome, Hailey. I'm going to put together a salad. Come on in the kitchen and I'll get us some wine."

"She drinks beer," John said.

"Actually, wine sounds good tonight," I said.

We could hear John and Derek regaling each other with racing exploits and storm stories. Can-tabs popped and we could hear them tuning up their guitars. As they chatted easily, bonding over a discussion of the best guitar strings and the finest music stores in Paducah, it struck me as it had many times before how nice Derek is to others. I can't say that it's phony. He's genuinely warm, sincere and courteous.

I wondered again why he was never that way with me. If Trish and Robin met Derek, they would probably think that I made the abuse up. They would think he was a nice guy, that I'm a drunken, nympho slut who brought trouble on myself.

Zip it, Hailey. They're your friends.

KC whines, a higher pitch. It's not my mind she's reading.

Robin stirs, sits up, face blank as if sleepwalking, and immediately lays back down, limbs stiff, eyes rolled back in her head.

KC jumps off the couch, the soft fur ruff around her neck electrified, standing on end. She barks, three short, staccato commands.

Robin seizes, limbs jittering, heels beating a macabre tattoo on the cushions. She stiff-arms a half-full can of beer off the coffee table. It rolls, leaving a wake of foam on the rug.

All I know to do is hold her firmly, to keep her from flailing off the couch. I tilt her head back and gently squeeze her jaw, reminded of a cat, Tina, who got hold of a baby bunny in our yard when I was a little girl. I had to beat Tina on the skull with a shovel to make her let go.

"Don't let her swallow her tongue," Trish warns, grabbing her cell phone and punching digits urgently. "I hope to hell they have 911 here."

The episode lasts about 30 seconds though it feels like much longer.

By the time Trish has gone up to the marina office at the head of the docks to meet the ambulance Robin is conscious, wrung limp but insistent that she doesn't need to go to the hospital.

"Bull," I say firmly, picking up the beer can. KC's already licked up the spill. "Let's at least get you checked out. Please!"

Her lips are a tinted a deathly blue-grape, color drained from the rest of her face save for hectic red mottling on her cheeks and over the bridge of her nose: the classic lupus butterfly rash.

"Is this a flare?" I sponge her face with a cool cloth.

"Ya think?" she chuckles weakly. "No, actually, the flare comes after the seizure," she says in a bone-tired, rasping whisper.

KC insistently shoves her head into Robin's dangling palm.

"S'OK, Kace, S'OK," Rob tells her.

From the salon window I spot the Emergency Medical Services crew rolling a gurney toward our pier.

"I will go," says Robin, "if you make sure she's fed and walked. Let her sleep on the boat tonight. It's supposed to rain."

"I'm going with you," I insist.

"They won't let you ride in the ambulance," she tells me, as one who knows. How many ambulance rides, I wonder.

She's right. The EMS crew is courteous but implacable. We are not next of kin. "We'll have her put you on the visitor list," they assure us.

The marina staff is understanding. "As soon as the courtesy van comes back — it's signed out 'til four-y'all can take it for the night," says the cute, pony-tailed dock attendant. "I cleared it with the marina manager, he said go ahead and stay in town for the night if y'all need to. We sure hope Miss Robin is gonna be OK. Send her our prayers."

It's 2 p.m. "Should I ask John if he'll take us now so we can get there sooner?" Trish says.

I'm tempted to say something smart-ass about Knights in Shining Armor on white horses, but I know Robin is Trish's main concern, so I don't push it. "It will take a while to get her checked in and examined. How about you go ahead and have dinner with John and I swear I'll call if I need you? I'll just wait for the van and take the GPS so I don't get lost."

Damn. I don't have a valid driver's license. The police cut it up. The Michigan Secretary of State's office won't even consider re-issuing a license for another year. I can't borrow the courtesy van without a license and proof of insurance.

"Wait a minute, change of plans," I say. "I'm a little shaky; maybe it would be better if John drove us."

I fill with self-loathing, especially since the lies are unnecessary. Robin knows about the drunken driving charge; I should have told Trish. Both of them have heard about the Four Lovers. And Joey's bullshit gang rape charge. We were headed down the Cumberland. Trish asked about the kids. What they were like. It just came out.

"She told him she was 17. He knew the Age of Consent rule. And both kids got multiple wear-a-condom lectures from Yours Truly."

"What a fun mom," Robin says.

Trish narrows her eyes. "Is it the same everywhere? The age?" I pick up a tone. The judgment. I don't think I can handle it again. The look. The turning away. Like you're slime because your kid fucked up. Fucked up while you were fucking around. And I'm the bad guy because I blame the girl.

"She took him over to the back of an SUV. She took off her pants. She unzipped his fly. He put on a condom. Entered her." I recite by rote from the police report. *I will never tell this story again.* "He pulled out right away. It felt wrong."

"I bet it did," says Trish.

"Can we talk about something else?" says Robin. For all her bawdiness, Robin's not comfortable discussing the actual mechanics of copulation.

"Yes. Please." I didn't like thinking about the women who came out to the Elbow for Friday night fish fry or post-ladies-golf-league cocktails. Serving the women I'd served with on Elementary PTA committees. Looking in askance at my low-cut hip huggers. Was my thong showing? Asking how I was. In that tone. Voices lowered. They all knew. They all judged. The Laundry Bitches are angels in comparison. But who was Trish to talk?

"I saw girls like her every day. At the Ranch. I hope she got help."

"Me too, Trishie, me too."

Trish thinks there are no secrets between us. Now I really do feel shaky. Lying to a friend will do that to you every time.

"We'll get back with you in a sec, thanks," I tell the dockhand. "But we would like to have the option of getting the van at four."

"No problem, it'll be here if you need it," she says.

"Let's talk to John," I motion Trish out of the office.

As we head down the dockway leading to the boatyard I blurt out the truth.

"I can't drive. They took my license when I was charged for impaired driving in Michigan. I'm an idiot. I'm sorry I didn't tell you earlier."

She hugs me. "Hailey, hey, it's OK. The picture's God-awful, but other than that my Nevada license is good to go. I can check out the van at four, no worries."

"What about John?"

"Him," she snorts. "Honey, the men will always be there. Nothing like a little delayed gratification to keep Mr. John on his toes."

John makes us promise to show up for the cook-out the following day. As we head to the hospital in Paducah I share the sordid details.

"My lawyer hanged himself just when I needed him most."

Trish clucks in sympathy, shivers at appropriate intervals and interjects "oh-my-goshes" and "you're-kiddings" as needed as I tell her about Ricky the Dick and my night in a jail cell. She isn't approving or condoning, just supportive. Like everyone else she wants to know what it was like.

"They put me in a woman's cell with white-painted cinder block walls. There was a barred window. In the right-hand corner of the cell someone had written 'I hate myself' in blue Magic Marker."

Wrapped in dark thoughts and a cheaply woven tatty brown blanket I sat cross-legged in half-lotus on a crackly blue plastic mattress the thickness of a yoga mat, waiting for dawn. It was so cold, one of those damp northern August evenings that foreshadow the coming of winter. Loathing my existence, utterly humiliated, my offense magnified by self-perpetuating paranoia, I irrationally began to wonder if anyone would come to get me out or if I'd just be left to rot. Would they keep me here all weekend and on into Monday and Tuesday until the usual Wednesday morning arraignments in the district court next door?

"I hated myself and I wanted to die."

I realized that even in a democratic society, when you're in police custody your power is gone. You're told what to do and if you do not do it of your own volition you will be forced to comply.

"At the station all the cops acted nice. But you knew they would slap you down if you tried anything funny. So I acted nice, too. I didn't have to pretend to be ashamed and remorseful. I was."

Trish nods.

Guilt and shame: although these buzz killers travel hand-in-hand, there is a difference. "The psychiatrist I went to for court-ordered counseling told me that guilt is healthy. She says shame is another story; it breaks you down."

Trish is nodding.

"My homework was to jettison the shame. Get rid of it by replacing it with behavior that made me feel good about myself. But every time I saw my mug shot on Derek's laptop, the shame came back."

"He didn't."

"Yep. Screensaver. Nice."

"We have all screwed up and been screwed over — that's the gospel according to Aunt Ada," Trish says. "What matters is picking yourself up, dusting yourself off and starting all over again."

"Thank you." I stroke her shoulder.

Chapter 12: *Blackout* to *Blackdog*

The regional medical and referral center known as Western Baptist Hospital is a huge complex. When we finally locate Robin in her private hospital room she's sound asleep, a round lime-and-white "I've Been Turtleized" Green Turtle Bay sticker firmly affixed to the center of her broad forehead.

"She insisted," the nurse says. "So we know where to return her." She is a pert brunette in sky-blue scrubs.

"I'm surprised she didn't order you to write 'This Side Up,' on her gown," cracks Trish.

The nurse whose nametag reads "Meredith" laughs softly. "Your friend said you were coming. She's doing much better, but we're definitely going to keep her overnight."

I look at the absurd sticker again; a pig-like snort escapes me. I've picked up Trishie's not-infrequent mannerism. The general laughter that ensues wakes Rob.

"Hi guys. Meredith here informs me that I am in the hands of 'the leader in cardiac coverage.' So no worries. Who brought the beer?"

"That's the last thing you need," says Meredith.

"No, the last thing I need is a cigarette to go with my beer." Robin winks. "I know, I know, you have your rules."

"We do," Meredith nods. "You ladies are welcome to stay 10 more minutes. Then this lil' booger bear has got to get some rest."

"Booger bear? Nice one," says Robin. "They want to do some bloodwork. I'm stuck here for at least one more day."

"Is there anyone I need to call?" I ask. "I'll camp out in the lobby. Trish can take the marina van back and pick us up when you're discharged tomorrow."

"My family isn't too thrilled with me right now," says Rob, yawning as if the subject tires her out. "No need to get big sister in panic mode. That's Renee. She considers herself in charge of the entire family."

"What about mom and dad?" Trish asks.

"Mom passed away four years ago this month. We lost dad last year. I'm happy they're together."

"My dad hated — hated — that expression," I say. "He always said 'when I'm gone, I won't be lost. I'm not like car keys.' And my mom went ballistic when I referred to her as 'beloved wife' in his obituary. 'Beloved!' she freaked. 'He would never say that!' So I changed it to life companion and best friend."

"Nice," says Trish, absently fooling with her phone again. "My mom referred to my father as 'your biological sperm donor.' He was out of the picture before I was out of diapers."

"Mine were so cool," says Robin. The mauve circles underneath her eyes make them look sunken and enormous. "They owned marinas in Michigan. Always had nice yachts. They would understand why I live on a boat."

"You need to get some rest, Skipper. I'll be just down the hall — Holla back!" I kiss her on the cheek; she squirms but is too exhausted to resist.

"You don't have to stay."

"I'm here. Don't argue. We are not leaving you alone in a strange place. Good night, Booger Bear. I'll check on you later."

Trish blows her a kiss. "Nighty night, don't let the bedbugs bite."

"Thanks." Rob scratches at her scalp, squirming. "Now I can lay here all night wondering if the bed is infested."

"Nope, it's not," says Meredith, returning to usher us out. "We're not some rinky-dink outfit here, we're — "

"I know, the leader in cardiac care," Robin intones in her deepest register.

Since I truly enjoy perusing *People, Architectural Digest, Southern Living, Lucky, More* and all the other magazines I can't afford, it's no trouble amusing myself with the waiting room archives until I fall into a light doze on a chaise lounge in the tastefully decorated, deserted waiting room.

I'm nodding over a back issue of *Better Homes and Gardens* when Meredith pokes her head around the corner. It's shift change. Gladys and Evelyn will be taking care of Robin through the night. I am assured that the patient is "resting comfortably in good hands."

I skate along the edge of consciousness. If I dream I do not remember. The air conditioning is blasting; it's too cold for night sweats. I get up a couple of times to use the restroom, stretch my legs in the corridor and peek in on Rob.

Trish is back in the morning with John, wearing the same clothes she had on yesterday. I whistle a snatch of "Johnny Angel."

"Oh shush," she whispers the minute his back is turned. "Is it that obvious?"

"Where are your panties? In your purse?" I hiss as John walks down the corridor ahead of us with, I note, a very satisfied swagger. "What did he pick off the pleasure menu?"

"Zip it," orders Trish. "Seriously!"

The first thing John says to me is, "Hey, how's Derek? Shame he couldn't make the trip."

"Jim Dandy, thanks for asking. I'll tell him you said hi."

"Do that. Would have liked to do some pickin' with him. Shame he couldn't make the trip. Work, right?"

"Yep. TCB." Lame. Not convincing. Why didn't I just tell him we're divorced?

"Is he meeting you down in Florida or what? Where's your boat?"

"We're still working out the details," I say. "It's going to be a couple of hours before they spring Robin. Want to go say hi?"

Rob's watching *Regis & Kelly* on TV. She's looking perky; what a relief.

"Hey Trishie, did you feed KC?"

"Yessir, Captain Rob, and I walked her too. She keeps looking around for her main lady. Gonna be hot today, so I left her inside with the AC and TV on."

"Wow, you must have been up and at 'em early," I drolly observe. Trish nudges. "Ow, watch it!" Trishie has very pointy elbows. I wonder if John has noticed.

The lovebirds head out for breakfast after I decline to accompany. "If you could bring me back some kind of breakfast sandwich, like a ham-egg-and-cheese croissant? Hold the mayo?" While not as extreme as Robin I've always been a plain Jane when it comes to condiments.

Test results won't be available for a few days. Robin's blood pressure is normal, she ate her breakfast and peed and pooped on schedule, so they're letting her go home, much to her delight.

I realize that I can't wait to get back to *Blackout*, either. Somewhere along the line she's become home to me, too.

As we roll along the highway in John's old, comfy conversion van, Robin comfortably ensconced in the rear seat, where she has already cracked a window so she can smoke, Trish switches on a country music station.

"What's a bedonk-a-donk, anyway?" Rob asks. "Can you turn that down a little? I have a serious question."

Oh no. Bad news. She's worse than we thought. Dying, maybe. And running out of money. Or patience for freeloaders.

"I'm changing the boat name. Perfect place to do it. John, that freehand boat painter still around?"

I stop mentally packing my bags. "Yeah, old duffer's still in the neighborhood," he says. "Only works when he feels like it. Hell, that's understandable. He's going on 90. Seth, is his name. Seth Wannamaker."

"Seth. He painted the original lettering on *Blackout*. His hand still steady?"

"Far as I know. Teetotaler. Lives in that little cabin in Grand Rivers just off the main street, the one with all the driftwood in the front yard." We've all seen it on our golf cart rides into town to eat at Kitty's, which serves some of the best Southern-style home cooking I've ever had the pleasure to tuck into. Robin is irritated by the lack of a cocktail menu in the dry county but is mollified by Kitty's warm-from-the-oven bread, individual loaves blooming golden out of clay flowerpots. My mouth waters just thinking about it.

"Can you get ahold of him? I'd like to do it right away."

"I'll check soon as we get back. You girls still on for the BBQ tonight?" he rubs Trish's knee with his free hand. "I got a mess of chicken and ribs ready to go on the grill."

Rob begs off. Me, too. I don't want to be the third wheel.

"If you're sure you don't need me," Trish purrs from the passenger seat. The sexual tension is palpable. Electric. I'm surprised their feet don't spark off the burgundy carpet.

"We'll be fine," I say. "Now tell us, Captain Rob. The suspense is killing me. Why do you want to change the boat name and to what?"

"I'll tell you when we get home," she says, stubbing out her cig on the rim of an empty Schlitz can. "Damn, I wish you had a full one around here, John. At this point even a warm Shitz would taste good."

KC is beside herself with puppy joy, nuzzling Robin and talking a mile a minute in her whine-growl. Robin looks up at us from the salon couch, propped with pillows, an afghan over her knobby knees. "There have been way too many blackouts in my life. From now on, this pleasure vessel will be known as *Blackdog*. One word. And Miss KC here is Official Mascot and Admiral."

"Woof!" It's only the second time we've heard her bark.

"That makes it unanimous," Robin says. "Done deal."

Robin is out of commission for the next eight days, hobbled by debilitating weakness and bone-deep aches. "I hurt everywhere," she says. Her stomach is also out of sorts. She attempted to sneak a couple of beers the first night back, subsequently alternating between nausea and diarrhea until there was nothing left to excrete, followed by dry heaving so long and virulently that blood vessels broke in her left eye, adding to her battered appearance. Administering the "little purple pill" prescribed by her doctor at the medical center turns the dull ache in her stomach into a stabbing pain. I don't realize how pissed off and worried I am until without thinking I chuck the "Nexi-bum" bottle overboard with the lid off, so the little purple fuckers are sure to sink.

"Hey, that's expensive!" Robin is flabbergasted. "And you shouldn't pollute the bay."

"Screw that poison!" I snarl viciously, before bursting into tears. "I'm sorry. I'll pay for them."

"Don't worry about it —"

"Don't every say that again. Please." I'm losing it. "Every time someone tells me not to worry about it, something to worry about happens. It's a stupid, fucked-up expression."

"Whoa. F-bomb!"

"I'm sorry, Rob. I'll try to get a grip. How 'bout a Pedia-Pop?"

"Why not. It'll be something different to throw up," she says, chuckling weakly. "Hey, maybe we're both having a nicotine fit?"

We made a pact. I won't smoke if she abstains. It's lasted 14 hours. I don't think either one of us can hold out much longer. Cigarettes are crazy cheap in Kentucky. Trish even remarked on it. "Gosh, maybe I should start." But she was only kidding because she still gives us those Lord Help Me looks every time we light up.

"Knock knock, here's your laundry!" The sotto-voiced singing-out is followed by a quick boarding. One of the Laundry Mat Bitches has come calling. Apparently Robin did it again: washed a load of boat rags, stuck them in the dryer and forgot they were there, causing great consternation in the floating hut crowded with two coin-operated washers, two dryers and a long line of women with their panties in a bunch.

"I've folded everything," the buxom middle-aged dyed-blond, visor-wearing Brunhilda proclaimed. She clearly has experience as a Welcome Wagon Lady. Robin remains prone on the couch as I lurch to the side door to intercept the invasion, grasping our bleached wicker basket by the handles. The bottom is filled with tri-folded hand towels that we use to mop up various boat spills.

"More rags," Robin mutters low to me. "No big deal." Louder she calls over her shoulder "Thank you, I appreciate that. Sorry I forgot to get the stuff out of the dryer."

"No problem," she says, "I just took care of it. I know you've been under the weather. They were sitting there for over an hour while we were all waiting to use the dryers."

"I'm so sorry," says Robin.

"No problem," she repeats. "Everything was dry so I just folded it."

"Oh, that was so great of you, thank you so much!" Taking Robin's cue I jump in with the praise. We'll never get rid her otherwise. She must have suffered greatly on the Mississippi, where there are no laundry rooms past Alton. Our own pile on *Blackout* was erupting out of the mesh bag when we sorted it for washing a few days ago. The vital stuff — undies, tees and sweats — was laundered long before we went to the hospital.

She wasn't going to let us down easy.

"I had four loads myself, so I just pushed you on through," she chortled, a laugh not really a laugh. "OK then, anything else I can do for you? No? You have a good night."

"You too," we echo sweetly. How can we miss her when she won't go away?

"Here's my boat card, we're on *Summer's Eve*," she says. "How are you feeling? Sounds like you had quite a scare the other day."

Again I lurch, grabbing the card, intercepting her before she can step into the salon. I hate having strangers on the boat, especially while Rob is recuperating. I can feel her unhappiness because we haven't welcomed her aboard for a tour. Tough.

I'm glad Trish is off with John. She'd scold us for our behavior and invite the dame in for coffee no doubt. Robin and I are at ease with being dismissive; as long as we're overly, ridiculously polite about it we figure no harm done.

"I'm fine, thanks. Just catching up on my sleep. We really appreciate your help. You have a good night now." Robin murmurs effusively from the couch. Nodding my head like one of those bobble dolls, I advance, smiling, and shut the door. In her face.

"Sincerity and brevity — you're my hero," I tell Rob, stuffing the rags back into assorted spots: under the galley sink, near the grill on the back deck and in the cleaning locker where we have stocked all manner of detergents, glass cleaners and polishes.

"I can't believe random women keep folding our rags. We've been here way too long," Robin says. "And if I ever get that OCD, smack me."

"Promise. No more laundry trips for now." I can see the veins under her alabaster skin, a frail road map. The view beneath her skin is stark, discomfiting. But the ugliest aspect of lupus doesn't show. Sufferers collapse in throbbing agony, but like lower back pain there's no way to x-ray or otherwise pinpoint the source. As I tend to Robin as she allows, I'm also reminded of CFS, chronic fatigue syndrome, another very real condition too often called into question as something a wilting-flower hypochondriac might claim, a lady lying in gentile repose on her fainting couch. When Cher started talking about her CFS, it gained more acceptance. After all, who could imagine Cher as a willingly lethargic poseur?

Each day Robin is a tad peppier. She's "antsy to get moving" before another wave of Laundry Mat Bitches arrive. The name-changing project is a healing diversion.

Green Turtle Bay is calm enough that Seth Wannamaker decides he can paint on the new name while the boat is in the water, saving the trouble of lifting *Blackout* in the hoist and positioning her on stationary stands in the boatyard. With his ancient, hooded eyes and habit of tucking his neck in as he lowers his head to his work, the venerable artisan himself bears close resemblance to a turtle. He has tied his beautifully curved white wooden rowing dory named *Carol Lee* (after his wife) to *Blackout's* stern rail.

Trish and I take turns standing guard for errant Jet Skiers and other rowdy water traffic that could rock the boat and splatter the paint. Seth is confident he can match the original gold lettering perfectly and congratulates Robin on a choice requiring only three letter changes. The previous day, he'd lightly sanded off the *o-u-t* and applied a black base coat.

In between pulling the boat apart to ensure that every item that bears the old name, from logbooks to the floating keychain to her *Blackout* cap and denim shirt, is either discarded or otherwise obliterated, Robin keeps examining the paint job from every angle. She even walked all the way over to the opposite docks to see how it looks from a distance. None of us can tell where the new black paint begins and the old paint ends. The job is seamless. Still, ever the perfectionist, Rob warns him more than once "if it's going to look cobbled together just repaint the stern and do the whole name over."

"Now, now Miss Robin, I did it properly once, I can match it properly this time," he soothes.

Seth entertains us with the long version of the story of how he painted the Coppertone Suntan Lotion billboards all around the south by hand (getting the exact flesh tone of the little girl's exposed hiney was particularly dicey), as well as the Weeki Wachee billboards featuring the famous mermaids. As he talks, his skilled fingers trace in a pencil outline barely discernible on the black hull before he takes up a series of brushes and applies the gold paint with exacting strokes. He's chosen early morning for the project, because the water is calmer and the rear of the boat is in shade. "The late afternoon sun will dry it nicely," he notes, "but you would never want to paint it in direct sun."

We invite Seth to stay for the denaming and renaming ceremony, but he declines. "A body gets to be my age, it's off to supper and bed before the sun goes down," he says. "Carol Lee is expecting me. After 50 years, I know better than to disappoint my bride."

As the shank of the day softens the light, cruisers curious about the ritual and willing to participate in anything that involves cocktails join Robin, Trish, John, KC and I on the pier. "Here," says Rob, thrusting the piece of paper into my hand. "You read it."

It's a copy of John Vigor's *Interdenominational Boat Denaming Ceremony.* They must have printed it for her in the office. Robin is not a computer-savvy person and does not wish to be. I realize that I haven't really missed being online myself, although e-mailing may be a good way to contact my mother and the kids. I'm going to have to let them know I'm alive. The truth is I've lost track of time, a common traveling-boater ailment or blessing, depending on whether you need to know what day it is. Since my immediate family and I speak so seldom, maybe once every couple of months, I doubt anyone has even gotten around to wondering where I am. Except for Derek.

But I don't want to think of him right now. Or ever. The boaters watch as I take position on *Blackout's* — soon to be *Blackdog's* — bow. I'm grateful I don't know any of them except John.

When I told Robin and Trish it would be best if I stayed in the boat during the ceremony they balked. "The Laundry Bitch recognized me. I should play it safe."

"She thought you looked familiar. Big whoop," says Robin. "What would she or anybody else do about it anyway?" Trish is nodding.

It's nice, feeling free. I savor that simple, unknotted feeling as I take a deep breath:

"In the name of all who have sailed aboard this ship in the past, and in the name of all who may sail aboard her in the future, we invoke the ancient gods of the wind and the sea to favor us with their blessing today.

"Mighty Neptune, king of all that moves in or on the waves, and mighty Aeolus, guardian of the winds and all that blows before them: We offer you thanks for the protection you have afforded this vessel in the past. We voice our gratitude that she has always found shelter from tempest and storm and enjoyed safe passage to port.

"Now, wherefore, we submit this supplication, that the name whereby this vessel has hitherto been known, Blackout, be struck and removed from your records.

"Further, we ask that when she is again presented for blessing with another name, she shall be recognized and shall be accorded once again the selfsame privileges she previously enjoyed.

"In return for which, we rededicate this vessel to your domain in full knowledge that she shall be subject as always to the immutable laws of the gods of the wind and the sea.

"In consequence, whereof, and in good faith, we seal this pact with a libation offered according to the hallowed ritual of the sea."

Robin insisted on a Miller Lite toast. "I can't stand champagne," she says. "And anyway, Miller is known as the 'Champagne of Beers.'" The assemblage whistles and claps as she cheerfully hoists a can.

"Do I pour it out West to East or East to West?" She asks.

"Do both," I advise. "Use a full can for each. The gods want only the best, and they want it all."

"Here's to you, Neptune, Poseidon, Eel-lust..."

"It's EE-oh-lus," I correct and for once she obligingly pronounces the slaughtered moniker properly without argument. The spectators cheer. One of the Laundry Mat Bitches waves her visor in the air.

A ruddy-faced, white-haired gent, from a 50-foot classic Trumpy Yacht named *Irish Eyes,* insists on passing up a bottle of Glenfiddich. "Add that to your christening liquids," he shouts over the loud crowd, smiling merrily. "We could all use a bit of the luck and a blessing from the gods. The bottle will break on the bow — a bit more smashing than an aluminum can, wouldn't you say?"

"Hadn't thought of that," admits Robin. "Thank you. But I have to tell you, I'm glad I don't have to drink it."

"Trishie, Hailey, come over here with me." KC is already sitting at her feet — actually *on* her feet-cowed by the crowd but excited to have her beloved's attention. "KC, move just a little sweetheart. There you go. Ahem," Rob rattles another sheet of paper. "Thank God this part is a lot shorter." The spectators laugh.

"I name this ship *Blackdog*, and may she bring fair winds and good fortune to all who sail on her!"

"Let's get the sheet," I nod to Trish. We board the boat amidships and head for the back deck, to the draped stern. We each grasp a lightly taped corner, pulling the tarp off to reveal the gleaming gold new name. "OK, Rob, let 'er rip!"

As we move forward to join Captain Rob and Admiral KC, we hear the busting glass of the Scotch bottle breaking on the bow, accompanied by applause, as John softly plays "Son of a Son of a Sailor," vintage Jimmy Buffett, on his guitar. A few people are clicking away with phone cameras and real cameras. *Shit.* Hadn't thought of that. By sheer luck I'm out of range, although I have gussied up for the occasion, digging out the peach sundress and espadrilles stuffed in the bottom of my ditch bag.

"To *Blackdog!*" Robin toasts.

"To *Blackdog!*"

"As soon as the shirts are done, we're outta here," Robin tells Trish and me. "I ordered them yesterday, along with a scarf for KC." There's an on-site embroidery and silk-screening shop. I should have guessed she'd need *Blackdog* replacements for her *Blackout* hat and shirts.

"Did you ask yet?" says John, stepping up next to Trish and placing a possessive paw on her derriere.

"What?" I'm wondering if Trishie's gonna jump ship. I can tell Robin's thinking along those lines, too. It would be a shame, but it seems to be her pattern, moving from guy to guy. Who am I to judge, me with my adulterous sport-fucking and drunken driving?

"Well I, that is we, were wondering — if it wouldn't be too much trouble — if John can travel with us down the Tennessee. You can say no, I mean, I know it's an imposition, but he could help at the locks and do some of the driving."

"I've got a couple of weeks of vacation time coming," says John. "Just an idea, but we thought it might be fun. And I can pitch in with expenses."

It isn't my place to say no, but I'm thinking "No!" as hard as I can. Doesn't do a bit of good.

"Sure, why not," says Robin. "As long as you remember who the captain is. And you bring your own beer." She winks. Trish squeals. I'm trying to smile.

The more the merrier. Yeah, right.

Chapter 13: Tennessee Waltz

"Lookout-Lookout-Lookout for godsakes woman! You're gonna hit it!"

We're not even off the dock before John is huffing and hollering, criticizing Robin's maneuvering and ordering Trish and I around as if we're rail meat on his racing boat.

I knew it was a bad idea to bring him along. And not just because my story could slip.

"Settle down there, Hoss," Robin calls to John. She easily clears the docks, not even close to banging into anything, extracts a pack of Marlboro Lights out of her *Blackdog*-embroidered denim shirt pocket and promptly lights up. Then says to me, "This is not the best idea I ever let myself get talked into."

"No kidding," I mutter, sticking my tongue out at John's back. He's standing at the bow urgently pointing to the green cans and red nuns that mark the winding channel as if we can't see them just fine all on our own. Trish scurries to the bow to nestle up against him.

"Smitten," I observe. "Next thing you know they're going to pose like Kate and Leo in *Titanic*."

Robin snickers, smoke curling out her nostrils. "She's got him so distracted he doesn't give a shit about you, so you can drop that wrinkling-the-forehead thing." I relax. A little. She's right.

Lake Barkley is lined with small, well-kept clapboard cottages and a scattering of palatial year-round homes, long docks with small boat-lifts in front of most of them. On this calm, clear Saturday morning, shiny, multicolored pontoon rafts, fishing skiffs and ski boats are out in full force, the lake dotted with flying spinnakers ballooning in the soft breeze as local sailors race their two-man vessels. John keeps urging Robin to steer closer to them, so he can hail his friends. Since we're planning to travel just a short way, to one of the dozen or so lush emerald coves on neighboring Kentucky Lake, we have time to putz around.

But I find the vanity show irritating. I feel like moving; an interior urging to move faster downriver makes me restless and impatient. I light a cigarette. If Robin's not quitting, I'm not either.

Eventually we come to the land cut leading to Kentucky Lake, following the coastline of the expansive, experimental forestry region known as Land Between the Lakes. President John F. Kennedy laid aside this land in 1963 for hands-on experimentation, tweaking the pretty peninsula's environment to suit deer, birds, fish, assorted rodents and other wild and domestic creatures that thrive when the right sorts of trees, ground cover and other habitats are provided for them. Forests are weeded systematically and clear-cutting is used; human visitors flock to enjoy the camping, fishing and pioneer re-enactments centering on farming life in the 1850s. Three hundred miles of coastline. You could spend a summer here. Or a year.

Despite my flight response, I know it would be wrong to pass by. We can afford to dally at least a day, especially since we don't have a schedule or a destination.

The change of seasons is pushing all of the Loopers and Snowbirds to keep traveling, fleeing frost, to the places where dolphins swim and it never snows. Some cruising newbies, including Trishie, dream of languid breezes and pina coladas, trop-rock music in the shade of the Chiki-Tiki bar, day after lazy day a rosy picture of sun-kissed serenity.

That's not what it's always like, down there, but she'll probably achieve some semblance of the tropical dream. In the Florida Keys it would only be a matter of time before Trish connects with a delightful new Sugar Daddy. I'm admiring but not jealous of that. What I'm jealous of, I'm ashamed to admit, is that John went for her and not me. Why is that? I don't feel attracted to him. I don't even really like him.

I'm sure I don't look particularly attractive just now, in my son Joey's castoffs, a very faded dark blue Nike pull-on hoodie sweatshirt and droopy gray sweat pants that bag in the seat after the first 10 minutes they're on. My hair is gathered in a low pony tail. We're freshly showered but no one primped. We were too busy cleaning and stocking the boat. Life on the move changes priorities. It's more important to have a fully stocked larder than it is to be groomed to the nines.

The general feeling is to just get through this patch on the river highway where the weather is often nippy and amenities are rustic to none. There are those couples on boats who buck the trend, creating detailed itineraries and stopping at every historical or artistic place of interest. Never minding the extra days or expense, they dawdle at will in quilt museums and old cemeteries. I think it's very sweet.

It reminds me of the times that I wanted to see or do something other than what Derek wanted to do. It happened often. Funny how you can miss the things you never had the chance to see.

Carefully steering a course around more trolling boats full of fishermen who don't want to get out of our way, Robin clicks along the narrow, well-marked channel into Kentucky Lake. Entering each new "pool," as the spaces between locks are called, on the way down the rivers is like opening a door into a different world. The trees change in their size or species; the flow of the water alters; there are more homes or fewer.

Once there was a town here. "They flooded Birmingham when they built the Kentucky Dam," John tells us. "You can see the foundations and streets when the water's low. A buddy of mine sailed too close to the north shore and got hung up on something, couldn't go forward or backward. They had to dive on the boat to figure out how to get it out; it was trapped in a breezeway between a house and a garage. Had to pull the boat out backward. A lot of underwater hazards; most never charted. They say you can navigate using an old township plat map."

"Like a redneck Atlantis," I say.

"Who you callin' a redneck?" He laughs. "OK ladies, I now declare it Beer:30."

"I'm way ahead of you," says Rob.

KC has found her spot beneath Robin at the steering station, her compact body neatly fitted between the rungs of the Captain's chair. She backs out, stretching her paws, hind end in the air, and slowly organizes her limbs to rise to her feet.

"A perfect yoga down dog," I tell her. "Nice job, Kace!"

"Don't let her go out without her life jacket," Rob instructs. In addition to our normal provisioning we have stocked Purina kibble, several varieties of canned dog food and white-battened potty pads for KC to use on the front deck. Just in case she doesn't like the pads, Robin also purchased a five-foot square of AstroTurf. We punched a hole in it and attached a long rope handle so the fake grass can be dunked overboard for rinsing after KC does her business.

KC submitted to wearing the pink life jacket when we tried it on at Green Turtle Bay but turned up her nose at squatting on the potty pad.

"She sees the land, so she's confused. Why would she go on the boat when she can pee under a tree?" Robin reasoned. "She'll be fine once we're out on the water and nature calls."

In our travels both of us have met cruisers with pets; we're adopting their strategies for the adopted black dog. There was never a question whether KC would come with us. Nobody answered the Found ad in the paper (much to our relief). KC is meant to be here.

The little Lab mix confidently prances out the side door onto the front deck, sniffing as she goes, and finds a spot to recline on the shady side of the deck. "Smart move for a black dog," Trish tells her. "Atta girl."

It's early in the afternoon when Robin steers off the channel into Clay Bay. Before I can move into position, before Robin's signal, John deploys the anchor close to the mouth of a quiet creek shaded by the surrounding oak, maple and evergreen forest. It's irritating. But the annoyance can't last in the kind of spot where you feel you could stay forever, just floating, without a care in the world.

KC won't pee.

"I've filled her water bowl three times today," I note. "She's got to need to go."

"Throw her in and let her swim to shore," suggests John.

What an ass. Before anyone has time to react he picks KC up by the life jacket straps, tossing her in the drink.

"What the hell is wrong with you?" Trish screams.

Rob and I are already over the rail and in the water.

KC is whining steadily, but also making a respectable beeline for shore 50 yards away, dog-paddling for all she's worth. We follow her, weighed down by clothes and shoes. All three of us fetch up on a sandy point, whereupon KC immediately squats and urinates, her relief audible.

As we huff and puff we can still hear Trish hollering and John laughing as she calls him every name in the book. It's reassuring in a way; she's still on our side.

"I'm glad KC got to pee," I tell Robin. "But I'm done with our friend John. Done."

The water is surprisingly warm for autumn, but now that the adrenalin has worn off we are both shivering.

"Here, sit in the sun a minute," I tell her. "Catch your breath," Robin's lips are that awful shade of purple.

"John is a Fucko. Drowned a whole pack of cigarettes," she gasps. KC is rooting around in the underbrush in preparation for taking a dump.

We sit and recover. "I wish I had my camera," I say. "The boat looks good from here."

"It does," says Robin. "But I can't even begin to deal with swimming back."

Problem solved. Trish in drill-sergeant tone is directing John to deploy the dinghy. In short order they row over to collect us.

"If you ever do that again, I will kill you," Robin tells him. "I want to be very clear: do not ever throw my dog off this boat again. Don't touch the dog. Don't look at the dog. Don't even think about the dog."

"OK, OK, sorry." John is not particularly contrite. "But we got the job done, didn't we Kace?" Wet-bellied sand-bedraggled KC wags her tail. She stinks like a wet dog. She rolls over to have her belly scratched.

Traitor.

Several beers and a grill-full of hot dogs later, it's time for bed. John's unrefrigerated Schlitz supply takes up a good portion of the V-berth floor. It forms a little step for me as I hoist myself onto the bed. I'm not drunk enough to block out the noises from the master suite. Roaming hands and tongues, moans and wetness, yes, yes, yes.

I wonder if Robin can hear. And then I play with myself, middle finger finding the magic button, and I come along with them.

It's going to be a long trip down the Tennessee.

Robin's up at dawn as usual, generator puttering, echoing in the still bay as she puts on the coffee. Downbound Canada Geese honk overhead. We hear heavy footsteps coming up from belowdecks.

"Good morning ladies. Beautiful day!" says John, walking past us to the stern deck. We can hear him pissing off the porch. He waits to zip up until he comes back into the cabin. He sees us looking as he ostentatiously closes his fly. "Ha ha, sorry ladies, but that's for Trish."

As if.

"Coffee's ready," says Rob, pointing to the mugs.

John pours his cup full and steps onto the front deck near the port side. As he is admiring the sunrise she shoves her palms into his upper back, right under his shoulder blades, pushing him over the side with more strength than I knew she had.

"Man overboard," she announces. And then, "Anchor up."

God, I love this woman.

"You bitch," John screams, treading in place.

Robin laughs, feet firmly planted, hands on hips, "bitch wings" deployed. "Shucky darn, Johnny Come Lately, you lost your hat."

"What the fuck?"

"That's for KC."

"There's something seriously wrong with you. Hell, you're probably not even a woman."

"Better get to shore and get some sunscreen on that shiny ol' billiard ball. Go on now." She shoos him away with one hand. And then to the tousle-headed, droopy-lidded, satiated Amazon goddess coming up the steps from down below, "Sorry Trishie."

Trish glances at her waterlogged lover and laughs at him.

Not getting sympathy from her, he lashes out, "Screw you, Trish. Oh wait, already did."

"Bet you're even smaller in the water," Trish observes. "Bout the size of my thumb, Hailey."

I can't help but giggle, and that turns his rage on me.

"Fuck you, too, Hailey. Derek know what nut jobs these bitches are? Wouldn't let my wife out to dinner with them, let alone on the river. I'd get off this boat at the next stop if I was you, Missus Hailey. Before you end up as fucked-up as they are."

My heart pounds. My head swims. My gut churns.

Robin engages the engine.

John rolls over on his back, stroking toward shore. He hollers skyward. "Gonna give him a call and let him know what's up."

Brainless with panic, I gulp and open my mouth. "Go ahead and call him you, you-Jerkwall!"

"Fuck you skanky old bitches. Go straight to hell."

Trish looks at me. "Jerkwall?"

"Cross between fuckwad and jerk?" I laugh. But it's not funny. "Oh shit, did I just tell him to call Derek? Oh shit oh shit oh shit."

As we head out of the cove I'm looking out into the channel, expecting Derek to already be there, waiting for me.

Robin apologizes again. Trish isn't expressing anger. She's meticulous in her polite exchanges and promptly follows orders from the Captain as we proceed into the navigation channel. Rob and I endure this for 10 minutes.

"Go ahead. I know you're pissed. Let it out!" Robin says. "He had to go. Sorry you lost your sport-fucking connection, but he had to go. We can ship his Shitz back. But I *am* sorry that it didn't work out."

"Don't even get me started," warns Trish, but Robin already has. "What? Didja think I wanted to marry his ass? When he threw this little booger bear off the boat I was over it," she says, stroking an appreciative KC.

"But girls," she sticks her hip out and curves her back. "I won't lie to you. He does possess a particularly pretty penis."

"Oh brother," says Robin. "Hailey, did you just snort again?"

"Yup. That's me, an old, snorty, skanky bitch. Bitch of the ditch."

It *is* funny. But now I know for sure that I have something to be scared about. The hazy what-if has shifted. "He was really pissed."

"Big whoop," says Trish. "It's not like he can call right away. Don't worry about it."

"Please, don't ever say that." A lot depends on whether Derek started down the rivers. Knowing him, he did. He always says he travels best solo. For the rest of the morning I'm continually scanning the river, the banks. The binos are never out of my hands.

"Fuggedaboutit," says Robin a few hours later. She knows my history with the other phrase.

"What, do you think they're coming to take you to jail?"

"I don't know." It's true. "But it feels like they're coming to get me."

"Who? Nobody, that's who," says Robin. She knows what I'm thinking. "So you moved a sailboat. No harm done. Nobody cares."

"They won't take you back there." Trish wants to make it all better. But they took Joey back again and again, just hauled him in on any pretext. No proof of insurance. Beer in the trunk. Dark-tinted windows. A dangling deodorizer 'blocking' the rear-view mirror. He had to move away to get away from them. And can never come back.

"I was only in one night. It was a lot worse for my son. Bad enough sitting in the waiting room on visiting day," I tell them. Visiting for last names A-Q was from 6-7 p.m. Mondays at the county lock-up. "I always brought two magazines. One to read and one to sit on." The purple-upholstered office chairs bore large, irregular brown stains redolent of leaky Pampers or Depends, sweat and soda pop. Friends and family there to see the inmates shared an unspoken bond of embarrassment and sorrow, which the young expressed in smart-mouthed bravado, the elderly in stoic silence. A couple of 60-ish grandpops and uncles occupied the chairs closest to the front entry most weeks, along with a fat, pasty-faced grandmother on oxygen; from time to time a pleasant-faced, overly made-up bleached blond female officer appeared at the Formica reception counter to accept money for commissary accounts or inmate packages.

"I was allowed to bring him three pairs of boxers, three t-shirts and three pairs of socks at the beginning of his sentence. A sweatshirt, during the winter." I shopped for the nicest things I could find, socks with extra cushioning and a star on the cuffs, soft cotton boxer shorts in subtle, non-provocative neutral tones, pristine white fitted tees that embodied the clean, new, shiny, under-the-radar life I wanted for my son.

"Derek told me 'you're not the one in jail.' But it felt that way. My son is a good person," I tell them, sounding like every jailhouse mamma cliché. "But he was also good at hiding his wild side." Recent findings that the impulse-control portion of the brain remains not fully developed well into the 20s don't surprise me. Passionate impulses, heedless rushing and full-throttle revving down roads best not taken are what trapped my son behind scratched and cloudy glass, a jail wall between us.

"So what's your excuse?" Robin says, brandishing a beer. I wave it off.

"That was my excuse."

The water does what it can to ease troubled minds. There's no sign of Derek. In the next few days the traveling pack spaces out, lulled into somnolent, good-natured lassitude with plenty of room to roam the dreamy emerald river framed by autumn's amber color show in an unexpected heat wave. We are carried down the winding water path, meandering from golden bay to golden bay. Soothed by the ceaseless murmur of cicadas the *Blackdog* crew takes turns taking naps. In the afternoon temps warm to the mid-70s. Trish and I pull man-shirts over our bikinis to fend off sunburn. We slather Robin in sunscreen as she strips down to her Guy Harvey tank top and Snoopy boxer shorts, her nose and cheeks white with zinc oxide ointment.

Some nights we drop anchor in peaceful forest-encircled coves; on alternate evenings — or when Robin craves something deep-fried — we motor in to one of the state park marinas, which in this neck of the woods always feature an A-framed lodge-restaurant-golf course that provides relaxed buffet dining and well-scrubbed albeit spidery clubhouse-style showers.

There are no treacherous narrows; on the wide Tennessee River waterway, tows pass by far less frequently than on the Mississippi and when they do are far and away.

"No locks," Trish happily intones at least once a day.

The immense relief is unanimous. By tacit agreement no one is talking about John — or Derek, or Robin's ex, whoever he is. No worries with KC and the call of nature; we haven't stopped anywhere where she can't get off the boat to do her business. There's always a spot of clay-pocked sand shore or a dog-walking expanse of grass at the state park marinas.

The Ahhh-not-Aha days and nights twine one into the other, as if we've been doing this forever and will never stop cruising the river. Mussel harvesters with red diving flags hoisted on their small skiffs surface and submerge in search of freshwater pearls. Pisgah Bay, Kenlake Marina, Pebble Isle, Cuba Landing — the names on the charts take on life for Trish as Robin and I revisit old haunts.

We bit into hot grilled burgers at Pebble Island Marina's floating café adjacent to its busy fuel dock. We'd earned a good lunch after once again flying practically blind inside the funhouse twists of a narrow channel into the marina in intense but short-lived fog. I heartily seconded Rob's motion to stay more than one night.

"We need a break."

Where else can you drive the owner's pick-up truck to the New Johnsonville Farmers Co-op to refill the propane tanks? The scenery is pastoral and the people are as nice as you'll find anywhere. The showers, primitive no-privacy cubicles in a cement-floored open-air summer camp-style block building, are a far cry from Alton's luxury suites. "At least they're clean, and there's plenty of water pressure," says Trish, who shows us how to cleverly rig an extra towel and two clothespins into what she calls "a modesty curtain." But not before we again spot the thin blonde line. "Did you know the clitoris has more nerve endings than the penis, ladies?" Trish notices us noticing.

"Yes I did." I laugh at Robin's discomfort.

"TMI." she says.

Rested and clean, we're prepared to put some miles behind us as we snake out of the twisting channel on a clear morning. But Robin insists on stopping at Mermaid Marina early in the day, as soon as we spot the curvaceous sign featuring a come-hither sea-goddess. The marina's motto is, "We will try to treat you like a rich aunt or uncle!" How can you pass up a promise like that?

"I don't see the point in rushing," says Rob.

"We can use the courtesy car to provision," she says, and I know it's time for a beer run again, seeing as we already have ample groceries aboard. She's grouchy; I wonder if another flare-up is imminent. There's certain twitchiness to her movements, the flushed butterfly patch across her nose and cheeks is prominent, despite the carefully applied zinc oxide ointment.

We anchor another short hop away at Double Island, where two beefy rednecks in an orange-and-white pontoon boat with ridiculously souped-up engines circle us for an hour, grinning idiotically. At first they pretend to fish, but after the first 20 minutes all they do is give us the fisheye. We wave once. After that, we try to ignore them.

"What do you think Ehnis and Roscoe are looking for?" I ask Trish, who's reading a glamour-girl fitness magazine.

"Well, according to this article, it could be one of four things: Friends with Benefits, Booty Call, F-Buddy or One-Night Stand," she says.

"What's the diff? I'm an Information Specialist, I need to know."

"Doesn't matter, cause it's not happening," she says. "But FYI, since we don't know them the only possibility is a One-Night Stand. All the other categories are for people who know each other or at least pretend to know each other."

I try to figure out which category my escapades with the Most Dangerous Lover of All fall into. I squirm with disgust, not lust, as I remember a thumb, a mouth, two tongues and inappropriate behavior on a waiting room couch in a deserted office. Lover Number Four, the Contractor, rich, handsome, blond, upstanding pillar of the community, diddling me and every piece of ass he could get, waiting for his wife to die. Making all "his" women feel special when the only thing we were really doing was unwittingly swapping body fluids. I didn't think about condoms or an AIDS test until I overheard some ugly, but I'm sure very true, gossip.

Our two nights together — and the build-up to them — were just another game on his sport-fucking circuit. For me it was something close to love, an envisioned future with an affectionate, considerate, demonstrative, sensual and generous mate.

"After the third lover, you'd think I'd smarten up," I tell Trish. "But each encounter dumbed me down another step."

"Thank God you didn't catch anything," she says. "That's the part I don't get; you lectured your kids on condoms, but you didn't follow your own advice. Well, now you know better."

"I sure do, Trishie," I mock. "I've now moved on to even dumber things, like trying to run away from my husband on a boat."

"Well, as far as we know that's not fatal," she notes.

"Not sure. Could be life threatening."

She swivels her head, sharply. "Do you really think he'd kill you?"

"I don't know. I don't plan to give him a chance. And I sure don't want to put you or Rob at risk. Maybe I should get off, head out on my own."

"Don't worry about it. We can take care of ourselves," Robin, coming out on the back deck, KC at her heels. "Sorry. Just slipped out."

Ehnis and Roscoe leave while it's still warm, sun just beginning its trek across the western sky. Trish wants to swim and so do I. Robin points out that we'd need a rope around our ankles or waists if we intend to stay with the boat.

"That's what Derek said," I remember. "He was right. About this." I demonstrate the "What Floats" game. There's a strong current here, 11 miles from the Pickwick Lock. When I peel the potatoes for dinner (homemade mashed potatoes, mind you), the brown skins are whisked downstream and out of sight within 10 seconds.

"So let me understand. You ate a plate of potato skins at the last buffet. But you don't like skin-on mashed potatoes?"

Robin shrugs.

As we draw closer the next morning the current makes itself known, crudely manhandling *Blackdog's* bow, slowing our speed. Pickwick is the last of the two locks that lead to and from that glorious valley of thick forest, rich fields and the ever-present energy of one of America's most noble and powerful rivers, the Tennessee. Bass boats are everywhere, anglers flirting with the current as flipping carp — excited by outboard-engine vibrations — spring out of the water, scales flashing as they catch impressive air. We never tire of watching the spectacle.

Each heartland river has a song; whether we can hear it or not over Robin's Kelly Clarkson CD is another matter. It doesn't matter. "The Tennessee Waltz" continues evermore.

Rob cranks down the stereo and the twin diesels as we approach the entrance to the Tenn-Tom waterway entrance. Next stop: Pickwick Lock.

Chapter 14: Tenn-Tom Transit

There's a bottleneck of boats at Pickwick, the lock at the end of the Tennessee River named for the *Pickwick Papers* of Dickens fame. The free-for-all is well underway before we enter the lock: 15 boats from 32 to 60 feet long jockeying around twice that many small local fishing boats vying for the lead spot closest to the lock gates.

The only sane rationale for being first into the chamber is that locking up closest to the downbound exit gate is generally less turbulent. The real reason boats are fighting for position is that subconscious desire among too many of the human species to be first, to lead the pack, to shoot out of the gates with all the other boats behind, eating your dust (or in this case, wake).

"More road rage on the rivers, bring it on!" says Robin, pumping a fist in the air.

The floating "ballards" as she still insists on calling them, will be at a premium. Obviously there are not enough to go around. Boats will have to raft two or even three deep to fit everyone in for the 55-foot lift. The sharp-tongued lockmaster is already warning boats to stay in line in their current position. It's mid-morning; the day is young but he isn't.

"No cuts, didn't you hear?" Trish hollers at a trawler about our size as it eases in stealth mode past us to port. The loutish brute manning the wheel flips her the bird. To starboard a couple in matching lime-green polo shirts stares resolutely forward as they attempt to sneak by, as if we won't see them if they don't look at us. They overtake and pass *Blackdog*, only to nearly collide with the encroaching boat coming around us on the other side. Evasive maneuvers prevent injuries but not inappropriate use of the middle finger again from the immature jerk on our left.

"You got a license to fly that bird?" Trish catcalls. "Wow, they're getting me wound up," she admits. "Is it always like this here?"

"Every time I've come through it's crowded and there's someone who wants to play games," I tell her. "Just ignore it. It's like the drivers who crack in a traffic jam. Boat rage is just another form of road rage. They think they're so important that the traffic should pull over and let them through. Like the world is their express lane."

Then more bad news on the radio: "All you boats waiting, we've got three bollards out of commission on the north wall. If you can't locate a bollard or somebody to raft to, proceed back out of the lock, next lock-through in two hours. Gates opening in five minutes. Stay back from the gates until they are completely open."

"Great," mutters Robin, idling in a lazy circle as we watch the boats that passed us come within inches of each other again in heightened haste to make their way to the front of the line. Passing other boats is against the rules. No one cares.

"A bunch of bullies," says Rob. "What a cluster F!"

"Why don't we just wait? It's gonna be a madhouse in there," Trish says.

There are no boaters that know Derek or me in this group. I think. You never know when a "hey, we saw you in …" will pop up. Somebody I never noticed. Somebody that noticed me.

Hiding in the crowd is a strategy. Rob thinks so.

"Derek could catch up. John's royally pissed and gossipy as a clucking hen," she says. Her simple acceptance ratchets my paranoia to a new level.

"Besides, I'm tired of waiting. We're going for it." She gooses the engine, timing the acceleration to swoop *Blackdog* through the narrow gap between the bully and the couple. Trish flashes the peace sign as we shoot ahead of our overtakers. As we maneuver alongside a Nordic Tug named *Sassy*, next to a sailboat whose name I can't see no matter what angle I try with the binos, Robin sticks her head out the pilothouse window, giving them a shout-out. "Hey sailboat — Nordic Tug — let's raft up on the south side."

"Aye," bellows the Nordic Tug skipper. "I'm heaviest; I'll go on the wall. Then you, then the sailboat. Acknowledge?"

Rob gives him a thumbs-up as the male member of the two-person crew on the sailboat *Baloo* nods. "I'll bet you five bucks his name is Bob," Trish says. I laugh longer than the lame joke warrants. So relieved.

The exhaust fumes in the canyon of the lock are a blue haze, thrusters employed, shouting matches both productive and destructive echoing off the walls of the man-made cavern. We carry out our plan flawlessly, rafting three deep, second bollard back on the south side, watching restlessness, anxiety and impatience surface without getting involved.

Trish and I count down the drop by the horizontal seams on the lock wall, blocks divided in five-foot increments. A nest of baby birds is dislodged from the bollard ahead of us; pity the mother sparrow that made an unwise nesting choice. The kindly lady boater closest to the bollard has tears in her eyes as the chicks drop into the water and the nest follows, bobbing uselessly. She grabs a net to try and scoop up the babies, letting her boat bang into the wall as her husband yells at her to pay attention. It's a futile effort.

"I had snakes on a ballard once," says Robin. "There was a whole coil of them. It was beyond creepy. You never know what's going to nest in the chamber."

The siren sounds, the gates open, presenting another new environment. The water color has shifted from gray to green.

We've had enough travel for one day. Just past the round, steel mooring cells located on the upbound side of the lock we hang a right, entering the starboard channel leading to Pickwick Landing State Park. The floating aluminum docks are easily accessed, pylons lassoed and cleats secured; with Trish and I manning the lines, we're tied up in short order. When she registers in the office Robin books the courtesy van for a trip to the Star in the nearby town called Counce.

The tiny Star grocery and hardware store is crammed with everything from fuel filters to piñatas, inner tubes to tiramisu, the fresh-made goods and produce supplemented by a mind-boggling array of canned stuff. The bakery and deli departments are a culinary revelation. Sue's cupcakes, Andy's BBQ ribs, Sara's Mac & Cheese, Mary's Pecan Pie — every dish is lovingly labeled by its creator.

As we unpack the provisions back at the boat we eat, testing Andy's Pulled Pork, Chocolate Cupcakes by Stacy and TyAnn's Lasagna, the latter on special with warm garlic bread.

"We'll do the buffet at the restaurant tomorrow," says Robin. "I can't believe I ate the whole thing!"

In bed by nightfall, we sleep like the dead.

No one has used or cleaned the showers here since Labor Day. The prolific spider webs are dusty but fully occupied. Trishie's screams make me grateful that the bathhouse is set back a few hundred yards from the docks so she doesn't wake everyone up. I run to her in my pjs, bare footed.

"Here, didn't I tell you you'd need a broom?"

"Oh my God," she gasps, "Are they poisonous?"

"Nah. Just brush them off and wash 'em down the drain. Here's the spray bottle, too."

A broom and a spray bottle of Clorox diluted with water will take care of almost anything you find in a marina bathroom.

Derek always says he does his best thinking in the shower. I do my worst, as in worst-case scenarios while I aim the nozzle to allow the hot water to pound the sides of my neck. Bleach smell lingers in the stall, reminding me of a hotel pool. *John called Derek, Derek called the lockmasters, the jig is up. All he has to do is report me to the county probation department for stealing that sailboat and I'm back in jail.*

"Knock it off."

I poke my head out of the stall. Robin's brushing her teeth at the sink. I'm eye-to-eye with her reflection.

She's right. I can't fix this. So there's no point in worrying about it. But tell that to my roiling gut. And the day sweats that are more about panic than The Change. Between the three of us we have a load of colors and a load of whites. No Laundry Mat Bitches in residence. "And not a spider in sight. Let us be thankful for small blessings," says Trish.

Replete with deep-fried dinner, KC included since we brought her a doggy bag from the lodge, we again retire at an absurdly early hour.

At 4 a.m. I feel energy next to my head. It's the barest touch, so light, so slight that it could be part of a dream. There are fingers on the hull. Someone is out there. I yank open the curtain and look out the porthole. All I see is plaid flannel. The national anthem blares from unseen speakers.

Stumbling topside in fleece pajama pants and long underwear top I discover an invasion. Hundreds of bass boats are covering every inch of the Pickwick Landing lagoon, engine vapors mixing with the steam off the water, the exciting odor of gasoline, testosterone and competition. No less than five bass boats are clinging to *Blackdog's* exposed side, anglers steadying themselves on the caprail as they rise to recite the Pledge of Allegiance.

How could anyone complain at awakening to such an extraordinary sight? Surrounded by passionate and elite fishermen, Robin, Trish and I join in the pledge and bow our heads for a fishing prayer. I tack a 'thanks' on to mine for an escape that's working. So far.

This is why we travel the river, to know that we are part of a larger world that latches on to us whether we like it or not. "America the Beautiful" blasts tinny from a sound system somewhere farther out on the sea of aluminum and fiberglass and I am reminded of the patriotic tunes that play from sunrise to sundown over the public sound system on the Joliet docks.

As we pass by Aqua Yacht Harbor mid-morning, I'm reminded of an equally startling but far less inspiring sight: the butt of *Mary Poppins*. It's warmed up nicely into the 70s. Amidst the bronzed bodies, ice-laden coolers and increased amounts of Confederate flags flown on a plethora of party boats, I spot Aqua

Yacht marina with its transient dock and all-too-public shower stalls. Bathers must contend with a shower compartment that while appropriately curtained opens into a common area facing the toilet stalls. Those emerging freshly showered are visible from every angle. No amount of extra towels or cleverly placed clothespin/shower curtain configurations will prevent a public display if anyone enters.

I made *Mary Poppins* scream when I opened the door to the ladies room on my second Great Circle Loop. Her blinding white derriere was amply presented to me, as immense and startling as a breaching whale's back, magnificent in its own way, astounding in its circumference. Her piercing shrieks drowned my rapid but sincere apology and continued for several seconds after I hastily shut the door. If you're going to be that upset at being discovered naked, chances are you will never find peace living on a boat.

Shaken by her virulent reaction I dashed back to *Chinook*. She had to walk on the long dock past my boat to get to her own, fully clothed, wearing a jaunty straw hat with cheerful blue ribbon streamers. She climbed into the trawler three boats up from ours named *Mary Poppins*.

I was glad that Robin, Trish and I didn't stop at Aqua Yacht Harbor, not only because of the shower situation. The nearby paper mill reeks. The magnificent homes on the shoreline hold no charm or value for me, considering the stench permeating the air.

"Finally, the Tenn-Tom!" Trishie announces, intent on the travel guides splayed across the chart table. "The guy who wrote the *Tenn-Tom Nitty Gritty* keeps his boat there," she points to Grand Harbor Marina.

"I had dinner with him once," Robin says. "He's a nice enough gentleman, but a little full of himself."

"Really, you met Fred?" I'm starstruck as only a cruiser who has traveled the rivers and lived by the instructions of the scion-guides can be. Boaters rely on the words of the classic guidebooks by Rick Rhoades, Skipper Bob, Claiborne Young, Fred Myers, following directions as faithfully as a new wife adheres to coveted family recipes the first time the in-laws come to supper.

"Fucko and I took him to dinner at the restaurant here. It's a nice marina. And no, I don't care to talk about my ex right now."

Or ever, apparently.

"Let's keep our eyes on the channel."

"Aye, Cap'n Robin," I say, saluting. She rolls her eyes. Trish snorts.

As we pass the dilapidated docks of the fully operational Spry Boatyard the scenery changes dramatically. The Divide Cut, 280 feet wide, reinforced by rock and rip-rap, was forcibly carved out in the late 1980s. The scars have abated and blended with the natural landscape over time, but it retains its crude industrial character. Trees cut to 2-1/2 feet above ground level protrude like the stubs of rotting teeth. Anchoring in this sector is both illegal and foolhardy.

Blackdog motors along the stump-lined channel, passing over forests and farmland flooded by the creation of the Tenn-Tom Waterway in 1985.

Trish eyes the rotting, sun-bleached, stubborn trunks protruding aggressively on both sides of the pathway and shivers. "Well, at least it's clear where we can't go," she says. "It's ugly, but Fern said we should be grateful," notes Trish. "If it wasn't for the Tenn-Tom we'd have to go down the lower Mississippi to get to the Gulf."

"Four-hundred-fifty miles to Mobile," I say. "And it gets prettier. Maybe by then we'll have figured out a way to get KC to piddle on the boat."

Commercial traffic is by necessity slower, smaller-sized and less frequent at the top of the Tenn-Tom, skinny by width but more importantly by water depth. Maintaining a controlling depth for tow-barge configurations drawing nine feet keeps Army Corps of Engineers dredging operations on constant duty. I show Trish how to watch for the long, partially submerged tube sections of dredge pipe protruding for hundreds of yards out from a working dredge. If boaters can't go around the tubes, the dredge team can retract them, but it takes time.

We hoot and wave at the truckers passing over the US-72 highway bridge and earn a couple of horn blasts for our efforts.

Trish points out the orange-and-white buoy marking the original site of Holcut, a town relocated to make way for the waterway.

"What is this, trivia hour?" Robin wants to know.

"I am an Information Specialist by trade." I grin.

"I thought you were a sport-fucking waitress by trade." Smart ass.

"I've always had a thing for history, nature and math," says Trish. "Figuring out this river traveling on a boat: how to be safe, have enough fuel, stock enough food, etcetera, etcetera is like a whole series of fascinating story problems! I can hardly wait to start factoring the tide in. Say," she says, "do you think somebody puts out a tide guide for dummies?"

The river widens into a deeper, more generous channel, opening into the clear waters of Bay Springs Lake. Rob lets Trishie take the wheel. We pass raw red outcroppings and sand-ringed marsh islands tagged fore and aft with official channel markers and gaudy, home-made trot line bottles. It is a strong, surprising pleasure to look into clear water for the first time since Lake Michigan.

"I can't see to the bottom but I can see my toes. Not too cold, either," I report after dipping my feet off the swim platform. As I return to the pilothouse from the back porch, Robin's outside, headed up to the foredeck. Trish and I watch as she squats on the green-turf potty pad.

KC follows her out, ears perked, eyes trained on her beloved mistress as Rob crawls on all fours, periodically dipping her nose to the pad and sniffing as if she's discovered the most captivating scent in the world.

"She gonna drop her drawers?" Trish looks around to see if anyone's watching.

"She might," I say, observing the demonstration with amusement.

KC is unimpressed. After a couple of minutes she eases back on her haunches, then inches down to her belly and closes her eyes, napping. "Oh well," I scan *Nitty Gritty* and run some mileage numbers on the calculator. "If she won't go, I suppose we can make it 52 miles to a marina today instead of anchoring out. If there are no delays at the locks."

"This first one is a biggie: Whitten Lock, an 85-foot drop," Trish announces. "I can't even picture how huge that is."

"You'll see it up close and personal soon enough," says Robin.

Mainly to irritate her, Trish and I embark on a lively discussion of the nearby Natchez Trace Parkway, a time-honored Native American trail and trading route from Natchez to Nashville.

Even jaded seen-it-alls are apt to pull out their cameras in Whitten Lock. It's the largest drop on the route south, providing before-and-after shots with impact.

It's all downhill from here, literally a 414-foot descent in increments to sea level.

Since it takes considerably more time to drop in the Whitten, in addition to singing our favorite, "Roll Out the Ballards," we're able to add a new tune to our repertoire, "I'm Going Down," complete with air guitars.

"Maybe we've got something going here," I joke in my radio-announcer voice: "Hits To Lock With, now available on K-Tel records. But wait … order now and receive 'Sweatin' In the Locks,' free, just pay separate shipping and handling…"

Creating our compilation of lock songs carries us cheerfully through the five miles to Montgomery Lock, where we drop down another 40 feet or so without incident. Then it's 8.3 miles to the Montgomery Lock. The upper Tenn-Tom locks used to be alphabetically named and were later rechristened in honor of notable regional leaders. Some lockmasters still prefer the plain old letters and are slow to answer if you use the honorary name.

"I can see why we have to call all of them on different radio channels," says Trish, working the dial and cueing the microphone. "They're all so close together, it'd be jibber-jab on the same station. Rankin Lockmaster, Rankin Lockmaster, this is pleasure craft *Blackdog* ...”

I pat her arm, reassuring that she's doing a fine job. Robin insists that we all take turns “yacking,” as she refers to it, on the radio. That way in an emergency any one of us would know how to operate and communicate using the equipment.

Trish is still a bit shy and tends to take it personally when the boater, tow or lockmaster she's calling doesn't immediately react. “Does the squelch button shut people up?” she wanted to know.

This lockmaster answers promptly, although his comeback is drowned out by the sudden blasting scream of a jet overhead. Aircraft from nearby Columbus Air Force Base strafe the sky often, always without warning, always ear-splitting. Some of the experimental flying machines are so bizarrely shaped it isn't accurate to refer to them as planes.

“This is getting old,” says Trish, as we steam out of the Rankin Lock. “Except I do like the part where the gates open and you enter a new world. It's like that Disney mermaid, Ah Ah Ah,” she trills.

“OK Ariel, get up on the bow, would you? These are fixed docks.” Robin's cutting *Blackdog* in for the approach to our next stop.

“I remember,” I say. “Yay! A break from floating docks.” It will be nice to tie to something stable that doesn't undulate underfoot like a Funhouse walkway.

Next to the long wooden dock there is a haunting, starkly beautiful tree stand of tall bald cypress bleached gray with age, riddled with woodpecker holes. I'd forgotten about that, too, and was glad to see it again.

On the dock there's another forgotten sight, none other than the bombastic Midway Marina dockmaster, who looks exactly like Billy Bob Thornton in tight jeans and white t-shirt. I scan the waterfront. No sign of Derek. Billy Bob's face is unreadable. *Relax Hailey. He's not coming. We would have heard him on the radio. Everybody has to check in on the radio.*

“Does he know Derek?” Trish wants to know.

“Yes, but that's not why you're gonna need to watch out for him,” I warn her. “He's a ladykiller. And he's very married. Don't flirt with him. Nadine — that's his wife-doesn't like it.”

“Gee, I'll see if I can manage to control myself,” Trish retorts, tossing her curls then tossing a line to Billy Bob.

“Well look what we have here,” he says, grinning. “It's my lucky day.”

Robin cuts the engine, steps out on deck. “I hate to cut this getting-to-know-you session short, but we need to get to a hardware store with a garden section or a nursery if there's one around here.”

"Sure," says Billy Bob. "Smithville Hardware's open for another hour. Keys are in the pick-up yonder. Need me to show you the way?"

"I think we'll be fine, thank you kindly," says Robin. "Hailey, will you stay here and walk Miss KC?"

"No problem."

KC meets Billy Bob's docile Doberman, Hooch, a young male with a constant erection and no idea what to do with it. As we're trying to convince Hooch that it's not a good idea for him to board the boat, Robin and Trish return from their mysterious errand. Before dark we have assembled a plastic-sheathed wooden framework, taking up most of the floor space on the rear deck, upon which Robin unfurls four rolls of sod.

As we sit sipping our beers in folding chairs placed around the border of the newly formed back yard, KC springs to the center of her own personal turf.

"Don't watch her," Rob instructs. "This could be the solution."

I close my eyes, a smart move considering the clod of grass and dirt that hits me between the brows. KC is fanatically burrowing through the fresh lawn, throwing grass divots willy-nilly into the air.

"What is she doing? Digging to China? KC, stop!" says Trish, laughing in spite of the mess. "You are one crazy mutt, that's for sure."

Panting, KC wags her tail.

"Back to the drawing board," says Robin.

"At least we got to pick some cotton," says Trish, holding up a plastic baggie full of fluffy balls fresh from the fields. "A first for me. Had to grab a souvenir."

The following morning we're off to an early start on the next round of what our guide Fred refers to as "The Not So Dirty Dozen." Technically the last two locks, on the Tombigbee River at Demopolis and at Coffeeville in LA (as Lower Alabama is known) are not an official part of the Tenn-Tom Waterway. But most travelers refer to it all as the Tenn-Tom anyway.

It is 14.7 miles to Fulton Lock. I wave at the Smithville Marina docks as *Blackdog* passes by. When Derek and I stayed here during the course of our first Loop we ate at a steakhouse named "Pete's" and picked our first cotton in the fields bordering the humble, hospitable marina. "Too bad it's too early to stop," I remark to Robin.

"Yeah, this is a cool spot. Ever been here for the Yam Festival?" Robin says.

"No. Do you know Log Cabin Debbie? She's an insurance agent who lives on her boat with two cats."

"Sure do," says Rob. "I still have the Woodmen of the World Life Insurance Society complimentary Presidential History ruler that she gave me. Very handy."

My worry level drops with each lock. It's not a lot of mileage for him to cover, but transiting these barriers takes more time than he has in one day. Each time I imagine him coming by land I delete the thought. Although if he docked the boat, then rented a car he could get ahead of us.

Delete.

After Fulton Lock it's 14.7 miles to Wilkins Lock and then 5.2 miles to Amory Lock. The monotony disappears as commercial forestry traffic increases, massive tree-chewing chip grinders eating pulpwood on the banks. The channel widens and the swampland retreats.

As we near the poetically named Aberdeen (actually it got its name because someone didn't like the way the locals pronounced "Dundee"), Trish marvels at the profusion of water hyacinths. A solid green-and-purple raft covers our path from bank to bank. "It looks like a scene from *The African Queen*."

In later years biocides would be employed to stifle the exotic invaders. But on this trip together, as we had done on our separate Loops before, Robin and I constantly obsessed over checking the strainer in the engine room — at least once every half-hour-while continually straining our eyes to scout a clear path, scanning for logs waiting to bang us and the other stealthy booby traps floating two inches under the flower-and-bulb infested water. "Give me lily pads anytime over these suckers," Rob comments. "They don't grow so thick and the flowers are prettier."

Finally we turned sharply to starboard into a narrow, black, mud-banked channel leading to Blue Bluff. There's a snug, picturesque cove at the base of the slate-gray sheer rock bluff. Trish remarks that it doesn't look all that blue, and she's right. On the opposite bank is a green park with symmetrical walking trails and picnic shelters.

The route in from the main river, unreadable water the hue of dark chocolate, is a scary path for anything larger than a bass boat. Once you commit there's no room to turn around. Sapling shoots grow tall on the shallow mud flats, skinny red whippet limbs close enough to touch.

"Are you sure we're going the right way?" Trish asks, just before a crude hand-painted sign, an old wood dock plank mounted on a stake, announces "Blue Bluff," the wavery primitive arrow below the lettering pointing left. She's only slightly mollified but cheers up as the depth sounder registers more water under *Blackdog's* keel. We're the only boat anchored in the cove; other river travelers must have gone to Aberdeen, home to some of the South's most impressive and well-restored antebellum mansions. Not really Robin's style.

Since KC destroyed her grass pad and continues to ignore the artificial turf, we row her to shore for her nightly constitutional. Several beers and a pork roast later, we're tucked in for the night. Trishie's magic menopause pills seem to be having some effect. Maybe it's just the general lack of stress and brisk pace of travel in the fresh air but I'm sweating less and sleeping longer. The night feels protective, the water surrounding our castle like a moat. One anchor light looks like another. I can't be pinpointed in the dark.

Tomorrow, after Aberdeen Lock, we'll trek the 22.8 miles to Columbus Marina.

Columbus Marina can't help but be upbeat. It's owned by a former Dallas Cowboys cheerleader, Barb, and her husband, the equally affable and enthusiastic Chuck. After a spate of uncrowded travel, we're caught in a bottleneck. Too many other cruisers had the same idea as us. Boats are rafting up two and even three deep on the long transient docks. When we call as we head down the runway to the entrance, with me once again scanning for my not-so-loving husband or his emissaries, I can't shake the feeling that the authorities are coming to get me. Not the men in white coats that take you to the loony bin. The men in blue, with badges and handcuffs, that take you to prison. It's not rational. It's just there. I'm sweating again.

Chuck tells us to hold off for 10 minutes. He's on the verge of losing his jollies when Robin asks about a covered slip, but brightens considerably when she tells him how much fuel we need to take on. "Be with you in a hot minute. Looks like I need a bigger shoehorn to get all these boats in here," he says, tone so chipper that you smile back even though you can't see his face.

The busy air-base town of Columbus has a Wal-Mart and numerous other big-box outlets, so it's off to town we go. Seven of us impatiently wait under the marina office for the courtesy van to return. The office, like most permanent structures here, is on stilts; insurance of sorts against rising water. From the grumblings, we learn an inconsiderate boater has kept the courtesy van way over the time limit (you are allowed one hour, he took five). When the van finally does arrive, one of the aggravated husbands rips the inconsiderate boater a new asshole. Far from being impressed, his wife is mortified.

I hang back, congratulating myself on my stealth, until one of the guys yells, "Short legs in back."

I keep my dark glasses on as I hustle, without a word, into the rear of the courtesy van. We speed off to pick up the necessities of life, in Robin's case that being a Wal-Mart kiddy pool plus five bags of white play sand and some fine pea gravel.

The light-blue plastic pool decorated with dancing turtles just fits on *Blackdog's* back deck. Between that and the Astroturf pad on the front deck this boat is definitely not what one would term "Bristol."

"We look like the Clampetts," I tell Rob.

"Nuh-uh," she says, singing the theme to "Sanford & Son" as we dump the play-sand in the pool. "Doo doo doo do ..."

Maybe KC will at last be inspired to pee freely.

"For Heaven's Sake, Robin, this dog is not a cat. She does not need a litter box," says Trishie.

Robin laughs. She's feeling optimistic and better yet, hungry. "Let's go up to the office and check the phone book," she says. "There's got to be a pizza place that delivers."

Chapter 15: Slickers, Mud Puppies
and Bumps in the Night

The channel broadens again after the Stennis Lock, the lock immediately adjacent to Columbus Marina. The wide-open river is deeper but no less hazardous due to the rainfall that caused the water to rise, washing debris into our path. I marveled at *Blackdog's* windshield wipers, a true luxury to a sailor used to peering through fogged-up plastic Isinglass.

There was no way to stay dry in the locks; Trish and I stood out on deck in the incessant downpour. I wished that I'd appropriated the foulie suit in *Seawind's* locker. Could it have made things any worse? I wonder if they'll press charges. Maybe they noticed what good care I took of her. Maybe they've let the whole thing blow over. Yeah. Right.

Robin has a couple of slickers but they're too small for Trish, so she's reduced to wearing a black garbage bag fashioned into a poncho. Our gloves are soaked.

"Are we there yet?" She rolls her eyes as we stand in the rain at Bevill Lock near the Mississippi-Alabama border. Robin's found a pop music station on the FM radio. "Feel the rain on your skin? Seriously, Rob, turn that off!"

There are fewer hours of daylight, reducing our travel time. Marina options are nil.

"Cochrane Cut-off is a decent spot," I tell her. "I've stayed there once; there should be at least 10 feet of water. There's some current but the holding is solid."

"Fine," Rob grumbles. "I won't sleep tonight, anyway."

"You were OK in Blue Bluff."

"We were off the river. Didn't have to worry about tows there," she says.

"Relax," I suggest. "We can set the anchor alarm and take turns on watch if that will make you feel better."

"I'd feel better is if this dog here would take a pee," she says.

"One day isn't going to kill her," I say, hoping that's true. "Maybe she'll have a breakthrough when she realizes she's got nowhere else to go."

Two other yachts have already tucked in for the night but there's plenty of room. Robin steadily works her way through several beers. Chilled to the bone, Trish and I opt for hot tea and canned chicken noodle soup.

"It feels like I'll never be warm again," Trish says, alternating sips between her Earl Grey mug and soup cup. "I wish this miserable weather would ease up."

"I learned a long time ago that swearing at the wind or cursing the rain is pointless," I say. "We don't control the weather." NOAA Weather Radio is forecasting more rain the next day, with no let-up until the following morning. I choose two marker points ashore: a tree with a pink piece of plastic tape tied around it and a giant tree stump with knotholes shaped like a grinning face. "These are our demonstration logs," I tell Trish. "To make sure we haven't moved. As long as we're in line with them, we're fine."

The rain tapers as the wind picks up around 2 a.m., the beeping of the anchor alarm interrupting our slumber. A scan with the portable searchlight shows we've merely reversed position, facing north now rather than south. Robin has it set it to go off if the boat moves 50 feet.

As the rain recommences in earnest I shine the beam into the back of the anchorage where the other two boats are riding out the weather. The light hits a majestically gliding trawler that is now much closer than it should be.

"Hit the horn," I yell into the cabin. "A boat is dragging down on us!" Rain drips off the tip of my nose as I wonder whether it will be better to fend off or raft up the runaway vessel. I'm soaked to the skin; no time to worry about that.

We left the marine radio on as a precaution; Trish simultaneously hits the horn on the steering console while grabbing for the mike. "Where are we, again?" she asks, frantic.

"Cochrane Cut-off," Robin says. "Five blasts on the horn, Trish. Do it!"

"To the boats in Cochrane Cut-off, one of you is dragging, repeat, you are dragging!"

The errant trawler is 20 feet away and closing fast when its cabin lights come on and we hear the engine engage. I swing the searchlight toward its bow; no sense in blinding them. "Idiyachts," says Robin, as we survey the anchoring setup. Rope-a-dope indeed. Rope is for dinky ski boats. Real cruisers hang to chain. All chain. And stay put.

The lights are on in the other boat, apparently a buddy to the trawler. We can hear them shouting back and forth as the people on the drifting boat pull in the anchor and prepare to re-deploy it.

"Thanks for the wake-up call, *Blackdog*," a hepped-up feminine voice broadcasts over the radio. "This is *Where's Linda*. Sorry to cause a ruckus. We're going to raft to *Brave Turtle* for the rest of the night. They're dug in good, lying to all chain."

"Roger that," says Trish. "That was a close one."

"This is why I don't like to anchor," Robin says. "Fuck me. Might as well put the coffee on."

"No rest for the wicked," I tease, toweling off. There are wet clothes hanging all over the salon. "We could sure use a dryer on this boat."

"Oh can it," she says, laughing in spite of herself. "And with 70 miles to go, there's no way we'll make it to Demopolis tomorrow. So I guess I'll just have to put up with anchoring."

"Aye, Cap'n," I say. "You might even get to like it."

"That," she says, "is highly unlikely."

There's nothing particularly beautiful or especially safe about Rattlesnake Bend, our anchorage the following evening, but we're running out of daylight and there isn't anywhere else to stop. Working tows motor through the narrow channel day and night. With little-to-no wiggle room, Rob nudges *Blackdog* as close to shore as possible. Working in the rain, we drop the dinghy into the water so we can row a line over and tie it to a tree, a classic mooring method that will hold the stern of the boat against the bank and prevent our vessel from swinging into the middle of the channel. Robin insists on taking KC ashore.

"Here's a word for you, Robin: Rattlesnake," says Trish.

"Here's another word: Mud," I add.

"She can't go two days without going," she announces in her sternest don't-argue voice.

"Then let me walk her," I say.

"Nope. It'll be quicker if you row us over and attach the stern line while I deal with Miss KC," she says, slipping the dog into the canine life jacket. KC whines.

"Yes, I know you don't want to get wet. But you gotta go, girl," she tells her, snapping on the leash.

"At least we'll get into Demopolis early in the day tomorrow." I unlock the oars.

We're ashore in short order, facing an impenetrable thicket of bracken tangles, shaded by maple, pine and oak. A sturdy willow leans over the water as if preparing to dive in. Robin points out a marginal landing spot underneath it. "Looks sandy," she says. "It'll have to do."

While I make the line fast to the largest willow branch I can reach, she carefully climbs out of the dinghy and is immediately ankle-deep in tan mud. KC jumps over the side of the dory, scrambling for the underbrush. Robin has a firm grip on the leash; her feet slide out from under her and she lands on her stomach in the mud that looked like sand.

She grunts, struggling to sit up while maintaining her hold on the leash. "KC, stay!"

Belly plastered with goo, KC obeys, and then blessedly somehow does her business.

We finally get them back in the dinghy, which is now smeared with sticky tan river mud inside and out.

"I guess we'll have to wait until Demopolis to clean up this mess," Robin says, exhausted. "Let's just tie the dinghy off. We can drag it. I don't want to put it back on deck like this."

Trish thrusts towels and rags at us as we climb aboard, neatly intercepting KC's mad dash to get indoors. "Not yet, you mud puppy," she says, tsk tsking as she towels away the worst of the muck. She has a bucket of river water ready for Robin's caked shoes. "Dawn is my middle name," says Robin, idly, squirting detergent in. She looks at us. "It really is."

"Well, Miss Robin Dawn, wait 'til the Laundry Mat Bitches at Demopolis get a load of this!" says Trish. "Mine's Lynn. Patricia Lynn."

"Marie." I say, and we all nod as if formal introductions have been made.

The power of the sun bright in the morning sky cheers everyone up as *Blackdog* completes the few remaining miles to Demopolis. We completed the 121 miles to Demopolis in three days of pouring rain and temperatures that never got much above the 50s, but the memories of our travails in that oppressive gloom are now fodder for jokes that bond us. As I grow old, the possibility and the desire for new friends fades. Can't have. Don't need. Yet here they are, two new friends that I will cherish forevermore no matter what happens in the future. It feels as if we've always been together and always will be. In their eyes I am capable. Their faith in my ability to run the rivers with them, taking on whatever tasks are required, has birthed a new confidence. They see me strong. Knowing. Worthy. Confident. As I am.

More magical thinking, I warn myself. But my open heart does not pay heed. To breathe easily, smile openly, to give and receive without fear — this is the happiness I've denied myself. It is impossible to resist basking in the light just a little bit longer.

Sure. He's coming. It's my job to be gone before he arrives.

Chapter 16: The Metropolis of Demopolis

Fast Eddy, Bobby Joe James or *Honest John*, pick your towboat crew, they're all in love with Trish.

"Clearly you've never met a John you didn't like," I tell her as she flutters her eyelashes and pops out what *America's Next Top Model* host, Tyra Banks, calls a "booty tooch" in direct view of the towboat crews. "Buns on parade, you go girl" I tease, "Betty Grable's got nothing on you. Next thing you know they'll have your picture up in the crew's quarters or painted on the bowsprit like they used to do on the nose of a plane."

"Oh shush," she hisses sweetly, not bothering to look at me because she's alternately watching the numbers on the fuel pump and exchanging goo-goo eyes with the guys unloading trash and re-loading provisions a few steps away on the other side of the wide-planked floating fuel dock. Here on the Demopolis gas dock, pleasure craft fuel to the right and commercial towboats to the left. It's no Fleet Week, but there are enough nice-looking men on *Fast Eddie, Bobby Joe James* and *Honest John* — vessels named for famous towboat captains — to make a girl take notice. They're all younger than us but who cares? Ah, those delicious 30s, when men are finally coming into their own and gaining brains while they still have brawn.

"Three hundred!" Trish yells to Robin, as the pump clicks on. We need to be full up for the next leg; between Demopolis and Mobile there's one lonely outpost where fuel is available.

"Where's our slip?" Robin says.

"Trinella put us off the end of the first dock, rafted to that sport fisher nobody's on. Fred's gonna meet us over there."

"Do you need me?"

"Only in the Biblical sense," says Robin, deepening her voice to the lowest tone. "They think I'm your husband."

Robin, Trish and Fred's marina crew can take care of getting *Blackdog* into her slip. I focus on getting the namesake of this crazy boat to poop in relative privacy. I'm the DD: Designated Dogwalker. I enjoy it. I've even considered turning it into a profession. I picture my business card in an easy-to-read Arial font, perhaps with a leash for a border. I picture and dismiss my maiden name. I don't want to be different from the kids.

Hailey Sanderson
Information Specialist
Dog Walking by Appointment

What color is my parachute, anyway? This is something I should have figured out long before fleeing my crappy marriage. Every day, between the fear that tightens my jaw and cramps my intestines, there are stupefying moments of winning-lottery-ticket magical thinking. The capering thoughts inform me that divine timing is in my favor. They tell me revelation will burst through at the most opportune moment and plop me in the right spot at the right time, somewhere where I can be as free and happy as KC as she joyfully galumphs down the dock, yanking me up the railed steel ramp to the solid ground she's been waiting for. A rip-rapped triangle of green turf jutting into the river, sodgrass newly laid in the brand-new RV park, demands her immediate attention, i.e.: copious urination. This is embarrassing and inappropriate, but the dog is so completely ecstatic that I cannot chastise her.

KC jerks me hither and yon, nose to the ground. I stuff the plastic bags more securely into my shorts pocket, glad to have more than one receptacle. I guide her past the Riverfront Motel. It's built on stilts with parking spaces underneath. Several signs are posted warning: "No dogs under building."

"KC, can't you read the signs, little girl? You can't go there."

We make our way to the grassy knoll overlooking the yacht basin. Ornamental kale, chrysanthemums and marigolds are blooming in a raised planter made of railroad ties. Herons crank, ducks quack, turtles stacked six deep sunbathe atop deadwood rafts. The pace of life in this tiny Alabama town slows everything down, relaxing dog and walker.

"If it's Thursday, it's dressing day," I tell Robin the following morning. "At Vowell's. There's a Champs Chicken counter. Butter beans, cornbread, okra, mac & cheese, fried chicken, ribs, you name it. On Thursday there's turkey and dressing with gravy."

"That's where we're having lunch and shopping," she says. The courtesy car is Trinella's 1996 cream-colored Buick Regal with the super saver discount card dangling from the keychain.

We dance up and down the aisles in the grocery store, grooving to the piped-in R&B Muzak, although Robin draws the line at holding hands. "I hate that touchy-feely stuff," she says. Every so often her upper-class breeding shows its snotty side; she's as aloof and out-of-place as the Vine & Olive French nobility that was dumped in Demop in 1817. The patrician exiles, arriving after Napoleon's Waterloo, were granted land by the U.S. government with the stipulation that they would plant olive trees and vineyards. It was a foolish venture. The upper-crust settlers were ill-suited to the task and so is the hardpan gray soil that turns to clay in rain and dries to dusty concrete in dry weather.

Modern-day settlers occupy the houseboats permanently docked in Demopolis Yacht Basin. Ranging from 53 to 80 feet in length and 14 to 16 feet wide, the floating homes feature everything from motorcycle garages to rooftop gardens. The houseboat we partied with at the Kaskaskia Lock on the Mississippi is docked here; it must have passed us up while we tarried at Green Turtle Bay. No one's aboard at the moment. There's a talkative couple living on the houseboat next to *Slo-Poke*. Their vessel is a long, glossy black beauty, its port and starboard walls emblazoned with large renderings of the classic Coppertone Girl, complete with the tugging dog revealing her tush-level tan line.

"Ain't she something?" the wizened riverboat dweller who introduces himself as "Mudbug" asks, obviously very proud of his vessel. "Those are hand-painted by the artist who did the original Coppertone billboards." He hasn't gone anywhere in decades, but Seth Wannamaker's art sure gets around.

"Maudie," he knocks on the patio-style sliding door peering inside. "Come on out, sweetheart, we've got company."

"Wow," says Trish, eyeing the homeport lettering. "Did y'all come up from Mobile?" Robin rolls her eyes. The farther south we go, the more Trish drawls and y'alls.

"I can't help it," she insists. "I'm a sponge when it comes to dialects."

"Young lady, the last time we went out on Mobile Bay was 30 years ago. We had us a time, didn't we, Maudie?" Mudbug says. "A line of squalls come out of nowhere, lightning, thunder. And those waves on Mobile Bay build up steep right quick. Shallow bays are the nastiest. This here 20,000-pound boat would rise up, then 'Slam! Slam!' she'd pound back down, hittin' the bottom of the bay. I want to tell you, I thought it would break this boat to pieces."

"I thought it would break me to pieces," Maudie chimes in, a bright floral chiffon scarf atop her curlers, eyes sharp and lively behind rhinestone-framed cats-eye glasses, a skinny, wrinkled sprite as full of vim and high spirits as her husband.

"Sixty years we've been together, and I always let him have his head 'cause he never steered us wrong."

"Until that day," he says, shaking his head. "Now I can't tell her anything."

"That's our arrangement," Maudie agrees, cackling. "You had your 30 years, Sugar, and now I got mine, ever since I told him to turn the dang boat around and skedaddle on back up the rivers. That itty-bitty sample of saltwater cruising was plenty for me."

There's a "Help Wanted" sign up in the grocery store window. I try to picture living here on a quiet side street, close enough to pedal a bike with a wicker basket and a shiny red horn to work. Or maybe I could rent one of the perennially for-sale houseboats in the marina. "I wonder if Wal-Mart is hiring."

"What's that got to do with the price of tea in China?" Trish asks, as we wait in line for our dressing and chicken.

"You're thinking about staying here?" Robin raises her eyebrows, frowns. "It gets cold here in the winter, Hailey, you know that. And the economy is dreadful, unless you're into cotton or catfish."

"At least it doesn't snow," I say. "And the Christmas on the Water parade is supposed to be really beautiful. The cost of living is affordable. I dunno, ladies, I'm just thinking that I need to figure out what I'm doing. It's not as if we can keep going on like this forever."

"Why not?" says Robin.

Chapter 17: Bobby's Fish Camp

The rock is hard but the river is patient, sculpting smooth the ivoried moss-veined walls above and below Demopolis Lock. The dam boils fiercely, mist rising from the roiling rapids of the man-made waterfalls.

"I feel like we're in a giant bathtub," says Trish.

Several miles past the lock the limestone basin softens to golden sand, carved into high mesas, banked into broad, flat beaches, lapped by the Tombigbee.

I dread the next stop: Bobby's Fish Camp. There isn't anywhere else to buy fuel before Mobile Bay, so I'm resigned to stacking up on the floating aluminum dock with a flock of fellow snowbirds and Great Circle Loopers, the latter to me now seen as naïve and knock-kneed as a gaggle of preteens attending their first boy-girl dance. Their self-important, excited chatter has been a plague on the radio all day, clogging Channels 16 and 68. "Turn that shit off," Robin said, but she knows we can't, there are too many blind corners. We need to hear the tows. I need to know if anyone is waiting for me at Bobby's. Derek would never announce his presence. But any little nuance, from who's on the docks already to who's headed in is a clue.

I anticipate Derek around every bend. The one-upon-another hairpin curves finally break into a straight stretch of leaf-dappled river.

"There's Bobby's. Whoop Dee Doo," I remark, deadpan.

"When did we get so jaded?" Rob crinkles her nose, squinting as she spots the filled dock in the distance.

"What's wrong with you two?" Trish runs around the deck whipping pre-tied bumpers over the side. It doesn't sound like any boaters I know from previous visits are around, but I rigged everything so I can duck below if need be. "We have to raft up, big deal. There are people — and a restaurant. Civilization!"

"Sort of," I caution. "Did you ever see the movie *Deliverance*?"

"No. Why?"

Robin chuckles. "Daduh dun dun dun dun dun dun dunnn …"

Silver Airstream trailers, Confederate flags flying, line the dirt banks facing the dock. A few full-size vintage Frigidaires are sitting outside the campers, power cords running to the common outlet on a telephone pole. It's late in the afternoon and very obviously Happy Hour has been going on for hours, with nearly all the aluminum green-and-white webbed lawn chairs occupied.

A motley assortment of lop-eared hunting hounds, beagles and pit bull-hybrids bark and bay at the busy docks, skulking amidst the aluminum trailers, ramshackle wood cabins, aging modular homes and the occasional Quonset hut. Several larger cottages are perched on the hill where the riverbank grades steeply up, mountain-like, following the curve of a hardpan gravel road. Every flat-topped roof is liberally salted with rusty beer and soda pop cans. Spanish moss drapes the oaks, hairy gray lace swinging in the strong breeze. Here and there small potted palmettos and the last of the season's marigolds cheerily nod from well-tended, pine-needle mulched flowerbeds.

"Charming, isn't it?" I say. "If you think this is a party, you should be here for Jefferson Davis Day."

Trish ignores me, clearly enthralled. KC wags her tail.

"Don't forget to leash Kace right away," I tell Trish. "Those hounds will eat her for supper."

I roll my shoulders, take a deep breath and whistle "Dixie." No sign of Derek or anyone else I recognize. Bobby and Betty June are sure to be around. But they won't remember little old me. On that I can rely. They've seen hundreds of boaters every year for decades.

About halfway up the hill in the low, white cement block restaurant with green shutters Bobby and his daughter Betty June serve the quintessential all-you-can-eat deep-fried catfish dinner complete with hush puppies and fresh coleslaw.

"I can't eat here," Robin says, claiming the 20-foot alligator gar mounted in the dining room ruins her appetite. Bobby himself caught the 137-pound beastie below the Coffeeville Lock. I agree it's the ugliest fish I've ever seen with its snakelike snout, plate-armor head, full mouth of narrow, pointed teeth and bulging tar-black torso. It's even uglier than the fat-tongued big-lipped invasive gobies of the Great Lakes or the tumorous 200-pound trout some fishermen pulled off the bottom of Lake Superior near Isle Royale when it should have been left to its moveless peace 200 feet down. A few years earlier, Derek and I had watched the hapless anglers on the docks at Chippewa

Harbor as they tried to catch-and-release. The ancient fish was too old to survive handling.

Trish wonders if the gar is still in the dining room.

She doesn't know. The only thing that changes on the Tombigbee River is the shoreline contour.

"Of course it's still there," says Robin. "Too frickin' gross for words. Get me a burger to go. Well done. Please."

"As if we need to be reminded you like your meat burned," I say, heading amidships.

"Elvis preferred his meat well done," Robin points out.

"Yeah and look what happened to him," says Trish, already at the stern, lines ready. Under our tutelage she's gained an easy competence handling basic boat skills. Teaching her what I know is deeply satisfying, this vast store of unacknowledged knowledge finding a willing outlet—with immediate, effective results. As Robin says, we know our shit, and anyone who underestimates our skills is quickly outmaneuvered.

She pilots past the 160-foot floating dock eyeing up the six yachts already tied to it, then pivots *Blackdog*, steering into the current, slowing as we pull into the middle. She aligns the boat with the notch alongside a 47-foot Chris Craft Cabin Cruiser, *Water Witch*. It's a roughly 50-foot inset, which doesn't leave room for error. The Chris-Craft is flying an America's Great Circle Loop flag with a white background, meaning the cruisers aboard haven't completed the circuit yet. Flags with a gold background are awarded to those who have finished the Loop. The wife, girlfriend or whatever she is hoists her glass of red wine so enthusiastically it splashes. She's wearing a golf visor atop short, curly gray hair. Hubby, boyfriend or whoever he is, stocky, full head of thick white hair, eyes hidden behind mirrored aviator sunglasses, stations himself at the outside rail, his easy smile indicating he's ready and willing to take a line.

Rafting is a House Rule at Bobby's. When there's no dock space left, incoming boaters tie to other boats, rafting out as far as need be. It's a relief to encounter amiable cruisers. Some boaters just don't get that they can't have the place to themselves; pointless grousing begins as soon as they see another boat heading for "their" dock. Bobby is famous for his mandate that no boat is ever turned away. He'll stack in as many as need be to get boaters off the river for the night.

There are only a few spots where anchoring is possible in this sector of Tenn-Tom waterway. Fern's river lessons still apply: only a fool would travel after dark. There are too many dangers, from submerged logs to tow-barge configurations as wide as the channel. Commercial traffic keeps moving 24/7 down here unless there's fog. But I've never heard of pleasure vessels being allowed to lock through at night.

"We're gonna raft to you if that's OK," Trish shouts to the Loopers. Our intention is clear but a courtesy notification is custom.

"Sure. As long as I can get out. We're locking through early tomorrow morning," the man says.

"Same here," I say. The more I see the better I feel. No one I know in the vicinity and we're on the outside, where it would be easy to escape. "We're all headed to the same place."

"We're gonna fuel in the morning if we fuel at all," Robin says. "We should have enough to make it to Mobile. Looks like the pump is gonna be tied up for a while."

"So the only reason we're stopping is to let KC pee. Great."

"We can fill the jerry cans if that'll make you feel better," says Robin. "And I *would* top off if this wasn't such a shit show." She gestures in front of us, at the single diesel/gas pump. That's why she picked the middle slot. Boats ranging from 40 to 60 feet in length are performing a perpetual switcheroo, pulling up to fuel and then rotating back into their assigned slots. The current runs hard here. Some of the boaters aren't used to steering to accommodate the push and pull, depending on whether you're with the flow or against it. There's more than one near-miss as they struggle to control their boats, a fair amount of cursing, and a lot of flailing rope tosses as those safely secured catch lines and pull vessels to safety. At least there's no need to fret over plugging and unplugging power cords. There's no shore power. There are also no showers. There won't even be a flush toilet available once the restaurant closes.

The last time Derek and I stopped at Bobby's — *Chinook* continuously undulating in the wake of local fishing skiffs, tow-barges and power yachts with the speed and fuel reserves to bypass the camp — I'd asked if there was anywhere to throw out the garbage. It was a fair enough question considering the $1.50 per foot we were charged to stay the night. For 50 bucks there ought to be a dumpster, right?

"Put it over there, honey," gestured one of Mr. Bobby's waitresses (the great man himself was not on the premises during this occasion). She pointed at a ditch behind the restaurant, where a passel of hounds was eagerly ripping plastic bags to get at the good stuff. Later that night we heard a piercing yip — apparently the gators were as attracted to the improvised dump as the camp dogs.

"The big one got Cody. Lucky them other dogs were smart enough to run," one of the teen-aged boys fishing on the dock next morning informed me.

Kerflumoxed, I reverted to a neutral non-sequitur. "What are you fishing for? Catfish?"

"Naw. Eels. They're real good eatin'."

"Say what?" Derek never had the ear or the patience for southern dialect.

"Eels," I interpreted. "He says they're delicious."

We couldn't get out of there fast enough. We laughed later, when I suggested reeling in some eels for breakfast. Yum. Eel omelets? Eel hash browns? My sister has eaten saltwater eel in sushi restaurants, but then Layla will eat almost anything. As a child she tried toadstools multiple times. She didn't mind having her stomach pumped after her experiments.

I miss Layla, even though we haven't been close the past 10 years. She pities me. I resent her for not rescuing me, even though I've never asked outright. I think she looks down on me, subconsciously or otherwise, for staying in a bad marriage and never doing much of anything with my life. I tell myself envy is a petty emotion. It's more like shame, anyway. Shame and blame for simply going wherever outside forces carried me, as thoughtless and meaningless as the rafts of leaves and water weeds transported by the current.

Still, I miss my family. The awful-awesome of being with the people you know best and who know you best, no matter how they treat you, can be a comfort. We don't check in with each other more than once every couple of months, so I know that right now they're not at all worried about me. More than normal.

Events that would bring other families to a celebratory or grief-stricken standstill are blips on Layla's screen. On one typical call her news, delivered in low-key, businesslike fashion, was that she had earned her doctoral degree. "That was fast," I thought but did not say aloud. She'd probably mentioned she was going for it in passing, years earlier. The content of our phone calls is always minimized to bullet points that efficiently cover the relevant territory where our family geography overlaps. Her big concern is guaranteeing that her teen-aged children, my niece and nephew, turn out the way she thinks they ought to. Not like mine. Or me. Boy, is she in for a surprise!

Derek hates my family. He isn't likely to call them to report that I'm missing. He'd have to explain why. He's a non-voting Republican. They're Union Democrats. He pees with the door closed; they pee with the door open. They hug. He hits. If my family has to choose between him and me, they would choose me. He's always known that.

I remember the way that we laughed at this crazy redneck river camp. "Oh Derek. We'll always have the eels," I say aloud, then snort at my own maudlin, perverse humor.

It's routine for nine or more yachts to nuzzle up to Bobby's during November migration. That's three-to-four boats deep and not for snobby anal retentive types who don't care for complete strangers clomping across their decks to get to shore. It's been muddy out and several boats are carrying red wine drinkers who add crimson splotches to the bits of dirt, clay, gravel and fallen autumn leaves tracked across the decks as hosts and hosted refill drinks and snack platters.

Robin laughs openly at the Clark Griswold lookalike on a magnificent 57-foot Nordhavn named *Avalon* as he vigorously swabs his deck with a mop after each of his neighbors step on and off his boat. There are drawbacks-besides the inability to escape-to berthing directly on the dock. Privacy cravers and neat freaks are better off in the outside position. The more sociable types enjoy the proximity to other ebullient boaters, trading cocktails and tall boating tales that grow in drama in direct proportion to the piles of empty cans and bottles before everyone walks up the gradually inclining, curving, tree-lined gravel-clay path to the restaurant for catfish.

Lack of privacy has advantages. I can see the wide-screen TV in the 53-foot Hatteras *Kendra* ahead of us well enough to read the news crawl on the bottom of the screen. I haven't looked at a newspaper or television broadcast since Hammond. Most boaters, if they watch anything on TV, are into boating movies or documentaries.

The crawl says nothing about a middle-aged female boat thief breaking probation. CNN hasn't latched on to my downriver run to perdition. What a relief.

On our first visit here Derek dealt with a blown fuse in a 60-foot Trumpy, the stand-offish neo-Cons aboard more than paying for our night's stay. Funny how snotty yachties turn right friendly when they realize that the middle-class jack-of-all-trades sharing the dock in a less-fancy vessel is their only hope to get the boat moving.

Strange things between strangers always happen at Bobby's.

"Don't let that dog close to the ponds. The 'gators got a dog last night."

"Gee, that's what I heard last time I was here," I tell the skinny, long-haired young man watching us with his duck gun in hand as Trish carefully leads KC over the two boat decks between us and the dock. *Water Witch* is rafted to a 48-foot Kadey-Krogen with the amusing name *Can't Anchor Us*. KC is a very calm negotiator of various obstacles, and since we know that she really, really has to go, her restraint is inspiring.

"You all have alligators around these parts?" Trish looks like she's ready to bolt back to the boat, hauling KC with her.

KC clearly doesn't care about hazards ashore. She's got number one and number two in her immediate future, predators be damned.

"Yes ma'am," he affirms. "Just keep her on a leash and away from the pond and you'll be OK."

Traveling incognito fed my paranoia; now the lack of recognition deflates my ego. So far John at Green Turtle Bay is the only face encountered to whom mine is familiar. "I can't believe nobody recognizes me," I remark to Rob as she comes up from below with another beer, a box of Cheezits and a bowl of Clementine oranges. Scanning the transoms of the boats at dock I don't recognize any names. In addition to *Water Witch, Can't Anchor Us, Avalon* and *Kendra,* five other boats have stacked in for the night.

The 35-foot Island Packet sailing catamaran *Menou* is snugged into the T at the end of the dock nearest the boat launch, the Cajun couple Dick and Dixie ensconced in folding chairs to meet and greet newcomers.

"Oh come on, Gil, give it up," the *Avalon* wife cackles, turning from her lively, laughter-punctuated conversation with Dick and Dixie. "We'll scrub everything after we're through with these dirty rivers."

"When you get done with your decks, c'mon over here bebe," Dixie called in a melodious patois. "There's plenty of dirt to swab darlin', but don't you touch my attack dust bunnies down below!"

The sturdy, dignified 40-foot Nordic Tug, *The Newfie Bullet,* is parked in front of *Can't Anchor Us.* Dee, the take-charge Admiral aboard, lets us know that we're all going up to dinner at the restaurant in an hour or so. On the dock, behind *Water Witch,* an elderly white-haired couple in a 37-foot Pacific Seacraft named *Wind Dancer* speaks quietly to each other as they make adjustments to more firmly secure their mast, which protrudes well off the end of the canoe-shaped stern. A younger couple on *Rough Draft,* the 39-foot Corbin cutter-rigged sailboat tied to them, offered advice and commiseration.

"I can't wait to step our mast," the vivacious, voluptuous brunette announces while her well-toned, athletic male mate nods vigorously. "It feels like our boat isn't whole with the mast down, you know? You know. When we can put the sails up again I'll be so happy."

Meanwhile the English couple on the 31-foot Camano Troll *Spirit of Whitby,* tied behind us to *Rough Draft,* is politely inquiring of all and sundry where to plug into electrical power. Temperatures are routinely dropping into the 40s at night and they are crestfallen when informed there is no shore power to be had. They have the effrontery to ask if they can plug into the sailboat's DC power. Of course not.

As I observe the interplay, I long to jump in, handing out boat cards and sharing my stories. I feel left out.

"Poor Hailey, does it hurt your pride that nobody knows you without your man? I guess you aren't that memorable," Robin teases. "Or maybe it's the clothes." I glance down at my nondescript plain white t-shirt and boot-cut button-fly jeans. There's a muddy orange leaf stuck to the side of my scuffed white high-top Reeboks and a tomato sauce stain on the left side of my shirt just below one breast. The sun is leaving us; I unknot the sleeves of Joey's faded Nike hoodie from around my waist and pull it over my head.

The evenings are getting cooler; we left the bikini weather up on the Tennessee, although the autumn color has followed us downriver. Amidst the tall red pines and towering oaks emerge patches of crimson, orange and walnut-brown foliage. The ground around the boat launch is littered with yellow leaves, gold the first to go as the season progresses. With a mountainous hill looming over us, it's easy to imagine that we are somewhere farther northeast in hillbilly country, the Smokies, say, or the Appalachians.

"Really, I wish that we could just keep going. I've never liked it here. You two go on ahead to the restaurant. I'll just hang out on the boat," Robin says.

"Come on, I need my husband's moral support to sit there and eat catfish with that butt-ugly alligator gar staring at me. Put down that beer and come on up to the restaurant. There's beer up there, too." I say. Trish has gone ahead with the group, promising to save us seats.

It's pointless to argue. "OK, I'll bring you that burger plain, well done," I say, sighing theatrically.

"Do you need money?"

"No. Thanks. You're doing enough. I can foot this bill."

"You take this." She hands me two twenties. And her credit card for the dockage. "You'll need everything you have once we get to where we're getting to, wherever that is. How much is it again?"

"One thousand five hundred and seventy-two, give or take the $72," I say.

"Well I'm just glad you didn't decide to take that Wal-Mart greeter job in Demopolis."

"Too cold. Rob?"

"What?"

"Thanks."

"You're welcome. Now scoot. I'm gonna take a nap."

As I step over our deck and onto the adjoining boat, I notice a new arrival parked behind us off the end of the dock. Or maybe this weird sailboat was already here and I'd missed it in the crowd. Once I've climbed over various obstacles on *Water Witch* and *Can't Anchor Us*, I walk down to the upriver end of the dock for a better look. The roughly 27-footer's decks and hull are carelessly sponge-painted lavender. The boat isn't tied to the dock, it's anchored off in the reeds and cattails bordering the drainage ditch that feeds the boggy 'gator pond. It's tethered to a floating laundry-soap bottle trip line, a trick river travelers use to retrieve their underground tackle if it becomes tangled in bottom debris. The gender-neutral assortment of medium-sized shirts and pants hanging from the rigging and lifelines doesn't offer further clues about the sailor aboard. A poetically curved old wooden rowing dory painted a deeper shade of purple is marked T/T (tender to) *Schizo*, home port New Orleans.

A creature of indeterminate age and sex in a voluminous brown turtleneck sweater and plaid polyester trousers wearing ripped black low-top canvas sneakers emerges from belowdecks, gesturing insistently. Its face — framed by short, black, wooly, frizzed hair with bits of line on the ends, like dreadlocks in training, framed by the fading sun — was slightly off in some way. Off in a way impossible to immediately define but instantly felt.

"Hi!"

"Hello," I said, noting the pilling sweater and stained pants. "When did you get in?"

"I just got here. I come here every night. Can I raft to your boat? Bobby lets me raft when every other boat is in for the night." The voice is a scratchy, whiny croak. I'm struggling with gender identification. The Pat character from *Saturday Night Live* comes to mind.

"No. I can't give permission; it's not my boat. I'd have to ask the captain, he's up at the restaurant. Everyone is. You could come up there and ask," I offer, hoping Robin, six boats away, will hear us and come outside.

The androgynous creature has already started the sailboat engine, a sputtering, puttering Atomic 4 from the sound of it. Black oily smoke belches out of *Schizo's* stern. In short order, the homemade anchor is hauled, a 30-pound spiked chunk of metal swinging wildly from the bow like a medieval battleax. In a matter of seconds, *Schizo* has wheeled out around the dock into the river, its bow pointed straight at *Blackdog's* starboard side. All of the boats are tied to face the current with their right quadrants exposed to the river, the bows (the pointy end is the strongest spot on any vessel) taking the brunt of Tombigbee current making its own run downstream to the Coffeeville Lock, less than two miles distant.

Blackdog is about to take the brunt of *Schizo*. The lunatic captain's current path and speed will slam the sailboat squarely into the couch where Rob sleeps.

"Robin! Prepare to ram!" I'm shrieking as loud as I ever have and I keep yelling as I climb back over the boat closest to the dock, banging my hip against the edge of the cabin bulkhead and knocking over a glass of red wine onto the holly-wood sole of the cockpit floor. Stubbing my left big toe on the rope-wrapped eight-inch metal cleats binding *Blackdog* to *Water Witch*, I swear and stumble down the side deck onto our back porch.

"Robin! Prepare for impact! Robin!" The bright pain of a self-inflicted injury screams in my toe and my brain.

"Sheeut! Hailey? What is it?" She emerges from the salon just in time to see the little sailboat heading directly toward us. "Heyyy — slow down," she yells. "Do you wanna kill somebody?"

"It wants to raft to us," I say. "Fend off."

"It?"

"I can't tell the gender," I say. "But I know crazy when I see it."

"Stop," orders Robin in her deepest, lowest voice, projecting louder than I've ever heard her. We're both so loud it's a wonder no one has emerged from the Airstreams or nearby cottages. I can see lights on in some of them. "Do not come any closer." *Schizo* is about four feet away, its unsecured anchor swaying like a lunatic metronome.

"Mister Bobby says I can raft up," the creature whined.

"Mister Bobby didn't tell me that," says Robin, calm but stern, like an elementary school principal quieting a child on the verge of a tantrum. "You'll have to go and get Mister Bobby if you want to tie up somewhere. You are not tying up to this boat."

As if to itself, the creature begins to mumble in its own jargon, laced with a few recognizable profanities. "Kill the assholes, kill the fuckin' assholes," it mutters, cackling mad whispers. *Schizo* backs away six feet, proceeding to run up and down the exterior line of boats at the dock, back and forth, circling. Rob grabs a boathook.

"Oh, man," says Robin. "Hailey, run up to the restaurant and find Bobby or Betty June or somebody while I fend off this nutbar."

A bandy-legged white pit bull mix splotched with brown and black patches gets up from his resting spot as I clomp down the ramp off the dock.

"It's OK boy, I gotta get some help," I say, startled but starting out friendly, which isn't going to do any good because despite the rakish RCA-dog pirate patch over one eye this is not a friendly dog. He's wagging his stump of a tail and growling at the same time, rumbling low in his throat as he moves leisurely directly into my path.

His upper lip curls into a snarl. Why would they keep a dog like that around? "You sure are a mean dog, aren't you?" I say, trying not to show fear.

I side-step into the grass, scanning the ground for a rock, a branch, anything to bop him with if he attacks.

"No!" I hear Robin order again, as if commanding a dog.

"No!" I mimic to the mean dog with the big head, massive jaws and the merciless eyes of a killer. He turns away to sniff at an interesting turd pile and I sprint up the crude road, slipping in the loose gravel, nearly taking off the swinging screen door of the restaurant. Behind me, the mean dog is meandering up the hill.

"Where's Bobby? We need him at the dock. We need some help, some nut in a purple boat is trying to raft up to us."

Twenty or so preoccupied, happy faces glance up from their deep-fried pickles, sweet tea and platters of catfish fillets.

"Mister Bobby went home," says Betty June from behind the counter, her head partially hidden by the ornate antique cash register. She punches a button and the metal drawer pops out with a chime and a solid chunk. "Somebody needs some help tying up; tell 'em I'll get to 'em after I ring in these tickets. They need the gas pump turned on?"

"No, it's some kook in a purple boat acting crazy. She, he, it — I can't tell-is trying to ram our boats." This gets the attention of two skippers sitting with their wives at a nearby table. I am speaking at the volume which throughout my life has prompted parents, teachers and employers to tell me to quiet down and use my "indoor voice."

"Oh, that one," says Betty June. "Bobby told it to stay away." She asks in a confidential tone. "Do y'all think that's a man or woman? We can't decide."

"Whatever it is, it's not sane. Please, can somebody help?"

The two skippers rise from their dinners. Both are tall, beefy men wearing West Marine foulie jackets. "Let's see what's going on," says the one I recognize from the boat in front of us.

Trish comes out of the ladies room. "Where's Robin?"

"She's trying to keep a wacko off our boat. Come on!"

I'm last out the door. I don't see the mean dog or even sense him until I feel a sharp pinch on my upper thigh just below my left butt cheek. The two-pronged puncture is like a hole-puncher or a stapler, neatly placing two round indents on the tight skin of a back thigh in motion.

"Son of a bitch!" The pain is a rusty nail, penetrating deep like the time I jumped out of my tree house when I was 9, one bare foot impaled on the tiny, dirty metal stake sticking up out of a discarded board.

Infuriated, I wheel around and kick the mean dog in the head. "Fuck off, Fido." I've got a thighs roundhouse going, adrenalin pumping. No flight. So fight. I kick him hard again, in the ribs. He yips, startled. I drive in another good one with a Reebok to the ass before he slinks away, howling monotonously. It sets off the other dogs, barking and hair-raisingly howling.

"Holy shit," says Trish. She must have turned around when she heard me holler. "You're bleeding. He got you good."

"Screw it," I mutter, stumble-running to the dock, catching up with the men.

In the fading light the full moon is up, clouds streaming by behind it. I can just make out the dim outline of the invading sailboat.

"What in God's name is this? That's no way to park," says one of the skippers.

Schizo is wedged bow-first into the five-foot space between *Blackdog* and the yacht in front of us, its anchor dropped on the yacht's stern deck. The skipper murmurs dismay as he gets a look at the trailing, gelatinous weeds, his Sunbrella seat cushions sullied with mud and other slop from the river bottom. A thin twist of yellow ski-tow rope is tied to *Blackdog's* stern rail, sloppily but effectively holding the purple sailboat in place, stern swinging out in the current.

"That's one heck of a way to raft up," says the other skipper.

"Where's Robin? Robin?" Trish is calling as I somehow make it again over two decks to the salon door. I hear Annie Lennox, smooth, low, powerful, controlled, on the stereo speakers singing "Mamma, where do I go," the "Diva" CD we were listening to earlier in the day. In the low lamplight I see a brown throw blanketing the couch. KC is cowering in the corner next to the armchair.

The brown throw is moving. I see the lint and fabric pills covering it, and hear a pig-like grunting. It's a brown sweater. Its hips — his hips — are moving in that age-old rhythm, obscenely bumping in time with the music.

He is covering Robin.

He is raping Robin.

I can't see her face, just one helpless inert bare foot hanging off the side of the couch, the sole plastered with a pain patch.

Without much thought I move around the coffee table, approaching the prone bodies feet first. I reach in under where the lower abdomens meet, my hand in a belly sandwich directed past the pubic bones. I know what it is the minute my fingers skim the pliable, rubbery skin. I close my hand around the penis that is about two inches inside my friend. How satisfying to pull it out hard and bend it down sharply, jamming it head first into the cushions.

That gets his attention. He stiffens as if stung by a million wasps, rising up on his forearms. He sucks in air but does not speak.

"Get off!" I hiss. He struggles to one knee, bracing the opposite foot on the floor as if paused to spring.

The Roomba zips from under the couch, clipping his inner ankle on the tender spot between sock and shoe. He groans, trapped between the coffee table and couch as the robot vacuum mechanically bumps and backs up, bumps and backs up.

Robin's eyes are closed. I can't tell if she's breathing. From the side table I grab the long-handled butane lighter we use to ignite the gas stove, brandishing the wand at his ugly, feral, inhuman face. I hit the flame button, searing one gaping, gasping nostril, and smell burnt hair.

"Uhhh," he moans.

"Get out of here," I hiss again, fierce and fearless.

"Everything OK in there?" Trish calls. She's still on the dock with one of the skippers. The other skipper's back on his boat, untangling the errant anchor. All three are trying to raise someone on the odd, purple, dangerously parked sailboat.

Fuck. How do I answer that without telling the world? "Some trash wandered onto our boat," I call back. "No worries. It's leaving. Now."

He has crawled out from between the couch and coffee table, panting, on hands and knees. I kick him in the ass. My foot's going to be as sore as my toe tomorrow. "Pull up your pants," I direct, keeping my voice low. The ornamental iron poker next to the Franklin stove comes easily to hand. Head down, muttering to himself, he yanks up the absurd plaid trousers as he lurches for the door, crouched low over his aching groin.

"Out!" I shout. He's through the door and into the cockpit, me close behind with the poker in bashing position.

I'm untying the ski rope. The skipper on *Kendra* is still exclaiming over his muddy back porch as he examines the bizarre anchor.

"Hey *Kendra*," I yell, "Could you toss that anchor off your stern?"

A spotlight clicks on, illuminating the scene and temporarily blinding me. "We got trouble here?" Betty June calls out.

Nice of her to show up. "This freak came on our boat," I inform her. "But he's leaving now. Keep that light out of my face, OK?"

Muttering at the mucky mess, *Kendra's* boat skipper manages to heave the anchor back onto *Schizo's* foredeck. "You're gonna pay for any damages," he warns the gibbering rapist as in obvious pain Robin's attacker attempts to raise a leg over *Blackdog's* rail to step onto his beat-up excuse for a boat. I help with a shove that sends him over the side into the water. He hangs on, grasping one of the many dangling lines hanging off his boat.

Robin, Trish and I have a good start on a Top 10 List of Creeps We've Offloaded Overboard.

"I saw your ladder, sicko. Swim for it," I shove the *Schizo* away as hard as I can. The current catches the bow, pushing boat and sailor out into the river. A tow-barge as brilliantly lit as a cruise ship turns the corner, searchlight sweeping the banks. Too bad it's so far away, I think, vicious in my need to obliterate the horror, picturing the smaller vessel crushed under the weight of a full barge load.

"That wasn't very nice," remarks Betty Jean.

I've had it with her.

"Yeah, well he wasn't very nice. And that mean dog you've got running around here isn't nice either. He comes near me again and I'll kill him." I'm huffing, short of breath. The bite isn't throbbing, it's banging. "Somebody needs to run me to the hospital."

"Which dog?" says Betty June. "Buddy? That's Mister Bobby's dog. He's a barker, that's all, he don't mean no harm."

"More like bloody Buddy," I say, showing her the bite and blood. "He snuck up behind me and latched on. Are his shots up to date?"

"Just got him a new set of tags," says Betty June, no doubt threats of a lawsuit dancing in her mercenary brain. "Let me get the pick-up. I'll run you to the Urgent Care."

"I'll meet you up at the restaurant," I tell her. "I'm going to pour some peroxide on this right away."

Robin can come with me. Surely they'll have a rape kit or know how to get one. She's still lying on the couch. "Rob, are you OK? Answer me."

She's rigid, eyes still closed. I bend closer, touch her cheek. "We both need to get to the hospital. Let's get you dressed." I pull up her Snoopy boxers, straighten her rucked-up t-shirt that reads "Carrabelle: A Quaint Drinking Village With a Fishing Problem."

She opens her eyes, colorless, no pupils visible, awash in trauma. "No hospital," she rasps.

"You have to. God knows what that monster is infected with. We've got to collect the evidence. Where else did he hurt you?" He didn't get in far, but she must be torn, ripped. There are fingermarks on her skinny neck.

"I am not going. Don't tell — anyone."

Trish enters the salon. "Oh my God, Robin, are you OK? What did he do to you?"

"Raped her," I say. "She won't go to the hospital."

"Don't tell." Robin repeats. She closes her eyes again. Trish grabs the tangled navy-blue blanket from the floor and covers her. KC pads over to the couch, carefully placing her snout on Robin's leg. "Good girl," Robin says.

"OK sugar. It's OK." Trish strokes Rob's forehead, nods at me. "I'll stay with her. Maybe in the morning ..."

"Grab the peroxide from the medicine cabinet, would you?" There are involuntary tears in my eyes. The bite hurts more by the minute. I lay prone on the floor, not bothering to take off my jeans. Trish pours the contents of a full bottle over the back of my leg. It foams; I squirm with the pain and bite my lip.

"Protect her, Trish. Watch in case that fucko returns. Don't let anybody near this boat. I'll be back,"

"We're covered," she says, brandishing pepper spray, poker nearby.

I limp across the decks again, tears still streaming, adrenaline crashed into organ-deep exhaustion. I realize I've left my purse aboard. Screw it. This repair is on Betty June's dime.

Funny how on the river you forget the land life nearby in towns beyond view. The white pick-up climbs the winding camp road up the mountain and in seconds we are on a flat University of Alabama Highway bordered by dormant fields, traffic zooming by and bright lights in the distance.

"You're going to need to quarantine that mean dog," I tell Betty June. "Unless you want to get it over with and put him down before he hurts somebody else."

"Bobby's dog wouldn't hurt a flea," she says.

"How many other people has he bitten?"

"Must have been some other dog. Buddy just barks. Y'all can show me in the morning. Might be Bob's hound. He don't let his grandkids around it."

With a population of 360 covering 4.5 square miles, Coffeeville doesn't have a full-fledged hospital. The emergency urgent care office on Highway 177 is quiet. Since I have no other pants they give me a pair of blue scrubs to wear home after the wound — two puncture marks already vividly bruising- are washed and dressed. Since I don't remember the date of my last tetanus shot (possibly after the tree house incident of long ago) one is administered in short order. I give my name as "Nora Jones" on the medical forms. I'm a big fan of her music. The admitting nurse practitioner is anxious to get the proper forms filled out regarding the dog and his distemper shots. Without proof, I am advised that I will need to return for a round of rabies shots. They also give me a packet of amoxicillin to fight infection.

Betty June promises to return the next day with the dog's proof of vaccination. She writes a check for services rendered.

Robin is still on the couch when I return. I stand over her, looking down with a tenderness not felt since Lisa and Joey were babies. I wished I'd stayed with the boat and sent her up the hill. That maniac would never have gotten a foot aboard. "Oh Robin," I whisper, like a prayer. I let her sleep.

We'll get her help in the morning.

I latch the cabin doors and check the windows. Across the river, a new mast light shines near the opposite bank. *Schizo?* I slump in the armchair, still-thumping leg propped on the ottoman, to keep watch. Fog rolls in, obliterating the mast light and the moon.

Chapter 18: Coffeeville to Three Rivers Lake

The morning fog is saturated cotton wadding, drops condensing on every exterior surface, obscuring the view from the windows, muffling the sky in the cold, sunless dawn. Typical for here at this time of year; if the weather stays true to pattern it will begin to lift after 9 a.m., reluctantly pulling away in upward-flying tendrils that spiral off the river, the dancing Indian ghosts of frontier legend whirling off the surface of the sparkling Tombigbee.

Robin wakes at dawn. "Hailey, you're drooling."

I pick my head up off my chest. There's a pool of spittle on the front of my sweatshirt. "Gross." When I stand up the dog bite reasserts itself. "Ow!"

"Nice pants," says Robin, eyeing my scrubs. She moves stiffly off the couch into the galley, starting the coffee like it's any other day. Apparently we're striving for normal. I don't know if I can go with that program.

I wipe the fog-sweat off the window and look out across the river. Nothing seen. "Where did it go?" I wonder aloud.

"Where did what go?" she says.

"Are you OK? I don't see how you can be OK."

"I'm definitely not. But will be once we get out of this shithole," she says, measuring grounds into the basket. "We are out of here as soon as the fog lifts."

"Don't you think we should stay? You need to see a doctor. We need to report this. He has to be caught and put away somewhere where he can't..."

She turns, eyes blazing, shutting down my self-righteous monologue. "Zip it, please. I'm not saying dick about shit. We're leaving. End of story."

"He could have killed you. He'll do it again."

"Not talking about this. Let your karma-thing get him." She flips the generator on, pushes the brew button, heads down the steps. "I'm gonna waste some of our water on a shower."

Washing away the evidence.

My mother is a rape and domestic abuse counselor. I'm a domestically abused Information Specialist as familiar with the cycle of grief, denial and anger as I am with the sorries that follow the beatings that lead to more beatings and more apologies. I just make it outside, every surface wet to the touch as I lean over the railing and puke yellow bile into the brown water. The current swirls it downriver before it can sink.

As soon as I lift my head, wiping my mouth on my sweatshirt sleeve, I see *Kendra's* skipper watching me from the stern of his boat.

"Rough night, hey?" he laughs uneasily, sipping from his Captain mug. He looks a little embarrassed for me, even sympathetic; maybe I'll be spared the spreading of tales about the drunken brawd on *Blackdog*. That would be better than the truth, anyway.

"Yeah, I guess I had a little too much." Heh heh.

"You locking through today?"

"Yep. As soon as the fog lifts."

***

Robin comes up freshly dressed from her shower. Trish is on her knees with a magnifying mirror behind me, scrub pants pulled down as she examines the bite. "Hoo-eee, those are some colorful bruises," she remarks as she tentatively prods around the puncture marks. "But no red streaks, that's a good sign."

I gulp my coffee. "I'll live. It aches like crazy, like I have a pounding headache in my upper thigh."

"Of course it does," Trishie says. "But it's healing well with no weeping or discoloration. We do need to find that dog and check his tags. Rabies ain't no joke."

"Betty June says he has his shots," I protest.

"Yeah, but she says that isn't the dog that bit you. We need to be sure."

"Well hurry up about it," says Robin. "I plan on a spot in the first group through the lock this morning." She pours herself a mug of java then carefully crouches, trying not to jostle any sore places, to rummage through a lower cupboard. "Here. Go find that fuckin' dog." Hands me a can of wasp spray after shaking it hard. "It shoots from 30 feet away. Give him something to remember you by."

"Bloody Buddy." I shiver. "Trish, will you come with?"

"Hell to the yes," she says. "Just let me grab the boat hook. Gonna whack his ass. And that other dirty dog, too, if he's still around."

"I popped his cock a good one," I announce. "He's feeling that this morning. Bent it backward."

The rapid descent into violent profanity is discomfiting, but it's working for us. I actually feel better. Robin is grinning and nodding.

"Then the Roomba got him." She laughs hysterically. We all do. We need to. It washes us cleaner than tears.

We are not in the mood to take abuse. I feel sorry for anyone who dares to confront *Blackdog's* crew today.

"Anticlimax," Trish announces after we march down the dock to the ramp. The lights are on in other boats now, generators grumbling as coffee smells distill and dilute in the moving mist. Low murmurs flow and ebb, early-morning conversation controlled by every crackle and burst of static from a baker's dozen of marine radios turned on to listen for the Coffeeville Lock announcement.

"I need to borrow your phone," I say.

I walk up the hill, wasp spray at the ready, stopping when I get a few bars on the cell. Praying the signal is strong enough. That I'm strong enough.

Nothing fazes my mom. Or at least that's how she comes off. Whether she's serving her signature chili at a church supper or driving a vanful of drunks to an AA meeting, everyone feels like they can talk to her. Except for her kids. My entire life she's been so busy counseling others that it never felt like she had time for me. This time it works in my favor. She kicks into bra-burning militant mode when I tell her Robin has been raped and won't go to the police.

"Of course she won't. You're in *Alabama*." She says it like there's shit in her mouth. "Only an idiot trusts the Good Old Boys."

Not what I expected to hear. "We fought to get police departments stocked with rape kits," my mother says. "But tens of thousands of rape victims across the nation go untested every year. No follow-through."

She tells me to let Robin do whatever she needs to do. To be OK with uncharacteristic behavior. To listen to her. "But don't try to make her talk."

"Jeez Mom, I know that much."

She ignores the jab. "Watch her. But don't be obvious. Don't bring up counseling again unless she does."

"I'd like to meet her," she says. "And you do whatever it is you need to do, too."

"I'm fine, Mom. Just a couple more days to the Gulf."

"I'm not stupid. How's Derek?"

"I can't go into it right now, Mom."

"Come home. We'll get the process started." Here we go. The spiel about breaking the cycle of abuse, blahdey, bla, bla, blah. "I can't do this right now, Mom. This is not about me. I'm fine."

"Talk about avoidance."

"I've got to go Mom."

"I know you think you do," she says. "I love you. Will you call me back when you can?"

"Love you too."

This lock is one of the smoothest running anywhere on the rivers. The lockmaster patiently announces the fog delay, predicts when the lock will open, calls out for and records every boat name and registration number and assigns vessels to the starboard and port walls in successive order beginning at the front bollards and proceeding to the back of the steel-and-wood lock gates where herons and egrets perch to eat the fish caught in the rise and fall. I hope *Blackdog* gets the sunny side to port, nearest the lock control office. We could all use a little sun, including KC, who seems afraid to leave the boat. She promptly peed and pooped five steps away from the dock ramp and obligingly climbed back aboard, curling up on the couch.

I wish she could tell us what she saw last night. As people do, I attribute human characteristics to her animal existence. She's scared, confused and I believe chagrined that she could not stop the base violation of her mistress. KC doesn't appear to be physically damaged in any way; her gait was normal when Trish walked her. KC and Trish have the only normal gaits on the boat. Robin and I have what my mom terms "hitches in our gitalongs."

Did somebody spread the word to hide the dogs? There isn't one in sight. I've lost my buzz for shooting wasp spray into Bloody Buddy's eyes. I think I did hear tags tinkle on his collar. Then I think I made that up to reassure myself. Trish and I leave a note on the restaurant door.

From her ever-present purse she pulls a cash-register slip from last night's meal at Bobby's and writes with a clicky pen from Mermaid Marina as I dictate:

Dear Mister Bobby,

I was bitten by your dog on your property yesterday. Please text, e-mail or call us with Bloody Buddy's dog-tag numbers and date of distemper shots. If I have to undergo rabies shots I will be sending the bill to you in care of this address.

Sincerely,

Nora Jones

Trish reads it over. "Where on God's green earth do you suggest we check e-mail?" She grabs the pen and crosses that part off before folding the note into thirds and sticking it into the center of the screen door's metal scrolling.

When we turn around, the white dog is lying there on the road, dead center, staring at us.

He barks.

"Hey, Buddy, cut that out," says Bobby. "Don't worry, ladies. He talks a lot, but his bark is worse than his bite."

The denizen of the Fish Camp looks the same as always, in his denim jacket and sneakers, wise face and knowing eyes shadowed by a ball cap. He's medium-sized but he talks like a six-foot man, an honest straight shooter.

"He bit me," I say, turning my back to him and pointing to the bite. "That is a mean dog."

"First I heard of that," he says. "Buddy doesn't bite, as a rule."

"Does he have all his shots? Rabies and everything?"

"C'mon over here," he orders Bloody Buddy, who complies completely. "Roll over." He's like a different dog. I hear the tags tinkle.

There are men of honor and chivalry on the river. We have to try to remember that.

We could not escape rape; but we have been spared rabies.

Coffeeville Lock is 600 feet long by 100 feet wide, large enough to fit eight standard-size barges. There are five "ballards" on each side. We ease in with the last of the flotilla arriving from Bobby's along with a few stragglers from a couple of nearby anchorages tucked just inside Turkey and Okatuppa creeks, part of the Choctaw National Wildlife Refuge, a 4,000-acre wilderness that borders the river along the stretch before Bobby's. At Trishie's excited direction we'd scanned in vain at mile 120.4 for a sign of the last Choctaw Native American Indian possession east of the Tombigbee River. "There was a village around here," she said, scanning yet another guidebook. "They kept thousands of turkeys, and ancestors of the flock are living in the refuge."

"So far the only turkeys I've seen downriver are the humans on some of these boats," Robin observes. Wry on toast. How can we help her when she won't talk about it?

There are 10 boats locking down. The *Newfie Bullet* is secured; Jack is playing "Amazing Grace" on his accordion. "I thought that song was for funerals," says Trish. "I'd plug my ears but I don't want to be rude."

"I'm wondering why the lockmaster allows it," I say.

There'd be an even dozen boats in Coffeeville Lock if *Spirit of Whitby* and *Menou* were joining us, but both couples opted to stay at Bobby's and let the crowd thin out before proceeding downstream.

"Tally Ho!" called the *Whitby* Brits, waving cheerily as we pulled away, an unevenly spaced line of floating homes motoring toward the lock.

"Again with the full house," notes Trish. "I'm just glad the lockmaster assigned rafting partners so it's not a free-for-all. Foxtrot Uniform Charlie Kilo that!"

"Oh brother," says Robin. Ever since Trish heard the *Avalon* crew laboriously spelling out "Alpha Victor Alpha Lima Oscar November" over the marine radio, she's been fascinated. And wouldn't you know it, the captain just happened to have a spare copy of the NATO Phonetic Alphabet that he passed along to her.

"Cool your Juliet Echo Tango Sierra, Robin," says Trish. "I'm only gonna use it for swear words."

It's a little disconcerting to be lashed to the *Kendra*, since her skipper is the gentleman who witnessed my early-morning stomach eruption. Clearly he's mentioned this unsavory sighting to his well-groomed, exquisitely polite wife. After I compliment her on the boat's sparkling white decks and ask her how they keep their bumpers so clean, she thaws slightly and explains how the boat was named.

"I'm Audra and he's Ken. Put two-and-two together," she says, before she abruptly stiffens to attention, pivoting her head toward the lock wall.

"Hey there. What do you think you're doing?"

Derek.

Above us.

Coming for me.

He swings down the ladder next to our bollard in the lock like an enraged gorilla cross-bred with a maladjusted chimpanzee. He looks like he wants to bite somebody. I've never seen him this angry. But I'm weary with anger; there's been so much of it that I just want to go to sleep under a soft blanket far away from nasty, unpredictable people and dogs. I feel blank.

He doesn't say a word, just barrels down the muck-slimed rungs.

"Sir? Sir! You can't come down here," Audra instructs firmly in a schoolmarmish tone. "Ken! Call the lockmaster."

"What's this happy horse poop?" Trish raises her sunglasses, peers out for a better view of my fast-approaching husband. Derek looms over the foredecks of the rafted yachts, staring down at us with hate. His pasty forehead is shiny with sweat. His ponytail is frizzy and his clothes bear a variety of engine oil, varnish and food stains.

I'm dead in his sights. Trapped on deck. I resist the urge to bolt. Surrender the notion that running away will save me. Locking myself in the cabin or curling up in a ball in the bathroom will only cause damage to the boat if he decides to come after me. Besides, I'm tired of making myself small so that he can be big. That's why I left him in the first place. But I don't know what to say. So I don't say anything. I take a really deep breath in. The dog bite throbs.

"Fuck me," Robin says, deadpan, then barks, "Derek."

He stops his descent at his name in a stranger's mouth. I breathe out.

"I know about you," Robin continues in her husband-voice. "You're a lowdown dirty dog who hits women. You do not have permission to board this boat. I'd go right back where I came from if I was you. I will personally fuck you up if you come any closer."

"You're not getting on our boat, either," says Audra, hands on her hips.

Derek looks down on us, his favorite position, narrowed piggy eyes crafty, mean, sweeping the decks to spot an advantage. Trish talks to the lockmaster on the radio. I can't hear what she's saying. Attendants in dark blue uniforms putt toward us in their government-issued golf cart.

The river doesn't care and the white birds don't care. But there are witnesses who do. I am safe. For the first time I'm safe with my choice. It's like the lock doors opening into a new pool. This world is opening like a gate unlocked.

"Hi. Bye." I wave at Derek, copy-catting those teens who waved me off so breezily from the Hammond breakwater. Remembering Robin and I on the river, waving at everyone, cracking ourselves up. We three River Queens with our disco call in the locks. "Oooh Oooh." I try it solo, looking straight into his ugly face. My battle cry bounces off the lockwalls. It doesn't disturb the white birds perched on the chamber doors. Robin laughs. "One more time!" Trish joins in.

I walk away. I can't stand the sight of my husband. I take my spot at the bow. Gloves on. Boathook ready to shove *Blackdog* off the wall.

"They're talking him up," says Trish, smiling, as if Derek was a suicide risk being coaxed from the precipice of a tall building. You can feel the fed-upness of the other boaters. Muttering. Engines running. Patience running out. We all just want to lock through and move on. He's holding us up. Boaters hate that.

"Hang it up, Derek," Robin advises. Then to me "They all know you now. Happy?"

"Yeah, actually. I'm really good," I tell her. "How are you?"

I don't wait for an answer. Mom's right. She's not ready to talk. We'll stumble and dance around it; if we love, the lines stay open. The uniformed men are losing patience. Derek is more firmly instructed to climb out of the chamber. He comes two more rungs down. "That's my wife," he pants, pointing. "She ran away. She just left. I had no idea where she was going."

This is it.

"Get ready," I tell Trish and include Audra, my voice loud enough for everyone to hear on the dark side of the chamber. Over on the east side, they're fidgeting in the sun and wondering what the holdup is. We need daylight to get to the next anchorage. Derek is a speed bump.

"Keep the hook handy. He likes to choke, don't let him get close enough." Trish nods, eyes hard. I think she's seen some things, sunny nature notwithstanding. Confrontations are in her lexicon.

But Audra's got this. We're in her wheelhouse. Before Trish can make a move, she whops Derek's knees with her own boathook, adding a quick jab to the balls. "No!" she yells as loud as she can, then again, "No!"

"Nice job, Audra!" Trish calls. "Someone's taken a self-defense class." We laugh. Derek's right foot slips on a greasy rung and he bangs his chin before clamping both hands back on the ladder. The bottom of his chin is bleeding. Judging by the motherfucker-cocksucker invective, he probably bit his tongue. God, I am so glad I'm not with him anymore.

Muttering, growling, he hovers between down and up as the courteous middle-aged dock attendants renew the urges to be sensible. "Come on up now, man, come on bud, you're fine bro," finessing him just as smoothly tow-barge drivers negotiating a two-whistle pass on a tight curve.

"Go away," I tell Derek.

"You could have let me know, Hailey," he yells at me, so Brando to my Stella. "You had no right to run off like that."

"I am done blocking your view," I say, snide and terrified.

"And there won't be any more choking," says Trish.

"Just leave me and my wide ass be."

"Oh, is that how you want to play it? Fine. I'm filing for divorce."

"Do what you want."

"You won't get support off me. Trust me on that," says Derek, hawking a coffee-colored loogie that lands on the *Kendra's* deck, Audra adroitly sidesteps the ugly splatter before raising her boathook. "Don't tempt me, mister."

"You always were a pig," I say. "I was never supported."

I'm weary. The biting and beating. The violence of last night and so many days and nights before.

"Just leave me alone. That's all I want," I say. "Leave me alone."

The men above never stop murmuring. Derek finally tunes in, blearily making his way up. I keep my eyes trained on his slow progress. I can feel the stares from the other boaters in the lock. They'll have plenty to discuss at tonight's cocktail hour.

"*Blackdog* is secured," Robin announces businesslike over the radio. The other boats chime in. Clicks on the mike switch for applause. A few glad-it-all-worked-outs and a couple of Atta Girls. A formal thank you from the lockmaster "for your patience."

The siren sounds and we drop toward tidal waters. Lord only knows what wild claims Derek is making up there. He was shuttled away in the golf cart; I did not see any police on scene. Will Trish, Robin and I be detained for questioning?

The gates open on a new vista. The mechanics of the hydraulics grant freedom. The open doors signal permission to proceed without exception, an enormous relief.

"How do you think he found you?" Robin asks.

"It had to be John," says Trishie.

She's right. "That's got to be it," I say. "John wanted someone to listen to him belly-ache about being tossed off the boat."

The traveling pack bunched in the lock thins out as the faster vessels increase to cruising speed, leaving the sailboats and slow trawlers who want to save fuel behind. There are only two boats behind us when I spot a flashing blue light on a silver-hulled craft with a small pilothouse zipping toward *Blackdog*.

"Shit and shinola," I mutter. I'd been thinking we got away too easy. The Alabama Marine Police are on our tail.

"Shit is right," says Robin. "Take the wheel Trish, I gotta dump my beer and get my papers."

"That's Sierra Hotel India Tango, to you."

Chapter 19: Cops and No Docks

"Good afternoon ladies," says the officer in khaki green shirt and black pants stationed on the bow of the police patrol vessel. "Where are you headed?"

There are two other water cops on board, one at the wheel and one to spare. One for each of us, I think, sweat breaking out at my temples, between my collarbones and trickling down my lower back.

Trish slows to idle as Robin approaches the rail. "We're on our way to Mobile Bay," she says. "We just locked through."

"Roger that," says our interrogator, a young, fresh-faced, clean shaven guy with a beautiful mouth full of even white teeth.

"Are you the captain of this vessel?"

"Captain and owner," says Robin.

"I need to see your documentation and registration," he says. "Also your driver's license if you have that available." Rob hands the paperwork over, which is promptly affixed to his clipboard. He begins filling in the blanks.

"Do I need to stop?" asks Trish, who cannot resist flashing a coquettish smile at the cutest cop.

"No ma'am, just proceed at this speed." Trish doesn't enjoy being called ma'am. She arches her back and tosses her hair. "We're just going to tie alongside here for a minute," says the cute cop, while the one not driving comes out to secure their boat to ours. After a few minutes examining and writing, the cute cop announces that they'd like to do a safety and sanitation inspection. This seldom happens on the rivers; rivers are largely overseen by the U.S. Army Corps of Engineers. I smell a rat. I'm sure they're just looking for a reason to detain us and drag the runaway wife back to her rightful owner. But I'm a good crew member adhering to the proper procedures outlined in maritime law. It is my job to keep my mouth shut and let the captain handle it.

The other, equally young officer who latched on to our boat gracefully swings a leg over and places a jack-booted foot on *Blackdog's* deck. His eyes are inscrutable behind mirrored aviator sunglasses.

"Where would you like to start?" asks Robin. "Obviously we're all wearing our PFDs." Life jackets are required in the locks and we haven't had a chance to shuck them yet.

They go below and Robin produces the flares, fire extinguishers, throw-able floating cushions and all other applicable safety equipment. Trish hits the horn as requested to demonstrate that we have a sound-making device.

"Looks like everything is in order," says the examiner, after emerging from the head where he has inspected *Blackdog's* through-hull valve fittings for the toilet.

"Hurray!" says Trish.

"Yes ma'am," he agrees. "One more thing — we understand there was a little trouble in the lock today. Someone tried to come on your boat?"

"Scared the heck out of us," says Robin. "Never saw him before in my life."

"Well he claims that he wanted to talk to his wife," the examining officer says. "And that she was on a stolen vessel."

"That would be me," I speak up. No use letting Trish and Robin get in trouble. "We're getting a divorce and he isn't used to the idea yet."

"I see. Did he threaten you with bodily harm?"

"Not really," I say. "I think he just wants me to come back to him."

"Can I see your driver's license?"

"Uhm, no," I say, but confess. "It's suspended."

He doesn't say anything, just looks annoyed as if I am being resistant.

"I have my passport though. Will that do?"

He nods and I try my hardest to walk smoothly into the salon to fetch my passport, the bandage hidden under my sweatpants. I definitely don't want to discuss Nora Jones and her dog bite.

He examines my passport and hands it back without comment.

"Are we free to go, then, officer?" asks Robin.

"Did you want to file a complaint? They're holding the gentleman back at the lock. He was trespassing on federal property."

"No, we don't want to press charges," says Robin. "Sounds like he's got enough trouble on his hands. Maybe he'll get the message and leave her alone from here on in."

"I hope so," I say.

"Well here's my card if you have any trouble or decide you want to report him." The cute officer hands it to Robin, who sticks it in her shirt pocket. "Domestic violence is a weighty crime. We take it very seriously."

"Thank you. I'm glad somebody does," Robin says.

The cop looks annoyed again. "You have a good day."

"You too."

And just like that, they pull away.

I've read about collective sighs of relief, but I've never really heard one until now.

"Thank God and Greyhound they're gone," says Trish, eyes on the river. "That first one was pretty cute, wasn't he? But the one driving, he was a mean sumbitch. Took a bunch of pictures of us with his camera phone. Tryin' to be all undercover with his dark glasses and his smart phone."

"I was so scared he'd bust me for probation violation," I admit.

I realize that we just missed another opportunity; clearly the rape is not going to be reported. It's been decided without discussion. Every day, every year, so many women don't report. I never understood why; now I see how even the thought of the telling and re-telling, the collection of evidence, could grind the desecration so far into the persona that it would leave a permanent groove.

Not reporting it isn't healthy, at least by conventional standards. I want to tell Robin again and again that it's OK to tell. But in these moments when she seems to be drawing strength in not discussing it, I hesitate to broach the subject. "Forget about it," she said.

"Oh, my God, never say that to me again!" It is probably written somewhere in a rape response document that one should never yell at the survivor. Fuck that. I'm treating her normally. The Robin-ness of Robin freed me. Why wouldn't it do the same for her?

"Derek wants to keep me. What's the point?" This need for possession and control with no sex, lust or passion is confusing and scary. It's like Robin's rape by a creature that is neither female nor male. Carnal confusion.

"We saw Johns like Derek all the time," Trish says. "What's so funny?"

Maybe we just need to laugh.

Even with the cop-stop delay we make Three Rivers Lake an hour before sunset, turning to starboard off the main river into a 60-foot channel with a minimum of swinging room and a narrow turning radius. The waterway widens a few miles back, expanding into a lake surrounded by modest cottages, but it's too shallow and stumpy for a yacht of any size to proceed much farther than just past the entrance. The tows won't fit in here. The only disturbances are fishermen whizzing by in small aluminum boats and Carolina skiffs, waving with no apologies for the noise or the rolling prop wash from their oversized outboard engines. The anglers are coming in for the night as we drop anchor in the shade of cypress oaks and poplar that arch over the narrows. Trish spots four turkeys nesting in the trees. A heron quocks.

Robin is taking another shower. We have plenty of bottled water if the tanks run dry before Mobile Bay. I can hear her talking to KC.

"Come on honey, you can pee in here. See?"

"Oh my God, is she demonstrating?" Trish asks in an undertone, putting together a salad and chicken strips for dinner.

"So what? Urine is fairly sterile, completely sterile before it comes out of your body," I say. "And if it will get KC to go, it's well worth it. She hasn't gone since this morning. As far as I'm concerned she can tinkle anywhere she wants to. She's got to go or she'll get sick. I've seen it before. A dog with a kidney infection or uremic poisoning is one sick puppy. If anything happened to KC, I don't know what Robin would do. Especially right now."

"What about tomorrow? Is there anywhere we can get the pup ashore?" Trish pops the strips in a fry pan, placing a grease screen over it and wiping her hands on a towel before whipping out the sparkly pink Hello Kitty notebook tucked in her back pocket. She's been keeping a short list of potential anchorages gleaned from the guidebooks. "What about this Ten-Saw River Cut-off that you two want to hit tomorrow? There's got to be at least a patch of dry land there."

"We anchor in Briar Creek there, about a mile down the Ten-Saw Cut-off. It's all marsh, palmettos and sawgrass along the creek. No solid land. They say mother sharks go up the Mobile River to have their babies there.

"But," I recall, "there are some run-down fishing camps on the Tenn-Saw, on the right bank; old wood cottages with rickety docks. We maybe could land at one of the camps, as long as we're watching out for snakes and 'gators."

"And sharks. Great," says Trish, turning the sizzling chicken strips. She's talking with the spatula. "I swear, this whole trip is starting to make me crazy. This river makes me crazy. Going down the rivers is a lot harder than it looks. A Super 8 off an Interstate would look like a Hilton spa to me right now."

"I can't figure it out," I say, "are you Thelma or Louise?"

"Neither. I didn't run away, I just went, remember?" she says. "And if you want to jump any canyons, count me out."

There are no gulches here, although there's the highest point on the Eastern U.S. coastline at Ecor Rouge on Mobile Bay, the red cliff that will guide us toward the Eastern Shore of that great brown expanse of water local sailors refer to as "the mud hole."

Otherwise, the world gets flatter and flatter as we drop to 23 feet above sea level, motoring at 7 miles per hour past distinctly more tropical flora and fauna, the first pelicans venturing 25 miles upstream from the Bay to bob in the chop like blow-up water toys, mindlessly smiling, drifting in the current.

Robin reports that KC had a thorough bath but did not pee. Then she asks if we have any rolls or bread. I assume she wants to feed the fish or birds or something.

"I think I have a mix in here," she says, joining Trish in the galley to scout the cabinets.

"What's this? Can't we just bake it?" Trish proffers a plastic-wrapped torpedo of bread dough from the freezer. "How long has this been in here?" she says, grabbing her cheaters from the pearled and bejeweled string around her neck. "Self-answering question: good for another year. But we can't have it tonight, it has to thaw and rise."

"Jiffy Mix," says Robin, handing a cardboard box to Trish.

Trish squints as she reads the package instructions. She cranks on the oven, taps Robin on the shoulder. "Well go ahead, Robin Dean — or should I say Robin Ray? Make muffins."

I'm really happy about the butter that Trish also found in the freezer. There's no margarine product comparable to real butter. The icy cold pats melt into the soft, warm, puffy blueberry muffins.

"These are so delicious," I nearly moan.

"Jesus, Hailey, it's not the second coming of Christ," says Robin. "If I feel like baking I'd appreciate you not making a big hairy deal out of it."

"Fine," I say, stung. "Sorry if I went overboard with the praise. Sheesh. But they are really, really tasty."

I'm reminded to focus on what Robin is experiencing rather than how supportive I can be. We're all so busy not talking about it that at times I can hardly breathe. That fabled elephant-in-the-room takes up a lot of space.

KC goes to sleep, which we hope means that she isn't completely uncomfortable. Robin puts a potty pad covered by a patch of green turf right next to the dog bed, which KC only uses sporadically. Most of the time she sleeps intertwined with Robin on the couch.

"Maybe we ought to put a diaper on her," I muse. Rob snickers, which I take as a positive sign. "I once met a poor little wiener dog who wore a diaper all the time. The boat was named *Sara*; her owners didn't have a dinghy and they anchored out all the time to save money so the dog never got off the boat."

"Not even to Papa Oscar Oscar Papa?" asks Trish.

"Nope."

"That's horrible," says Robin, shivering. She remembers the fishing cabins on the Ten-Saw, too. "I'm sure we'll find a place to get her to shore," she says.

"Dinner was really good," I say. "Thanks, you guys. And thanks for sticking up for me when Derek showed up."

"That's what friends do for each other," says Trish. "I'm just glad that gob of spit didn't hit me."

"So gross. I'm sorry," I say.

"Hailey, it's not your fault he's a jerk," says Robin. "Quit apologizing for him."

"Maybe he'll leave me alone now," I say, swigging the last of my beer. How many tonight? Truth be told, I lost count.

Trish is over her limit as well. I hope it helps us sleep.

Tomorrow, the river again. It's wearing on all of us.

"I'm so tired," I say. "Tired of bullshit."

"Bravo, Uniform, Lima, Lima-"

"Can it, would you Trish? Anyway, we're almost to Mobile Bay," says Robin.

"Yeah. Then what? Do we just keep going? What am I doing, anyway? I've got fifteen hundred bucks to my name. My kids have no idea where I am, not that they care, but..." I say.

"Better than me, hon, I'm down to $500 until I get to the secret stash in my safety deposit box and I have no one to call," says Trish. "Time to get a job. What are my options for hooking or hairdressing on this here river?"

We can't stop laughing and don't want to. Robin is rolling on the rug. "Put up a sign for the towboats," she chokes out. "Haircuts and Hooker Here. Two-for-One Specials Available."

"I've got you covered, top to bottom," announces Trish, between gasps of giggles.

"And Robin can bake her muffins and I'll be the receptionist and waitress or whatever you call the person making the appointments and collecting the fees," I say. "I'm awesome at prep, customer service and ordering supplies."

"Think bigger. If you're handling the money side, that makes you a pimp or a madam," says Trish. "Or COE. Chief Operating Empress. We'll call the business 'Robin's Muffins.' You'll be the Muffin Madam."

"So are you the Muffin Mistress? The Muffin Magician?"

"No, yuck," she wrinkles that pretty little nose of her, tosses her curls. "I'm the Muffin Top!"

We stayed up all night talking about "Robin's Muffin Top," our fictional business that heals us as we dream of a house of women living together on the river taking care of the motherly needs of its travelers — and making a bundle doing it.

"Coloring alone can net a thousand or so per month," says Trish. "Have you seen some of these women boaters and their roots? No wonder they get nasty in the laundry rooms. They're feeling low because their hair isn't happy. You have to fight to beautify on this trip, that's God's honest truth."

"When I was in the Caribbean, the local kids would row out in their canoes and bring boaters bread or fruit or whatever," says Robin. I hadn't known she had made longer passages to foreign lands. "We could do that with the muffins."

"Coffee, too," I say. "Derek always made a great pot of coffee in the stovetop percolator, but a lot of boaters don't have that luxury. I cannot believe people still drink instant coffee with hot water. Barf!"

A debate on the various types of coffee cups ensues: Styrofoam vs. plastic vs. Robin's idea of a $5 "Robin's Muffin Top" mug with each cup of coffee. "We'll fill thermoses, too," she says.

Trish and I are hesitant to ask her how much money she has, but after this suggestion Trishie can't hold back. "Who's gonna bankroll this mug manufacturing? Are you made of money?"

"I have enough to do what I want," says Rob. She holds our gaze for a moment, realizing she can't dodge it anymore. "I'm what you'd call well off. Not rich but nowhere near broke."

Turns out she started the whole folding camp-chair revolution by buying one of the first prototypes, setting up a manufacturing plant and selling the hell out of the innovative product before anyone else had caught on to the potential. Eventually folding chairs went into mass production overseas and the retail price dropped drastically. "When they first came out I was selling them for $50 apiece," Robin notes with amusement and pride. "Made a bundle while it lasted."

Plus there's the family inheritance. Plus the divorce that included an airtight pre-nup agreement.

"You never talk about Fucko," I say.

"That's right," she says, winking.

The fog curls in around 3 a.m., the coldest time of every day on the river. Wrapped in fleece blankets with the generator purring and the Franklin stove emitting small, blue, regular flames, we abide in our small, warm circle, content and comforted in a river cove in the middle of nowhere. Three a.m. is a good time to pray, to plan, to count blessings while the rest of the world sleeps.

Chapter 20: Coming Home

"14 Mile Bridge, 14 Mile Bridge, this is downbound pleasure vessel *Blackdog* requesting your next opening…"

We're elated by the sight of the old railroad swing bridge, the last of its kind on the lower rivers and the last moving obstacle in *Blackdog's* path down the Mobile River to that great port city on the bay leading to the Gulf of Mexico.

"Why do they call it the 14 Mile Bridge?" Trish wants to know. The span is located at mile 13.4.

"This is the 14 Mile Bridge to the downbound pleasure vessel," the bridge operator answers back on Channel 13. "We'll open 'er up for you in about 10 minutes, Cap, got a shift change comin' up. Gotta get home to watch some football."

"Roll Tide!" Trish cheeps back enthusiastically.

"Talk about taking one for the team." I remark. She's figured out priorities.

Northerners accustomed to Sunday football rituals learn quickly that Saturdays are sacred in LA. Forget the pros; it's all about college games — most specifically the University of Alabama — in these parts. Sundays are for church and family dinner. The bars are closed and liquor sales are prohibited.

Kingfishers chitter along the shoreline, hovering above the river surface in search of dinner. The yellow-billed common egrets are wading, white silhouettes poised along both sides of the banks as the tide drops and tasty live morsels are revealed. A tow-barge arrives on the other side of the bridge; Rob knows without asking that it gets to go first, so she eases *Blackdog* over to the green buoys to give it room to pass.

There's a faraway look in her eyes. *Come back to us Robin.* "Whatcha thinkin' about?"

"As soon as we anchor I'm gonna make some more muffins," she says. She baked a batch first thing this morning. We're running low on butter. It's not the eating that seems to interest her, although I've seen her run a finger around the mixing bowl, licking the batter with real gusto.

"Good deal," I say. "Maybe there will be some other boats in the anchorage to share with. Test run for the Muffin Top, right?"

"That would be good," she says. "Very good."

The center section of the bridge swivels with an audible creak, as if groaning in protest as it moves from horizontal to vertical, presenting two parallel channels. After the tow proceeds through the starboard channel, we line up for the pass through, waving up at the bridge operator in his rusty control shack. He offers a lackadaisical two-fingered salute. He's likely engrossed in listening to the game on the radio.

"Thank you, 14 Mile Bridge, you have a nice day!" Trish transmits on the radio, before waggling her hand at the water ahead of us. "Look, girls!"

"Now I feel like we're truly headed for the tropics," I say, watching the young, brown, smiling sky pilot swoop low over the water, wide wings whooshing wind as he wheels over the foredeck and hovers beak down over the water before dive-bombing with an ungainly, ungraceful splash. He pops up empty-beaked but seemingly unperturbed.

"Look at him, just bobbing along. Most years I haven't seen them until Mobile Bay," I say. "From his markings he's a young one."

"I think it's a lucky sign," says Trish.

"Well if pelicans are lucky, we'll have all the good fortune we need for the rest of this pleasure cruise," says Rob.

To port we see the curving entrance to the Ten-Saw River cut-off, bordered by marsh to the left, scrub pines and palmetto forest to the right. I feel the rush of excitement that always radiates through every cell of my body upon arriving at a new portal, a new entrance. In just these few weeks of learning that I know more than I think I know, the dread that accompanied every stop and the waiting for something bad to happen is done.

I know how to run this entrance. I know exactly where to turn at the broad, welcoming intersection of Big Briar Creek. The water will never be less than nine feet deep. The tide is negligible. Fifteen yachts or more will fit in this bonafide hurricane hole. But because so many boaters sprint for the marinas on Mobile Bay, there are never more than a half-dozen large vessels parked up the cut-off. It's a strategic starting point for an easy trip through the Port of Mobile and halfway down the bay-a very sporty and capricious body of water, to beautiful downtown Dog River on the western shore or our marina of choice, Eastern Shore.

Robin also has Eastern Shore on her mind. Should have known she'd be a fellow FOC, Friend of Chuck. The official marina mascot is a tiger-striped, real-life version of Garfield the cat, not as chubby or orange but a dead ringer when it comes to attitude.

In later years Chuck merited his own Facebook page, with more than 1,000 human friends following and "liking" his posts on a daily basis.

"I wonder how Chuck and KC will get along?" I ask Robin. Just three batches in and she's perfected the muffin recipe; they're golden, symmetrically puff-topped, evenly bejeweled with cranberries.

"Who would have ever thought I'd run out of muffin cups?" she asks. "They should get along fine. KC is anything but aggressive." KC wags her tail agreeably, eyes intent on the warm muffin Trish is systematically disassembling, breaking off tiny pieces with her still well-manicured fingers.

"There it is." I'm smiling. "Hello."

Just ahead to my right the single-story gray cottage is as it ever was, set in a small clearing at the river's edge, sagging slightly on a crude, exposed foundation of strategically placed concrete blocks no more than a foot from the water. Five steps railed with two-by-fours lead from the warped, slightly sloping, unpainted wood deck down to a time-warped wooden dock affixed by six small timber pilings. A configuration of white PVC pipes protrudes from the water, marking the deeper water, a makeshift channel leading into a boat slip. The tiny clearing is overshadowed by a forest of massive water oaks and spindly loblolly pine, palmetto scrub poking from the kudzu-covered underbrush. A lone, waterlogged cypress stands sentinel a foot from shore, roots immersed in the shallows to the left of the dock.

The jaunty elbow of an aluminum stovepipe pokes skyward from the right side of the black-shingled roof as if waving to passersby, a rudimentary but functional chimney. In one of the narrow rectangular windows on the left side of the structure, a chunky circa 1980s metal air conditioning unit protrudes.

"I can see under that shack," Trish notes. "It looks like a place snakes would like. I bet it would just float away in a flood. I wonder if anybody lives there."

"It's probably a hunting or fishing camp," says Robin. "There are a lot of them scattered out in the bush around here. The river leads back into a network of lakes and streams," as she points down the waterway, we see a bass boat and a pontoon boat heading our way. "Looks like we're in the middle of nowhere, but you'd be surprised."

Before the little boats reach us, she's wheeled *Blackdog* into the creek, lining up with the gray cottage on the opposite shore. Three boats are rafted together at anchor 100 yards further up the creek. *Blackdog's* anchor is deployed in short order. Even when we swing with the tide I will be able to watch "my" house.

Keeping it in sight comforts me. I remember picturing myself in it the last time I was here, smarting from harsh criticism over the marks my shoes had made on the deck of the sailboat, over the pork chops I'd pan-fried for dinner that were pronounced tough and inedible, over the inordinate amount of time and water that I'd wasted on brushing my teeth and several other shortcomings that Derek had once again summed up as "I should know by now, you can't do anything right."

I'd retreated into the cockpit after dinner, staring hard at the placid, primitive abode even as the light faded and it was no longer visible.

"I could live there," I tell the girls. "I could be happy there."

"Bet it's a mess inside," says Trish. "Although there must be electricity, or at least a generator to run that rickety air conditioner."

"Let's take a look," says Rob. "Grab us a couple of fresh beers. Plenty of daylight left. I don't see anyone around. If somebody catches us snooping we can blame it on Miss KC, here."

KC wags her tail frantically, her entire hind end switching rhythmically to and fro.

And so we cross the river, landing at the surprisingly sturdy fixed dock. The front door is secured with a new-looking chain and padlock. Emboldened by the solitude and the lack of a no-trespassing sign, Trish peers into a window. "I can't see anything," she complains. "The blinds are pulled."

KC yanks me around the back of the house, where the clearing is larger than expected, although the kudzu is encroaching. There are no windows. A concrete-block fire pit and well-scorched burn barrel are ringed with fan-backed, rust-flecked, pink-painted metal patio chairs. A two-track black dirt road — sporting humps of grass and bracken down the center line — leads into the woods and presumably to proper roads and civilization. A tire swing dangles from a fraying length of hemp rope tied to a massive branch on a majestically spreading oak.

"And you thought we were the Clampetts," Robin says, surveying the scene as she takes a long draw of her beer. "Looks like we got competition."

"Let's go, ladies!" Trish hasn't left the dock; in fact she's already back in the dinghy. "Not loving those noises in the underbrush. Gators, snakes, boars, whatever, I don't want to be here when it comes out."

"Don't soil your shorts, we're coming," Robin hollers. "Chicken!"

With a plastic-bagged hand I gather and fling KC's droppings into the woods. "What was that? Did you hear that?"

Robin's laughing hard. It's a beautiful sound, washing away some of the worry that constantly niggles in the back of my mind since her rape.

"Calm yourself, wimp," I call to Trish. "I was just cleaning up after the dog. Sheesh."

"You won't think it's so funny when Bubba and his buddies show up," Trish shouts back.

Before we head back I climb up to the porch to examine a moisture-warped, crumbling piece of poster board lying face-down by the door. I can barely make out the "For Sale By Owner" lettering; the phone number is indiscernible.

"I would buy this," I say. "We could establish Robin's Muffin Top right here. Think they'd take a fifteen-hundred down payment on a land contract?"

"Hailey my girl, dreaming is free," says Robin, raising her voice as Trish gives the outboard engine a pull and it ignites with a roar. "But I wouldn't get my hopes up. That sign looks like it's been there a long time."

KC's already on the bow, pointing like a hunting dog, ears flapping in the wind that has picked up as dark clouds scud overhead in the emerging twilight. I scan the sky in all directions. A solid bank is coasting in from the west, blotting out the first stars of the evening. "Think it's gonna rain?"

"Judging by those clouds, yes, Captain Obvious," Robin responds. "Kick 'er in the ass, Trishie!" Trish obligingly gooses the throttle as we shove off. Since KC's enjoying the ride so much, she arcs the dinghy around in a deliberate circle.

"Doing a donut!" she hollers like some hopped-up teenage motorhead. Robin claps her hands with glee.

Since the Whaler is already in the water, it's no prob to stop by the boat to pick up the remaining muffins and zoom over to visit our neighbors on the rafted-up boats *Water Witch*, *Can't Anchor Us* and *Newfie Bullet*, distributing the treats to the appreciative crews. We're invited aboard for cocktails, but the wind is continuing to pick up, so we decline with regret and zip back to our Mother Ship.

"The lady from *Water Witch* says it's supposed to blow even harder tomorrow," says Trish, tuning in the NOAA weather radio forecast.

Sure enough, six-to-nine footers are predicted for Mobile Bay by early morning. Conditions aren't predicted to improve until the day after tomorrow.

Big Briar Creek is an ideal spot to ride out nasty weather. We stay put until the storm passes.

Chapter 21: Damn the Torpedoes

It takes two days for the front to pass. And another before Robin gives the thumbs-up. "The waves need time to lay down," she explained numerous times to an antsy Trish. "We need a two-day weather window. Or at least a full 24 hours." The plan was to cruise on through Jimmy Buffet country down Mobile Bay to Gulf Shores, where the panhandle beckoned just across the Floribama line.

Mother Nature wasn't hip to the program.

A procession of Mare's Tails marched across the sky as *Blackdog* entered Mobile Bay Ship Channel. The cacophony of the waterfront: spewing grain chutes, warning horn blasts and the ever-present low vibration of machinery, was fading faster than the hot-tar scent of industry. But the clouds were telling a story that couldn't be denied. It was about to get loud.

"Shit." Robin flicked on the radar. She didn't have to tell me to get out the life jackets.

"Well, they're not black," she says, eyeing the thin and wispy cirrus clouds.

"Make sure everything on deck is either tied down or stowed," I told Trish.

Robin and I know the signs. Ignoring them won't make them go away.

The pelicans haven't retreated. Yet. They're still piloting the sky, climbing high then crash-diving straight down into the water in that clumsy, comical way they do, fishing in the wake of shrimpers steaming toward the sentinel cliffs of Ecor Rouge. Following the fleet home.

"All the boats are headed in," I say, reminded of the Coppertone houseboat couple. It didn't take them more than one storm to skedaddle back upriver.

The flat, beer-bottle-brown water gathers up the wind. Foam-tipped whitecaps form as delicate as cat's paws, growl in ever-increasing gusts. As if orchestrated right on cue the ominous sky darkens to dull cobalt. The wind shrieks. "We can make it," Robin says.

"Well kick 'er in the butt then." I've heard these ridiculously optimistic predictions before. And been knocked around because Derek misjudged conditions. He'd never admit he was scared. But he'd reduce sail, and sometimes turn back. If I begged. If he could blame it on me. It was easy, during the tale-telling later, to attribute the retreat on my cowardice. "Hailey's a fair-weather sailor," he'd say.

That was better than the times it was too late to turn back. In the middle of the Gulf. In the middle of Lake Superior. In the middle of maelstroms with waves washing over the dodger that shades the cockpit, water up to my waist and nowhere to hide.

At some point all Captains lie. They're forced to. It's the only way to keep their shipmates from freaking out when the shit hits the fan.

We click along the red-green picket fence of close-spaced channel markers — green going out (that's to the right, to you landlubbers) until we reach the point in the bay where it's deep enough to leave the channel and cut east. The upper reaches of Mobile Bay are so shallow that the bottom is visible in some places at low tide. Exposed shipwrecks demonstrate the folly of turning too early. Even midway down the bay there are humps and bumps and spoil dumps to avoid. Depending on the tides, the controlling depth is still only nine feet. Shallow doesn't mean safe. A boat caught in a storm on Mobile Bay will founder as easily as an unsteady toddler left alone in the bathtub. Robin kicked up the engines. *Blackdog* sleighed steadily toward Eastern Shore, rolling on the growing waves, pushed by the west wind behind us. The wind howled. We rolled on. Every so often a rogue wave, larger than the others and from a slightly different angle, would smack her steel ass. *Blackdog* could take a spanking. But the sound was disconcerting.

"Should I be scared?" Trish had to shout over the wind and engines to be heard.

"Nope." Robin was right. By the time the full brunt of the front ripped in we were up the creek, Fly Creek to be exact, securely tied at Eastern Shore Marina, a configuration of fixed wooden docks huddled at the base of Sea Cliff. It's always harder to dock a boat in a strong wind. The marina owner, Ed, had a couple of dockhands waiting for me to toss the lines. Got 'em on the first throw. Trish deployed the extra bumpers I'd rigged for additional protection. I'd come to believe *Blackdog* could take almost anything. She could definitely take a bite out of a wooden dock.

Surrounded by water oaks, azaleas, gracious mansions and the gentle, courteous attentions of staff and local boaters, we quickly renewed acquaintance with Eastern Shore's sleek mascot Chuck the Cat. He and KC formed an uneasy alliance. KC was too shy and Chuck too well-bred to fight. Robin greased the wheels of friendship with smoked oysters and Liv-a-Snaps. The hurricane did damage here. The watermarks are above the clubhouse windows. No functioning washer and dryer. But we're grateful for the new fiberglass stall and shiny commode in the still-under-construction bathrooms.

On our second day at the Eastern Shore docks, the incessant west-blown waves of that great brown bay found their way into Fly Creek, jangling and sloshing the vessels contained therein, from the sailboat fleet at the Yacht Club to the working shrimp boats tucked around the corner at the commercial dock.

The sailboats *Rum Line* and *Chip Ahoy* tied to the outer piers ahead of us were hobby-horsing so violently that the hapless occupants became a spectator sport. Local folk from the utopian-settled town called Fairhope came down to eat lunch at the shaded picnic tables, exclaiming over every pitch and yaw.

"Kinda makes you seasick just to watch it," one of the spectators told us.

"I forgot how exposed this spot is in a west wind," Robin said.

We're wide open to the full fetch of the bay. So we let the prevailing winds dictate our fate.

It hasn't affected her baking. Batch after batch. Warm-muffin-smell wafts all the way down the pier to the parking lot as Trish and I walk to the showers. "Reminds me of this young one at the ranch. Tara. She would do anything on the menu. And then some. The M in S&M," she says.

"Tara never talked about the rough stuff. She crocheted. She watched re-runs of *The Bachelor*, we had every episode TiVo'd, and she'd go to town with a ball of yarn and the crochet hook. Started with potholders. Then hats and scarves. Everybody had slippers. Afghans for the beds. It was some kind of therapy."

Bake on, Robin. Bake on.

***

We couldn't catch a weather break. Which was fine. It felt good to rest, to think about what-nexts without the pressure of daily travel. Until the day, a week after the storm, when I spotted my old sailboat coming into the channel. I'd just finished a yoga practice on what I liked to refer to as my private beach. I felt peaceful. Loose. Free.

Shit. Am I ever going to be able to relax?

I'd know *Chinook* anywhere. I belly-crawled from the beach up to the tall grasses bordering the creek, startling an egret. I watched my old boat's progress. My lower belly cramped. Sweat popped at my hairline. It's that visceral dread you get when a cop is behind you and you think he's going to pull you over. Even if you haven't done anything wrong, you feel sick. You feel guilty. Trapped.

As *Chinook* moved farther into creek I paralleled behind the water oaks rimming the inner basin. Hiding. I had to expose myself to get from shore to *Blackdog's* pier. I move as quickly as I safely can, praying Derek is too busy navigating the channel and getting ready to dock singlehanded to pay attention to anyone on the piers.

Robin is stretched out on the couch with KC, watching a snowy TV picture. "The reception here sucks," she says.

"Derek's here."

"Fuck me." Robin laughs.

"What's so funny?" He's going to find a way to hurt me again. Make me be with him again. Trap me again. I need to get away.

"Screw it. Let's deliver some muffins," Robin says.

"If he tries anything," Trish offers, "I'll shoot him with the flare gun."

She's in the galley, where she roots out a plastic container and lid to pack a half-dozen from Robin's morning batch.

"Maybe Robin should make some special muffins for Derek. Do we have any arsenic on board?" I say.

"Not funny," Robin says.

Great. Now I've upset Robin.

"I'm sorry. I don't want to use your muffins for evil," I tell her. "And I don't want to kill Derek."

"Are you sure? I've got no problem with poison," Trish teases. "We'll pack a lunch...just like that Dixie Chicks song."

I realize that if I don't talk to my husband, I, he, can't put this to rest. Be done with the way things were. Be with the way things are.

And that's how a real woman grows a pair. Not balls. Tit bombs. Chest out. Heart open. No resistance to confronting what is. Taking back my power.

As we draw close to *Chinook*, tied up two slips over, I gasp at the slime-streaked bumpers hanging over the sides, uncoiled ropes strewn about the deck, flies buzzing around the black garbage bags piled near the chain locker. Empty beer cans roll on the cockpit floor.

I shudder, imagining what she looks like down below. Lacking a hapless swabbie to order around, Derek has apparently been forced to lower his sanitation standards. I wonder if he's kept up with maintenance. Robin handed over the oil changes, stuffing box adjustments and other mechanic chores to me. I can help my boat, still my boat, if she needs me.

I place my palm on *Chinook's* spattered white hull, caressing her port side near the curve of her elegant bowsprit, where it swings close to the pier.

"Hi, sweet girl," I whisper. "I'm sorry."

Then to Robin, "Wow, what a mess. I've never seen her so trashed."

Robin looks at me, jerks her head toward the cockpit. I shake mine. She gestures again. Hands on hips, bitch wings deployed.

Fine. I call out the traditional boater's greeting.

"Ahoy, *Chinook*. Anybody home?"

And there he is, whisker-stubbled face peering out from the companionway. He looks defeated.

"What do you want?" There's no anger, just beaten-down resignation and a hint of embarrassment.

"We brought you some muffins," Robin announces diplomatically.

The offering is reciprocated by an invitation to come aboard, which we decline. I still don't trust him fully and never will. "I can hear you just fine from the dock," I say.

After paying a hefty fine for his lock invasion (now we're even: we've both spent a night in jail) he boarded *Chinook* and followed me down the river.

"It's no fun singlehanded," he admits. Apparently that solo trip down the river was an eye-opener. He ran aground twice, hit a few logs and resorted to pissing in an empty pop bottle because he couldn't leave the helm without some sort of crisis cropping up.

"Oh, so I can't be replaced by an autopilot?" I marvel.

"No Hailey, you can't. So I guess you're happy that you ran away."

"Shoot, I didn't run away. I just went," I say, winking at Trish.

"The student learned her lesson," she says. "Gold star!"

"I've learned a few things, too," he says. Here it comes. I'm over it. "Can you leave us alone, ladies?"

"No, stay," I say. This strength is new to me. I'm reveling in it, but I'm not sure how to fully deploy it, or what I'll do if Derek decides to get nasty. I want back-up.

"You're forgetting how much I annoy you and make you yell and make you do worse than that. I don't think I can forget."

"Well, I'm sorry about that. Maybe things could change," he says softly, hopefully. I know this contrite phase. He'll return to his same old badgering ways eventually. Pushing his buttons is something I know how to do in my bones with no effort. I know how to make him hurt me. Still, the question vomits out my mouth.

"Why did you ever want to hit me in the first place?"

"I wanted to keep you. I didn't know what else to do to make you stay," he says.

Chapter 22: Resting Place

"Corky knows all about that fish camp," says Ed, when Robin and I look him up in the boatyard. We cornered Corky at the local Wal-Mart, where he works as a greeter. "I don't need the money," the courtly, white-haired gent wanted us to know. "This lil' old side job just gets me out of the wife's hair."

Turns out the Tenn-Saw fish camp was for sale, for, as they say, a song. Robin wouldn't take more than $500 from me when we got around to making it all legal. "I don't like to sweat," she told me. "That's your equity. The perspiration."

"But Robin—"

"I believe the sun has set on this particular conversation," she informs me in Aunt Ada's strictest tone.

The next favorable forecast put the Fairhope town gazebo and the red cliffs of Eastern Shore at our stern as we motored back toward the skyscrapers of Mobile. Clothes laundered, cupboards bursting with provisions that would feed a fleet of towboat crews, we head 12.2 miles upriver to a new beginning.

***

Laugh if you want. The sky doesn't care. The seagulls don't care. The sun doesn't care. These entities do what they do whether anyone is there to see them or not. I take great comfort in this.

The world does not revolve around me, Miss Hailey Marie. My little shack on the river is off the radar. Hence from 50 forever known as a mortal woman of a Certain Age, I spend a great many hours looking at the sky or water. Most mornings, I meditate with the heron who favors this swampy shoreline. We stretch together, a mix of yoga and Tai Chi. By the time he's caught breakfast, I am ready for a raspberry-cranberry yogurt.

When I first settled here on the Tenn-Saw Cut-Off, I worried about being watched; worried that someone might see and jeer at my gyrations on the porch. The indifferent creatures intent on their own ministrations gradually reassured me that no one cares if I twist myself up to stretch myself out, shoulders crackling, hamstrings yawning on the first Down Dog. Falling is part of the practice. I laugh with no shame for my stumbles. The heron, oblivious to competition, maintains perfect balance, intense stillness and laser concentration. He's my demonstration bird, his steady gaze as useful, if not more, than any human guru.

Living on the mucky banks of a brackish river 12.2 miles upstream from Mobile Bay has both charms and drawbacks. Flushes of freshwater dilute the salinity in rainy season, but the influence of the Gulf of Mexico is ever-present in the flatulent sulfur aroma of low tide. My mother calls it "a good stink." Mother sharks sometimes venture many miles from their normal cruising grounds to give birth in the diluted saltwater upriver. I've never seen one but don't doubt it. There is so much life in the water here. It takes courage to be as shy and powerful as the snakes, which never really intend to bother anyone but will strike when ambushed.

The old porch creaks and flexes in the after-waves of passing towboats, sloshing over the dock, rocking my clay geranium pots, bouncing the fishing poles. I have learned not to place anything too close to the edge; if something falls in the water a net is handy, but if it's not an important item I let it go. Chances are I'll find it washed up somewhere later.

The tow drivers who throw a wake are generally young bucks learning the ways of negotiating the river. Like a 16-year-old boy in his first Camaro, these dudes occasionally get out of hand on an open stretch and almost always exceed the speed limit, ignoring my boldly lettered "No Wake" sign. Robin says we should declare it a manatee zone, but I don't think that will fly.

The speedboys are easier to understand than the veteran curmudgeons who deliberately disturb this abode because two uppity white women had the audacity to buy a broken-down old fishing camp in the middle of nowhere and turn it into a year 'round home. They steam on through as if those prissy geranium pots are a personal affront.

Robin's latest plan for counterattack involves mounting a water cannon on *Blackdog's* bow. "They don't pay any attention to signs; let's see them ignore this," she says, pantomiming a full-frontal strafing. "Or what about a giant slingshot and some cantaloupes?"

This is her house, too, technically and legally. But since we both need solitude for healing she spends most of her nights aboard *Blackdog*, tied off from shore 300 feet downstream, at the line of the parcel we purchased on land contract. The little dock won't hold 30,000-pound *Blackdog*; we're building a bigger one. A proper pier.

"This way we can be alone, but never lonely," says Robin.

Living alone offers many opportunities to feel true freedom. Eat whenever, sleep whenever and set your own schedule. I refuse to have another argument about passing out on the couch or the porch glider if that is where my body drops itself for the night. I cannot get over the fact that I can work out or bust a few dance moves to a pop song on WAVE radio whenever the mood strikes. I can sleep with the TV on all night or burn the lights until the wee hours consuming a good book. There are no critics to comment on my habits, demeanor or attire. I enjoy walking around naked.

Once you hit 50, there's a pain somewhere every day that cannot be ignored. Dancing and yoga are necessary to work out the kinks. It is my firm belief that every woman should stand on her head once per day. The recipe continues as thus: Once upright again, put on some shuck & jive music and perform at least eight high leg kicks on each side. Dance full-out to at least three songs. That's the medicine. It requires the right type of music, which varies daily. On Monday "Mustang Sally" may be appropriate. The next day, "Little Bird" by Annie Lennox. The next it may be Justin Timberlake, Britney Spears, Johnny Cash, Johnny Rivers or Roy Orbison, Lady Gaga or Michael Jackson. The Black Eyed Peas if you please. Led Zeppelin if you will. There is enough music to dance to for the rest of our lives and it does the music a dishonor when we don't dance. The oldest, saddest people I know don't dance any more or have sex any more.

When I danced to the tunes of others, I was a sailor but not captain of my own ship. I was considered too flighty and impractical to be in charge. Physically and mentally abused, I cowered before everything, including nature.

The yoga came organically into our lives. The only station we could pull in with the ancient TV antenna was PBS. Robin was fascinated by Wai Lana, that flower-bedecked sprite in shouting colors (our favorite Wai Lana outfit is a flowered pink, yellow, green and purple jumpsuit) who bends, stretches and breathes atop Hawaiian cliffs. Her program airs at 6 a.m. weekdays. One morning we just started following along with her, Trish first, egged on by Robin. "If you think it's so Echo Alpha Sierra Yankee, then you try it," she said.

"That's not a curse word," Robin pointed out.

"Kiss my Alpha Sierra Sierra," Trish responded smartly.

"In that position, you're not asking for the impossible," I said, resting my head on the floor and enjoying the inverted rush. It feels good to be goofy. Even Robin has to admit it's "almost" as relaxing as a cigarette. Breathing and stretching while the morning coffee perks has become a replacement habit. Nature abhors a vacuum.

We miss Trish. She still comes to visit, at least once a week, but it's not the same.

Trish pretended to be excited. She couldn't fool us. Life in a ramshackle cottage at the edge of a quiet river is far from her idea of paradise. It was only a matter of weeks before she secured a chair at the hottest salon in trendy downtown Fairhope, along with a hunky boyfriend who crews on the *Bobby Joe James*. She insists on retouching our roots once every five weeks and ensures a regular supply of female caps to keep the hot flashes to a minimum. There are still those white nights when I have to have the talk with myself: "This is your last chance, mind! You go to sleep or else!" It's the same for Rob.

But thanks to Trish we are the most serene middle-aged babes on the Ten-Saw River Cut-off. We often send her hair-dressing clients, but sometimes she'll come to them by appointment, cutting, coloring and curling at Robin's Muffin Top, LLC. We made the business official, and it's doing better than projected in our small business plan. We bake several dozen muffins each day; but the enterprise turned out to be more than that, a sort of concierge service involving everything from selling bait and garden produce, to partnering with fishing guides to offer boat rentals and day trips on Briar Creek. One of our favorite services is dog walking for boaters: Do It Yourself on our property or let Robin and me fight over the job.

I just spoke to my mother last week about a loan for miscellaneous equipment, including another skiff with an outboard, a dozen life jackets and a new stove and refrigerator for the muffin end of the operation. It's so good to be in touch again. I got the promissory note yesterday. She's fine and well and promised to come and see the operation firsthand next winter.

Robin still won't talk about what happened at Bobby's. Both of us tense each time a dark-hulled sailboat enters our stream. I couldn't murder Derek but I do think about killing, about how easy it would be to bury a body in these woods, kudzu covering the grave of the monster. When we hear the guns of duck and deer seasons cracking the air in every direction, we think about timing. At least I know I do. I believe Robin does, too.

The only thing she's said to me recently is, "He should be dead." We haven't yet had the conversation I need entitled, "What if he does it again?" I'm going to give it a little more time.

It sounds improbable, but I can feel Robin's happiness, her calm as she stirs the batter and spoons it into cups. When she is making her muffins she is at peace, drinking and smoking less, smiling often.

Firmly ensconced in my river refuge, I remain safe and sane, making a living by the sweat of brow and brain in equal measure. Despite the indignity of having both wrinkles and zits, grace has come to me on my dock on the river and for the first time I truly find myself beautiful. I shine. The sun has come into me; my life is golden. As I swim in long strokes toward an inner core of peace, through the banked fires of various desires, I have regrets.

I regret the days when I was gorgeous and I didn't know. As penance I constantly remind my young friends to consider themselves gorgeous early and often. "Don't look for compliments from others, see for yourself how beautifully you have been put together, how dewy and supple your skin, how unfettered your mind. Appreciate it! Twenty comes but once. Thirty is full bloom. But after 40 is best, because you will finally know who you are and what you can be in your second half of the century. By 50, if you've made it that long, you will look back and marvel at your beauty. And you will still be beautiful."

The cosmetic changes of age still scare the Sierra Hotel India Tango out of me. Just when I think I can't get any pouchy-er or withered, I do. I tell myself that these physical erosions are outweighed by the gift of wisdom. But all people are vain to a certain degree. The left-handed compliments catch me off guard. Being told "you look 10 years younger" after an appointment with Trish is as disconcerting as the upgrade from Miss to Ma'am.

Bah to the Botox; I am not allowing anyone to inject botulism spores into my forehead any time soon. I'll just have to look like I look, although I do take very good care of myself. Thyme and lavender facial steams once weekly, followed by aloe vera gel slathered on straight from the plants I grow out back.

Sunscreen is mandatory for Robin and I follow suit. The cottage is comfy but tiny and unless it's raining we're both outdoors. Here I farm, growing all sorts of unconventional things, tending the fenced-in plots in between the chores involved with helping Robin deliver her muffins to the masses. Well, not masses, exactly, but we cleared $1,500 the first month off sales to boaters craving baked goods. Trishie's hair-dos added an additional $500 to the general fund. It takes time to grow a business. As Robin always adds like she made the adage up herself, "It takes money to make money."

Bankrolling such a wacko idea is proving to be "a once-in-a-lifetime golden opportunity" (thanks to my family she's grown fond of mixed clichés). So far our growth projections are dead-on accurate.

Farmer's markets turned out to be an extremely profitable venue for my fresh herbs: basil, thyme, cilantro, coriander, dill and parsley. I sell lavender in gallon pots. The sunflowers cultivated purely for pleasure turned into another money maker when I harvested and roasted the seeds.

"If this keeps up, by next summer we'll have to hire help," I tell Robin. Wistful, I imagine Joey and Lisa coming to stay for the season. I would gather my chicks under my wing, reveling in the simple pleasure of looking at them, feeding them, hugging them. I have written letters; they have not responded.

"Don't be such a wuss, you should call," Robin advises. "Kids don't write letters these days. They text."

"I put your cell phone number in the letters. Maybe they'll text. And then I'll have to figure out how to text them back," I say. My children have not had children. Never having been one of those women who yearn for progeny upon progeny, I wait for the issue of my loins to be happy. I expect their happiness: it is there and they will find it. It is taking them a lot longer than it took me. I'm impatient. My greatest failure is as a mother. I adored doing all the right things; I can't put my finger on what I did wrong.

I'm sure they think of me as a weird old woman, twisted in some way that other mothers aren't. But in so many ways I am comfortingly conventional, washing clothes, administering advice and aspirin, always wanting to touch them more than they wish to be touched. Their standoffish body language, the instinctual stiffening, is, I think, so much like Derek. Some of us are born to touch and be touched. Others flinch. It is the way of the world. They know I will hug and kiss and fuss over them when they come to see me, if they come to see me. They will know that I love them and I will know that they love me. All other things pale before this simple wish.

I still seek my bliss, torn between the stable mother I should be and the sport-fucking temptress that I still haven't worked out of my system. I think I am too damn old for hijinks. Often I resent having to surrender the things of youth gracefully. Why should lustful, moonlit nights come to an end?

The man challenge is more easily solved. Released from an abusive marriage, I continue to sample lovers, some of whom are or become friends. I do not consider myself sluttish for doing so. In fact, the idea of polygamy does not repel me, as long as it is the woman doing the picking.

And, as Trish notes, "For a woman your age there's still plenty of action in the boondocks." Gives whole new meaning to BFE.

I think it would be quite handy to have several men as companions on the journey of life. With this one, you could read and discuss great books, ramble through museums, debate the news of the day. That one would install new floors, maybe some new kitchen cabinets and take you boating on the weekends, all the while looking like a *Playgirl* centerfold. The third one would be a gourmet cook with a four-star sensual appetite. The fourth would be an affluent businessman so infatuated that your every wish was his desire ...

If there is one thing I have finally learned about men, the secret to the whole find-a-guy-game is never being the hunter. I do not hunt. Find me if you wish to see me. I am not prey. I do not seek to harm, but will attack as required. I can live with that. I do live with that.

Who knew there would be so many men who wish to see me, some of whom are, as Alanis Morissette puts it, "Friends with benefits?" If they don't like visiting me, they don't need to come back. And if I don't like it, they won't be coming back.

Derek comes back. As many broken couples find, we are better apart than we are together. He can no longer yell me down with his raised fist and red face. No one hits me. No one. No one ever tells me that I am worthless because I don't fit into his particular agenda. I'm immune to such ridiculous drama. I don't run my legs or life by his clock or his cock.

The gaslighting is over.

He's living on the boat at a marina in Dog River, on the west shore of Mobile Bay. I tell him he should continue heading south, as he'd planned, or go north back to what's left of his life in Michigan. "I'm not going with you. Hurricane season is over, so there's nothing stopping you from sailing where you want to sail," I tell him. "My sailing days are done."

But he keeps coming back.

One evening after a scrumptious dinner featuring Key West pinks, my excellent herb-garden salad and fresh-mint mojitos, Derek asked me why he shouldn't just move in. It wouldn't be moving back in, because he's never lived here. We never did the legal paperwork for a divorce. I don't need to be divorced because I'm never getting married again. Our familiar closeness is sometimes thrilling and always comforting, but in general I really like being alone. In his favor he does make excellent coffee with a never-the-same grind of specialty beans. And his morning face is the sunniest I have ever seen, beaming with the promise of a new day.

"A lot of my stuff is here anyway."

"But not enough that it couldn't be moved out in about 10 minutes flat. You just had a good dinner and we're having a nice time but May is coming and we always fight in May." Having switched to vodka I tipped back the icy lime dregs of my Grey Goose vodka tonic for one last quenching swallow. Two is my limit.

"I am not going to get any easier to live with and I like things the way they are," I tell him. "Let's leave it at that. I am sorry that I couldn't be a better wife, but about one week per month spread out is all I can take. I mean the days spread out, not me." I laugh. Derek's mind didn't go there but mine did. Sex has always been on my mind just as much as any male. I severely distrust the celibate lifestyle. Such monkish behavior reminds me of the boxers saving their semen in abstention before championship bouts. People that are so closed to the animalistic side of our beings have my sympathy. Engaging in sexual activity is healthy. Love is sex and music and dancing. I say shoot your wad whenever you can. But this attitude sometimes results in double entendres that I do not mean to introduce into conversation.

Derek withdraws, retreats, waits.

Women friends come to the river more often than men do. They understand. We are simpatico. There will always be a whistling teakettle, a bottle of wine, an iced tub of beer for my fellow runaways and other females who flock to our pine-carpentered dining table with the red-checked runner in the aromatic great room to talk about where we've been, where we're at, where we strive to go next. We don't bash men, but often we hammer at each other. We are scarcely moved in when Trish brings Aunt Ada, the Florida Cracker who gave us our rallying cry, "I didn't run away, I just went."

"Honey, you got to use him for whatever he's worth," she tells me, after eyeing Derek up and down. "But now that you got up the gumption to leave, don't let the dirty dog come crawlin' back like nothin' happened."

Ensconced on the porch slider, she clucks at the proximity to the water. "This is the dry time in a drought year, Miss Hailey. You want to live on the water; you could end up living *in* the water."

"I know, it's a gamble," I say. "But for now, this is where we landed and where we stay. More tea?"

She nods. "Bring the sugar bowl with you, darlin'," she instructs. "You Northern girls need some lessons in sweet tea."

I envision this house of supportive women as it grows through the years. Some of the women will be sad and lonely when they arrive, but it won't last. We'll laugh and sing, gathering at my table, sitting on my porch or lolling on chaises in the "guest" gardens, divided into flower and vegetable plots. We'll track the scents in the herb garden and baby the tender fruit trees — orange, apple and loquat-that I've planted and that no one but me expects to thrive.

Susan has promised to come soon. She's bringing a special crystal with exceptionally powerful energy and is bound to have a few good dating stories to crack us up. Her May-September adventure with a 25-year-old Chinese university student is a favorite, a classic referred to as "Looking for Love in All the Wong Places." I can't wait for Robin and Trish to hear that one.

The water flows past my bedroom just off the porch-dock, undulating with tides and tug wash. Heeding Ada's admonition and knowing all too well that the water is not always kind, I am grateful for the temporary occupancy permit granted by Mother Nature. The water may someday drive me and that which I hold dear from this cabin. My "camp," my enclave, my cottage, my gardens remain a work in progress that may have to be abandoned at any moment in this impermanent world.

Here I never look for black trucks other than my old F150 parked out by the barn. The obsessive compulsive jerk reflex to examine every large truck, searching for a glance of the Most Dangerous Lover of All passed on the day I took title of the black beast. It is a relief to let go of the what-could-have-been addiction to focus on what is now. Maybe all that I ever really wanted was that truck. The dangerous lover, the fourth lover, was just an accessory. It is a relief to stop looking.

But what to do with the guilt? The distractions are many; I've no time to wallow in the residue of my many messes and mistakes. The garden needs tending and the bulk of my day is spent taking care of family. If I can forgive others maybe one day I'll be able to forgive myself.

Robin still talks about taking the boat farther south. If she wanted to leave now I'd just let her go. True friends are like bobbers on a fishing line. Sometimes they just float out there and you wait for the bobber to go under to let you know it's time to reel in. Whenever she talks about going away, she always asks, "If I call you from wherever I am, will you come?" Yes, I always say. Yes. "I will come to you wherever you are."

Robin won't be going anywhere until KC has her puppies. We spotted the telltale teats one morning when KC rolled over for a belly scratch at Eastern Shore.

"Holy Sierra Hotel India Tango!" Robin exclaimed. "I guess she and Hooch touched more than noses at Midway."

On her bad days, Robin looks like she's about to die, pallid, skeletal with mottled purple-and-white skin and deep ebony-grape circles under her eyes. We've made more than one trip to the nearest hospital. But she's not dead. Not even close. The flares are few and far between, and for that we are both thankful.

There is a certain class of people with life-threatening illness who simply go on and on, having frightening medical episodes and somehow surviving. Robin is my Elizabeth Taylor/Liza Minnelli, Queen of a thousand medical procedures and a couple of bad husbands (just found out there's more than one). There are days when she won't do yoga, when the Miller Lites have rendered her insensate, all chain-smoking bravado and hectic butterfly blush fluttering across her steroid-plumped pixie cheeks. These are the days when I cannot halt her headlong rush into self-destruction, basically flipping the bird at the Grim Reaper.

I admire her bravado even as I gather her tiny whip of a body into my arms, such light bones holding such a big personality. As physically weak as she is, I still feel like she could kick my ass or cut me to the marrow with a single nasty comment. She never does, because she would never hurt me.

It's like the vintage hair-color commercial: My husband. I think I'll keep her. This is one of the healthiest relationships I have ever had in my life.

We have lived through biting dogs and insane rapists, lurking husbands and alligators waiting to strike. We know each other at the gut level. There are many things we need to talk about, talk out. And we will, in time.

We both know when to back off. And I like having me to myself. The Haileyness of Hailey is enough. Solace doesn't come easy, even up a backwater creek. Constant interruptions continue to punctuate my day, most often when I'm trying to meditate but at other intimate times, too. It's enough to make me envy the monks.

There's a universal Murphy's Law that draws visitors to the human being looking forward to totally private time. Caught naked, caught masturbating, caught dirt-caked in the garden or mowing the one small patch of conventional grass in my back yard, it's all the same to me. One simply shakes off the previous private mood and plays the gracious host, rising to any occasion. Getting older is a quest for the serenity beyond embarrassment, a place where order emerges naturally from chaos. I ponder the compost pile, proof that messes left to percolate are transformed into a rich and invigorating catalyst for growth.

Oh, great revelation, being myself seems to attract the kind of creatures and friends that suit me best, although sometimes I have to shake my head at the characters who fly in to see me, sleeping in the trees and using the dock as a toilet — and it's not just the birds who accomplish these feats of disruption. Love comes to me on the river every day in every way.

The hot flashes continue. But the mental pause is over.

Acknowledgements:

Guidebooks are the angels sitting on the shoulders of boaters who wouldn't dare travel the Heartland Rivers without copies of the following aboard: Skipper Bob's *Cruising Lake Michigan, Cruising from Chicago to Mobile* and *The Great Circle Route*; *Cruising Guide: Lake Michigan to Kentucky*, by Rick Rhodes; *An Illustrated Cruising Guide to the Great Loop Inland Waterway: Chicago to Mobile, Vol. 1: Chicago to Paducah*; *Quimby's Cruising Guide*, by Waterways Journal Inc.; *Waterway Guide: The Cruising Authority, Northern Edition*, publisher Jack Dozier; *Tennessee River, Tenn-Tom Waterway and Lower Tombigbee River*, by Marian, Thomas W. & W.J. Rumsey; *Tenn-Tom Nitty Gritty* by Fred Myers.

The U.S. Army Corps of Engineers takes the lead role in maintaining the Heartland Rivers for commercial and pleasure traffic. The Corps charts for the Illinois, Ohio, Mississippi, Cumberland, Tennessee, Tennessee-Tombigbee and lower Black Warrior-Tombigbee Waterway to Mobile were consulted often during the writing of this novel. The *Rand McNally Road Atlas* also served as an essential primer for pinpointing towns near the river system.

The hundreds of boaters I've met during 17 years of Lake Superior boating, five years of southern cruising and two 6,000-mile circumnavigations of the entire America's Great Loop have graciously and generously shared their knowledge, their humor, their equipment and many Happy Hours. I'm in their debt.

Discussion Questions
for Killing Time on Long Voyages

More Than You Think You Know centers on a trio of women in their early-to-late 40s who have decided to flee the status quo, heading from Illinois toward an undetermined destination at the end of the Heartland Rivers. Have you ever wanted to run away?

What role does menopause play in the story? Have you experienced hot flashes, mood swings and other hallmarks of "the change of life?" If so, how did you ameliorate the symptoms?

Statistics show that a shocking percentage of rapes go unreported. What do you think is behind Robin's decision to keep silent about the assault? Do you think Hailey and Trish should have pushed her to report the attack? What self-healing methods does Robin use to aid in her recovery?

Hailey's husband is mentally and physically abusive. Her methods of retaliation are infidelity and alcohol abuse. How does her lack of control and passive-aggressive response ultimately affect her life? Does she deserve sympathy or empathy?

Early on in the book we learn that both Hailey and her son Joey have spent time in jail. The situation reflects a reality in the U.S., which imprisons more of its citizens than any other developed country in the world. Have you seen any evidence of this "incarceration nation" phenomenon in your community?

Trish seemingly embodies the stereotype of the "hooker with a heart of gold." A man magnet and accomplished flirt, she continues to attract male attention throughout the trip down the rivers. If you met someone like her, would you be drawn to form a friendship? Or would moral scruples or jealousy be a barrier?

To dye or not to dye, that is the question when a woman of a certain age begins to go gray. Trish, a licensed beautician, is a firm believer in cosmetic enhancement. Hailey, confounded by the double-whammy of wrinkles and zits, discovers the joy of looking good for herself rather than worrying about how sexually attractive she is to men. Robin either doesn't care or is pretending not to care how she looks. How does aging affect the way women look at themselves? Does getting older really mean getting better?

All three women drink to excess on occasion. Robin, who has lupus, exhibits many alcoholic tendencies. How does alcohol consumption affect their decision-making and well-being? Why do you think Robin drinks so much?

Each autumn hundreds of boaters head down the Heartland Rivers for warmer climates, experiencing the power and beauty of the Illinois, Mississippi, Ohio, Cumberland, Tennessee, Tenn-Tom Waterway and the lower Tombigbee and Mobile Rivers leading to Mobile Bay and the Gulf of Mexico. Many who make the trip vow "never again." Does a river journey sound like fun — or Hell on Earth — to you?

"You know more than you think you know," an Ontario sailor tells Hailey. How does she discover the truth of this statement during her escape down Lake Michigan to Chicago?

The estrangement of adult children from their parents is reportedly on the rise. Experts advise patience, avoiding guilt trips and doing more listening than talking in reaching out to children who have "divorced" their parents. Do you think there's hope that Hailey will reconnect with her kids?

Robin takes delight in her androgyny, willingly playing the role of Hailey's "husband." How does her masquerade affect the interactions between *Blackdog's* crew with boaters, marina operators and other people that they encounter during their travels? Do you think that being able to imitate a man would come in handy (for example, when you're getting a repair estimate for your car?).

Boat collisions, close encounters with giant tow-barges, raging water, mean dogs, violent intruders and medical emergencies are among the crises Hailey, Robin and Trish encounter head-on in "More Than You Think You Know." When were you most scared for them?

Do you think Hailey will find permanent peace in her cottage on the river? Does the idea of a "house of women" appeal to you?

About the Author

Award-winning journalist and long-time magazine writer Cyndi Perkins writes and edits print and digital media for Michigan Technological University. The former Houghton, Michigan *Daily Mining Gazette* reporter and editor wrote the popular "Line of Sight" column for nine years.

Cyndi has sailed Lake Superior, the Heartland Rivers, and the Eastern Seaboard since 1995. She and her husband survived two 6,000-mile circumnavigations of America's Great Loop aboard their 32-foot DownEast sailing vessel *Chip Ahoy*. (And yes, she gave her boat a cameo in her own novel. Sailors are like that...)

Keep up with her writing and adventures at http://cyndiperkins.com and on Instagram and Twitter: @cyndiperkins